RUSSIA

Amur River

Vladivostok

Sea of
Japan

JAPAN

Tokyo
Yokohama

HONSHU

Kanmon
Straits
Moji
Hiroshima

Fukuoka
KYUSHU

agasaki

Pacific Ocean

0   100   200 Miles

0   100   200 Kiometers

Map by Gene Thorp

The
Fox
Wife

The Fox Wife

A NOVEL

YANGSZE CHOO

HENRY HOLT AND COMPANY
NEW YORK

Henry Holt and Company
Publishers since 1866
120 Broadway
New York, New York 10271
www.henryholt.com

Henry Holt® and Ⓗ® are registered trademarks of Macmillan Publishing
Group, LLC.

Distributed in Canada by Raincoast Book Distribution Limited

Library of Congress Cataloging-in-Publication Data

Names: Choo, Yangsze, author.
Title: The fox wife : a novel / Yangsze Choo.
Description: First Edition. | New York : Henry Holt and Company, 2024.
Identifiers: LCCN 2023017093 (print) | LCCN 2023017094 (ebook) |
    ISBN 9781250266019 (hardcover) | ISBN 9781250266026 (ebook)
Subjects: LCGFT: Detective and mystery fiction. | Novels.
Classification: LCC PS3603.H664 F69 2024 (print) | LCC PS3603.
    H664 (ebook) | DDC 813/.6—dc23/eng/20230417
LC record available at https://lccn.loc.gov/2023017093
LC ebook record available at https://lccn.loc.gov/2023017094

Our books may be purchased in bulk for promotional, educational,
or business use. Please contact your local bookseller or the Macmillan
Corporate and Premium Sales Department at (800) 221-7945, extension
5442, or by email at MacmillanSpecialMarkets@macmillan.com.

First Edition 2024

Designed by Meryl Sussman Levavi

Map by Gene Thorp

Printed in the United States of America

10 9 8 7 6 5 4 3 2 1

This book is for Mika, who loves stories about foxes.

The
Fox
Wife

1

Perhaps you know this story: Late one evening, a beautiful woman comes knocking on an unsuspecting scholar's door.

"Who is it?" the young man asks, peering out into the neglected garden where flowers and shrubs bend into strange shapes in the moonlight.

"Let me in." She has a bewitching smile and a jar of his favorite rice wine.

And he does, hesitant at first because he's supposed to be studying for the Imperial examinations. Why is she alone outside this remote country villa, and why do her eyes gleam strangely in the rain-wet darkness? But he tells himself it's all right; she's likely a prostitute sent by his friends as a joke. They drink the wine, one thing leads to another, and despite her blushes and his untouched pile of books, he has one of the most enjoyable evenings he can recall.

Except he can't really remember it. The details are misted in lamplight and laughter. But he must see her again; he seizes her hands (such long-fingered, sharp-nailed hands) and won't let her go.

"My home is over there," she says, pointing at a curious little hill. "If you follow the road, it's the fourth house from the top."

The next night, he sets out after his old servant has gone to bed. If he paid attention, he'd see that the road peters out until it's barely a trail through overgrown grass, but he doesn't notice, so besotted is he. There are many curious houses along the way, all with darkened windows like empty sockets. Fine mansions, little hovels. Each with the name of a family prominently written on its lintel. The fourth house from the top of the hill is an imposing mansion; the name on its gate is *Hu*.* *Fox.

Again and again he visits her, neglecting his studies while a pile of unopened letters accumulates from his angry parents. His skin shrivels like a withered leaf, his tonsils swell, and his spine curves. Finally, the worried old servant brings in a monk to exorcise evil spirits. When the spell is broken, the scholar howls and weeps in humiliated fury, tearing his clothes with trembling hands. A raiding party is made up of local peasants who swear there are no houses or grand estates on that crooked little hill. Only a long-abandoned graveyard. The fourth grave from the top is constructed, as Chinese graves are, like a little house half sunk into the hill. Using hoes and spades, they break into it to discover that it has become a fox's den.

THIS STORY USUALLY ends with the shape-shifting fox boiled to death or skewered by an angry mob. That shouldn't happen, however, if you're careful. Most foxes are. How else could we survive for hundreds of years? The fox in that tale was greedy and stupid, giving the rest of us a bad reputation.

Foxes, people say, are wicked women.

Even in the best of times, it isn't easy for someone like me to make a living. To catch a train from Mukden to Dalian, for example, I had to make my way out of the grasslands of Kirin. The first day was the hardest, as I required clothing. I ended up dragging a peasant's blouse and cotton trousers off a washing line. A virtuous fox should not steal, but I needed the clothes desperately. Appearing by the roadside as a naked young woman is just asking for trouble.

I exist as either a small canid with thick fur, pointed ears, and neat black feet, or a young woman. Neither are safe forms in a world run by men. Frankly, I'd prefer to look like someone's grandmother; that would at least give me some dignity appropriate to my years. Which leads me to note in my diary that though most tales focus on the beautiful female foxes who live by devouring *qi*, or life force, little is said about the males. Women who run around willfully doing whatever they please are bound to be censured. A handsome, cunning man is a different matter. Most male foxes are only forced to retire or fake their deaths when their uncanny, ageless looks start to disturb people. Don't get me started on the unfairness of this—I generally avoid males of my own race.

Once I had clothes, I continued along, begging for rides. I had no money, of course. That was the consequence of living in the grasslands, watching the clouds drift across the wide blue sky and eating field mice. I hadn't been to a city in ages. When I reached Mukden, there were foreigners spending money in the streets and starving peasants fleeing famine. Before Mukden had become the old Manchu capital of the north, it had been Shenyang, the garrison stronghold of the Ming Empire. The world kept changing, but battles for cities remained the same.

It took me longer than I'd expected to settle some personal business, about which I'll tell you more in the future, but I managed to get onto a train by allowing a pimp to hustle me. I told him I urgently wished to go to the port city of Dalian.

"I see," he said, stroking my arm. Gauging the quality of meat. "You look very healthy. You don't have tuberculosis, do you?"

I shook my head. "I'm strong. I can pull a plow as well as any ox."

"You won't be the one doing the plowing," said he, smiling. "Come with me, I've a good job for you as a nursemaid."

He bought us tickets. Third class, hard seats. Scent of sweat, salt fish, the iron tang of hot metal. The train was a revelation. I'd seen it before, charging across the grasslands like a metal horse, snorting billows of black soot. I'd thought about riding it, but I'd been busy then. Too busy, and too happy. With a snarl, I turned away from the window. I didn't want to think about what I'd lost. At least we were traveling fast. My heart thrummed with impatience; I was eaten up with rage and anxiety that my prey might escape me if I didn't get to Dalian soon.

The land raced by, outpacing the cloud shadows as the grasslands fled away. The unchanging landscape of Northeast China stretched out in flat shades of brown and gray, broken by avenues of poplar and willow trees. The pimp watched as I pressed my face raptly against the glass.

"Aren't you afraid to leave home?" He had a friendly manner.

Girls, be wary of men who smile with their mouths and not their eyes.

"No." I usually tell the truth. It's too much trouble to lie. "That's not my real home anyway."

He smiled indulgently, no doubt thinking of a stricken hamlet clinging to a mountain. "Why are you alone, with no family?"

"Oh," I said, "I've been married before."

A frown creased his forehead as he calculated rapidly. Not a virgin.

"I had a child, too."

Even worse. My price was sinking by the minute. I covered my smile modestly with a sleeve. Discomfited, he said, "What happened to your husband?"

"I'm no longer married," I said softly. "And I'm looking for a man. A Manchurian photographer named Bektu Nikan. Have you heard the name?"

"No." When the train paused at a station, the pimp bought pork dumplings made from pigs raised on garbage. "You eat very daintily," he said.

"What do you mean?" Pause. Mouth full of dumpling.

"Such pretty white teeth." His eyes devoured my smooth skin, unscarred by pox. My bright eyes. I stared at the pimp and his pupils dilated. Gripping my elbow, he hustled me into the corridor. I had a moment of doubt—had I timed my ambush too early? There was no stopping him though. In the corridor, he shoved me against the swaying wall. One hand seized me by the hair. The other groped roughly under my blouse. I struggled instinctively but was too weak in a woman's body. This is always the most dangerous part for any fox. If I wasn't careful, he might break my neck. Panting, he shoved his mouth on me, breath stale as a sewer. I closed my eyes, inhaled slowly, and focused.

A little later, the pimp lay on the floor, the whites of his eyes rolled up. He was still breathing. Searching his pockets, I removed his wallet and dragged his body towards the carriage opening. My stomach heaved. Was someone coming? The train leaned into a curve, yawing and shuddering. I gave the pimp a mighty shove. He rolled off like a sack of meal and tumbled down the embankment.

Returning to my seat, I wiped my face surreptitiously and rearranged my hair, tied in two neat braids like any servant. A girl traveling alone attracted attention. Leaning my head against the window to still my racing heart, I considered my options. This third-class carriage was loosely packed with Manchu soldiers known as bannermen, with their distinctive half-shaven heads and long hair plaited in queues.

It was a dangerously unstable time. The current Manchu, or Qing, dynasty, a non-Chinese dynasty founded in the north, was in decline. Though they had ruled China for three centuries, the population still considered them invaders and was seething with restlessness. It didn't help that the throne was currently occupied by the Dowager Empress, a onetime concubine rumored to have poisoned her enemies. Meanwhile, the Russians and Japanese, who were busy carving up the northeast, were all sitting in first-class carriages. China, I thought gloomily, was being devoured like a roast pig. I'd better be careful that didn't happen to me.

One of the Manchu bannermen finally made his move, sliding down beside me. "Where are you from?"

"Kirin."

"You don't look like a local girl. Are you Manchu?" A glance at my unbound feet in woven straw shoes.

The Manchus don't practice foot-binding, though the Han Chinese had done so for almost a thousand years. A terrible custom, I always thought. No other creature hobbled its females like this, breaking the arch of a child's foot at the tender age of four or five and binding it into a hoof, so that little girls could only creep along, wincing as they grasped chairs, tables, to take the weight off their broken toes. Poor little girls, biting back tears bravely in the belief that they'd be chosen for a fine bridegroom.

I shrugged, avoiding his question, but he wasn't deterred. "Are you going to Dalian?"

"Yes."

"What for?"

"I'm looking for a man."

At this, he laughed, slapping his stomach. "There's a good one right here."

"I'm not looking for a good man." I smiled. "I'm hunting a murderer."

2

"A body was found in the snow."

The man rubs his face. His left eyelid twitches.

The detective leans forward. It's early morning, and the rising sun paints the opposite wall blush gold. They're sitting at an empty table in a popular restaurant that caters to the wealthy and fashionable in Mukden. Red lanterns hang from the eaves, and large round tables with rosewood chairs wait expectantly, as though at any moment, a well-known politician and his entourage might slide in, laughing and blowing clouds of cigarette smoke. Gu, the restaurant proprietor, has called him in: six weeks ago, the body of a woman was discovered in a nearby alley.

There was no sign of foul play, Gu says. She likely fell asleep and froze to death. That's the best scenario. He bites his lip. Local officials were alerted and the body removed to the city morgue. It's a sad but common story, the detective thinks, especially in this freezing city in the far northeast of China, the ancient capital of the Manchu dynasty. But why has Gu requested his services in such a secretive manner?

"The truth is, her body wasn't found in the alley. She was propped up in a seated position against the back door of my restaurant. My staff notified me early in the morning, and we secretly moved the body to the next street. We didn't do anything wrong." He's defensive, eyes sliding away. "But if word got out that she was found on our doorstep, people would gossip."

A corpse is bad luck, especially for a popular restaurant like this, which specializes in hosting wedding and congratulatory banquets. Doubtless, Gu paid off officials to keep the case quiet. The detective wonders why he's been called in if the corpse was moved without incident.

"I need you to identify her. We had a kitchen fire recently—

exactly a month after it was found—and my wife believes that moving the body disturbed her spirit. She consulted a monk who said we must find the woman's name to conduct a religious service." He blinks nervously. "She was dressed like a courtesan; I didn't want to get involved with a runaway from the brothels."

Many are connected to organized crime. The detective, a small, sturdy man with a doglike air, tenses. "What happened to the body?"

"Buried. It's been a month." Gu's fingers drum on the polished table, as though he'd like to be anywhere but here on this chill early morning.

"Where was she found?"

The restaurant proprietor stands abruptly. "I'll show you."

A dark passage with greasy walls leads to the restaurant kitchen. There's a door that opens on a narrow lane, barely four feet wide, between the double-storied bulk of the restaurant with its open-fronted upper pavilion where, in good times, people sit at the railings and drink tea behind hanging reed screens. But the alley is on the side, hidden from prying eyes. It follows the long length of the restaurant all the way back to the kitchen. The opposite side is a blank wall.

"The cleaner found her when he opened the door. Fortunately I was here—I'd stopped by early that morning to check the account books. Otherwise he might have lost his head and run screaming around the neighborhood." Gu hunches his shoulders against the blast of wintry air as he opens the door. It sticks a little. "She was huddled on the step. When he yanked the door open, she fell inwards. He gave such a shout!

"My first thought was to notify the authorities, then I realized how bad it looked for us. I'd never seen her before, so I don't know why she chose to freeze on our doorstep. I had to take out a big loan on the restaurant and we're barely making our monthly payments. If business falls off, we're doomed, so I got the cleaner to help me lift her. We moved her to the street corner. Luckily it was so early in the morning that there was nobody around. The cleaner who works for me is a bit simple, so I made him swear not to tell anyone. That's also why I asked for your help." He looks imploring. "You have an excellent reputation."

The detective nods, understanding his meaning. "Detective" isn't quite the right way to describe himself. He considers himself more of a fixer. Someone who smooths feelings, arranges deals. But his true value is his ability to spot a lie.

SINCE CHILDHOOD, HE'S been able to discern falsehoods. Nobody else seems to hear this mysterious sound, a faint warning when a lie leaves someone's mouth and hovers, like a bee, before their lips. When the detective was young, he briefly attended a school on the outskirts of Mukden. An older boy brought three steamed buns for lunch, stuffed with juicy meat, and the envy of other children. But when the bundle was unwrapped at lunchtime, there were only two buns left.

Accusations had flown around the schoolyard until the detective had piped up, "You ate it yourself. Don't pretend it was stolen."

He was eight years old at the time, small for his age, with a large head like a watermelon, and he still remembers the shock, then hatred on the face of the older boy who'd accused the others of theft. Two seconds later, his face was pressed against the dirt, blood seeping out of his left nostril.

To this day, he's never figured out exactly why the older boy lied. Was it to accuse another boy whom he disliked? Or was it simply one of those inexplicable impulses: the desire to stir up the classroom and their meek, sad-looking schoolmaster? In any case, that first lesson, bitterly learned in the dirt, has drilled into him the importance of keeping his knowledge secret.

He's older now, bandy-legged with a face like a loyal dog, and people ascribe his skill to wisdom and experience. Coincidentally, he has the same name—Bao—as the legendary Song dynasty judge who solved crimes. Judge Bao was so famous for his deductive powers that he was even deified as a god. And so, whenever a new case comes his way, the detective can be sure that there will be jokes, remarks, and even superstitious terror that Bao Gong himself is coming to investigate.

Now Bao glances swiftly around. He's seen a thousand alleys like this. The only interesting feature is that no other buildings open into it, as the proprietor pointed out. An unknown woman freezing to death on his back doorstep is ominous. Has Gu's conscience afflicted him for secretly moving the body, or have there really been uncanny events, like the kitchen fire he mentioned?

"She was lightly dressed, no outer jacket."

"What were her clothes like?"

"An apricot silk *changyi* embroidered with flowers, loose trousers, and gilt hair ornaments. Flashy clothes like a professional entertainer. Snow had fallen on her like a layer of rice flour; I couldn't understand why she'd go out dressed so lightly."

"Was the body stiff when you moved it?"

Gu closes his eyes, trying to remember. "Her hands were icy, and her features had stiffened, but the larger muscles hadn't seized up." He looks ill.

So, she hadn't been dead very long. Perhaps only a few hours.

"And you're sure there was no foul play?"

"I heard later that the medical examiner found no wounds. It was a natural death." He sounds defensive. "Besides, there was that look on her face."

"Did she seem frightened?" Bao knows that the last expression on the faces of the dead can be pained, even uncanny.

"No, she looked delighted. She was smiling." Gu rubs his face. "I can't tell you how terrifying it was. There was a dusting of snow on her face and open eyes, so she looked like a bride on her wedding day, gazing through a veil—like she'd seen something wonderful."

Taken aback, Bao says, "You're sure she looked happy?"

"Yes. At first, I told myself that she'd had a good death, so it didn't matter that we moved her body. But when I mentioned it to my wife, she was extremely upset. Said it was the work of a fox."

Bao exhales slowly. Since ancient times, foxes have been feared and revered. The very earliest ones, the celestial foxes, were regarded as divine beasts. In the Tang and Song dynasties, they acquired a reputation for trickster cunning and the ability to turn themselves into humans. Still, it's mostly peasants who believe in their supernatural powers.

Gu grimaces. "My wife comes from the north, where they believe in foxes who lure people to their deaths. She cries every day, saying we're cursed; I shouldn't have touched the body or moved it. I'm at my wit's end! This restaurant is popular, but I borrowed heavily to open it. We're just beginning to break even."

At Bao's pause, he adds hastily, "I heard from our mutual connection that you were personally interested in foxes. Otherwise I wouldn't dare trouble you, especially since I heard you were thinking of retiring."

A shiver prickles Bao's scalp. For years, he's investigated any hint of foxes in unusual happenings. His friends laugh and refer to it as his hobby, while clients pass on rumors of twilight visitors. Bao merely smiles.

It's true, he's deeply interested in foxes.

3

Lots of men like to tell you they are bad. Often this is said with a wink and smile. *Little lady*, their eyebrows suggest, *you'd better be careful with a virile fellow like me.* But change the subject to murder and they back off. As I recall, the punishment for murder in Imperial China has always been gruesome. No wonder my statement about hunting a murderer made the Manchu bannerman get up and leave, ensuring a peaceful journey until we reached Dalian.

When the train stopped in a billowing huff of steam, I got off amid the rush of passengers. One woman had a pair of trussed live geese for sale, long necks protruding mournfully from her basket.

"How much?" I asked, running my finger down a feathered neck. The goose flinched. A gleam appeared in the woman's eye. Brusquely, she named a price that I paid without haggling from the pimp's wallet.

YOU NEVER KNOW how things will work out. The slightest change creates a swirl in the snowstorm of possibilities. Because I decided to buy two nice plump geese, the entire course of my investigation (that sounds so much better than words like "revenge" and "blood debt") shifted. As I lugged the geese away, I wondered what had possessed me to buy them. Perhaps dealing with the pimp had shaken me more than I cared to admit. My initial plan of finding a quiet alley to eat them was laughable. Dalian, or Dalniy, as the Russians like to call it, was now a large modern city.

Situated on the tip of the Liaodong Peninsula in the far north of China, its deep, ice-free harbor was prized as far back as the Tang dynasty, passing through Manchu, Russian, and now Japanese hands. The Russians had laid out a Western-style city, but lost Dalian after the recent Russo-Japanese War.

As I observed from the wide boulevards, the Japanese had been busy adding to its construction.

I'd underestimated the speed at which things had moved. Living in the grasslands and watching the clouds drift had made me soft, I decided. And what had I been thinking, that I could set my hissing bundle down somewhere and eat it? That might be true in a village, but not in this bustling modern city. The sun was setting, flooding the street with a bright, sad light, the color of yellow forsythia blossoms. In the past, I'd watched it gild the grasslands. Instead of an angry goose, I'd held a child in my lap. Warm, sleepy. Full of milk and sweet dreams. It's when you least expect it that sorrow returns, like a thief who steals joy.

The ache in my chest would never go away; a hollow, bloody darkness that had swallowed me for the last two years. Grass had grown on my child's grave in the far north. I'd lain on top of it every night for months, in vain hopes of keeping her warm. It was so cold, and she so small, lost to me forever. Burying my face in the dry clods of earth, I thought I'd die of grief and fury. But unlike the dead, living creatures recover. I clung to my vengeance grimly, that thin vein of blood that pulsed and kept me alive. The man who'd commissioned her death was a Manchurian photographer named Bektu Nikan.

His trail had vanished for two years, but I'd recently discovered he'd gone south to Dalian. Hastily pursuing him, I was dismayed to discover this city was far larger than I'd expected. How was I to find Bektu while securing shelter for myself? The incident on the train had underlined how dangerous it was to appear as a lone young woman. If two or more men assaulted me together, I might be overcome.

As I gazed despondently at the road, a middle-aged woman and her elderly maidservant stopped in front of me. Catching my eye, they hurried off. A few minutes later, the maidservant returned. Thin and nervous, she looked like a hare with large bulging eyes. "Are these geese for sale?"

I nodded.

"Where do they come from?"

"The north," I said. They looked like village-bred birds to me: small and rather tough.

"Is that where you're from?"

"Yes, from Kirin."

For some reason, that seemed to please her. In fact, if I were willing to carry the geese to her mistress's house, I'd be paid extra. Having nowhere to go, I agreed. As we walked, she plied me with questions: Where did I come from? What did my family do? To which I answered vaguely, for I had questions of my own. Whether, for instance, she'd heard of this new art called photography and if anyone practiced it in Dalian.

She said, "Oh! That's our young master's hobby. He knows many photographers since his friend runs a studio."

Eagerly, I quickened my pace. With any luck, I'd soon hunt down a photographer who'd come from Mukden.

OUR DESTINATION TURNED out to be a traditional Chinese medicine store. The sharp, bitter smell assailed my nose from afar: *dang gui* for menstrual irregularities, ginseng, red dates, and other herbs to be boiled with pigs' trotters or sea cucumbers for medicinal soup. Constructed of gray bricks with a curved-tile roof, the building's eaves were adorned with decorative rainspouts in the shapes of animals. The shop seemed prosperous from its wide frontage and the steady stream of customers exiting, clutching folded paper packets of dried herbs and roots. Behind the imposing double-storied shop front peeked the lower roofs of inner courtyards and a family home.

The front entrance was reserved for customers, not bedraggled peasants carrying geese, so we entered through a side gate. I was instructed to release the geese into a large poultry pen behind the kitchen. The bitter scent of medicine had given way to the aroma of braised pork belly wafting from the kitchen. My stomach growled as the maid told me to wait in the courtyard, before she returned with her mistress, the same woman who'd first spotted me with my geese. Her clothes were silk and fine cotton, appropriate for the wife of a wealthy merchant. On her finger was a ring of pale white jade, like a nugget of mutton fat.

The mistress studied me carefully. She had a smooth plump face and oiled black hair. Between her eyebrows and the downturned corners of her mouth were creases exactly like the pinch marks from tofu pressed and drained in a cloth.

"I heard you came from Kirin—are you looking for work? It's very easy; you'll serve an old lady."

"How old is she?"

"Over sixty."

I stifled a snort. Sixty isn't old to me. At sixty, humans are just beginning to understand that the weather will never obey them; that true love strikes at most twice in a lifetime; and that by saying yes in your youth, you may bind yourself unwisely to another's cause. But that was beside the point.

"Why me?"

Most people don't choose servants by picking up itinerant poultry sellers off the street. This woman didn't seem a fool; her downturned mouth suggested she was capable of counting every pair of chopsticks in the kitchen.

"My mother-in-law has been very picky about who attends her. But if you're from the north, she may agree. She's from that region herself." She pursed her lips. Clearly, there was more to the story, but it solved my urgent need of shelter while searching for my prey, so I nodded.

"She'll want to see you before she decides."

Before my interview, they agreed to provide me with clean clothes, a hot bath, and a good meal. They must have been completely desperate to offer such terms, and I began to wonder just what sort of terrible job this might be.

"Her first meeting with you must be at night. That's one of her conditions before hiring anyone."

I raised my eyebrows. Now that I was here, in this interesting house behind the medicine store, I could almost sniff out an aroma of mystery that curled through the winding passageways. Or perhaps it was just stewed pork belly.

AFTER A HOT bath, I was given clean clothes and a bowl of rice mixed with barley, topped with stewed pork belly and mustard greens. It was late, and the household had fallen silent when the maidservant finally led me through passageways and up a steep stairway of polished wood. Made for little bound feet, each step was no wider than the palm of a hand and led to the women's quarters.

Upstairs was a living area with a balcony that looked down onto a courtyard. The windows were open, bringing in the spring night, and a lamp was lit beside a rosewood chair. A little old woman was sitting in it. Her upright carriage reminded me of those small dogs that sit by the window: alert yet timid.

That timidity surprised me. From the mistress's words, I'd assumed a harridan who ran the household, but she almost looked frightened. And when our eyes met, hers widened.

4

When Bao was a child, his old nanny took him to a fox shrine in the back of their neighbor's house. It was a god, she told him, folding his small hand in her roughened red one.

The fox god lived in a little dark shrine, hardly more than a box with an open front, behind the neighbor's house. It was built some fifty years previously, after a severe illness had almost carried off the grandfather of that family.

"He was very sickly, and him the only son," said his nanny. "His mother prayed to the *huxian*, the fox spirit, and one night she had a dream."

They entered through a small back gate. Apparently, his old nanny was in the habit of visiting this shrine with the tacit permission of the other household's servants. It lent the whole enterprise an air of suppressed mystery. Bao's own household was strictly Confucian; his father would never countenance the worship of beasts, complaining it was nothing more than a peasant cult. In northern China, the fox, hedgehog, weasel, rat, and snake are considered the *wudamen*, or Five Great Households—minor gods of wealth and prosperity. Ridiculous, according to his father. Why would a wealth spirit slither around on its belly or live in dank holes? Bao had to agree with this logic, though tagging along with his nanny that day, he felt a frisson of wonder.

"What was the dream about—the one about the neighbor's grandpa?" he asked her.

"Oh," she said, "so you were listening after all?"

He'd laughed a little timidly. Tightened his grip on her hand. He felt uneasy about sneaking into their neighbor's rear garden, though they were on friendly enough terms.

"At that time, he was just a little boy like you, though he had fits and foamed at the mouth. His mother dreamed that an old man in a silk robe appeared before her and said if she raised a shrine to him in the back of their house, her son would be cured. And he was!" He remembers the smile in his nanny's voice, though her face has completely faded in his memory. "So today we're going to pray to the *huxian* to take your— . . . —away."

Strange how he can never recall exactly what she was going to pray for him. The words are blurred, like a smear of sound, or perhaps he wasn't paying attention. He was so very small at the time, young enough to reach up for her hand. Lower than the height of the bolt on the wooden gate. But he remembers the sunlit leaves and the huge bamboo culms that grew in this neighbor's back garden. Bao spent his time wandering in that grove, picking up leaves and jumping over the young shoots, while his nanny busied herself at the fox shrine.

A dark box with a sloped roof, it was open at the front and made of weathered gray wood. Inside was a small stone statue, upright and slender. It looked more like a cat than a fox, he pointed out. "Hush," she said hastily, apologizing to the deity for his rudeness. That's what he remembers, the way her pressed hands trembled slightly as she'd offered sticks of incense.

And now that Bao thinks about it, it was after this visit that he began to hear truth from lies. What exactly happened to him, that sunny morning under the bamboo leaves? The memory vanishes, and he turns his thoughts back to the current situation.

A WOMAN'S BODY found in the snow.

Waves of famine have driven peasants to the city, where they die in alleys and freeze in makeshift shelters. Yet this body belonged to a young woman who was neither starving nor ill dressed. As Gu, the restaurant owner, suggested, she was likely a courtesan from the pleasure district. Booked for parties, they sing, play the *qin*, and banter coquettishly as they pour wine. Important guests choose girls to take home as though they're desserts or afterthoughts.

Bao sighs. Recovering runaway women is a business that he usually avoids, but this nameless girl deserves a memorial. Her light clothes and lack of an overcoat are surprising. It was freezing that night, Gu told Bao. So cold that the snow slid off the curved-tile roofs in powdery drifts. Why did she fall asleep in the snow in a delirium of happiness?

Gu's wife insisted it was the work of foxes. On hearing those words, Bao's heart gave a curious, twisting leap, as though he were a child again in a rustling bamboo grove. Foxes and his strange ability to hear truth feel entwined—it's a mystery that has gnawed at him for most of his life.

Quickening his steps, Bao walks to the red-light district, felt boots slipping on the icy cobbled street. Here in the north, the buildings are brick and gray stone, tiled roofs slick and dark with melting snow. Rows of red lanterns hang between the buildings and across the street. They're lit at night, giving this district a rosy, optimistic glow. Very different from a morning like this, when clotted rags and torn paper plaster the wet pavements.

Bao checks with the staff at different establishments, asking if any women have recently gone missing. A bookkeeper says two women in the district have died of tuberculosis and another girl ran away. He pauses, one hand suspended over his heavy black abacus beads. "The girl who disappeared was from the Phoenix Pavilion."

"Have you heard any rumors of foxes?"

"Foxes?" The bookkeeper looks up, surprised. "You mean the normal kind or *hulijing*, the spirit foxes?"

"Either. Anybody mention them?"

"One of our porters swore he'd seen a white fox outside a teahouse late at night. I heard about it when he came in to be paid at the end of the month."

"What day was that?"

The bookkeeper flips open a ledger and names a date that's exactly the same night the woman's body appeared on Gu's back doorstep.

Bao inhales sharply, stomach clenching. "He's sure it was a fox?"

"I thought he must have seen a white dog, but he was insistent about the tail. A proper fox's brush, he said. Asked for extra pay so he could go to the temple and be exorcised. I told him no, of course." He glances shrewdly up at Bao. "If you're interested in foxes, you should talk to Bektu Nikan."

"Who is he?"

"A Manchurian photographer commissioned by a few establishments to take pictures of courtesans for a catalog. He stopped by when he heard our porter had said he'd seen a white fox. A strange man, with an uncomfortable stare. The girls didn't like him much."

"Why was he asking about foxes?"

"He wanted a white fox skin. Said people would pay good money to be photographed with it." The bookkeeper makes an involuntary face.

Foxes, Bao knows, are feared and worshipped as deities. They also steal the breath of living men—their *qi*, that vital force that animates everyone. The famous scholar Ji Yun, who was obsessed with foxes, said: *Humans and things are different species, and foxes lie between humans and things; darkness and light take different paths, and foxes lie in between darkness and light.*

"Between darkness and light" implies shadows. The uneasy realm of the believer. Sometimes Bao wonders if he falls into that category. Certainly he doesn't have the faith of his old nanny, who trudged to the fox shrine every week with small offerings of cake or fruit. She'd hardly anything of her own— she didn't even have a room to herself, but slept on the floor next to his bed ever since he was a baby. She was a stubbornly superstitious peasant who loved Bao dearly. That, he can't deny.

And he remembers his childhood and the day he first discovered he could hear lies.

5

We foxes have an appearance that elicits strong emotions from humans. It's the same quality that leads us to be trapped in boxes or put to death. So when the old lady's eyes widened when she saw me, I immediately felt alarmed.

Northeast China is full of villagers who still worship at fox shrines, consult mediums who claim to channel fox spirits, and invoke exorcists to drive them out. It's a love-hate relationship. Foxes used to be considered sacred, but where once we were revered, we're now reviled as seductive tricksters. For all intents, my prospective employer resembled your average granny. Small, upright, and rather sweet, despite her daughter-in-law's characterization of her as picky. But I knew better. That look in her eyes, the surprise and half recognition, made my ears tingle. It was the look of a believer: someone who had encountered one of us before, though she might not realize it herself.

"Madam," said the elderly maidservant, "this is the young woman."

The old lady tilted her head. "Come closer, into the light."

She had a quiet, reasonable voice. All the more reason to be careful since she didn't sound crazy. (Crazy, by the way, is helpful for us. People who act like madmen are seldom believed. The term "crazy like a fox" is something we're quite proud of.)

I stepped forward into the circle of yellow lamplight. There was really nothing to fear, I told myself, despite my racing pulse. She was just an old lady and not a Daoist exorcist, though I didn't really want to think about why an old lady would be conducting job interviews "only at night."

"You're from the north?" she asked.

"Yes, *furen*." I addressed her respectfully as missus, or the lady of the house. I had a whole story prepared about having come from the countryside to work as a nursemaid and having been hustled by a pimp (all true), but she didn't ask me any of that.

She simply said, "Has spring come to the grasslands already?"

"The plovers are calling, and the sheep grass is pushing up green shoots." I could almost smell the rich scent of the soil. It made me inexplicably sad.

"Could you please turn around?"

I did so, puzzled. The elderly maidservant looked unaccountably nervous.

"You have a shadow," said the old lady.

"Everybody does, *furen.*"

"No, not everyone. And yours is nice and solid."

The maidservant caught my eye and coughed, embarrassed. But I instantly understood what the old lady was doing. She was concerned about spirits. I felt like laughing. If that was the issue, there was no problem with my taking a job like this, for I was assuredly a living creature.

But I didn't laugh. I looked serious, and that seemed to please my prospective employer. "I'm not afraid of ghosts."

Which is absolutely true.

THAT'S HOW I got a job serving the widowed mother of the medicine shop owner. The interview had ended so late that I was starving again. Outside, I bought lamb skewers from a thickset man who was grilling them over a charcoal brazier. According to the skewer seller, the medicine shop was famously prosperous and had been established by a family of Han Chinese doctors from Mukden. Though for all their cleverness at curing other people's diseases, they themselves weren't long-lived.

"The heir to the house always dies young. It's said that the eldest son never survives. In fact, the current head is the second son," he said.

"They're unlucky, but they can cure others," said another. He was eyeing me in that acquisitive way, so I hastily made my departure, being sure to lose any pursuit by scrambling over a couple of walls.

I won't go into details, but one doesn't switch from fox to

woman and back on a whim, so it was extremely important to find a safe space to pass the night. I was grateful for this job, which would provide shelter while I hunted Bektu Nikan. I hadn't forgotten him. Not for a day, or even an hour. The image of my child's broken little body haunted me; I would not let it fade. Crawling under a bush in the courtyard of a deserted, half-built house, I curled up. Always choose the most haunted-looking place that others avoid. Chinese cemeteries are especially good. That's why people say that foxes live in graves.

Early next morning, I presented myself at the medicine shop. I was to address my new employer as *tai furen*, or Elder Mistress, to differentiate her from her daughter-in-law, who was the current owner's wife. This lady—Madam Huang—the pale, tofu-mouthed woman I'd first seen on the road, received me in the main house.

"What is your family name?" she asked.

"Hu," I said. There's another name, "Hu," which sounds exactly like fox but is written with a different character. That's the one that we often use to disguise ourselves.

"And your personal name?"

We foxes tend to have very simple names. Nothing fancy—in fact, I once knew a fox with the unfortunate name of Spot. When you live for a long time, it's best to keep things straightforward.

"My name is Snow"—"*xue'er*" in Mandarin, "*tsas*" in Mongolian, "*nimanggi*" in Manchurian, "*yuki*" in Japanese. It's a beautiful, poetic name, and one that I've never tired of.

"Snow . . ." Madam Huang frowned. In the thin morning light, filtering through the carved transoms lined with oiled paper to keep out the cold, she clearly thought my name too alluring for a servant. "Not Snow. We'll call you Ah San," which means "number three" in Chinese. Many peasants barely had names at all: numbers were common, and so were animals like "Ah Niu" (cow) and "Ah Gou" (dog), to ward off evil.

"All you have to do is take care of my mother-in-law," she said.

Previous candidates had apparently been dismissed shortly after being hired. Madam Huang looked unhappy. She didn't say why, other than to repeat that her mother-in-law was picky, but as her husband was very fond of his mother, there was nothing to be done other than to keep hiring and firing servants.

Besides the elderly maidservant Ting, there were many maids and menservants in the shop. It was so large that it was more accurately called a medicine hall—an echoing space, very dim and dark, with counters running along the sides. Behind them were hundreds of small wooden drawers, each holding dried roots and rare ingredients. There were shelves with jars of ginseng and dried mushrooms, including the famous *lingzhi*. Light filtered in from the top of the double-height hall, and the upper gallery was lined with dusty red lanterns.

Of my new mistress, Ting said, "She's been wary of people lately."

In fact, the old lady's reluctance had led to her recent retirement, a pity as her advice and financial acumen had long been the backbone of the business. I'd come just in time, said Ting defensively. Just because the Elder Mistress was moving to the back courtyard didn't mean she wasn't important.

Her new quarters consisted of a small courtyard with a two-room annex, formerly used for storage. It was dim and smelled of dried radishes and yellow dust from the plains. I didn't mind; I see very well in the dark. Ting hurried off, her mouth a pursed line. She'd probably said more than she'd intended. Most people do if you keep quiet for long enough.

If my new mistress felt any sadness or regret about being put out to pasture, *tai furen* said nothing. Indeed, when we were alone, she mostly talked about her childhood in the far north. Northern China is a mixture of many tribes, including Mongols, Manchus, Koreans, and the now-extinct Khitan. And that's not even counting the ambitions of Russia and Japan. Despite this, I find people remarkably similar, especially in their fears.

Most men fear darkness, decline in physical strength,

ruthless women, and children not of their own blood. There's more, though they'll go to extraordinary lengths to deny it. Frankly, I've always thought that admitting you're terrified of something is a good first step. But then, of course, I'm not a man.

I WANTED TO search for Bektu Nikan as soon as possible, but nobody let me out for a week. At night, all the outer doors and gates were locked, and a watchman patrolled outside—to prevent theft, they said, since many of the rare tonics and medicines were worth more than their weight in gold. Despite my gnawing impatience, I was relieved to have a safe place to sleep and plenty of food. I'd been alone for so long that the chatter of this large, lively household warmed me. There were many young ladies, including cousins, aunts, and friends, staying over. Waiting for my mistress, I overheard their gossip.

"Is the girl outside Grandmother's new servant?"

"She's suspiciously good-looking, like a fox."

My ears twitched in alarm. No, no. That was just one of those common jokes.

"We mustn't let Bohai see her. Or maybe we should!"

Shrieks of laughter. Pining away like birds in a cage, they could hardly be blamed for being silly. At this point, my old lady appeared on the veranda. Embarrassed, she explained, "My grandson, Bohai, is studying Western medicine in Japan."

Many young Chinese had gone to study in Japan since its rapid modernization and embrace of Western science. They were disillusioned with the crumbling Qing dynasty and its increasingly corrupt bureaucracy. The old Imperial literary examinations for government posts had fallen into decline, and nobody knew what the future held.

"I heard that your grandson knows all the new photographers in the city."

"Photography is his passion." She smiled. "Would you like me to ask Bohai if anyone new has come?"

Yes, yes, I would. As for Bohai, the only son of the house, I learned he was twenty-three years old, unmarried, and due to return to Japan as a medical student at the end of the month. How curious that there were so many young women in the family and almost no men. I recalled the lamb-skewer seller's words, that the eldest son of the household always died young.

My mistress said, "Since you've been asking so much about photographers, it's probably time to take my portrait before I die."

Old Chinese people love to talk about the span of their lives. In many villages, a sure sign of filial piety is that one's children have already bought a carved wooden coffin for you. It will be kept in a back room, and I wondered suddenly if, in one of these annexes, a wooden shell was awaiting her final journey.

My old lady's decision to have her photograph taken was extremely helpful in my search for Bektu Nikan. He couldn't have gone too far, not if he'd continued to ply his trade. I bared my teeth in a snap.

"You look so fierce, Ah San," she said, surprised. "Has anyone troubled you?"

"Troubled" could hardly describe the sorrow and rage in my heart, but I said merely, "It looks like rain."

When I'd ensured she was well wrapped up, she said, "Tell Ting that I'd like Bohai to accompany me."

6

Soon after his old nanny took him to the fox god's shrine, Bao fell ill with a high fever. His skin turned yellow, his stomach hurt, and he cried for hours. The whites of Bao's eyes were yellow as lanterns, and his parents feared the worst. But his old nanny continued to pray fervently, going to the fox shrine daily. Each time she went, she brought back a little gift for Bao: a bamboo leaf, a pebble shaped like the hollow indent of a chicken's pelvic bone. He wasn't sure whether this was to assure him of her pilgrimages or distract him from crying.

"He has too much heat and wind in him," said the doctor who examined Bao. "The spleen and gallbladder are blocked—see the yellow in his eyes?"

He prescribed capillary wormwood and poria mushrooms decocted with herbs. Bao drank the bitter medicine with tears streaming down his face.

Whispered conversations in the next room. His father, a government official, came to look at Bao. His mother, usually more concerned with Bao's older brother, a promising student, sat by his bedside with red-rimmed eyes.

"What's this nonsense?" said his father, glancing at the leaves and pebbles by his bed. "Throw it away, it's dirty."

His mother swept it off, and together they bent over him.

"Am I going to die?" asked Bao. The last time his father had leaned, peering ominously like this, over someone had been at Bao's grandfather's deathbed.

"Don't worry," said his mother. "Nobody dies from a sickness like this."

There it was. A strange, high-pitched buzzing that accompanied his mother's words. Startled, Bao looked around, forgetting his misery for a moment.

"Of course. You shouldn't worry," said his father.

Again, the buzz. It followed the movement of his father's lips exactly. Bao stared, mouth agape.

"What's wrong with the boy—has his mind been affected?" said his father sharply. No, the sound was gone.

"It's just the fever." His mother rested a defensive hand on Bao's head. His head, he knew, was very important to both of them. It was the first thing they always talked about, how many poems he had memorized, or how quickly he could calculate sums on the abacus. His father had taken the Imperial exams in his youth and had come away with an official assignment to this far-northern town. *If only I hadn't had a stomachache on the day of the examinations, I'd have done even better,* he'd said once. Bao and his older brother had glanced at each other. Bao knew from his brother's quick, frightened frown that this was serious business.

As was his illness now, no matter what his mother said. The pain in his abdomen was so piercing that he wanted to vomit, only there was nothing in his stomach, just the parched bitter bite of his own tongue.

Eventually his bloated belly subsided, the ache in his limbs ebbed away. Studying and memorization were out of the question; days were spent lying in bed, watching the sunlit leaves flicker in the courtyard beyond. It was almost summertime— the short, surprisingly hot summer of the north that came with clouds of yellow dust. Cicadas sang, reminding him of the buzzing whine he'd heard in his parents' voices.

A few days later, he heard it again when their maidservant was talking over the wall. She called out to their neighbor's cook that they were all out of eggs and had none to spare that day. This was clearly a lie; on the ground next to her was a bowl of fresh eggs laid by their own chickens. Bao was fascinated.

"Say it again," he asked her.

"What?"

"That we don't have any eggs."

She refused, thinking he was making fun of her, but later that day, he repeated the experiment with his nanny.

"Let's play a game," he said. "You say something, and I'll tell you if it's true or false."

His old nanny was the only one who'd stayed calm during

his illness. In fact, he had a dim memory of his mother scolding her one night when he was extremely sick—*You heartless woman, my son might die!*—and then her muffled reply that he couldn't make out.

"How old am I?"

"Seven."

"How old is my brother?"

"Eleven."

"No, no, that's not right. You have to lie!" he said indignantly.

"All right. Your brother is four years old." She was indulging him, but he heard it. A faint, telltale hum.

"Tell me something I don't know," he demanded.

"I washed your blue trousers yesterday."

"False."

"When I was a child, I gave my lunch to a beggar and my mother beat me."

"True!" Bao's eyes shone.

His old nanny clucked; she didn't want him to overexcite himself. "Last one."

"Were you worried when I got sick?"

"No."

"Why?"

She looked away. Strange how after all these years, even in his memory, he can't recall her face. Only the sharp, medicinal scent of the white flower oil she used for her arthritis. "The fox god told me that you would definitely live a long life."

BAO IS NOW sixty-three. He wonders if his nanny would consider that a long life. Perhaps he's the same age now that she was, or even older; it's hard to tell, as in his childhood memories, all adults are ancient. Bao considers himself agnostic about foxes. After all, among the educated, foxes are considered folk superstition, though he can't deny the peculiar yearning he feels whenever he hears the term "*hulijing*," or fox spirit. It's as though his chest is the hollow body of a lute, whose strings vibrate to an invisible breeze. Lately, this urge feels stronger, as though time is running out for him to meet the fox god.

The bookkeeper in the red-light district mentioned that a girl had gone missing from the Phoenix Pavilion. When women run away, the news is often suppressed lest it encourage further escapes. Others die from disease or suicide. There's no official body count in this district, where officials are routinely bribed.

With that in mind, Bao heads to the Phoenix Pavilion, where he asks for Qiulan, or Autumn Orchid. She's a woman he once did a favor for. It's just after lunch and the smell of *pao cai*, pickled vegetables, wafts into the room.

Qiulan is buxom and blousy, her once pretty looks beginning to fade. Never very skilled in conversation, she compensates with good humor, so when parties are being made up, her name inevitably comes up as the fourth or fifth choice. Every time they meet, Qiulan seems sadder and heavier. The rouge on her lips is smudged exactly in the shape of the thin stem of an opium pipe, and when she sees Bao today, she can barely muster a smile.

"Uncle Bao," she says, calling him by the familiar honorific for an elder, though they're not related. "What are you here for?"

He sets a gift of *laopo bing*, flaky pastries stuffed with candied winter melon, on the table. Qiulan's eyes look tired and puffy. Bao fears that she'll soon have to retire or be thrown out.

"I'd like to know about a woman who went missing six weeks ago. Maybe from a high-class establishment."

"What makes you think I can help—do I look high-class to you?"

He won't lie. That's the one thing that Bao can't bear to hear from his own lips, the faint whine of falsehood like an untethered bee, so he keeps quiet. Qiulan laughs shortly. "Well, I don't have much longer in this profession anyway."

Bao doesn't ask if she's paid off her debts. Girls sold into brothels must shoulder the cost of their own imprisonment, to which is added, month on month, the cruel price of interest, room, and board. Asking servants to run out and buy snacks and hairpins requires tipping to keep the relationships sweet. There are so many ways they're bled dry. Bending his head, he stares at the wooden tabletop. An ant crawls over it, a small traveler heading nowhere.

"Listen," she says, half jokingly. "I'll tell you what I know if you'll buy my debt out." They both know that he can't afford it. Besides, they've never had that sort of relationship.

"I'm old enough to be your grandfather." It's the reply he always gives her.

"I don't care. I'll make a good wife. Don't you want a son to carry on your family name?" Qiulan sounds more desperate each time. Her looks are fading, her good humor barely maintained under the spell of her opium pipe. Sometimes when she coughs, bright blood speckles the mucus.

"I won't marry again," he says gently.

"Who is it that you're still thinking of?" From time to time, Qiulan puts on coquettish airs, like the mannerisms she uses with clients, though it seems that she really wants to know all his secrets. Bored with her own life, terrified of her future, she spends her time needling him when he drops by from time to time.

Bao shakes his head. He knows this game. Qiulan trades in personal information. But she's useful, since she plays the *qin* well and gets invited to many parties, where she won't outshine the top courtesans. And she's truthful.

"Tell me, have you ever been in love, Uncle Bao?"

"Yes, I have."

"Who was it?" Qiulan's eyes light up. Strange how, despite her own disappointments, the rumor of love still sparks an interest in her.

"It was a long time ago. She and I were childhood friends, but she married another, and so did I."

Qiulan breaks off a piece of flaky pastry. *What a boring story*, her plucked eyebrows seem to say. With a sigh, she answers his original question, "The one who went missing was a new girl, Chunhua."

Beneath her brittle exterior, Bao senses she's upset. "Were you close to her?"

"She reminded me of myself when I was younger. Eager to please, hoping someone would fall in love with me and buy me out. Why are you asking about her, anyway? I thought you would never work for a brothel."

"You're right, my client is someone else."

"Is it Mr. Wang?"

At Bao's surprise, she says, "He's a wealthy man who often hires professional entertainers for his business events. In fact, Chunhua disappeared during his last party at a teahouse." She names a place two miles from Gu's restaurant.

Bao notes the address. It's walkable, though unpleasant on a freezing winter night with no overcoat. No one in their right mind would embark unnecessarily on such a journey, especially a woman alone.

At his frown, Qiulan says abruptly, "Something's happened to her, hasn't it?"

"The body of a young woman was found frozen in a doorway. I've been asked to find her true name so that a religious service can be said for her."

Qiulan's throat moves up and down. She's trying not to cry, though her eyes brim dangerously. "Was it Chunhua?"

"I don't know. She was buried already, and since it was outside the pleasure quarters, they might not have been notified." Bao doesn't mention that Gu, by bribing the officials, hushed up the incident. "I only have a secondhand description from the person who found her. Medium height, dressed in light apricot silk clothing. Fancy hair ornaments. Early twenties?"

"That could be anyone," says Qiulan defensively. "And not just from here. Many merchants keep mistresses. Chunhua was nineteen."

"Do you recognize the clothing?"

"I don't know what she wore that night. That week was busy as several girls were out sick. They wouldn't have picked her for that dinner if we hadn't been short-staffed. Mr. Wang is an important client. He always asks for professional singers and musicians, even for small parties."

"Did she seem excited or depressed in any way?"

"Not that anyone noticed. She wasn't an accomplished

singer or musician, as Mr. Wang prefers, but she was young and cheerful. She offered to run errands for me—little things like that. Other girls, when they see you're on your way out, want nothing to do with you. But she was good-natured. We got along well." She swallows.

"Did she have any particular weaknesses?"

Qiulan stares at the carved screen behind him. A fly buzzes drunkenly over her head. "She didn't take opium, but she was a fool for handsome men. That's how she ended up here. A pimp recruited her the usual way, with promises of love and marriage. You know the story." She sighs. "I hope it wasn't her. Speaking of handsome men, there was one guest who attracted attention that night. He was all the girls could talk about when they came home. Nobody missed Chunhua until later, thinking she'd returned early. The next morning, she still wasn't back and that's when the alarm went out. They don't like it when women go missing."

That's an understatement, as Qiulan's lowered glance tells him. Still, Bao has a problem. He has no way to confirm that the missing woman was Chunhua, though it still seems like the most likely scenario. It's too bad that the restaurant owner's description was scanty, but he was likely too shocked to examine her properly. A corpse is considered a repository of *yin*, or negative energy, and thus deeply unlucky. No wonder Gu has been so terrified in the weeks since.

"Was Chunhua her real name?"

"No."

"Chunhua" means "spring flower," just as "Qiulan" means "autumn orchid." They're the sort of light, floral names given to women of the pleasure quarters. Often there's a theme, chosen by the establishment.

"Do you know her real name?"

Qiulan shakes her head. "Our house doesn't keep such records, to prevent trouble from relatives."

"Did anyone ever take a photograph of her?" If so, Bao can ask Gu to confirm if it's the woman he found. Photography is a new art, and though some are afraid of having their likenesses captured, fearing it will snatch away their souls, it's increasingly popular. The Dowager Empress herself has posed for photographs, dressed up as the Goddess of Mercy.

"Yes. The owner had some pictures taken for a catalog. Chunhua was in the group photograph, taken by a Manchurian named Bektu Nikan."

It's the same name mentioned by the bookkeeper—the one who asked about a white fox seen by a porter.

"The group picture with her wasn't selected as a print. You'd have to ask Bektu for it." Qiulan drops her eyes. "There's a rumor going round that maybe Mr. Wang took her to his villa. At a previous banquet, he remarked that Chunhua resembled one of his favorite opera singers, which made some of the other girls jealous. That's why they didn't want her picked for the last party, the one where she vanished. I've heard that Mr. Wang has a secret courtyard at his country villa where he keeps women. What if she's not dead, but there instead?"

Bao pencils this into his notebook. Qiulan would rather think of her friend as alive in a rich man's house rather than frozen in a doorway. They both know which is more likely though.

"If you want to know Chunhua's real name, she told me that she came from Wu Village to the west of the city. Her family were ragpickers, reselling old cloth. She fell in love with a pimp and ran away with him." Her shoulders sag. "She had a younger sister that she didn't dare contact. Said she was ashamed. Like I said, she reminded me of myself when I was younger. What a stupid girl."

Tears fall from her eyes. Bao is unsure whether Qiulan is weeping for her lost friend, or herself.

7

S o there we were, my old lady and me, waiting in front of
the medicine shop for Bohai to accompany her to visit
photographers. Finally, the door opened and out came the
young master. I almost burst out laughing. Bohai looked like
an egg. He had a pale oval face, small eyes, and thin flat hair
combed severely into a fashionable side part. On top of that,
he wore a suspicious expression: very hard-boiled.

"Grandmother." Even his voice was slightly squeaky. "You'll
catch a chill. Must you take your photograph today?" For all
his grumbling, Bohai seemed fond of her. When a rickshaw
arrived, he helped her into its swaying height and climbed in
after.

My mistress peered worriedly at me. "I want to take Ah
San, too."

"She can walk," he said, so I was forced to scamper after
them. I didn't care. As the breeze stung my cheeks, I had a
fiercely joyous feeling that I was getting closer in my hunt
of Bektu Nikan. He'd eluded me once, in a far-off northern
village when I'd heard falsely that he was dead. And, recently,
a second time when I'd tracked him to Mukden.

From what I overheard as I ran behind the rickshaw, the
photographer we were going to visit was a Japanese man named
Oda. "That's your friend's shop?" said my mistress.

"Yes," Bohai said. "Grandmother, your new servant—you
haven't noticed anything odd about her?"

The wheels rattled over a bump, so I missed part of my
mistress's reply. "—Bohai, I want you to be very careful. You
know why."

THE PHOTOGRAPHY STUDIO was neat and prosperous;
clearly there was demand for this new art, which captured
your likeness forever. A painted backdrop gave the illusion

of a faraway landscape, with various props to pose with. The hairs on the back of my neck stiffened; mixed in with the smell of furniture polish, darkroom chemicals, and a large bouquet of wax flowers was a faint musky scent that made me uneasy. That's the problem of living a long life. One can't help running into old acquaintances.

My mistress leafed through the album of photographs proffered by Oda, the proprietor. His Chinese was excellent, though he spoke Japanese to Bohai.

"If you like, I can take your portrait today at a discount for friends," he said. That was enough to make my mistress smile and agree.

"Where's Shirakawa—isn't he staying with you?" Bohai peered at the doorway curtain in the back of the shop.

"He's not here today."

"Oh." Bohai looked unaccountably disappointed. My stomach fluttered in alarm. "Shirakawa" means "white river"—a common enough Japanese name. However, any name with the written character for "white" in it is immediately suspect to me. As is "black," for that matter. But more about that later.

Oda looked up from the camera at Bohai. "Be careful at night; don't go drinking with strange companions. There's been another death."

"Who died?" A note of dismay in my mistress's voice.

"A student. He was found in an alleyway. Shirakawa told me."

Oda might have thought he was merely relaying news, but from the trembling of her lips, my mistress was worried. She glanced at Bohai and twisted her hands in her lap. Recalling the rumors of how the eldest sons of this medicine shop died young, I wondered if that accounted for Bohai's peevish air of anxiety. I, too, was on high alert.

Sudden, inexplicable deaths were of great interest to me.

As we left, I lingered to ask Oda if he'd heard of a Manchurian photographer named Bektu Nikan. He gave a nervous start. "I've no idea what you're talking about." Turning abruptly, he went outside to where my mistress and Bohai were waiting. I narrowed my eyes. Oda and his studio put me on edge; I had the gnawing feeling that I'd missed something. Perhaps I ought to come back. Alone.

I wasn't the only one feeling suspicious. At home, my mistress asked me, "You seemed to understand Oda and my grandson at the shop. Do you speak Japanese?"

When you live a long time, you learn many languages, but I gave her the same vague story I've used before. "I came from an orphanage in the north, where there were Japanese and Russian settlers. Koreans and Mongolians, too."

"Was it hard for you?" She looked worried. That was what I was beginning to like about her; there was no reason for a well-off widow like her to care, but she had a kind heart.

"Sometimes." I sighed, in a way calculated to put off questions as we went back to carding embroidery thread. I hate embroidering, by the way. But it's one of those womanly arts that you must endure to pass as a proper lady.

"Why aren't you married?" she asked.

"I've been married before. I've no interest in marrying again."

My mistress nodded mildly. "I see." She probably assumed that I'd been widowed or had run away. "Since you understand Japanese, could you do me a favor? I'd like you to keep an eye on Bohai's friend Shirakawa. I fear he's taking advantage of Bohai. Sometimes, he almost seems bewitched."

I kept my face deliberately blank. Words like "bewitched" are bad news for foxes. After all, it doesn't take long for rumors of devilment to set off literal foxhunts.* But I was curious about this Shirakawa myself, including the mention of sudden deaths that the photographer Oda had made.

AND SO MY mistress decided to hold a small dinner for her grandson and a few of his friends. It was to be an intimate gathering: Bohai, three of his friends, his grandmother, and his father, the master of the medicine shop. Madam Huang, his mother, had declined to attend. She gave vague excuses,

*I once spent five months hiding in a turnip cellar in the ancient walled city of Ping Yao, when disease killed off one-third of the male population and rumors blamed licentious fox spirits.

but I suspected she meant to keep the young ladies in the house from spying. They were at a dangerously marriageable age; it wouldn't do to have them involved in some unsuitable love affair. It has always amazed me how people lock up their daughters but not their sons. If they locked up the young men as well, there would be a lot less trouble. But who was I to interfere? I was simply there on my own quiet path of revenge.

Dinner would be in the main dining room, where an enormous round table made of rosewood was used for formal meals. I was to attend my mistress. There were no constraints about female servants being in mixed company. We were considered too low-class to be restricted, and gentlemen could be expected to take their pick from service females. I bared my teeth just a little.

Besides, my mistress had asked me to listen in on Shirakawa. As she explained, "My grandson often speaks to him privately in Japanese and I want to know what they're discussing."

The cook had been busy all afternoon. Dalian is a port city, famous for its seafood. Fish, clams, and sea urchins grow deliciously plump in its frigid waters, so there were oysters folded into delicate chive omelets, and sweet-fleshed croaker fish panfried, then braised with garlic and fermented black beans. There was also drunken chicken, steamed, salted, and doused with rice wine, with thin curls of green onions on its glistening golden skin.

It was dusk by the time the dinner guests arrived, and the dining room was brightly lit with oil lamps. So bright, in fact, that coming in from the dimly lit corridor made people blink. That was how I observed each of them enter, eyes scrunched up and slightly dazzled. An odd parade, made more so by the sharp shadows cast by the light.

Bohai's father looked harried and tired. He gave my old lady a questioning look, as though wondering why she'd arranged a dinner like this. Next was Bohai, ushering in a couple of friends: Lu Dong and Chen Jianyi. Lu was very tall and thin, with a downturned lip like a camel. Chen was so ordinary that it was hard to describe him. Medium height, medium-wide face. I'd passed a thousand Chens before, from princes to melon sellers. Standing quietly behind my mistress's chair, I noted how she leaned forward to scrutinize the young men. She was more concerned with their shadows than their faces. Each shadow was sharp and black, crisp as a sugar wafer, and I saw her shoulders relax.

"But where is your friend Shirakawa?" she said.

Bohai said, rather ungraciously, "He'll be a little late. He said to send his apologies." I was beginning to understand Bohai better. He didn't mean to be rude; he was merely anxious. But his father frowned.

"Who is Shirakawa? How long have you known him?"

The answer to this was confusing. Both Lu and Chen appeared to know Shirakawa as well, but their accounts were vague and contradictory. One said that Shirakawa had gone to school with them, the other that Shirakawa had done them all a great service in the past. The one thing they agreed on was that he was very charming and erudite, perhaps the cleverest person they'd ever met.

My skin tightened. I felt the warning tingle of running into someone you wish to avoid, of hoping that a description is just mere coincidence. And why shouldn't it be? I'd only the character 白, or "white," in his name to go by. There were thousands—no, hundreds of thousands—of people with names like this.

"When are you going back to Japan?" my mistress asked.

In a few weeks, it seemed. The Japanese academic year began in April, and all three young men were university students. Chen said, "I can't wait to get away from my father."

"You'd better make sure he doesn't know what you've been up to," said Bohai. A joke that fell flat. The young men laughed uneasily.

Lu said, "Speaking of trouble, remember Bektu Nikan, the Manchurian photographer who took pictures for Chen's uncle?"

I inhaled sharply.

There was the slightest freeze, as though he was warning

his friends. "I heard he's gone on to Yokohama, so we may see him again."

Their talk devolved to other matters, but I gripped the back of a chair in fierce triumph. Who knew why the young men were nervous about him, but I was glad that my mistress had hosted this dinner. Now I knew where Bektu Nikan was, I just had to figure out how to get there. It's said that foxes are deterred by running water. This isn't true, though we tend to be horribly seasick; it would be most troublesome if Bektu had run away to Japan.

Lost in thought, I forgot to heed my earlier unease. If I'd been alert, I ought to have excused myself and gone to stand silently in the corridor. When you live by your wits, there's no such thing as being too paranoid. But I was so pleased with having picked up Bektu's trail (in our own dining room, no less!) that I simply stood there, grinning like a fool. I'd utterly forgotten about Bohai's latecomer friend.

"Shirakawa!" Bohai stood up, and so did the others. There were smiles, apologies. The gift of some very expensive wine and little cakes. Everyone was charmed, including Bohai's grumpy father and my mistress. Everyone but me.

How to explain that feeling of irritation and despair when someone you neither expected nor particularly wanted to see again enters a room? Shirakawa was very much as I remembered him. In person, he has thin, humorous eyes and a pale complexion. Clever hands that move gracefully. He has a peculiar two-faced quality, meaning you can read two different emotions on his face at the same time. When he smiles, his mouth curls, but his eyes—very light, tea-colored eyes with sharp pupils—remain deadly serious. It's unsettlingly provocative; most people respond by laughing nervously.

"Shirakawa" was, of course, an alias, his real name being White, or "*shiro*" in Japanese. I told you that foxes have simple names.

Also, that I tend to avoid males of my own species.

8

Bao sits at the writing desk in his rented quarters: the large front room of a two-story shophouse, narrow and high-ceilinged. His landlord, a tailor, retains the rest of the long skinny shophouse for his family. He's been living here for the last three years and enjoys the clear, cold sunlight that streams through the windows in the morning. For that pleasure alone, he's willing to take on more jobs. Like this one. Opening his notebook, he jots down:

1. The young woman frozen in the doorway is likely Chunhua, a courtesan from the Phoenix Pavilion who disappeared that evening from a party two miles away. But if so, how did she end up at Gu's back door?
2. "Chunhua" isn't her real name. She came from Wu Village outside the city.
3. The quickest way to prove her identity is a group picture taken by the photographer Bektu Nikan.

Like a curling wisp of smoke, this case is already shaping into an uneasy tale whispered late at night: a woman found frozen in a doorway, a restless spirit. A shiver tightens Bao's scalp as he recalls Gu's words, *This is the work of a fox*. He adds another note:

4. Bektu Nikan was looking for a white fox skin.

BAO PUTS ON a quilted jacket padded with fine silk floss, a gift from his older brother, now a retired official. In the distant bluing of the sky, he senses spring's arrival in this northern region, though the wind still cuts like a knife. He's restless; the rumors of foxes drive him onwards, with the unsettling feeling that this might be his last case.

He's already canvassed the area near the restaurant, though Gu assured him that nobody saw anything. "I asked around myself," he said, looking guilty. No doubt he'd feared witnesses to his moving the body. Today, Bao starts from the teahouse where Chunhua was last seen. Hopefully he'll turn up a witness along the route between the teahouse and Gu's restaurant.

The area is a warren of streets and alleys, a mixture of restaurants, bars, and shabby courtyard dwellings behind them. Bao's inquiries if anyone saw a young woman lightly dressed in apricot silk late at night are met with stares and headshakes. Who can recall what happened more than a month ago? But finally, a boy sweeping a doorway nods. "Yes, I saw her."

"Was she alone?" Bao can hardly believe his luck.

"No, she was walking with a handsome gentleman." He's so scrawny that Bao guesses he's an indentured servant, sold by a starving family who can't afford to feed another mouth. Scabbed toes poke out of his straw shoes.

Bending over, Bao tucks a coin into the boy's cold hand. "It's yours," he says gently. "Buy something nice to eat."

Shyly, the boy puts it away. "It was late at night. That's why I remembered them. Nobody else was out because it was freezing."

"How do you know?"

"I sleep in the doorway," he says. "On the floor just inside. That night it was so cold that I woke up."

Many people treat their servants like dogs, making them sleep in the front entrance to alert the household to any thieves. Bao's heart twists with pity. At least this child was indoors, but it's small comfort on a snowy day, when freezing air seeps under the gaps.

"I heard her laughter, so I got up and pressed my eye to the door crack. She sounded happy."

"Do you mean drunk?"

"Giddy, like something good had happened to her. They were walking down the street, arm in arm. He was holding an oiled paper umbrella. Loose snow was blowing off the roofs, so it was all black and white."

Bao thinks this is a curiously poetic scene. "What did they look like?"

"The gentleman was dressed in white; his clothes looked expensive. The lady was wearing a thin *changyi* and trousers—I couldn't tell the color in the moonlight, but it was light."

"Did she look like a professional courtesan?"

The boy frowns, unsure. "She had a lot of hair ornaments. And no coat. I thought she'd be cold, but she was laughing and clinging to his arm. All the shops were silent and shuttered, the windows dark. Nobody was on the street, just the moon shining down on them and the silvery snow. I had the strangest feeling that I was in the wrong place or a different time. In fact, when I woke up in the morning, I thought I'd dreamed it."

"You said the gentleman was handsome?" Bao thinks of the party that Qiulan told him about, where the other girls were excited over a good-looking guest. "How old was he?"

"He seemed like a young man. As they passed, the wind raised a snow flurry and he looked straight at me, as though he'd spotted me peeping through the crack, though I don't know how he could see in the darkness."

"Were you frightened?"

"Yes . . . no." Pause. "He smiled. Such a sharp smile, with gleaming white teeth. I wanted to open the door, like something was calling me out. I think," he says, his voice getting smaller with shyness, "I think he was a fox."

Bao wants to ask why he's come to this odd conclusion but is interrupted as a burly man pokes his head out with an unfriendly glance. Bao introduces himself, explaining that he's looking for a young woman who's gone missing.

The man shrugs. "There's always girls going missing. Servants who can't take the work or get pregnant. It's none of my concern."

He ushers the boy in with a glare and Bao trudges off. A chill breeze is blowing, icy needles stinging his face. The boy's comment about the gentleman holding an oiled paper umbrella lends it an odd air of veracity. Why did he call him a fox? Those words linger with the clear tone of truth, though the boy's phrasing, *I think*, muddles the meaning.

Sinking his chin deeper into his collar, Bao imagines a winter's night where a sleepless child peers through a doorway at either a man or a creature in the semblance of one. If there ever was a time for ghosts and foxes to appear, it's now. The Qing dynasty that has ruled China for the last three hundred and fifty years—a foreign dynasty headed by non-Chinese Manchus—is in its death throes. Insurgents plot its downfall; young scholars flock to Japan to join revolutionary cells.

Every dynasty rises and falls with portents. Black and white foxes were viewed as omens in the past and sent to the emperor as tribute. Now the current young emperor is under house arrest, and the Dowager Empress, a former concubine who has grasped the reins of power for decades, is ailing. Warlords and foreigners circle like wolves. This case, with its constant mention of foxes, stirs Bao. He's restless, feeling the pull of doubtful belief. For hasn't he himself lived for a long time with a secret ability that he can't explain, either to himself or others?

BAO DISCOVERED HIS ability to hear lies also applied to himself soon after his old nanny was dismissed. His mother had never liked his nanny, having inherited her from his father's distant side of the family. Not one of her own people, but an old woman from a far village, who spoke a rough dialect that no official's wife could be expected to understand.

Bao's childhood sickness had more serious repercussions than either of them could have imagined. When his skin turned yellow and his stomach swelled, his mother had accused his nanny of being unfeeling, a wicked woman not to cry or show sadness when the child was so ill. Bao knew the truth—his nanny had been assured by the fox god that he would live a long life—but that was never communicated to his mother. Why would it have been? After all, his father was against such superstitious nonsense. And so, a month after Bao recovered from his illness, he returned home one day to discover his old nanny gone.

"Why? Where did she go?"

He'd wept for days. His mother gave him one explanation after another, lies spilling from her lips. So many that Bao heard the hum of their poison echoing against the walls of his small room. His nanny had been called away to nurse a sick relative. She was too old to take care of a big boy like Bao. And finally, that she'd taken ill and died. This last, an unwilling shriek from his mother when Bao wouldn't give up his relentless questioning.

"That old woman must have bewitched him!" she said. "How could a child question me like this every day?"

Lies. They were all lies.

The more his mother lied to him, with her soft hands and sheltered complexion, which showed she was an official's wife who never had to work, the more Bao wept for his old nanny.

But his tears had no effect. If anything, they hardened his mother's resolve. "Just think what would have happened if I'd left him under the care of that woman for any longer," she said to his father. The murmur of her angry words, nursing her own hurt and bitterness at Bao's rejection. The furious adult stare he gave her, knowing she was withholding the truth from him. Why did she care anyway? She already had his older brother, the favored one, the scholar. Bao was the spare.

"Listen," said his mother. "You'll never see that woman again. But I'll get you a playmate instead."

The companion that she'd promised him turned out to be not the stray puppy that Bao had coveted, playing by itself in the dust by the side of the road, but a child. A little girl who lived a few streets over. She was the daughter of someone's concubine and would normally never have encountered Bao except his mother had desperately combed the neighborhood for suitable playmates.

The little girl was the same age as Bao, though very small with bright eyes. He didn't want her. No playmate would make up for the loss of his old nanny, with her rough warm hands and her stooped back that had carried him since he was a baby. When they brought the girl over one morning, he shut the door of his room against her. The room that he'd shared with his old nanny, whitewashed walls, with a mat on the floor where she had slept at the foot of his bed since he was a baby. Now there was nothing, not even her thin bedroll. It had been bundled up and cast away with her. Bao imagined his old nanny trudging away, her tiny figure bent under the bedroll, and fresh tears stained his cheeks. No girl could replace her.

The little girl stood in the courtyard outside for a long time. It wasn't clear whether those were her instructions, that she must stand and wait until he came out, but she did. Faithfully, for more than an hour, until Bao, curious, peeped out at her. She looked like a chipmunk in her brown clothes. And she was even more miserable than he was.

"Go away!" he'd shouted at her.

She shook her head stubbornly. Her braided hair, bound up in big loops over her ears, quivered. The next day she was back again, and when Bao came out to chase her away, she stood her ground.

"I'm not allowed to leave until you play with me," she said.

"You look like a baby. You're so small."

She drew herself up. "I'm almost seven. Just like you. My name is Tagtaa."

"What kind of name is that?" It didn't even sound Chinese.

"If you come out, I'll write it for you." And she did, scratching it on the dirt with a twig in curling Mongolian script. "*Tagtaa*," meaning "dove" or "pigeon."

"I don't want to play with you," Bao said. Then stopped in wonder as he felt the buzz of a lie vibrate on his own tongue.

9

Across that bright, lamplit dining room (so bright that it was almost like the stage of an opera performance), I stared at Shiro and he at me. Naturally, his expression didn't change. Neither did mine, or so I hoped. Perhaps a muscle in his jaw twitched, very slightly, in amusement.

Mentally, I shot daggers at him. *Go away. Why are you here?* Unfortunately, foxes aren't mind readers, though I suspected that Shiro knew exactly what I was thinking. Well, unpleasant encounters are part of life. The first course of cold dishes—drunken chicken, translucent jellyfish served in wine, cold pork dressed with pungent raw garlic and a drizzle of soy sauce—had almost been finished, and I'd been so busy giving Shiro the evil eye that I didn't realize my old lady was talking to me.

"Ah San, can you serve my grandson and Mr. Shirakawa?"

I knew she wanted me to eavesdrop on their conversation. Earlier, I'd agreed, never suspecting whom I'd have to stand behind. Sometimes I think that my life will end not in some grand reveal or treachery, like being shoved off a cliff or shot through by crossbow bolts (very sad outcomes that have finished off several foxes I know), but by simple, stupid household drama like this.

But I couldn't very well refuse her, so I shuffled off gloomily to do my duty. Passing the soup and deboning the whole steamed fish that arrived, mouth agape on a huge platter, were tasks that I busied myself with in silence. I also served the other young gentlemen, Lu and Chen, who were seated nearby. Lu, after glancing at me several times, brushed his hand against my thigh. I moved away.

Partway through the meal, Bohai's father excused himself on business matters. With the departure of their host, the young men became more animated. This excitability is common in the presence of a fox, particularly if he's exerting his charm. Shiro spoke very splendidly about the poet Li Bai and spring evenings. Utter nonsense, of course, as I know Shiro won't read a menu if he can get someone else to do it for him, but foxes are good mimics.

"Favorite son-in-law" is what I call this role, in which the fox becomes fast friends with a scholar, swearing brotherhood and even marrying the daughters of rich families. Naturally, it has its dangers if people start poking around to see if this handsome stranger has a decent background. Many a fox has had to flee with his tail between his legs or been chased away by a keen family hound.

The medicine shop didn't keep any dogs, but for an instant, I quite wished they had, even if it resulted in my own eviction.

"Shirakawa, your insight is amazing!" exclaimed Bohai admiringly.

The other two nodded. Chen's wandering hand rested on my leg, sliding up to my hip. I took a quick sideways step, only to encounter Lu's foot, rubbing familiarly against my ankle. When I glanced at him, he smiled secretively. There was no choice but to move over again so that I stood right behind Bohai and Shiro.

"How have you been feeling lately?" said Shiro in an undertone.

"I'm managing. Though sometimes I have that sensation again."

They spoke softly in Japanese. I thought Shiro would have his guard up against me, but to my surprise, he went on talking to Bohai. "The same as last time?"

"Yes. Nausea, chills. Don't tell my grandmother. She'll never let me resume my studies. I wish you'd come with us, Shirakawa! I feel better when you're near; I forget my troubles."

Shiro laughed. He has a pleasant, musical laugh. If you imagine gently colored lights drifting upwards, that's the effect that Shiro's laugh has. I disapprove of such flashy techniques.

"What are you discussing so earnestly?" said Chen, gesturing me to refill his wine cup.

"I was telling Bohai a story," said Shiro smoothly. He turned slightly so that everyone could admire his profile.

"Oh! We want to hear it, too."

"Yes, please do," said my mistress. "I've heard so much about your stories, Mr. Shirakawa."

"Very well," said Shiro. "It's a tale about foxes. As you know, they can be found everywhere from Korea to Japan, but this part of northern China is their heartland."

"I read Pu Songling's tales and always wished to meet one of those beautiful fox women," said Lu.

Shiro smiled. "Perhaps you'll be lucky—tonight?"

Everyone laughed.

I wanted to smack Shiro's head down into the bowl of sweet red bean soup that had just been set in front of him. The first rule of foxes is that *you don't talk about foxes.* The second rule is—well, I shall tell you when we get to that part, but I was so incensed right then that I almost walked out. And perhaps I should have. Turned around, and vanished into the rain-scented night, leaving Shiro smiling in that ring of rapt faces, the bright oil lamps making a charmed circle against the dark.

But curiosity has always been my weakness. It's the same for most foxes, and why we often linger, wondering what that peasant is planning to do with his pitchfork, or if one's head will really fit into this jar. It's part of our quick-wittedness, our dizzy charm and carelessness. The way we live, always on the edge, running along the tops of stone walls and fences. Between civilization and the wilderness.

Of course I stayed. Shiro knew I would.

Also, I wanted to find out about Bektu Nikan, whom they'd mentioned at the beginning of this dinner. I wasn't going to be cheated out of that by Shiro. So I stayed, even though Chen had, under the pretense of a dropped napkin, leaned over and lightly pinched my left buttock.

"THE STORY I'M going to tell you is about the foxes who live among us. There are foxes even in a new city like Dalian. They come from the countryside, burrowing under disused houses and living in people's backyards. Of all these foxes, only a few—very few—are the kind that can turn into beautiful women."

I noticed that he'd carefully failed to mention male foxes. But at that moment Lu said, "Aren't there also men who are foxes? The wife of a merchant from Chu was seduced by a fox who visited her night after night."

"Why don't you tell us your story first," said Shiro. "And if mine is better, you'll owe me a favor."

"Very well." After some throat clearing, Lu began. "There was once a merchant whose wife was possessed by an evil fox spirit. Appearing in the shape of a young man, he entered the woman's chamber night after night until she was exhausted."

"Was the wife pretty?" asked Chen.

"Probably not. I mean, her own husband couldn't be bothered with her, and foxes are just animals." They laughed. I saw Shiro's lip curl, very slightly.

"Anyway, as you can imagine, this wicked fellow kept troubling her. When her husband came home, the fox would slip out the back of the house and enter a large bottle in the form of smoke. One day, when the fox had fled in this manner, the woman rushed out and stoppered the bottle. Then she put it into a large pot of water and placed it on the fire. When the water began to boil, the fox started to scream, 'Let me out!' The shrieks grew louder and louder, until there was silence. When the woman opened the bottle, it was filled with fur and blood."

There were groans and shivers from the audience. Shiro's nostrils flared. "That's quite a story."

Lu laughed. "I'd like to hear anyone top that one!"

"I've changed my mind," said Shiro. "I think I'll tell a different story. But it's still about foxes."

There were whispered giggles in the corridor; the young women of the household were peeking in and making breathless comments. Mostly about how handsome Shiro was, and how they'd just *die* if he happened to see them. Really, I thought, they'd no idea what they were dealing with. They might actually die. I was starting to get worried for my old lady. If Shiro was in one of his capricious moods, who knew what he might do to her household?

He raised his wine cup elegantly. "Once there was a rich man named Lu, from the old town of Caozhou in Shandong province."

Lu said in surprise, "Why, that's where my great-grandfather comes from."

"What a coincidence." Shiro was smiling again, that lopsided smile that's so charming and unreliable. "The Lu family owned a large estate, half of which was left untended. It was a good piece of land with a stream running through it and a grove of pine trees."

Lu's lugubrious camel face looked more astonished. "My great-grandfather's estate also had a pine grove and a stream."

Bohai leaned forward, and even my old lady looked surprised.

"One evening, an old man appeared and asked if he could rent the unused portion of the estate, along with the derelict villa that had been long abandoned. 'I'll pay you one hundred ingots of silver,' he said. Now Lu was a man with an eye for a bargain, who insisted they prepay the rent."

Lu frowned. "I don't recall anything like that happening to my great-grandfather."

Shiro continued smoothly, "As promised, the very next day the old man brought the silver, as well as many workers to rebuild the rundown villa so that it rivaled Lu's own mansion. Every time he went to visit his tenant, the old man treated him with great courtesy. Yet Lu was unhappy. Perhaps because his tenant's wealth was greater than his own. Or perhaps because his wife—" And here he paused.

I dug my fingernails into my palms. The color was beginning to rise in Lu's face.

"What about his wife?" asked Chen.

"His wife—ah, she was very fond of the old gentleman, and consulted him on everything."

There was a sigh, almost of relief. But I knew better. Shiro is very good at winding up people. To my knowledge, he has started at least five small wars.

"So," he continued, "Lu decided that the old gentleman and his entire family of hardworking sons and daughters must be foxes. After all, such unexplained good fortune must surely be the work of evil creatures." Shiro's eyes glittered in the lamplight.

Lu said awkwardly, "Well, that would be jumping to conclusions."

"Indeed. But that was not what your ancestor—forgive me, I mean, Lu—decided. He bought sacks of gunpowder, which he distributed secretly around his neighbor's estate. When everyone was asleep, he lit it. There was a tremendous explosion as flames leaped into the dark night, along with the screams of a thousand voices, young and old, burning alive.

"It took almost a day for the fire to burn out, and when Lu went to investigate, he found hundreds of dead foxes, charred into grotesque shapes. Big ones and little ones, even cubs drowned facedown in ornamental ponds, seeking their mothers."

Unbidden, a different image caught me. A small broken body lying in a hole. My breath stuck in my throat; a piercing pain, even though I knew that Shiro was playing all of us. Everyone at the table was silent, staring at him.

In a quiet, languid voice, he continued, "As Lu stared at this devastation, the grief-stricken old man approached. 'What harm did we do you? We even paid you far more than your useless property was worth! How cruel of you to destroy my family.'"

"That's horrible," said my mistress.

Lu shifted uncomfortably, his long face red. He was about to say something when Chen interrupted, "But they were foxes, right? It was not wrong to kill such beasts."

"No," said Shiro softly. "I don't think you would find any man who would say it was *wrong*."

His smile was like a knife. This is the terrible thing about Shiro. The more deadly his intent, the more seductive he appears. From the corridor, I heard a muffled thump. I was quite certain that at least one or two young ladies had fainted in admiration.

Shiro, I thought furiously, *stop this at once!*

I recognized the tale he was telling; it was "The King of the Nine Mountains," and it goes on to describe how the old fox takes revenge by duping the landowner into starting a rebellion, which ends with the landowner's execution for treason against the emperor. Shiro had repurposed it to deliberately offend Lu, and if he continued, there would be oaths sworn tonight and friendships broken. All for what? Because Lu had told a story about foxes that Shiro didn't like? Well, I hadn't liked it either, but I'd more sense than to casually explode people's relationships. Especially when I was so close to finding out more about Bektu Nikan.

So I picked up the tureen of sweet red bean soup and threw it at Shiro.

THE ENSUING CHAOS was quite satisfactory. Everyone jumped up, there were cries and shrieks, and the mood—that dangerous, silken mood that Shiro had been stoking—was shattered. Shiro was covered in soup, but he was unexpectedly charming and good-natured, telling Bohai and my mistress that it was his fault for talking too much. "It's my punishment," he said, laughing. "I've lost the story contest."

Bohai, red-faced, wished to send me out to stand in the courtyard. "All night, if need be!" he said. But Chen, who was holding my wrist a little too familiarly, said there were better ways to discipline me.

"She's my servant," said my mistress. "I will deal with her."

The dinner party broke up. Clothes must be found for Shiro, and he was led to Bohai's quarters with the other young men. I was wiping up the spilled red bean soup (very sticky and sweet—it was going to be quite a job) when my mistress told me to come with her.

"You did it on purpose, didn't you?" she said softly. "Good girl."

I'd done it because I wanted to get rid of Shiro, but she must have thought I was preserving the peace.

"Lu and my grandson have been friends since childhood. I'm glad you stopped them. If they were to quarrel, Bohai would take Shirakawa's side, though he hasn't known him long."

I was struck by her unwitting perception. As I'd suspected from the first time I saw her, she was one of those people who aren't completely fooled by foxes. There was red bean soup on my rough cotton blouse. Back in her quarters, my mistress rummaged around and pulled out a long Manchu dress.

"Wear this," she said. "It was my daughter's."

I protested that it was too good for me, but she told me to hurry before Shirakawa and the others left.

"What were they talking about at dinner?" she asked as we hastened back.

"Your grandson said he'd been feeling ill, and that Shiro—I mean, Shirakawa—made him feel better."

"What kind of illness?"

"Nausea, chills." I tried to recall what else Bohai had said. "He doesn't want you to know about it."

We crossed over to another part of the household that I'd rarely entered. This was the men's side, with a wider courtyard and a reception room for guests. As we approached, Bohai suddenly threw open the carved wooden screen doors.

"Shirakawa is leaving," he said to his grandmother. He seemed unhappy about that, but despite protests that he should stay, Shiro was indeed getting ready to depart.

"Please excuse me," he said. "I've an early appointment tomorrow."

He was wearing one of Bohai's best outfits; I saw my mistress note it, even as she politely saw him out. "I apologize for my maid's clumsiness. We'll wash your soiled clothing and return it to you."

Smiles, bows. Once he'd made up his mind to leave, there was no stopping him. Very soon (too soon, from Bohai's disappointed looks), the heavy front door had clanged shut behind Shiro's straight back.

After counting to one hundred, I set off after him.

10

The servant boy's tale of a woman dressed in light silk on a snowy street at night is the only eyewitness account Bao has turned up. It's likely the same woman found frozen on the back doorstep of Gu's restaurant, though whether she was the courtesan known as Chunhua is harder to prove.

For that, Bao needs the group photograph that Qiulan mentioned. His inquiries about the photographer, however, hit an impasse. Bektu Nikan has left town with no forwarding address.

"You're not the only one looking for him," says the sour-faced landlord who rented two rooms to the photographer. "Debt collectors have come, too. He still owes me a month's rent."

Bao walks through the rooms, bare as though their previous tenant had no intention of returning. Nondescript and shabby, one has clearly been used as a darkroom. The sharp smell of chemicals lingers in the damp interior and stained plaster walls. A wave of disappointment washes over him. It won't be so easy to identify the dead woman, let alone find her real name.

Hearing that Bao is a private investigator, the landlord is eager to talk, hoping that he'll track down his missing tenant. "I'd no idea he'd gone until I tried to collect the rent. Bektu liked to name-drop about his connections, but in the end, he was just a cheap nobody who ran away in the middle of the night."

"What connections did he have?"

"Claimed he was close with some rich men's sons. Also, that he was the personal photographer of Mr. Wang, the one with a garden villa out in the Willow neighborhood."

There are many men named Wang, but this sounds like the wealthy businessman who hired entertainers for a party— the same party that Chunhua abruptly disappeared from.

"Was Bektu good-looking?" asks Bao, remembering the boy's description of the gentleman who'd accompanied the girl on a snowy street.

The landlord snorts. "No. He was a big man, used to wrestle in his youth. Small eyes, cauliflower ears. Sometimes he was flush—last year, he bought six hairy crabs for me and my wife—but mostly he was broke."

Hairy crabs, trussed like neat packages and steamed for their luscious red roe and golden crab fat, are a delicacy dipped in cold vinegar sauce. The memory makes the landlord's face soften. "He got into debt over his mother's illness. When she died, he owed a mountain of bills. Whatever his faults, he was a good son."

"I heard he tried to acquire a white fox in some outlying area."

"It was Wu Village, to the west. He almost died coming back from that trip two years ago. Came down with pneumonia. He wasn't afraid of foxes though. It was the opposite, in fact—as though he had something to prove."

Wu Village rings a bell. Bao thinks of Qiulan's soft, heavy face, the words she'd said about her missing friend at the brothel. Chunhua came from Wu Village.

"Are you afraid of such creatures?" Bao is curious.

The landlord laughs shortly, eyes sliding across the bare room towards the open window. The shadow of a crow swoops past with a harsh croak.

"Foxes are unlucky. If anyone was crazy about them, it's that Mr. Wang. Bektu said so himself. Mr. Wang commissioned him to photograph his collection of antiques and rare plants, so Bektu sometimes stayed at his country villa." The landlord hesitates. "If you're looking for something shady, Bektu said that Mr. Wang might be keeping women locked up."

Bao's thoughts leap to the missing courtesan from the restaurant. Is it possible that she's been taken away by Mr. Wang, and Qiulan was right after all? "Why did he think so?"

The landlord scratches a mole on his cheek. "He said there was a locked courtyard in that villa that nobody was allowed into. Mr. Wang had been acting strangely recently, as though he was bewitched by a fox."

The term "fox" is used to describe any willfully devious woman, so it's hard for Bao to know if the landlord is referring to a haunting or just a run-of-the-mill gold digger. This case is riddled with foxes.

"If Bektu sometimes stayed at Mr. Wang's villa, could he be there now?"

"A privately guarded villa would be the first place I'd go if I were running from debtors. I tried to find him myself, but they wouldn't let me past the gate."

IT'S TOO BAD that Bektu has fled, taking all his photographs with him, but Bao is undaunted. The mansions of the wealthy are not easily breached, but there are ways to enter. As he hurries along, considering his options, a sparrow darts boldly towards spilled grain. Bao smiles at its bravery. Most people only notice eye-catching birds like eagles and swans that have auspicious meanings, or geese, mandarin ducks, and doves that signify fidelity.

The little girl named Tagtaa, meaning "dove," whom his mother insisted on bringing over to replace his nanny, was also faithful. She came daily, waiting in the courtyard to play with him. To this day, he still doesn't know how his mother managed this, for Tagtaa wasn't a servant, but rather the daughter of a neighboring household. By the third day, Bao had started to look out for her, though he didn't want to appear too eager. That was less to do with Tagtaa than with his mother. Some part of him, that stubborn, furious part that still resented her removal of his nanny, didn't wish to give her any satisfaction.

One afternoon Tagtaa asked, "Why do you hate your mother so much?"

"Who says so?"

They were playing inside a large rhododendron bush. By parting the branches and burrowing deeply, you found yourself in a hollow space at the center. If you kept quiet, you could stay there all day undetected. It was Bao's second-best hiding place, and a mark of favor that he'd shown it to Tagtaa.

"Your mother does."

In the twiggy half shadows, Bao grimaced. He knew exactly what she was referring to, his mother's complaints: *The child doesn't listen to me. He hates me now.* He understood it was her way of communicating her feelings to him. Later, from an adult's vantage across the chasm of years, he'd come to sympathize with her frustration, but in that moment, his resentment boiled to fever pitch.

For what his mother said was lies.

He hates me now. The words slipped off her tongue, vibrating in the air like mosquitoes with a tiny poisonous bite. Even she didn't believe them. But after a while, they would come to be truths.

Tagtaa, seven years old and solemn with braided hair, was diplomatic enough to keep quiet. She focused on the stones they were collecting in the small clearing at the center of the bush. "What are we making?"

Having begun with no particular plans, Bao now felt pressured to respond. "An altar."

"To what?"

"The fox god."

That's right. He hadn't been back at that little box shrine in his neighbor's back courtyard since his nanny had left, though he'd glanced longingly at the bamboo grove over the wall. It swayed in the wind, a mysterious living screen of green stalks and rustling leaves.

If he could go back to the fox god, he would ask for the return of his nanny. Though if he was honest, there were longer stretches of time now when he didn't miss her so desperately. It was because of Tagtaa's small, steadfast friendship. Despite being a relationship forced on both, it had turned out surprisingly well. That's what his mother had planned, though Bao refused to give her any credit.

"The fox god?" She had a tidy way of sitting on her haunches; Bao was reminded of his first impression of her as a Manchurian chipmunk. He glanced away, afraid she would make fun of him, but Tagtaa simply said, "That's good."

"Do you know about the *huxian?*"

"Yes. I've seen one of them before."

"Really?" A thrill shivered through Bao's veins. She'd seen one! "Was it an old man?" That's what his nanny had said about the guardian of their neighbor's fox shrine.

"No, he wasn't old." Tagtaa's eyes were a clear dark brown. Years later, he still remembers them vividly.

"Where did you see him? And when?"

"When I was small."

Bao opened his mouth to say that she was still small but caught himself. Nobody likes to be teased about their size.

Tagtaa rested her head on her knees as though she was deciding how much to tell him. She lifted up all five fingers. "When I was this age."

"How did you know he was a fox?"

"I just knew. Also"—in an embarrassed mumble—"he didn't look like an ordinary person."

Bao, his eyes shining with excitement, drew nearer, but at that moment there was a shout. "Tagtaa! Tagtaa, your mother is here!"

It was time for her to go; the afternoon had passed too swiftly, like all afternoons spent together. She got up and began to back carefully out of the bush. It wouldn't do to have a grown-up see them coming and going.

"Wait!" He clutched her sleeve.

Tagtaa gave him a faint smile. In that moment, she seemed grown-up and slightly pitying, as though she'd seen through all his protestations about his mother. Girls were like that, his nanny had said. They matured faster, age for age.

"Will you come back?" Suddenly hesitant, Bao remembered how rudely he'd rejected her day after day. Had even shouted at her as she stood in the courtyard.

But she nodded. "Let's make an altar to the fox god."

11

I set off after Shiro, having whispered to my old lady that I was going to follow him. She didn't stop me, saying only that she'd leave the back gate unlatched. The street was dark as a wolf's stomach and I had no lantern, only the icy halo of the moon gleaming off the puddles. It was also cold. Spring nights in the north of China are no joke. Well, it couldn't be helped if I wanted to catch up with Shiro.

There were several directions he might have gone in, but intuition said he'd head to Oda's photography shop. It was a gamble, but that's the nature of the hunt; anyone who has waited outside a hole for a nice fat marmot understands this. So I cut through several back alleys to get to Oda's shop as quickly as possible. The other reason I hurried was because a woman alone is prey for drunk soldiers, beggars, and young men spoiling for fun.

It's hard for some men to understand how a simple act, like walking down a dark street or drawing the attention of the wrong man, can be so fraught for women. I've given up trying to explain. Instead, I make my own arrangements, which include climbing over walls and trespassing through other people's property. In this manner, I soon arrived at the rear courtyard of Oda's shop. All was quiet and dim, save for a single lamp flickering through the reed blind in the back. There was a sturdy wisteria vine that snaked its way up to the second-floor balcony. Discarding my damp straw shoes, I climbed it as quietly as I could. Halfway up, I remembered that I was wearing a borrowed dress (a rather nice one, too), but it was too late by then.

Most people don't latch upstairs windows. I pushed it open, the wavy green glass panes cold against my fingertips. In the old days, windows were screened with oiled paper, which made them ridiculously easy to open. Of course, in the old days, nobody lived very long either. Crouching on the window ledge, I peered into a bedroom. Moonlight shone on rumpled bedclothes and a few items of men's toiletries on a side table. Carefully, I tiptoed across the wooden floor. At the door, I paused, then opened it abruptly, smack into somebody's chest.

Men do scream, by the way, and this one was no exception. A shriek of surprise and panic. I must confess that I screamed, too. I hadn't expected this; he must have just laid his hand on the door when I'd flung it open.

It was Oda, his eyes gummed up with sleep and terror. He started yelling at me in Japanese. "Who are you? What are you doing here?"

Running back and jumping out of the window seemed like a recipe for a broken neck. Besides, Oda had seized me by the wrist.

"I'm looking for Shirakawa," I babbled. "I was waiting for him, in his bed."

"That's not his bed, it's mine!" he shouted. Then he took a good look at me and started to calm down.

"Aren't you the girl who came with Bohai the other day—his servant?"

He was still holding my wrist. I tried to twist away. No good.

"How come you speak such good Japanese? Why are you here?"

Clamping my mouth shut, I averted my face.

"Hey, hey," he said. The smell of *shochu*, liquor made from sweet potatoes and barley, clung to his clothes, together with urine. Likely, he'd come from the outhouse. "If you're going to play with Shirakawa, you should know he's not the only one. I'm lonely, too."

"All right," I said, pouting prettily. "I'm sorry I scared you. Will you let me go now?"

Instead, he grabbed my waist with both arms. Nuzzling his unshaven face into my neck, he said drunkenly, "Why do they all come for Shirakawa? He's no good, you know."

"I know!" I said, elbowing him sharply in the chest. "He's absolutely no good."

"Is that what you think of me?"

We'd been making so much noise, struggling and tussling,

that I hadn't noticed Shiro's quiet appearance at the head of the stairs. He looked delighted. That's always a bad sign.

"Oda, let go of her. Please."

He did, reluctantly. I straightened my clothes and tried to look dignified.

"Ah. I'm sorry to intrude on your rendezvous." Oda rubbed his face. Tomorrow he'd be confused about this incident, I was sure of it.

"Not at all, I'm sorry she disturbed you." Shiro yanked open the opposite door on the landing and bundled me through, throwing me unceremoniously onto the bed.

Inside, he lit an oil lamp. The yellow flame flickered, shadows dancing and receding across the ceiling. I narrowed my eyes against the brightness. "Blow it out."

"No. I want to look at you. It's been a long time."

"Don't be ridiculous. I just saw you half an hour ago."

Shiro smiled, a secretive half smile. "I thought I'd have to call on you another day. How convenient that you spared me the trouble."

"What's your business with Bohai?"

"Why should I tell you?"

"All right, then." I stood up to go.

"Are you going to climb out of the window? This one doesn't have any wisteria." He leaned against the door and folded his arms. "I heard you climbing, you know. I'd just come in through the front door when there was a rustling at the back. Too large to be a squirrel."

I wasn't going to get out of that door while he was leaning on it, so I decided to wait. Shiro has no patience. Five minutes is a long time for him to spend in silence. I could hear him fidgeting around, so I sat down again on the narrow bed.

"Don't you have anything to say to me?"

In answer, I snorted and turned my back. That was my error. Shiro pounced on the bed, pinning me against the wall by winding his hand through my hair. Lots of people have been beheaded like this: a twisted grip, the whistling swing of a blade. I tensed my neck, but Shiro simply twined my hair tighter through his fingers.

"I want to know what you're doing in Bohai's house, too," he murmured into my ear.

"I went there to sell geese, and the grandmother offered me a job."

"Really?" Shiro examined me carefully to see if I was telling the truth. Then he burst out laughing, so much so that he released me. "Only you would do that. You were selling geese?"

"The two in the kitchen courtyard are mine. I haven't been paid. Yet."

Briefly, I gave him an outline of my arrival, omitting, of course, all the important parts. Shiro thought it was so amusing that tears ran out of his eyes. That's the other thing about him. He's easily distracted. At last he said that he'd go down to the kitchen and make me a snack of dried squid. I said I'd go, too. If you roll around for too long in someone's bed, they might get the wrong idea.

I was also very hungry.

Foxes have a tremendous appetite and will eat several meals a day if we can get them. In order to sustain ourselves, we require *qi*, or life force. *Qi* is everywhere. In the green shoots of plants pushing up through the earth. Pulsing in the veins of animals, fluttering in the night sky as moths. The reproductive act, of course, guarantees that an enormous amount can be collected, which is where many foxes get their lascivious reputations from.

However, a wise fox should refrain from such lazy methods, especially since overcollecting results in death. Generally, I manage by eating large quantities of food, such as pork buns, lamb skewers, and crispy pancakes filled with hot sugar syrup. Dealing with people is troublesome, especially in a city where news travels fast. Besides, I don't wish to add to my sins.

THE LOWER FLOOR of the house was narrow and dark, consisting of a few rooms behind the photography studio. The kitchen had an earthen floor and an enormous brick stove called a *kang*, the type that's common in the north. Part of it was flat so you could sleep on it during the winter, warmed by the hot air circulating through flues in the bricks.

Embers were still glowing in one of the stove holes, and Shiro took a wire grill and placed it on top. Then he rummaged through Oda's pantry and produced several large dried squid. He put one on the grill to toast and opened a jug of rice wine.

"To old friends!" said he, handing me a generously filled earthenware cup.

We are not old friends.

At least, I have never really considered him a friend. What Shiro thinks of me, I don't care to know. But I took the cup and carefully sat on the flat part of the *kang*. A blissful warmth seeped into my damp clothes. The fragrance of roasting squid filled the kitchen as Shiro took a pair of chopsticks to turn it. I noticed that he wasn't drinking, so when his back was turned, I emptied half my cup into the ash bucket.

"I really don't understand you," he said. "What are you doing working for Bohai's grandmother?"

"I told you, it just happened that way. You haven't said why you're hanging around Bohai."

"We're friends," he said, smiling. "Also, when I'm with him, he's not afraid of ghosts."

That's very true. Ghosts and foxes, though often confused by people, are quite different. For one thing, ghosts belong to the world of the dead and are therefore *yin*, or negative energy. Some people think foxes are similar because we go around collecting *qi*, or life force, but nothing could be further from the truth. We are living creatures, just like you, only usually better-looking.

I say this without particular pride, since it's a survival mechanism. There are so few of us and we're constantly persecuted. The worst was during the Song dynasty under Emperor Huizong, when Daoist masters were all the rage; every one of them wished to show off by putting a dozen foxes to death. Whenever humans encounter something strange and novel, their first instinct is to kill it.

Shiro's remark about ghosts, however, reminded me of my old lady's worries. "And what's in it for you?"

"I heard that Bohai has four sisters."

"Two of them are spoken for already," I said in alarm.

He narrowed his sharp tea-colored eyes. Then he gave a lopsided grin. "I'm glad that you're concerned about me. But marrying into a medicine shop, no matter how prosperous, is hardly my idea of fun."

I tried not to look relieved. My poor mistress—I shuddered to think of the havoc that Shiro might wreak between four sisters.

He said, "Bohai has offered me a boat ticket to Japan. It's time for me to leave."

I didn't ask him why. Having to leave town is a recurring problem for someone like Shiro. Instead, I asked if he knew Bektu Nikan, the photographer they'd been discussing at dinner.

"He left for Yokohama recently. Why?"

"I'm looking for him."

"Really? I was certain you were here to ask me about someone else. Not a half-rate Manchurian photographer."

I flushed. I'd drunk only half a cup of rice wine, but Shiro's needling was getting under my skin. That, or the warmth of the *kang* I was sitting on. "I've no idea what you're talking about." A wave of exhaustion rolled over me. I really wasn't up to playing more games with Shiro. And I was still hungry. A few pieces of dried squid weren't going to cut it. Pulling my legs up, I rested my head on my knees.

"Hey!" He sounded alarmed.

I closed my eyes.

"Are you really going to sleep now?"

THE TERRIBLE THING is that I did fall asleep. Right there on the *kang*, in Oda's house. I've seldom done such a thing; it can be a death sentence to fall asleep in a strange place. But I was so tired, not just physically, but from carrying my sorrow and grief over many weary miles. And even if I didn't trust Shiro, he was still one of my kind. It can be very lonely, living among people and always pretending. That's why I prefer the grasslands.

And I dreamed.

Of sunlight seen through swaying seed heads. Of the sweet smell of my baby, her soft, sturdy weight against my chest. The steady profile of my mate, nose up and alert. Wind blowing through the shining blades of grass, bringing the scent of early summer. Vivid and incandescent, the colors brighter than life. I was filled with unbearable joy and sadness; tears ran down my face and trickled between my breasts, so I wasn't sure, even in this brief, dazzling haze, whether I was nursing a baby or simply overcome.

I MUST HAVE dropped off for about half an hour, for I woke with a panicked start. How much time had passed? But the fire was the same, and the night beyond the half-open windows silent as a pool of ink. What had roused me was the scent of hot oil and blistering green onions. Shiro, his back to me, was frying noodles in a clay pot. From the aroma, he was doing a rather good job. I lay there watching him, feeling the wetness on my cheeks and trying not to sob. It had been a long time since I'd fallen asleep in someone else's company, and it took me by surprise.

When the noodles were done, Shiro set the sizzling clay pot on the wooden kitchen table (neglecting, of course, to put any sort of trivet under it—I was sure that Oda's furniture had horrible burnt rings). He laid out a bowl and a pair of chopsticks. Without looking at me, he said, "Eat while it's still hot."

Wiping my face on my sleeve, I sat sheepishly at the table. The noodles—tenderly chewy, drenched in hot oil and Sichuan peppercorns—were unexpectedly good, though perhaps I shouldn't have been surprised. When Shiro sets his mind to do something, he is mercilessly thorough. I'd devoured almost the entire pot when I realized he hadn't taken a bite.

I glanced at him, but he shook his head. "It's not poisoned."

He had a curious expression; if I didn't know better, I'd say it was almost sad. Well, it was his loss, so I polished off all the noodles. Feeling better, I stood up.

"You still haven't asked me," said Shiro, "about Black." The Japanese word he used was "*kuro*," for the character 黒.

"Thanks for the noodles," I said, ignoring the question. "I owe you a meal."

"You can owe me a bed, too." He jerked his chin upstairs. "Go to sleep. You look exhausted."

"My old lady will worry if I don't go back soon."

Come to think of it, she might be waiting up for me in the chill night air. In any case, I had no intention of getting into Shiro's bed, no matter how generous his offer, so I said a hasty goodbye and let myself out of the back door.

Then I ran all the way home.

12

According to his landlord, Bektu Nikan might be hiding from debtors at Mr. Wang's country villa outside the city. A little digging turns up that Mr. Wang comes from an illustrious family. He's forty-nine years old and has two official wives and six children. Cross-checking the address confirms that Mr. Wang is indeed the same man who hosted the party from which the courtesan known as Chunhua vanished.

Time is slipping away, and Bao is keenly aware that he still hasn't discovered the real name of the corpse found on Gu's doorstep, though he's almost certain it's the same woman. Another investigator might simply give her brothel alias to Gu, but Bao won't lie. He's scrupulously, almost compulsively honest. The dull buzz of falsehoods makes him physically ill.

Truth is a green garden hedged thickly with bamboo that he can't escape. At times he envies those who seem unfettered by it. Hearing lies is painful and lonely, especially when no one else can. Bao winces, noting a twinge in his chest that has recently sharpened; he is reminded of his mortality. If his ability has been caused by a fox, what is he to do with it? He feels he's drawing closer to an end, but whether it's his professional career or his life, Bao isn't certain.

On a gray morning buffeted by a light drizzle, Bao arrives at Mr. Wang's villa wearing a straw coat worn by peasants to keep off the rain and a bamboo hat. He's arranged to work there as a gardener for the day.

"Why did you bring such an old fellow?" the house steward grumbles when he opens the gate. The regular gardener, a taciturn man who agreed to bring Bao along for a fee, shrugs and claims he's his uncle.

Dropping his head, Bao follows the gardener down winding paths of pebble mosaics in the shape of coins with pierced centers, inviting fortune when you step on them. The unfolding gardens imitate miniature landscapes. A lotus pond echoes the shape of Lake Taihu in the south, and weathered boulders stand in for mountain ranges. These gardens are laid out according to the elegant life of the Chinese literati, like the famous villas of Hangzhou. One courtyard is filled with rows of *penjing*, or bonsai, placed on low trestle tables for leisurely enjoyment. Bao notes that the dwarfed trees, arranged in shallow pots to resemble windswept pines and ancient maples, are very old and fine. The collection is so large and valuable that it borders on obsession.

Bao looks around carefully while he works. The villa is so quiet that it seems deserted; the only sounds are the snip of shears and the rattle of the rake on gravel. At the noon break, they sit down to eat cold scallion pancakes produced from pockets. Pleased with Bao's diligence, the regular gardener asks him, "What are you looking for?"

"A Manchurian photographer named Bektu Nikan. I heard he sometimes stays here."

"If you want to know about houseguests, you should ask one of the maids," says the gardener. "She comes from my hometown."

He introduces Bao to a middle-aged woman with a soft face like a steamed bun. Like the gardener, she's willing to help in return for a fee.

"That photographer stayed many times, though he's not here right now. He was photographing the master's collection of rare plants and curios for a catalog."

Bao is disappointed. "He hasn't been here in the last month?"

"No, he came and went as he pleased. You're not the first one to ask about him."

"Who else was searching for Bektu?"

"His landlord, but the porter wouldn't let him in. And before that . . ." She frowns as though she can't recall who it was.

"Did Mr. Wang bring back a girl named Chunhua?"

The maid purses her lips, shakes her head when he explains

he's looking for a missing courtesan. A bright glint appears in her eyes, the gleam of the fortunate. *I may just be a maid,* it says, *but at least I haven't been sold to the pleasure district.* That's how humans are, Bao thinks. We're happy as long as we're better off than others.

"The master is very particular about the entertainers engaged for his private business parties at the villa. He prefers good singers and musicians."

This doesn't seem to fit the description of Chunhua, a new girl not known for her accomplishments. "Has he kept any of the women?"

"You mean as unofficial mistresses? There were three in the five years that I've been here," she says. "He had to be careful though. His First Wife is from the wealthy Chen family. She's prickly and easily offended."

Bao says, "What happened to the women whom he kept?"

"I'll show you."

THEY WALK DOWN a cloistered promenade under a bare wisteria trellis with the promise of buds. In the watery spring sunshine, the villa has an expectant hush. Chinese scholars have always idealized country retreats, though few of their so-called mountain or fishing huts are actually rustic, Bao thinks. They're artificial constructs, just as the owners of these estates like to imagine that the young girls brought in as concubines or entertainers have fallen in love with them.

It's so quiet that he can hear the crunching of their feet on gravel and the piping notes of a bird. When the master's two official wives come in the summer, they bring a retinue of their own trusted servants. In the meantime, the suites of empty rooms and green courtyard gardens are maintained by a skeleton staff. They stop at a wooden door set into a brick wall. The maid fits a key in the lock. Within is a little courtyard fronting a suite of rooms.

"This is where he kept them."

So this is the secret courtyard that Bektu Nikan mentioned to his landlord. Silence and the smell of dust greet them. Bao thinks about Qiulan at the brothel and her sad hope that her friend is alive and well at Mr. Wang's house. He'll have to tell her that there's nobody here. The maid casts a quick, nervous glance around as she pushes the door open to the empty room. Against one wall are several large wooden chests. They remind Bao of coffins.

Foxes, he knows, are also said to live in graveyards. There are tales of foxes that acquire human form by placing human skulls on their heads and bowing to the moon at midnight. An eerie image, combining all the things that Chinese fear: decay, darkness, moonlight. Bao once asked his old nanny about this, wondering that she was worshipping such creatures. She'd remarked it wasn't true. Some foxes might do that, but not the *huxian* whom she was devoted to.

The word "*xian*" can be taken to mean "immortal, transcendent being," or even "fairy." But there are other names for foxes as well, ranging from "*hujing*" (fox spirit) to "*huyao*" (fox demon) to "*hushen*" (fox god). Just like people, foxes seem to come in all shades of gray.

The *huxian* that his nanny had prayed to so diligently had, according to her, taken the form of an aristocratic old man, healing the sick and bringing riches to the house. But his neighbor's fortunes had eventually declined. Gossip claimed it was because the riches brought by foxes were illusory. Or perhaps they neglected the little shrine in the bamboo grove, and the fox god left them.

The maid opens the nearest chest. Inside its shadowed depths is what looks like the truncated head and torso of a person. Bao gasps, before realizing it's a costume: an elaborate Chinese opera headdress placed on top of stage armor.

He wrinkles his face, that sad, doglike countenance that inspires trust in others, and the maid says, "Mr. Wang is a collector."

"And the women he kept?" he asks. "Who were they?"

"The first one was an opera singer; when the master wouldn't marry her as an official concubine, she got her old troupe to make a scene outside until he let her go for fear of scandal. The second woman died of a fever. But the third one—now I recall that she was the other person who came looking for Bektu Nikan."

"Why?"

"She never said, but it was the first thing she asked when she came: 'Is there a photographer called Bektu Nikan staying here?' She was clever and bright-eyed. Her name was—" She frowns. "How strange, I can't remember. But it definitely wasn't 'Chunhua.' She didn't stay long. Not even a month."

Bao rubs his jaw. He's hit a dead end, since neither Bektu nor Chunhua are here in Mr. Wang's secret courtyard. Still, he's curious about who else might be searching for the photographer. "What happened to her?"

"She disappeared one night. From inside a locked room."

Bao's head jerks up. Perhaps he was wrong after all.

13

As I feared, my mistress was still awake when I returned late that night. She was sitting up in bed in the dim halo of an oil lamp. "Ah San! Are you all right?"

I must have looked a sight; there was a black smudge on the side of my face where I'd fallen asleep on the *kang*, and my clothes were stained from scrambling up the wisteria vine. Also, I'd abandoned my straw shoes in Oda's back courtyard.

"Yes, I found out where Shirakawa lives."

"Did he catch you?" She looked anxious, a little bird in a rumpled nest.

Explaining my previous acquaintance with Shiro would only complicate matters, so I gave her an edited account of how I'd followed him home and climbed a balcony to eavesdrop. "It sounds like he's planning to go to Japan."

"I see. Thank you."

I'd have thought she'd be delighted to hear of Shiro's departure, but she looked even more worried. I was anxious, too. If Bektu Nikan had gone to Yokohama, I needed to find a way to get there.

The next morning, I was in the kitchen helping the cook marinate raw crabs in rice wine and soy sauce when I was abruptly summoned to the women's receiving parlor. It was spare and plainer than the men's one, furnished with stiff rosewood chairs with perpendicular backs, as if to discourage visitors from staying long. My mistress was sitting in one, and in the opposite chair was Chen from the dinner party. At my appearance, he gave an awkward twitch.

"Ah San, do you remember Mr. Chen?" said my old lady.

"Yes, *tai furen*." I had a bad feeling about this. Had Chen been scalded when I'd flung the red bean soup at Shiro, and was he now here to demand compensation? When our eyes met, he turned red. Not what I'd expected from someone who'd spent half of dinner trying to feel me up.

"Mr. Chen is looking for a servant for his aunt and has asked after you."

I stared at him. That was a lie if I ever heard one. Chen looked even more embarrassed. "I was struck by your maid's quickness and diligence," he said. "My aunt is in need of services. I'll pay a good wage."

"No, thank you." The only person in need of female services was obviously him. I glanced at my mistress, and she nodded imperceptibly.

"There, I told you so," she said. "I'll listen to Ah San's wishes on this."

When Chen had gone, my mistress said, "Are you all right about refusing?"

I was surprised she'd even asked my opinion.

"He'd pay more, but it might be a different sort of job," she said.

I knew very well what sort of job it would be. Many employers considered female servants fair game. Maids who got pregnant were dismissed, yet some girls were willing. They fell in love or thought they could better themselves. And sometimes, it worked. So I understood her meaning immediately.

"No, no, no," I said.

She looked relieved; I felt a twinge of guilt. If I left abruptly for Yokohama in pursuit of Bektu, she might be very sad.

CHEN'S UNEXPECTED OFFER was all over the household within half an hour. Even Bohai's sisters got to know about it, and I was forced to fetch tea and embroidery thread just so they could ask me all sorts of inappropriate questions, including whether Chen had already seduced me and if I was pregnant.

Their questions were ridiculous, yet also a peek into the sheltered world of these young ladies, who were pining for love and gossip though confined to the upper floor of the house. To pass the time, they read romances, including a couple of vaguely pornographic novels written on yellow paper that described the pleasures of the flesh in completely unrealistic terms. Sleek and plump, they reminded me of young chickens. A fox like Shiro would snap them all up.

The servant who'd been helping clean crabs in the kitchen also plied me with questions. Her name was Ah Lian, and she was due to be married soon. "Why did you refuse to go with Mr. Chen?" she asked.

"Because he's an idiot."

"Oh!" She confessed, "I don't want to get married. I've never even met my fiancé. He was supposed to marry my cousin, but she died of fever last year."

"Is he from your home village?"

"Originally his family was. But I must go far away, to Malaya. I don't even know what country that is."

Malaya was a British colony with a large overseas Chinese population. I'd seen it on a map, looking like a sweet potato hanging off the end of Siam.

"I see," I said. Lots of men requested brides from China; poor Ah Lian clearly had no other options, especially if her family insisted.

"I'd rather go with Mr. Chen."

"No, you wouldn't." I said. "He's just playing around."

"They say the Chen family's wealthy, though his father is a frightening man. But I don't want to go on a ship by myself. I can't sleep, I've such nightmares about it." She did indeed look sick with dread.

"Wait here." I scampered off. Swiping a square of writing paper, I wrote a single character on it.

"Here you go," I said.

"What's this?" Ah Lian couldn't read, so I told her it was the character "*mo*," 貘, for "tapir."

"*Mo* is a dream eater," I explained. "Put this under your pillow when you sleep and call the *mo* three times to eat your nightmares. Though if you call it too often, it will gobble up your hopes and dreams."

She looked happy. "How do you know this?"

Meddling with fate might come back to bite me, but I said,

"If you have a child who has nightmares, you can give it to them."

"If I have a son," she said, "I'll name him Shin, or 'xin,' for integrity. Because I hope that my husband will be faithful to me."

I don't know why I added that last comment about a child with nightmares. For my own baby never had any, at least that I knew of. She was too young. When she slept, she dreamed, legs kicking occasionally. Pleasant dreams, I hoped, and not nightmares. I still remembered her chirping cries, her nuzzling warmth. I refused to forget, imagining her still with me. Now she might be walking on unsteady legs through the grass or crouched observing a frog. All those nows that never came to pass. They had been severed when a shovel had dug her out of the den in the snow.

I squeezed my eyes shut. If Ah Lian was to be married off to a man far away in Malaya, I hoped she'd have a responsible husband and a child who outlived her.

THAT EVENING, THERE was another visitor. This time Bohai was at home; we heard him hurrying down the stairs and calling out a greeting. Shortly after, he sent for his grandmother.

"Shirakawa wants to speak to you."

Oh no. I'd hoped that Shiro would leave us alone, but it seemed I didn't have the sole provenance of meddling. That's the problem of foxes; we can't help sticking our noses everywhere, even when it ends in a snap trap.

Bohai seemed put out that Shiro had come to see his grandmother and not him. Folding his arms, he sat sulkily next to her. I stood outside in the corridor. This, I wasn't going to miss.

The room was full of shadows and moths that were drawn by the oil lamps. Their powdery wings fluttered, casting odd shapes on the white plaster walls. Occasionally, they flew into the flame and burned up, leaving a nasty smell. Shiro's good looks were more striking than ever in this half-light, and I wondered cynically if he went around paying evening calls out of sheer vanity. But no, he'd likely spent most of the day sleeping in Oda's house, eating Oda's food, and carelessly burning rings on Oda's furniture. I felt rather sorry for Oda.

He'd brought back the clothes that he'd borrowed from Bohai the other night, but that was clearly a pretext. What if, despite my warnings, Shiro had decided to ask for one of Bohai's sisters? They made small talk about the unseasonably cold spring, and Shiro and my old lady traded meaningless compliments. I was beginning to relax when I heard him say briskly, "And now I'd like to buy your servant."

"What?"

"The one who poured red bean soup on me."

Bohai looked shocked. "Why?"

"I took a fancy to her. Please, sell her to me."

Shiro leaned forward, one elegant foot crossed over the other. I could tell he was exerting an undue amount of charm. A look of confusion passed over Bohai's features. "Well . . ."

"She's not for sale. She's not indentured." That was my mistress, but even her voice was wavering.

"Then send her to me as a gift. I'll treat her well."

"Call her in." My mistress was clearly at a loss as to what to do. I went straight in since I was already standing in the corridor.

Shiro said, "Yes, that's the one. I'll be taking her with me."

"I'm not going," I said.

How dare he try to purchase me like a slab of pork? Though it was true that women were bought and sold every day, sometimes for less than that. You could argue that Chen had tried the same thing that very morning, but I was particularly galled because if I'd tried to buy Shiro (another homeless person with only his looks and no family to vouch for him), everyone would have laughed at me. In fact, a woman couldn't hire a male prostitute without being maligned for the next five hundred years. People still haven't got over Empress Wu and her male lovers.

"Not even to Japan?" he said slyly.

Ah. He had me. Bektu Nikan had fled to Yokohama, and I'd been wondering how to get there. I'd need money for a ship's passage in addition to all sorts of bureaucratic hassles like papers and passes.

While I was waffling, Bohai said, "Have you finally decided to come with me then?" He sounded jubilant, all resentment forgotten.

"Yes, I think my business here is almost done," said Shiro.

Amid the subsequent rejoicing from Bohai, I was momentarily forgotten. I glanced at my mistress.

"Ah San," she said quietly, "do you want to go with Mr. Shirakawa?"

I didn't have the heart to let her down. At least not right then. "Of course not, *tai furen*."

"Then," she said, "would you go with me?"

The conversation ground to an abrupt halt.

"Grandmother, what do you mean?"

"I want to travel with you to Japan, Bohai."

"Why?"

"It's my last wish. I've been thinking it over, and if Mr. Shirakawa is also accompanying you, then I feel more at ease about the journey."

There was such an uproar over this that I was sent to fetch the master, and so wasn't privy to the end of the conversation. Still, I was most surprised. How long had she been considering this, and why?

THE ANSWERS ALL came out, though long after Shiro had left, taking Bohai with him. They were going to meet friends. Whether this involved wine, roast duck, or an expensive teahouse was undetermined, though Bohai's flushed, sullen face indicated his unhappiness at his grandmother's proposal. Still, household gossip agreed that the oddest thing about it was that the master had acquiesced. Had, in fact, seemed unsurprised by his mother's request.

Even his wife, Madam Huang, who'd hired me in the first place, objected.

"How can you send your old mother to Japan with Bohai?" she'd said, loud enough that her words spilled into the courtyards and drizzled into the waiting ears of the errand boys, so that news of the medicine shop's family quarrel spread even to the lamb-skewer seller and the tofu peddler.

Confucianism demanded respect for the aged and filial piety to parents. Sending an old lady on a ship to a foreign country sounded like a death wish. But the master only said that he'd talked it over with his mother.

"Why? What is there possibly in Japan, that dreadful country that Bohai insists on studying in, that could interest your mother? If she should die en route, everyone will say that we sent her to her death."

Madam Huang was likely feeling guilty about how the Elder Mistress had been recently moved out of the main house to smaller quarters. I didn't hear the master's reply, but his wife lowered her voice and no more was heard of their conversation. Meanwhile, my mistress had begun preparations. She'd asked one of the clerks to fetch two woven bamboo trunks from storage. When I came in with an armload of clothes, she was bent over like a cricket, wiping them with a damp rag. Despite secretly rejoicing that this was all very convenient for me (far better to travel with my mistress than to arrange other passage), it also screamed suspicion. I didn't trust Shiro.

"Why are we going to Japan?"

She smiled. "Today has been quite a surprise, hasn't it? Yet I feel that you were sent to me. I've been waiting for a capable servant like you, to travel with me to protect Bohai."

"Why does he need protection?"

"Perhaps you've heard that the eldest son in this family dies young. It's a curse that I now know to be true."

A shadow passed over her face. Though her travel plans to Japan dovetailed with my hunt for Bektu Nikan, I felt suddenly uneasy. My ears itched with the ominous feeling that trouble lay ahead.

14

"Vanished from a locked room?"

Bao feels the rushing thump of blood to his head. Another missing woman.

"She was locked in here one evening, but the next morning there wasn't a trace of her." The maid warms to her tale.

"Why was she locked in?"

"Because of the opera singer Mr. Wang kept before. She managed to leave by getting her old troupe to make a huge scene, beating drums and shouting outside the gate. Mr. Wang didn't want that to happen again, so he gave orders that Miss—" Here, her gaze goes curiously blank for an instant. "—that the young lady must be locked into this courtyard every night."

"And the woman, was she willing?"

"She came looking for Bektu Nikan. That's the impression I had, anyway. When she first arrived, he wasn't here. She was deeply disappointed, but Mr. Wang didn't notice, he was that besotted by her. We all were, a little." A flush appears on the maid's doughy cheeks.

"Where did she come from? Was she a professional?"

"The master requested entertainers for a party, and she came with them." The maid names an establishment that's pricier than Qiulan's brothel. "The other thing I remember was that she asked about foxes."

"Foxes?" Bao inhales sharply. "What about them?"

"If Bektu Nikan had ever brought in any fox skins. The steward said Bektu wasn't a member of the household, just a photographer commissioned by the master to catalog his collection. The master said if she wanted a fur stole, he'd get her one. She blanched then, like she was going to faint."

"When did she vanish?"

"More than a month ago. Mr. Wang had to return to the

main house, which makes me wonder whether she timed it that way. I don't think he even laid a hand on her—she said she'd be his only after a proper wedding, so there he was, ordering furniture and clothes like a crazed man. He babbled about foxes, deer, and snow. The only thing that he was strict about was that she must be locked in every night. 'Make sure she stays here,' he told us sternly."

"Did she meet the photographer after all?"

A frown creases the maid's forehead. "I can't remember. Isn't that strange? It feels like she was here for a long time, but also a very short one." She gives an embarrassed laugh. "But I do recall that morning when the steward opened this door."

Bao examines the lock. It shows no marks of being forced. The walls of the courtyard are eight feet high. Within the suite of rooms, the windows are barred save for a small window like a moon, higher than his head. "The inner suite door was also locked?"

"Yes, both courtyard and room," she says. "But the lady never complained about being locked in every night. I remember how bright her eyes were. They sparkled in the darkness like those of an animal."

An animal. Bao glances up at the single high window. Around the wooden lintel are faint scuff marks. To scrabble up the wall, squeezing through that tiny window, then running along the top of the courtyard wall, sounds almost impossible for a woman. Even if she were a trained performer. He recalls Mr. Wang's passion for Chinese opera, famed for its dazzling acrobatics.

No wonder the staff at this villa have been flummoxed. Yet how does this odd tale align with the discovery of the frozen body on Gu's doorstep? Perhaps it doesn't. He thanks the maid. "I'm afraid that doesn't sound like the same woman I was looking for."

Bao pays her the promised fee. As she leads him back out, he notes that though this elegant villa could easily house fifty peasants, it's kept empty for the occasional pleasure of a rich man. "I heard Bektu Nikan left his lodgings in the city—are there any other places he might have gone?"

"Wu Village was one location he liked to take photographs, half a day's journey from here. It has a beautiful view of a valley."

Wu Village is where Bektu's landlord mentioned he'd tried to buy a white fox skin. It's also the same place that the courtesan Chunhua came from. Bao wonders at this coincidence.

The maid says, "I heard that Bektu sometimes scouted girls for brothels. He traveled to rural villages, and if they had pretty daughters to sell, he'd let the middleman know for a commission."

Bektu's landlord said he'd been a good son and that his debts were due to his mother's illness. Bao is struck by how a man may be a monster to other people's daughters, yet filial to his own family.

He should investigate Wu Village if there's any chance that Bektu might be hiding from his debtors there. There's also the curious reference to foxes again. He's surprised that the maid doesn't seem to have noticed how many times she's mentioned them, as well as by her inexplicable memory lapses when she talks about the lady who disappeared. Yet other parts of her story are clear and sharp, like bright shards of glass.

The maid shows Bao out through a side gate. "Will you be searching for the lady who disappeared?"

"No, I'm investigating a different matter."

"I think the master would like to find her. Shall I put in a word if he asks about hiring a detective? I won't mention you came today."

Likely nothing will come of this, but Bao gives her his card.

"I wonder if she'll ever return," she says.

Her wistful expression reminds Bao of the boy who told him about the gentleman in the snow. *I wanted to open the door, like something was calling me out*, he'd said. Both reactions strike him as slightly abnormal. Just enough to set off a warning tingle that hints at secrets, of devotees who have been lightly touched by the divine.

And he remembers a girl, long ago, who told him about meeting a god.

IN OLD TALES, foxes are masters of duplicity, hiding their beast natures behind charming faces and fancy mansions filled with gold cups that don't belong to them. Families that worship foxes are rewarded with stolen goods, spirited from other people's storehouses. The fox gods provide, but only through sneaky means; thus, some people don't consider them proper deities. But Bao's childhood experiences with the fox shrine behind his neighbor's house instilled him with awe. The very simplicity of the worn wooden shrine, under the rustling bamboo leaves, impressed him. Secret, intimate. Not like the terrifying, gigantic statues of the Buddha, two stories high, in the city temple. In fact, he and Tagtaa made their own fox altar in the heart of the rhododendron bush. They spent the whole summer on it, collecting stones and choosing pieces of wood. She said they must put fresh flowers on it every day.

"Why flowers?" Foxes, Bao thought, might prefer offerings of fried tofu, said to be their favorite.

"They like flowers." She spoke with great certainty, and Bao had grudgingly nodded. Flowers it was.

"Tell me about the fox you met," he said. "I promise not to make fun of you."

Tagtaa, crouching over their altar, was silent. She'd brought three plump yellow daylily buds. Now she arranged them carefully, snapped stems juicily green. They had no water to put the flowers in, so they withered every day. This was part of the charm and responsibility of looking after the altar.

"It was because I got lost," she said. "My mother took me to visit relatives in Inner Mongolia."

"How old were you again?"

She held her hand out with five fingers like a starfish. "I told you that last time."

Of course Bao remembered. He was just checking, but there was no need. His ears, still new to this peculiar ability to hear falsehoods, told him that she wasn't lying.

"We went for a family picnic. Or maybe we were going to visit someone. I don't remember, except we stopped in the grasslands to eat. Then I got lost."

"How did you get lost?"

She flushed. "You said you wouldn't make fun of me!"

"I'm not. I just don't understand how you can get lost just walking around the grass." Bao imagined a picture from one of his brother's books: a flat, wide meadow sprinkled with wildflowers under a milky blue sky.

"It's not like that! Some parts have trees and shrubs, hollows and dips, and everything looks the same. If you wander too far and the grass is tall, you get confused." Exasperated, Tagtaa clamped her mouth shut, and Bao was afraid she'd stop talking about the fox.

"Sorry," he said. "I really am sorry."

A quick glance at him from under her bangs. "You are the only boy who says sorry to me. My half-brothers and cousins never, ever apologize."

This admission made Bao happy that Tagtaa was pleased with him, yet worried that he'd somehow emasculated himself.

"So you were lost," he prompted instead.

"I walked and walked. We'd stopped to eat our meal, and the grown-ups were resting. I was afraid that they'd leave without me."

Her small face, brown and smooth-skinned, furrowed at the memory. Bao felt a pang of sympathetic terror. He'd been lost before, when his father took him to the city temple to worship at New Year's, and he recalled the crush of crowds, men in identical fur-trimmed tunics and boots, burning incense making his eyes sting. Terror rising like a suffocating clot in his lungs when his hand slipped out of his father's, and the shameful tears he shed until he was retrieved. And that was in a city; he couldn't imagine how Tagtaa felt alone on the wide plains.

"When I thought they might leave me behind, I panicked," she said. "I ran and ran and put my foot into a marmot hole. My ankle was twisted, so I sat down. I was so thirsty that I started to cry. That was when the fox came."

Bao straightened, a thrill shivering through him. "What kind of fox?"

"I saw it standing a little way off in the grass. Maybe it had been watching me for a while. It was a black fox."

"There's no such thing!"

"Yes, there is! I saw it, clearly as I can see you. Very dark, with a pointed nose and bright eyes. The tip of its tail was white."

"All right, maybe there are black foxes." Now that Bao considered it, his brother had mentioned that whenever either a black or white fox was found, it was considered an omen and sent as tribute to the emperor. "What did the fox do?"

"It looked at me for a long time, then it walked away. I followed it."

"Why?"

"It wanted me to. It kept looking back over its shoulder, like a dog."

Bao's mouth opened in an O of astonishment. "Did it take you all the way back?"

"No, I couldn't walk much. I told you, I'd twisted my ankle. I kept sitting down, and I was afraid I would lose the fox. And I did. It went away into the long grass until I couldn't see it anymore."

"Then what happened?"

"I started to cry again, but then he came back."

"He?"

"The fox came back as a man."

Tagtaa's cheeks were pink, her eyes bright as she recalled this event. "A tall man. He looked at me and I knew it was the same fox. Then he gave me a piggyback ride, all the way back."

"Did he say anything to you?"

"No."

"Then how did you know it was the same fox?"

"I just knew," she said stubbornly. "The way you do, like you can recognize your brother from the way he walks. It was the same fox, only as a man."

Bao was overcome; he desperately wanted to believe her,

but the logical part of his brain protested. "What was he wearing, what did he look like?"

Tagtaa tilted her head, thinking. "Black clothes or dark gray. They looked old-fashioned somehow. And his hair wasn't shaved in front with a Manchu queue. It was just"—she frowned—"long, like pictures of men from the Ming or Tang dynasties. Tied in the back. He was rather strange-looking."

"Perhaps he was an outlaw or a bandit?"

"I thought about that, too, later," she confessed, "but there was nobody else around. No tents, no people, no horses. Nothing. Anyway, he gave me a ride on his back. His clothes had grass seeds and burrs on them, and he smelled like earth and a sort of musky scent."

"He could have kidnapped you!" Bao imagined bandits living in rebel camps. "Or you could have been sold. Weren't you frightened?"

"No, I wasn't. Maybe because he was a god. It didn't take very long to get back; he walked much faster than me. We went over a couple of rises, and then I heard them. My relatives were still finishing their meal, packing up, and nobody had even noticed I was gone. The fox put me down when we were still far away from people. He nodded at them. I knew he wanted me to go by myself. I tugged his hand. I wanted to show him to my mother, but he wouldn't come. Maybe he didn't want them to see him."

"Are you sure he was a god?"

"Yes, or some kind of *xian*, or spirit. I'm sure." Tagtaa's face flushed again. That happy excitement that came over her when she talked about the fox.

"How are you so certain?"

"Because." She looked embarrassed. "He was different. His eyes were clear, like a dog's. I knew he meant to save me."

"Aren't foxes supposed to be tricky?"

"This one wasn't." She set her small jaw. "Also"—her voice dropped to a mumble—"he was very handsome."

That sounded in keeping with the tales that Bao had heard. Foxes have a charming appearance. For some reason, there was a pang in his chest as Tagtaa continued, "I've never seen anyone as good-looking, even though he was wearing old clothes and his hair had leaves and grass in it."

"Did his face shine?" Bao thought of the wall paintings of deities riding cloud boats, with slender, cherry-lipped heavenly nymphs and page boys accompanying the Queen Mother of Heaven. The murals were touched up with gold leaf, the faces of the deities ringed with rays, their lidded eyes half closed and smiling with distant secrets. Nothing like the description of this strange fox person that Tagtaa described.

"No. In fact, his face was rather dirty. There was a smudge on it," she said, "but I'm sure he wasn't human."

And with that, Bao had to be satisfied.

15

I don't believe in curses.

Humans, however, are obsessed with patterns, ascribing meaning to randomness. To them, the past dictates the future, and the way a tortoise shell cracks in the fire predicts the rise of a future king. Or something like that.

My mistress was so sure there was a curse on the medicine shop that my curiosity was piqued. That's the weakness of us foxes. Think of us as amateur magicians who are always wondering whether there's a particularly good trick to be learned.

"Listen, Ah San," she said. "I'll tell you the secret history of this family. Then you'll understand why I'm worried about Bohai.

"I was seventeen when I was sent to this household. I wasn't their first choice. In fact, the first, second, and third wives had all died. One in childbirth, another from sepsis, and the last from smallpox when she'd gone to visit her parents. This medicine shop was originally a branch in Dalian; the main store was in Mukden and was quite well-known. Still, the shop had a reputation after losing three daughters-in-law so quickly. Especially since there were always few descendants.

"Most places have too many children. That dilutes the wealth, especially if there are many daughters to be married off and quarreling sons each demanding an inheritance. But not this medicine shop. Some said it was because of a bargain they'd made. This shop began five generations ago, when the founder was just a peddler selling herbs and cure-alls. By all accounts, he was very successful. And he only had two sons and one daughter.

"What's more, every subsequent generation of this shop has had two sons and one daughter. The elder son dies young, and the second one inherits. Within a few generations, people started to get suspicious. After all, you can't have exactly two sons and one daughter unless you're deliberately choosing which children will live. But the shop prospered, becoming famous throughout the northeast. However, the elder sons died younger and younger. And none has lived beyond the age of twenty-four."

In the south, "twenty-four" is the Cantonese homophone for "easily dying." In Japanese, it sounds like "you die." Also, Bohai was twenty-three this year. That might explain his general skittishness.

"By the fourth generation, rumors had spread, especially after three wives died early. People started to look askance at the medicine they sold, saying it was corpse bones and hair that brought about such miraculous cures."

"Bones and hair don't cure people," I said. No fox goes to a graveyard to collect *qi*, that vital life force. It's entirely the opposite.

My mistress smiled suddenly. "I'm glad you're with me, Ah San. When you're here, I don't feel afraid."

That was exactly what Shiro had said about Bohai's attachment to him. I was starting to feel uneasy.

She went on, "I was the fourth wife. Normally, I wouldn't have been considered for a principal wife. My mother was Mongolian, and my feet were unbound according to her tradition. They could have just taken me as a concubine, but my future mother-in-law said that they might as well marry me in so that any children I bore would be legitimate heirs. I think she thought I wouldn't survive the year.

"My husband was much older—over forty, with two children already. A boy by the first wife, and a toddler girl by the third. The girl was so young that she'd been sent away to be nursed by relatives after her mother died."

She bowed her head. Through the open window, a bird swung from a slender branch.

"I couldn't understand at first why they were so anxious about children. They already had one son, a fine boy of nine. Because he and I were only eight years apart, he was more like a little brother than a son. Initially, he didn't warm to me, but I was used to boys. I'd had four half-brothers, as well as a childhood friend, a neighboring boy. My stepson and I spun tops, played chess and even *jianzi*, kicking the shuttlecock back and forth. That, my husband really disliked, since it showed off my unbound feet, so we only played when he was out of the house.

"As the days passed, I noticed they were extremely anxious about my young stepson. And they also constantly checked to see if I'd become pregnant yet. When I finally did, everyone was delighted, with a sort of hysterical relief. I wasn't allowed to run outside with my stepson anymore. Poor child, he was very kind to me. Though he said something strange: 'If you have a boy, I won't live long.'

"'Why?' I asked.

"'It's what they say.' He looked upset, so I said I'd have a little sister for him instead.

"'Oh no,' he said. 'Then she won't live either. They won't let her. I've already got a sister.'

"I asked my husband about it. I was a little afraid of him because he was almost as old as my father. He said I wasn't to listen to such rubbish, but I remember the look on his face, the darkness passing behind his eyes.

"The other thing I noticed was that no matter how good or clever my stepson was, my husband never praised him. It was almost as though he didn't want to get too attached to him. The whole household was like that—waiting, waiting for something to happen. I was waiting, too, to give birth. As the time drew nearer, I grew more fearful. I begged them to let me go home to my mother to have the baby, but my husband said no. The last time one of the previous wives went to visit her family, she'd caught smallpox and died."

Giving birth is terrifying. Many pass over from life to death in the space of a few hours of blood. I remembered myself the pain and fearsome joy of it, and squeezed my eyes shut.

"I forgot you said you had a child before," said my mistress. "I'm sorry."

"No, go on."

"So we waited, in that house in Mukden. The main house, not this one. Afterwards, my husband closed that business. As my time drew near, my belly and feet were swollen, so I could hardly sleep. My little stepson couldn't sleep either. He said he'd started to see them.

"'Who?' I asked. We were sitting under a tree in the courtyard. He'd just returned from school, his face drawn and peaky under his cap.

"'The people with no shadows.'

"What did he mean by that? It seemed that 'they' had very pale, almost indiscernible shadows. In the daytime, you couldn't tell because they moved around. But at night, bright lamplight from a single source was the best way to notice. I don't know where he got these ideas from, but they made me shudder, though it was a blazing hot day. The cicadas were screeching away and the stones in the courtyard were too hot to touch, yet I had chills as though I were running a fever.

"'What sort of people?' I asked him.

"'All kinds.' He thought they might have recently died and were collecting more folks, as a sort of job to lighten their sentences in the underworld. We huddled together, my stepson and me. I held his hand and he squeezed mine tight, so tight. 'I'm frightened,' he said.

"'Nothing will happen to you.' Seeing how terrified he was, I tried to comfort him. Even the servants had started to leave us alone. If I gave birth to a girl, she'd likely die. If I had a boy—the second son—then my poor stepson was doomed. And yet nobody said anything. It was just the terrible feeling of waiting, like pressure building before a storm."

My mistress pressed my hand, forgetting momentarily that I wasn't her stepson from almost fifty years ago. Her hand was small and dry.

"But you can't avoid certain things . . ." Her voice dropped to a whisper.

Yes, I thought. Giving birth is an appointment you can't walk away from. The moment of a child's birth is also when its mother draws perilously near to the boundary between death and life.

"Finally, my time came. I had a very hard labor. So hard that I thought I'd die. The baby was stuck; my hips were too narrow. It went on for hours until I was exhausted, my throat hoarse from screaming. The midwife fell asleep in snatches. Later, I heard my mother-in-law lost hope, telling my husband that it would be difficult to find another bride if I died.

"After a day and a half, I gave birth to a son. Everyone was relieved and delighted, but I burst out crying. 'I wanted a girl,' I said, thinking of my stepson, and how frightened he'd be to hear the news.

"'How foolish of you!' the midwife said. 'You have a son. An heir. Why would you want a girl? Otherwise I'd have to drown her for you.' She was exhausted, too; otherwise I don't think she'd have been so careless with her comments.

"'What do you mean?' I asked.

"She pointed at the basin of water at the foot of the bed. 'That's for a girl.'

"After that, I had a dreadful fever. I was sick for a week, and everything passed in a daze."

"What happened then?"

"Ah." She blinked. "That's a story for another time, Ah San. I'm tired now, thinking of the past. Sometimes I feel I've lived too long." She looked small and frail. As I got her ready for bed, she said forlornly, "Will you accompany me to Japan?"

"Yes."

I hadn't meant to get involved with the medicine shop's secrets, but my hunt for Bektu Nikan seemed headed for Japan, along with whatever fears she had about Bohai. So I patted her hand and told my old lady again that she needn't fret. I'd take care of her the best I could. It was an honest promise.

16

Disembarking from an ox cart, Bao climbs into a hired rickshaw for the last leg of his journey to Wu Village. According to the maid, Bektu Nikan was fond of its picturesque scenery and often went to photograph it. Perhaps he's there, hiding from debtors. Bao smiles ruefully as he pictures a burly Manchurian photographer huddled in a damp hut. He's going to great lengths to locate Bektu's photograph of the courtesan Chunhua so that the frozen body on the restaurant doorstep can be identified.

This case, with its overtones of foxes and lost girls, fills Bao with strange urgency. He has the uneasy sensation that he's walking into a shadowy realm. No longer a child, he's an old man now, setting out into an unknown forest of lies and half-truths. Somewhere within this tangle is the name of the woman who died on a restaurant doorstep.

The rickshaw puller is lean and knotted like an old rope. It's said that the working life of a rickshaw man is only five years. The best can trot forty miles a day; they also drop dead of heart and lung diseases. Bao tries not to think about that. If he doesn't take a rickshaw, there's no choice but to walk instead, and who is he to deny a man his livelihood? He surveys the landscape. The unpaved road is white and dusty. Fields of barley and sorghum stretch out under the wide sky, dotted in the far distance by the country villas of wealthy men.

"Going to Wu Village?" the rickshaw man says as they jog along.

"I'm looking for a Manchurian photographer who took photographs there."

The man shifts the rickshaw poles. "I gave him a ride before. Heavy fellow, lots of equipment."

"Is he still in Wu Village?"

"No, said he had creditors on his tail. You're not one of them, are you?" The man laughs, showing blackened teeth.

Bao is disappointed, but has other questions. The courtesan known as Chunhua was said to have come from here as well. "Are there any girls who've left the village this past year?"

"Are you recruiting? You don't look like a broker."

There are always middlemen looking for young women to place either in service or brothels. Often it's both, a game of bait and switch. Bao shakes his head. "I'm trying to identify someone who might have run away to the city."

The rickshaw man falls silent, guessing no good news is forthcoming. At length, he says, "There were two girls who left last year. Word gets around in a small place like this. But one went to get married, and the other came back recently, so it can't be either."

"Which girl hasn't returned?"

"That'd be the secondhand cloth dealer's daughter."

WU VILLAGE HAS one main, unpaved road, and several side streets of brick houses with traditional curved-tile roofs, leaning against one another in the hobbled fashion of Chinese shophouses. Business is conducted on the ground level, where sliding doors open to display baskets, dry goods, and iron nails, while the families live above. The farther you go from the main street, the more disheveled the houses appear, until there are only hovels petering out towards the grassy hillocks.

Copses of birch trees dot the distance between fields of rapeseed. A small temple stands near the end of the street, wooden guardian statues glaring under peeling paint. It's devoted to the Buddha, though Bao has the feeling that there are probably fox shrines here as well.

The secondhand cloth dealer's shop is dark after the dazzling midday sun. So dark that Bao blinks twice before he spies anyone. Bolts of cotton line the walls; the floor is hidden by an enormous pile of rags. A woman with a lined, sad face is sitting on a stool, trimming the rags and repacking them for sale as quilt scraps.

When Bao introduces himself, her face creases abruptly in alarm. "My daughter? What about her?"

Bao explains, as gently as he can, that he's trying to identify the body of a young woman from the city who froze to death. "The restaurant owner on whose premises she was found would like to have a religious service said for her."

The woman shakes her head vehemently. "No! That's not my daughter."

She's agitated; Bao is sorry to bring such news. "Did your daughter have any distinguishing physical marks?"

"She was perfect, no marks at all. Pretty and plump-cheeked, with a mind of her own. She ran off with a sweet-talking peddler from Jilin, so there's no way that she's dead now."

"How old was she?"

"Nineteen. I was wrong to scold her. I told her that man was no good, she'd better stay home." She bites her lip, hard. "This girl who was found, what makes you think she was my daughter?"

"She was working in the pleasure district. Someone said she came from Wu Village." There's no way to sugarcoat this, and the effect, as Bao feared, is immediate. The woman's face turns beet red; she drops the scissors with a dull clank.

"Other villages have similar names, and besides, there was another girl from here who went to the city three years ago. Old Wu's girl—she's the one who became a prostitute. My daughter is married in Jilin."

Her eyes dart to the back of the shop. The stained door curtain is pulled aside, and a hard-eyed man emerges angrily. "I've heard enough! Talking about brothels and prostitutes—how dare you spread stories about our family?"

"Won't you at least tell me your daughter's name?" Bao says, but the man's face contorts with fury.

"Get out!"

OUTSIDE THE SHOP, Bao pauses. From behind the wooden shutters, he hears a long, broken wail. The woman is weeping, her husband shouting. Bao grimaces; the twinge in his chest that he noticed earlier seems to be getting worse; he takes shallow breaths until it eases. He doesn't like to eavesdrop, but he's come all this way and still hasn't learned their daughter's real name. Walking back along the side of the long dark shophouse, he leans against the window. Snatches of conversation drift out.

"... you'd better make sure it isn't her."

"I'm sure it isn't. It can't be!" That's the mother, her voice strained.

"It's because of that fox. Ah Yan!" Raising his voice, the man addresses someone else. "I told you not to bring it into the house! I should have killed it myself."

A slap rings out. Muffled crying, then running footsteps. The back door slams open and a girl tumbles out. She's about thirteen, hair braided untidily, face swollen and tearstained. When she sees Bao, her eyes widen. Seizing his sleeve, she tugs him away from the house.

"Uncle!" she says, addressing him as an elder. "What happened to my sister?"

Bao's face wrinkles in distress. His plain, honest-looking face, which is probably what made the girl dare to ask him. They walk away from the shophouse in silence, up a steep broken path to an overgrown, weedy area. The girl breathes heavily, holding back sobs. Once they're away from the main street, she stops. Behind her fierce, squinched expression, Bao senses she's frightened.

"You think it's my sister?"

"I don't have a lot of information to go on." Sighing, Bao sits on a rock. She's probably overheard the entire conversation in the shophouse.

"My sister ran away last year," says the girl. "We haven't heard from her since."

Children and wild animals are similar in many ways. If you sit down, they'll approach you slowly. "My name is Bao," he says. "I've been hired by the restaurant owner to look into this."

"I'm Ah Yan." She looks away. "There's nothing much to tell. My sister fell in love with a peddler who sold ribbons and hairpins. She hated living here, especially since my father was trying to arrange a marriage for her with the pork butcher. He's old and his breath smells like rotten meat. Sister said she'd never marry him. Her head's been full of romantic fancies forever, and she wanted a handsome man."

Ah Yan stares at the thin branches above Bao's head. Not yet in leaf, they cast faint shadows that tremble in the breeze. "She was the prettiest girl around. If anyone was going to marry well, it should have been her, but there aren't many young men in this village. They've gone to the city to find work. The ones who are left, like Jiang, are all taken."

"Who's Jiang?"

"A hunter. He should have married my sister. She liked him, but he got engaged to her friend instead. Her family owns land, so he must have decided it was a better deal. My sister was heartbroken. She was wild to get married after that and leave this village, but it's not like there's much choice here. I didn't think that peddler was that good-looking, but he had a smooth way of talking. My father said no, and Mother agreed. Nobody thought she'd run away."

"Did you know?"

Ah Yan shakes her head. "She didn't say anything to me. But the night before, she took out her second-best dress and gave it to me. And she combed my hair and braided it. Sometimes she was sulky and in a bad mood, but I miss her. I hope she's married somewhere and has a baby. You don't think that was her, do you?"

Bao thinks these details match forebodingly with what Qiulan told him, about the courtesan called Chunhua who'd come from this village, sold by a pimp. His sad expression upsets the girl, who gnaws her lip until it turns white.

"I don't know," he says honestly. "But I'll try my best to find out."

"Father says it's my fault, because I let a fox into the house."

Foxes again. Bao leans forward. "Does this have anything to do with a Manchurian photographer who was here?"

Ah Yan's eyes open wide. "How did you know?"

"I heard that he tried to buy a fox skin in this village."

"There's a mound behind the village called Fox Hill. Since

long ago, black and white foxes have appeared there. Most locals avoid it, but the photographer said he'd pay good money for a fox. The only one who took him up on it was Jiang."

"The one who didn't marry your sister?"

She makes a face. "Yes. It was two winters ago. Jiang went hunting but only managed to dig up a fox cub from a den. He brought it to the inn where the photographer was staying and tossed it on the table. I was there with my sister. She'd gone to buy noodles, but mostly, I think, to see Jiang. At that time she was still hopeful that he liked her."

Bao nods sympathetically. He remembers when he, too, was young, and the glimpse of someone's face was enough to set his heart beating.

"It was the wrong season for fox cubs, so I don't know how he got this one. The photographer said it wasn't worth the money since it wasn't white, but Jiang said all foxes are born dark. They handled it roughly, tossing it back and forth." Her square face flushes with indignation. "Jiang got paid, though less than he wanted. I was afraid the cub would die. It had soft fur like floss and was trembling.

"I burst into tears and my sister told me not to make a scene. The photographer came over to talk to her. Like I said, she was pretty, and she knew it. In the end, he said he'd give me the cub if she'd let him take a photograph of her."

Bao listens intently. So, perhaps the rumors were right and Bektu occasionally scouted girls for brothels. It's possible that the so-called peddler who took her away the next year was tipped off by him, but Bao doesn't want to mention this to Ah Yan.

"What happened to the fox cub?" he asks gently.

"Do you think my bringing it into the house was bad luck? Everyone said so when my sister ran off later. Other peculiar things happened, too—there was the lady who came for the cub, and also Jiang's misfortune." Ah Yan's voice trembles.

"What lady are you talking about?"

"I took the cub home and put it in a wooden box next the stove. When Second Brother returned, he examined it and said its legs were broken. Then he said that one of his friends had met a strange woman walking from the northern grass-lands towards our village. Twilight was falling and he didn't recognize her. 'I'm looking for my pet,' she said. 'Have you heard of anyone taking a fox cub?'

"He replied that Jiang had taken a cub from a den earlier, but it couldn't be her pet because it was a wild fox. After that, he must have fainted, for he found himself lying in the snow alone. Mother was afraid it was a *hulijing*, a fox spirit. I was lucky Father wasn't home that evening, otherwise he'd have thrown my cub out into the snow. Second Brother said his friend was likely drunk, and everyone laughed. I didn't think it was funny though. Not at night, with the snow falling."

Bao pictures this rural village on a winter's night. A cold wind is blowing; the air is filled with whirling flecks of snow. The windows are patched with paper and shutters drawn to keep out the darkness.

"The next day was bitterly cold. I was digging up a jar of pickles from the empty lot where we bury them when I heard the snow crunching as someone approached. To my surprise, it was a young woman I'd never seen before. She wore a man's quilted cotton jacket and mismatched trousers. No shoes, even in the snow. I couldn't stop staring. I'd never seen anyone like her. Such bright dark eyes and a lovely profile, her eye-lashes like a deer.

"She gave me a watery smile, as though she'd been crying. 'I'm looking for a fox cub,' she said. 'I heard that someone in this neighborhood has one.'

"If she hadn't looked so sad, I might have been frightened. My aunt told me to be careful if any strangers came talking about foxes, because you never know what they might be. 'Why do you want to know?' I asked.

"'It's mine. My . . . pet. I heard it was injured.'

"The more I looked at her, the faster my heart began to race. 'I have a fox cub in our house.' I said slowly. 'I rescued it from a photographer.'

"The expression on her face was both terrible and hopeful. I've never seen anyone want something so much. It was like a flame behind her eyes. 'Please, please bring it out to me.'

"She used polite yet old-fashioned language. For some reason, she didn't want to enter our house. So I ran inside, leaving her standing in the snow, twisting her hands. She had very slim, delicate hands, with no rings or jewelry.

"*Please don't be dead*, I thought as I took my fox cub out of the box. It looked very poorly, and I felt like crying, as though it was all my fault. I wrapped the poor cub in my shawl. As I carried it out, Mother stopped me. 'Where are you going with that animal, wrapped in your good shawl?'

"'A lady has come for it. She says it's her pet.'

"My mother frowned. 'Wasn't it a wild fox cub found in a den? Who's this lady?'

"She followed me out to the back. As soon as the lady saw the bundle in my arms, she let out a cry and stepped forward. Then she saw my mother. '*Furen*,' she said, 'thank you for rescuing my fox cub.'

"I was afraid Mother would start asking difficult questions, but she paused with her mouth open, her face blank. Since the lady seemed so anxious about the cub, I passed it to her in the shawl. She looked like she was going to cry, holding it tight yet tenderly.

"'I'm really sorry,' I said, explaining about the Manchurian photographer Bektu Nikan. She listened very carefully and asked me to describe him. After thanking us again, she left, cradling the cub and walking so swift and straight that we were left staring after her. Later, my mother said she couldn't imagine where she came from.

"'Why do you call her a lady?' my father said.

"My mother stopped with a blank look on her face. 'I don't know, she just struck me as one.'

"'Maybe she's a fox spirit—I told you no good would come of bringing that cub home!' And they started arguing again. My brothers said she was likely a fake medium who'd tricked me into giving her the cub. Father was irritated, saying I should have asked for money. I glanced at my mother, but she was looking off in the distance, as though she was beginning to forget. But I didn't."

Ah Yan falls silent, eyes shining.

Her excited face reminds Bao of his childhood friend Tag-taa and her encounter with the fox god. There's an inexplicable, envious pang in Bao's chest.

"You mentioned that something happened to Jiang, the hunter who brought the cub in?" he asks.

"Yes." Her expression grows fearful. "He died."

17

As soon as my mistress decided to follow Bohai to Japan, matters moved swiftly. Reams of paperwork were filled out and stamped. I've always been wary of official documents; most foxes are terrified of bureaucracy since we're undocumented vagrants. I wondered how Shiro had set up his current identity as Shirakawa. Perhaps he'd taken it over from a deceased victim or won it in a gamble. Thoughts of Shiro made me frown. I hoped he'd change his mind and go somewhere else, but he seemed as determined to stick to Bohai as my elderly mistress was.

"Ah San," she said, directing me to the chief clerk, "he needs to fill out your personal details."

I'd been dreading this.

"Place of birth?"

"Qiqihar," I said. Even farther than Kirin; most people hadn't traveled there.

"Age?"

How old did I look, anyway? I said, "Thirty-two," then revised it downwards at the clerk's look of surprise. "I mean, twenty-three. Ha ha . . ." That was a pity though. Thirty-two is in many ways a far better age than twenty-three.

I saw that he'd written *spinster* and didn't bother to correct him. Instead, I peered at the forms he'd already filled out. They were my mistress's traveling papers, and according to the forms, she was sixty-three years old. Next to her official Chinese name was a note: her name written in Mongolian as Tagtaa.

"Tagtaa," meaning "dove." How unusual. I wondered if her mother had given her this nickname and if she'd kept it all these years.

"And your name?" said the chief clerk. He looked impatient, and I realized he'd asked the question twice.

I debated for an instant. "Ah San," which was what the medicine shop owner's wife had decided to call me when I was hired, simply meant "number three." I disliked the notion of getting onto a boat as a number. For all I knew, it might be the last record of my existence; better to use my own name in case we capsized and drowned. I told you before that foxes dislike open water.

"Snow," I said.

OUR PASSAGE WAS confirmed on a steamer bound from Port Arthur to Japan. We'd go via Moji, a port at the northernmost tip of Fukuoka that had been developed for the purposes of shipping coal. I listened to this with surprise. Why not go straight on to Yokohama? It appeared to be Bohai's idea.

"We'll visit a friend in Moji to discuss some business."

Bohai had adopted the classic scholar's stance, feet apart, hands folded behind his back as he talked. I couldn't help sniggering and he frowned.

"How long will you stay in Japan, Grandmother?" Bohai asked.

"As long as you need me."

I listened covertly. This delay in getting to Yokohama made me uneasy. After all, Bektu Nikan was said to have gone there, and I wished to settle my business with him quickly, though I couldn't turn down free passage. Still, there were too many unexpected variables for my liking.

It was obvious that the master was unhappy that his mother was going. I was standing outside the open windows of the master's study, pretending to water some plants. "Mother," he said, "let me keep Bohai at home, then neither of you need travel."

"Ever since you told me about the baby, you knew it would come to this," she said.

"If it's a girl, then it doesn't matter."

"But if it's a boy—you still haven't told Jinghua?" That was the name of the wife.

Silence. I stood on my tiptoes closer to the window.

"Then the sooner I leave with Bohai, the better. You know she'll be furious."

"Mother! Won't you help me manage her?"

My mistress said, "You're a grown man already. But I'll take care of Bohai as best I can."

Clack! went the study door, and out she came. I sprang back and pretended to keep watering. Everyone, it seemed, had a secret agenda for this trip.

I DISLIKE PACKING, but it's another thing I've trained myself to do quickly. My mistress's traveling wardrobe and other necessities were neatly packed into a wicker trunk. As for myself, I had barely anything. Two sets of cotton clothing, one pair of straw shoes. Brushes, ink, and writing paper for this diary. All my belongings fit in a bamboo basket, a gift from my mistress, who was aghast that I planned to bundle everything up in a cast-off tablecloth.

"You certainly are careless about the way you present yourself," she said with a sigh. "Are you sure you don't mind accompanying me?"

"Of course not! I want to go to Japan."

I wasn't joking. It had been a long time since I'd been to the land of Yamato. It was wonderful that I was getting free passage on a steamship, but it would be even better if Shiro wasn't going, too. Perhaps he would fall off the side of the boat and drown.

THE STEAMER WE were taking was the *Shinanomaru*. Originally British, it had been sold to a Japanese merchant line and refitted. The bottom of the ship was dark red, then painted black to a white line two-thirds of the way up. I'd never been on such a large ship before—other vessels I'd ventured on were mere washtubs in comparison—and was amazed by the lack of sails.

We arrived at the docks on a bright morning that smelled like seaweed and rotting fish. Besides Bohai, our fellow passengers included Chen and Lu, who were also returning students to Japan. Chen flushed as our eyes met. It hadn't been so long since he'd offered to "employ" me as a servant for his aunt. There was the usual goodbye group of relatives, the shaking of hands and promises to keep in touch. The young men were eager to be off, and that included Shiro.

To my great disappointment, he'd shown up with two enormous steamer trunks and a coterie of doting women to see him off. One was the widow of a prominent dry goods store, another a passionate-looking lady in furs. A third was the rumored mistress of a Russian financier. She wore a pair of shiny leather shoes with buttoned ankle straps, and when she thought nobody was looking, she slid her hand up under Shiro's tailored jacket and gave his waist a sorrowful squeeze.

Poor lady. Or perhaps I should say "ladies." Well, they were all grown women and their hearts were their own responsibilities. At least they were still alive.

BOHAI AND HIS grandmother shared a second-class cabin, as did Chen and Lu. I had a berth in steerage, but I'd no time to rejoice in my free ticket, for as soon as the ship cast off, I was dreadfully seasick. Alas, it's true that foxes are particularly susceptible to water. All I could think, while I watched my breakfast of scallion pancakes disappear over the railing into the churning froth, was that I'd never manage the two-day voyage to Moji.

My mistress came over. "Ah San, are you all right?"

Assuring her I was merely seasick, I staggered off to my berth. Third-class steerage was divided into single men, families, and single women, the single sexes separated at opposite ends of the ship for morality. The day passed in a queasy battle with seasickness. Despite this, by dinnertime there was a ravenous gnawing in my gut. Forcing myself up from my narrow bunk bed, I grimly swallowed whatever they heaped on my plate at the communal dining hall. Ten minutes later, I bolted to the deck to throw it all up again.

Afterwards, I hung despondently over the railing. Dusk was falling, and the Yellow Sea was dark and wrinkled as a sweat-soaked bedsheet.

"Steerage passengers aren't allowed on this deck."

I didn't bother to turn around. "Go away, Shiro."

"I will. Back to my first-class cabin."

"Good for you. Who paid for it?"

Ignoring the question, he said, "Have you eaten? Oh, I forgot, you just threw it all up again."

"So did you, probably."

"But I can order room service."

I wrinkled my nose. Lack of food is very dangerous to foxes.

"Come to my cabin," said Shiro. "I have a proposal for you."

EVERYTHING WAS BETTER in the first-class part of the ship, including the corridors (wider), flooring (walnut and brass-tacked carpet), and lighting (fancy lamps with glass shades). Shiro's cabin was the same size as my steerage compartment, but without the eight bunk beds. Instead, he had twin beds and a small dining table with two chairs, all covered extravagantly with brocade. What delighted me most, however, was the porthole, which opened.

"Where's your cabinmate?" I asked, struggling with the stiff catch.

Shiro murmured seductively in my ear, "Don't have one— yet."

Bracing his arms on either side of me, he gave the window a hard shove. It opened with a gust of freezing salt wind. The fresh air made me feel much better, enough to duck away under his arm and sit at the table.

"Shiro," I said, "stop acting like a cheap gigolo. Let's order room service and get to the point."

With a sigh, he snapped open a menu in front of me. "Order whatever you like."

"What did you want to discuss?" I said, after we'd selected steak, grilled lamb chops, sturgeon, and roast pork loin.

"No small talk or asking how I'm doing?" he said, raising his eyebrows.

"Oda mentioned that people were dying mysteriously in

alleyways. Has that anything to do with you?" I'd had a bad feeling about that rumor as soon as I heard it. A virtuous fox ought not to prey on people; it's precisely this kind of behavior that gets us hunted down and skinned.

"How rude! As if I'd be that careless." But of course he would. You should never trust Shiro, particularly when he's looking relaxed. He's also good at changing the subject, which made me even more suspicious. "I heard Chen tried to hire you the other day."

"Yes, for his 'aunt.'"

"He's very taken with you. I want you to persuade Chen to abandon his studies in Tokyo and stay in Moji with us."

"What? Aren't we all going to Tokyo?"

Shiro leaned back, admiring his own reflection in the porthole. It was dark outside now, only the sharp smell of the ocean and the steady thrum of the ship's engines reminding me that we were on a voyage. "We're not. Bohai, Chen, and Lu have decided to give up their studies. They plan to become revolutionaries, supporting the overthrow of the Imperial Qing government."

"And you didn't stop them?" I was indignant. My mistress would be heartbroken.

"If they want to expend their money and lives on building a new society, then I can only offer my advice." He gave me a look. "I promise to be good. Get close to Chen, persuade him to stay with Bohai and Lu rather than change his mind, since he's wavering. His family is the wealthiest among them, though he's terrified of his father, the senior Mr. Chen."

"What's in it for me?"

"Bektu Nikan." Shiro waited to see if I'd take the bait. "Chen and Lu are also acquainted with him. Don't you want to know how? I can deliver him to you in Moji—if you wish."

There was a tap at the door.

"Time to eat," said Shiro. He smiled hungrily, and I remembered I mustn't underestimate him.

18

"Jiang, the hunter who brought in the fox cub, died?" asks Bao.

Ah Yan nods uneasily. "He disappeared on a hunting trip. Before he left, there were rumors that a stranger had been asking about him—Jiang thought it might be a debt collector, so he went to the wilderness to trap sables. But he never returned. A search party found his body by a burnt-out campfire, as though there'd been a fight. Jiang was killed with his own hunting knife.

"Nothing was taken, not even the valuable sable pelts he'd stretched. Father said it was brigands, or perhaps Jiang, being quarrelsome, was settled by an old score. I wondered if it was the strange lady who came for the cub, because she'd asked who had trapped it and I'd given her both Jiang's and Bektu Nikan's names. I felt so guilty! Second Brother said that Jiang was strong and experienced. No woman could wrestle or pin him down with his own knife, but what if she really was a *xian?*"

Bao is fascinated by this odd tale. Yet he agrees that it's most likely another hunter with a vendetta. "You mustn't blame yourself. You did a good deed rescuing that fox cub."

Relief floods her tearstained face. "About my sister who ran away—you don't think she's dead, do you? I tell myself she hasn't sent a message because she's afraid of Father."

Bao doesn't trust himself to speak. The details given by Qiulan at the brothel about her missing friend dovetail ominously: the daughter of a secondhand cloth dealer; seduced by a sweet-talking pimp; even the point about not wanting her little sister to know. Bao no longer needs the photographic verification from Bektu. He has the sinking feeling that he's found the right woman.

"What's wrong, Uncle? Are you feeling sick?" Ah Yan looks worried.

"Ah, I'm getting old, that's all." Bao gets up with a sigh. He presses one hand to his chest. That pain again. "I'll try my best to find out. What was your sister's real name, by the way?"

"Feng. Her name's Feng. Do you think she's happy, wherever she is?"

Bao thinks of Gu's description of the body found on his doorstep, and the unearthly expression of delight on her frozen face. He nods gently.

THE JOURNEY BACK from Wu Village is long and tiring; Bao spends it reading a book of poetry. He doesn't want to think about dead girls enticed away from villages or little sisters still waiting for them. Only after a hot soak at the communal bathhouse—where for a fee you can wash, get a shave, and relax on a reed mat afterwards, listening to the singing of caged songbirds—does Bao feel up to examining his thoughts. His conclusion from talking to Ah Yan still stands; her sister is very likely the courtesan Chunhua who was found frozen to death. And he knows her true name now: Feng.

"Feng" means "phoenix," while "Ah Yan" means "swallow." It's not surprising that siblings would be named after birds, though it's ironic that Feng ended up at a brothel called the Phoenix Pavilion. Did she find that bitterly apt, or did it strengthen her desire not to let her family know what became of her? Whatever happened in the year since she left Wu Village, Bao hopes that she's at peace now.

The girls' names also remind him of his childhood friend Tagtaa, whose name meant "dove." They were close for many years, longer than his mother expected. In his mind, he sees her, still small but growing taller by the day. Her smooth brown skin had a healthy glow, like the bloom on a fresh-laid egg. Her small bright eyes laughed easily. "That girl is too dark, like a peasant. It must be her Mongolian blood," his mother said after Tagtaa left one day.

"I think she's pretty," Bao blurted out, and immediately regretted it. His mother's plucked eyebrows and sharp stare turned to him. Bao was furious with himself. He should have known better than to praise Tagtaa in front of his mother. Now that they were twelve years old, she'd surely come up with some pretext to separate them. The idea of them forming an attachment was an uneasy worm in the back of his mother's mind. How could Bao, the second son of a local magistrate, marry the daughter of a Mongolian concubine? It wasn't that Tagtaa's father was low status—he was a moderately wealthy merchant—but her mother wasn't an official wife. She wasn't even Han Chinese.

Bao knew all this, even without his ability to hear lies. Who needed that when he could read his mother's mind clearly? Her thoughts flitted between his older brother, the studious hope of their family, and Bao, the backup. Neither son must make a mistake.

So Bao pretended to be somewhat disinterested in Tagtaa, though he couldn't hide his happiness when she came. She was his dearest friend, though he'd never admit it. His feelings for her were muddled, filled with unspoken longing and fear for the future.

Occasionally, they visited the fox shrine they'd made, hidden in the rhododendron bush. They'd grown too big to squeeze comfortably in, but it was still a refuge. The altar to the fox god received occasional flowers from Tagtaa. He himself had never been in the habit of making regular offerings. Without knowing exactly why, he traced it to her confession of meeting a fox god. That tale of a black fox that returned as a man lingered in the back of Bao's mind. Only years later did he understand that his ambivalence was due to the blush on her cheeks when she mumbled, "He was very handsome."

What would it take to have Tagtaa refer to himself in the same way? The thought made Bao excited yet uneasy. And so, that day when they crouched in the heart of the rhododendron bush, he brushed his shoulder against hers. She didn't notice, focused as she was on the altar. On it she had laid one of his mother's roses, the white kind known as *shui meiren,*

or "sleeping beauty," hybridized during the Tang dynasty.
Tagtaa's lips moved soundlessly.

"What are you praying for?" Bao asked.

She dropped her eyes. "They're talking of marrying me off."

"But you're only twelve!"

"I know, it's just talk."

Bao knew that talk of marriage could begin years early, but he was filled with a choking sensation. Tagtaa took a tortoiseshell pin from her hair, laying it on the little altar. She murmured faintly, "Please, please let me find a good partner." When she left, Bao stopped to pocket the hairpin. Later, he didn't know why he did such a thing. Yet Tagtaa's hairpin—and her wish—was something that Bao desperately wanted for himself.

WHATEVER HAPPENED TO that hairpin? Bao kept it for years, tucked into the cloth wrapping that held his writing brushes. At some point, it simply vanished. Just as he stopped thinking about Tagtaa for several decades. This case stirs up old emotions, with its lost girls and whispers of foxes.

The lady who came for the fox cub. Could she be the same woman who disappeared from Mr. Wang's garden villa a month ago? Bao sits up, struck by the thought. No, it's absurd. There's a gap of almost two years between the events, yet he can't shake the idea that they're connected. After all, the maid at the villa also described the lady as bright-eyed and charming—and unusually focused on Bektu Nikan.

Bundled up against the spring chill, Bao walks home from the public bathhouse. His skin tingles from the hot water and his shoulders are pleasantly loose. *Two years*, he thinks. Assuming it's the same woman, what would account for that gap? Perhaps she lost Bektu's trail and only picked it up later. Bao shakes his head.

Tomorrow he'll go and make his report to Gu, the restaurant owner. Tell him that he's discovered the true name of the girl who died so that he can hold a religious service for her spirit. Chinese believe that those who die unknown and unmourned become hungry ghosts, destined to linger forever in this world. And when a little more time has passed, he'll return to Wu Village and notify her family properly.

Perhaps by then, they'll accept her passing.

19

"Stay," said Shiro after I'd wolfed down an enormous dinner and risen to leave.

"Only if you tell me more about Bektu. You said Chen and Lu were also acquainted with him."

"Did I?" I put my hand on the door, and Shiro said, "Oh, very well. But you haven't explained why you're looking for him."

"To repay a debt."

"Whose?"

"Mine." Which was close enough to the truth. A benevolent fox shouldn't seek vengeance, but there were such things as honor and principles. Or so I hoped.

"If it's for you, I'll tell you what I know." Shiro gave me his earnest look, the one that makes young ladies fall in love. I waited in stony silence.

"Bektu did some freelance work for Oda's photography studio, between his trips to Mukden on commissions for rich patrons. But they had a falling-out and Oda wants nothing to do with him now. That's how Bektu knows Bohai, Chen, and Lu. In fact, he's known for some . . . unusual photographs." Shiro watched me, a slight smile on his face. "Did he by any chance"—he leaned forward suddenly—"take a picture of you?"

This is why I dislike dealing with Shiro. Half his portfolio is composed of shrewd guesses. "He did."

"I can't imagine why you were so careless. I thought you were going to stay in the grasslands forever, Snow." The word he used for my name was "*yuki*," which means "snow" in Japanese. Of course, neither Shiro nor I am Japanese or Chinese or Mongolian. We just happen to resemble such people enough that we can speak their languages and live quietly among them.

"I'm planning to go back."

"But I don't want you to leave. When it's night, aren't you lonely?"

His words sank in like sharp teeth. I closed my eyes. Behind them it was dark, black as a late winter's night in a village in the northeast of China. Snow was falling, a thick curtain of blowing white. The wooden houses with their leaning eaves were shuttered against the wind from the grasslands. Nothing stirred as I wandered desperately up and down, listening for the faint cry of my child. Just a whimper, to let me know where she was.

But I wasn't here to confide in Shiro. I'm not that stupid.

"Don't pity me," I said. "I can take care of myself."

There was a knock at the door. We both jumped.

A faint voice said, "It's me, Bohai."

Shiro shoved me behind the door as he opened it partway. "What can I do for you?"

Peeking through the door hinges, I wondered what had brought Bohai here. His breath reeked of liquor. "I didn't see you at supper," he said to Shiro.

"I was feeling seasick."

"So is Grandmother's servant. That girl has been laid up since we got on this ship and has neglected her duties."

"Is that so?" Shiro sounded amused, though I knew it was all at my expense.

"Grandmother is too softhearted," Bohai mumbled. "I don't want to worry her, but it's happening again."

"Do you mean the people with no shadows?"

"Yes, at sunset, there was a man on the deck . . ." His voice trailed off. "I'm terribly anxious; I can't sleep at all." Bohai let out a groan so piteous that even I felt sorry for him, though my nose tingled with curiosity. My mistress's tale of how her young stepson had complained of such creatures rose vividly to mind. Pressed behind the door, I considered what I knew of ghosts.

Foxes and ghosts have fascinated people for centuries; the writer Pu Songling filled an entire book with tales of bewitchment by spirits, foxes, and flower nymphs, all of whom seem too willing to be men's playthings and mistresses. I enjoy reading these ridiculous stories because they make me laugh.

Obviously, they're the fantasies of a frustrated man. Pu Songling himself never did well in the Imperial examinations. I doubt he ever met any of our clan, but thanks to him, foxes and ghosts are linked in the public imagination, though they're entirely different.

In any case, I myself have never seen a ghost.

"Let's look for this man on the deck," said Shiro.

Bohai looked unhappy; I couldn't blame him. Searching for specters late at night was unappealing, no matter how much liquor he'd drunk. Shiro didn't seem worried. In fact, I've seldom seen him show fear. Mostly, he is the one terrorizing others.

"Well," said Bohai hesitantly, "perhaps I should hire someone to follow them, next time this happens. Just to see if they're real people or if I'm going mad."

"A discreet servant could do some detective work. In fact, I have someone in mind for you. But for now, let's go hunting for these no-shadow people."

Seizing Bohai's arm, Shiro propelled him down the corridor, shutting the door behind him. I knew this was to allow me a quiet getaway, but since he'd left me alone in his cabin, I made a quick search of his belongings. There was nothing of interest other than a Japanese detective novel in the drawer by his bed.

I wondered whether this novel had put the notion of detectives into Shiro's head. I wouldn't put it past him; he's easily swayed by the latest fashions, though all foxes are interested in trickery and tales of the hunt. I replaced everything neatly. There was nothing to indicate how Shiro meant to get in touch with Bektu. No notebook with a convenient address in Yokohama. A pity, as I meant to finish my business with Bektu swiftly. It was two years overdue.

Ah. It pains me to even think of that time. A wound so agonizing, it was like disembowelment. I'd felt like dying myself. A parent should never bury a child; it feels wrong, though in nature many cubs die. I told myself I mustn't fall into this spiral again; my grief must be channeled to better purposes.

After a final glance around Shiro's cabin, I let myself out. Just as I was closing the door, Bohai appeared in the corridor, having escaped being dragged around by Shiro. "What were you doing in Shirakawa's room?" he said suspiciously.

The liquor on Bohai's breath made me avert my face, though I suspected he wasn't as drunk as he appeared. The passageway was dimly lit; in the flickering shadows, Bohai's grip tightened on my arm. "Who are you really? You don't behave like a normal servant, and my grandmother is unnaturally fond of you. Oda also said you spoke Japanese."

So Oda had gossiped about the night I'd been caught climbing up the wisteria into his back bedroom. How troublesome!

"I'm not really a servant," I said. "I'm an investigator." Of course I'd been standing right behind the door when Shiro had proposed hiring one, but Bohai had no idea I'd overheard their conversation. "Shirakawa asked me to look after you and your grandmother. Because he was worried about the people with no shadows."

At this, Bohai's egg-shaped face turned pale. "I see," he said. "That's very good of him."

Goodness had nothing to do with it, though seizing on this sudden outpouring of trust (or perhaps the drink had finally caught up with him), I escorted a now chastened Bohai to his cabin. Then I went back down to steerage to throw myself on my hard, narrow bunk bed and think furiously.

People with no shadows.

I'd never come across this in all my wanderings. People with too many shadows, people who feared they were overcome with darkness, who couldn't sleep without burning lamps, and who were terrified of the moon and all ghostly *yin* things—that I'd heard plenty of. In fact, Chinese traditionally consider shadows part of the soul. Harm done to a shadow, whether by pinning it to the ground or stepping on it, was considered spiritual damage to the person. Of course none of this really works. But the mind can certainly affect the body.

Why, I could tell you about a stout Turkic merchant in the walled city of Luoyang who wasted away from sheer terror after his enemy stabbed a dagger through his shadow. I had nothing to do with this, by the way. I'd been working as a dancing girl to earn my passage home to the north, and just happened to be one of the poor man's attendants the night that this happened. I tried to tell him that he should really be looking out for poison, especially from his business partner, but unfortunately, he didn't believe me.

Anyway, it's usually *too many* shadows that people dread. Some are even terrified of opening umbrellas, fearing that their shadow creates a doorway to the netherworld. So by logical deduction, people with no shadows ought to be the opposite— like heavenly beings, I supposed—in which case they ought to elicit cries of delight, but that didn't seem to be Bohai's reaction at all.

Shiro was right. A fox was uniquely suited to investigating such creatures, being both insatiably curious and not easily fooled. Besides, the meek way that Bohai had acquiesced reminded me of a half-grown whelp trotting behind me. And since I'd declared myself to be his protector, I felt a certain amount of responsibility.

Helping others, by the way, is one of the duties of a virtuous fox. Others include abstaining from lying, money-laundering, and killing people. It's all part of the journey towards enlightenment. As for me, I'd turned aside onto my own path of thorns, though sometimes I feared where it was leading me. Revenge is a terrible dish to consume. It eats one from the inside out, no matter what they say about it being best served cold. As the Chinese saying goes, "When a gentleman takes his vengeance, ten years is not too late."* But you and I know that chilled food inevitably leads to an upset stomach.

·君子报仇,
十年不晚

BY THE AFTERNOON of the next day, the port of Moji was in sight. The railings were crowded with excited passengers, eager for a glimpse of land. Having recovered from my seasickness, I was attending my mistress. Fortunately, she seemed unaware of Bohai's adventures last night, and Bohai himself, standing a little apart with Shiro and the other young men, was uncharacteristically polite to me. He looked nervous, glancing warily at the other passengers. As we rapidly approached the docks, the scent of land wafted towards us in the brilliant, late-spring sunshine. Closing my eyes, I inhaled the smell of pine trees and seawater. It had been a long time since I had come to the land of Yamato.

Moji was very modern and tidy, with European-looking buildings and a customhouse built of red brick. It looked like a toy port glittering in the sun amid waves of beaten bronze. As the ship prepared to dock, I gazed down at the crowds of waiting people. Customs officers, longshoremen, and relatives calling out and bustling here and there. I stiffened. There on the dock, standing a little apart as if observing, was a tall, wide-shouldered, painfully familiar figure.

"Shiro!" I hissed, turning on him. "How dare you!"

"What?" he said silkily. "I thought you'd be happy to see him again—our old friend Black."

20

That night, Bao dreams.

He's standing in the weedy clearing where Ah Yan told him about her runaway sister and the strange lady who came to retrieve a fox cub. Only this time, it's deep winter and snow covers the ground. The moon has an icy halo. In his dream, Bao is glad that Ah Yan isn't here. It strikes him as no place for a thirteen-year-old girl or even himself.

As Bao peers around, looking for the lights of Wu Village, he fears suddenly that he'll come upon the dead hunter Jiang, propped up eerily by a deserted fire in the woods. Or perhaps a wooden box where a tiny fox cub whimpers, legs broken and sides heaving. A howling wind of despair fills him, a raging sadness that threatens to swallow him.

He wakes with a start, pressing his hand over the sharp twinge in his chest. Bao thinks of the lady who came looking for a fox cub. Perhaps he's been so taken by the story that he's imagined her in the snow at night, wandering around the silent village. Though it doesn't make sense that Jiang, the hunter, would be dead. That happened later, as did Ah Yan's sister running away. It's muddled, as dreams often are. Unable to fall asleep again, he pads down to the silent kitchen and boils water for tea. Sipping it, he waits for the gray dawn to arrive.

BAO HAS SENT word to the restaurant owner that he's found a name for the body left on his doorstep. They've arranged to meet discreetly early at the restaurant again. Buffeted by a sharp spring breeze, he taps on the shuttered door. Gu, the owner, greets him with a nervous look.

"How's business?" asks Bao.

"Middling." Gu drops his eyes. Despite his best efforts, word has seeped out that a corpse was found nearby. "Though not on our doorstep," he adds hastily.

They sit at the same empty table as last time and Bao explains his findings. "So you see, I believe the woman you found was named Feng. Also known as Chunhua, from the Phoenix Pavilion."

Gu is impressed. "I heard good things about you, but I didn't think you'd find her name so quickly. I'll get a monk to say a service for the dead then." Suddenly cheerful, he gets up and offers Bao a dish of cold, thinly sliced pig ears tossed in spicy *mala* chili oil along with the payment for his services. As Bao leaves by the side door—the same doorway that the young woman's body was huddled on—he pauses to say a brief prayer. *I hope you're happy, wherever you are*, he thinks, remembering the smile on her face.

Why was she there anyway? What led her to leave a teahouse with a handsome guest, and why did he abandon her in the alleyway? The more Bao uncovers, the more questions unfurl, like paths that twist in a dark forest. There's the fox lady, too, whom Ah Yan told him about. Bao remembers his dream and the wild sorrow in it. The description of the strange woman haunts him, though he wonders whether that's only due to his own childhood fascination with foxes. Well, he'll likely never hear of her again.

As it happens, Bao is wrong on that count.

THERE'S A LETTER waiting when he returns to his lodgings, dropped off by private courier. Bao skims it quickly: *Having heard of your talents, Mr. Wang would like to meet you concerning a matter of great personal importance.* Its brief, hurried nature suggests that it's been personally written, not dictated to a secretary. The address on the back is in the city, but he recognizes it instantly as the official residence of the same Mr. Wang whom Bao investigated earlier.

Surely that's no coincidence. The maid at the garden villa had requested Bao's business card, saying her master was much troubled by the disappearance of a lady. Could she be the same woman who'd gone to fetch a fox cub in Wu Village? Bao's pulse quickens. The possibility is intriguing enough that he sits down and pens a reply to Mr. Wang right away, agreeing to meet him.

Next, a shave from the street barber. It's been a year since Bao cut his hair short. Nobody has remarked on it in this northern city, where there are many foreigners, including Koreans and Japanese. The young men who study abroad return with cropped hair and dreams of revolution.

Bao felt relief when he cut off the heavy weight of his long pigtail, a symbol of Manchu overlordship. If he were young, he, too, would have liked to go abroad to study. Not the classics of Chinese literature, the backbone of the old examinations, but to learn about electricity and bridges made of steel. Who cares how many lines of poetry he can recite? This restlessness was what made his elder brother frown the last time they spoke.

"We need a new ruler," his brother had said. The Dowager Empress has put the reform-minded Guangxu Emperor under house arrest, and continues to rule as though she'll never die, although rumors abound that this year she's very ill.

"Not a ruler," Bao replied. "A constitutional monarch. No more emperors."

His brother's eyes had widened. "Don't say such things in public."

I've become an insurgent in my old age, Bao thinks. Why didn't he have more courage when he was younger?

After his roadside shave, Bao walks up the narrow, dark stairs to his front room. The scent of grilled skewers and fried dumplings wafts up from the street. As part of his board, he gets one meal a day from his landlord, but today he doesn't feel like joining them. Not that they're unfriendly; far from it.

"You must have come from a good family!" the wife often says, praising Bao's polite manners to her children. Bao smiles and doesn't answer. Yes, he did come from a good family. His mother would have been horrified at the idea of her younger son boarding at a tailor's shophouse in his old age.

The path she'd planned for him was identical to that of Bao's older brother. Constant study, success at the Imperial examinations, and promotion to an official rank surpassing his father's. Bao's mother would have expected to see him ensconced in his own home with a wife or three and many grandchildren by this age. On his sixtieth birthday, which represented the completion of a full cycle of the twelve lunar animals, there should have been a celebration with peach-shaped buns to symbolize longevity. An enormous live fish would be carried in an enamel basin of water to present to the guests, then later exquisitely steamed and dressed with soy sauce and ginger.

All those things did come to pass a few years ago—for Bao's brother. Bao attended as a guest, as he always did. Played with the grandchildren (not his) and talked politely to the wives (also not his). His older brother, drawing him aside, asked discreetly if Bao needed money.

"I'm fine."

"You say that, yet you're living in rented lodgings."

"I still have a house." That was true, a small house that Bao had lived in with his wife out in the countryside.

"Is it rented?"

Bao considered telling his brother that it was but decided not to. The numb sensation of lies still bothered him after all these years.

"No, there's a caretaker who comes from time to time."

"If you rented it out, you'd have an income. You wouldn't have to do these jobs." His brother's distaste for his occupation made his brows draw down. "Why don't you return to teaching?"

"Brother, you needn't worry. You've been very good to me."

His older brother has been exemplary, bearing the burden of family expectations and succeeding modestly as a local official. Through diligent study, he secured a rank just slightly higher than their father's. Because of this, Bao's own shortcomings were overlooked.

Bao, too, was a scholar in his day. In fact, his tutor once told his mother, "I believe the younger boy is more talented than the elder." Bao, eavesdropping surreptitiously, was taken aback by this praise. Especially since there was no lie in his tutor's words.

"Is that so?" his mother had said. Triumph in her voice,

yet also perverse rage. "Why doesn't he apply himself better then?"

"His poetry is good, and he has original thoughts. But he's easily distracted."

"It's that girl."

Crouching below the raised veranda, Bao couldn't see his mother's face, but he could imagine the compression of her lips. This conversation was taking a bad turn.

"The one who comes to play—the daughter of a neighbor's concubine. Although she's too old for childish games, as is Bao."

Bao dug his nails into his palms. *No, no.*

"Bao is too attached to her. He's unwilling to leave home for his studies, like his brother did."

"Youth frequently form attachments that don't last," said his tutor, who went on to speak of green plums and bamboo horses: a reference to a poem by Li Bai about childhood sweethearts. For some reason, this made Bao flush. To be discussed like this was humiliating, but even worse was to have his affection for Tagtaa widely known. He'd thought he'd concealed it so well.

"Well, hopefully that girl will be married off soon. Bao, too. He's not too young to think of an alliance."

In that moment, Bao swore silently that he'd never fulfill his mother's dreams. He would not be an examination candidate; he would not marry the girl of good family she chose.

Of course he was wrong in all those predictions.

Remembering this now, Bao can't help but smile at his childish folly. He did sit for the examinations, though he didn't do as well as hoped, having come down with a fever that day. And he married a young woman of good family, his wife of many years until she died nine years ago.

And Tagtaa, what happened to her? For decades, he put her in the very back of his mind, not wanting to pain his wife. She was a nervous, timid woman. When relatives suggested that he put her aside since they had no children, Bao resisted. His wife had done no wrong; if she wasn't the one he'd have chosen, it was through no fault of her own.

In fact, the fault was Bao's.

There was a moment—a brief window—when Tagtaa might have been his. Sitting at his desk, he takes out the memory and examines it, recalling a stiflingly warm afternoon, ringing with the sound of cicadas.

Tagtaa sits opposite him in the pavilion in their garden: a conceit that looks good from a distance but is hardly ever used, due to the number of spiders that descend from the roof. Her visits have lessened. Lately, when she does come, she's accompanied by a maid, who's thankfully friends with Bao's cook and leaves them alone.

"I don't know why they bother," Tagtaa says, biting into a plum. It's late summer, almost unbearably hot. The air is filled with swarms of flies that multiply on the donkey dung in the street.

"It's because you're almost a young lady now," says Bao.

Tagtaa laughs. Her eyes crinkle into half-moons; her skin has a clean glow. There's a dusting of freckles on her face, like the faint speckling on an egg, and Bao has the urge to touch them. But he doesn't. All their meetings will come to an end if he doesn't continue to play his role as a childhood friend.

Mostly, that's not hard. It's easy to talk to Tagtaa because she's naturally thoughtful. Bao is the one with the more exciting life, with lessons and excursions to all parts of the town with his father and brother. In comparison, she's constrained to her walled compound, the misdeeds of her half-brothers, and the occasional visit to a temple. Despite this, Tagtaa is never silly. She also doesn't lie.

Bao knows by now how rare that is. Everyone lies. Well, almost everyone, the easy words slipping off their tongues. Even Bao does, though he despises himself for it. Once, frustrated with this strange gift of his, he decided to tell nothing but lies from morning till night. The result was a swollen tongue, numb lips, and a feeling of disgust.

"What are you thinking?" Tagtaa says. He realizes that he's been staring at her wide forehead and the clean sweep of her brows.

The words tremble on his tongue. *What do you think of*

me? But he's terrified to hear the answer. It's too obvious by her unruffled acceptance of him.

"Is there any news about your marriage?" he asks.

She shakes her head. Her hair, its characteristic two braids looped up over her ears, is shiny and soft. "Last year's discussions fell through. Besides, I'm just a concubine's daughter. I'll be lucky if anyone wants to marry me."

Bao leans forward. *I do*, he wants to confess, but instead, he says, "Well, you're almost fourteen."

"So are you. And your mother is already talking to the Zhou household."

"How did you know?"

"Everybody knows." Tagtaa laughs. A guileless laugh, with no shadow of jealousy. Bao is good at detecting jealousy because he himself suffers silently from it. Yet he can't declare his affections.

Part of it is Bao's own ambivalence. What is love, anyway? The feeling he has towards her is elemental, a "youthful attachment," as his tutor said. Tagtaa is the person he almost always wants to see. Without her, he feels unmoored. The books that Bao has read about love use literary allusions and courtly language. They dwell on the size of a woman's feet, her fainting, seductively tottering gait. None of them refer to freckles or the ability to listen solemnly. Perhaps what he feels for Tagtaa isn't love but something else.

So he keeps his mouth shut, never telling her about the thrill he feels whenever the main door creaks open and the gatekeeper calls out to him from his post, "*Xiao pengyou lai le!*"—"your little friend has come." Technically, they're too old to keep meeting like this, but it's been so many years that nobody comments. Still, Bao has the feeling that things are coming to an end.

The air is thick with the hum of insects. Tagtaa is silent for a long time. Then she says, "I wish I didn't have to get married." Her head droops, and Bao knows she's looking at her feet.

They're unbound, in the Mongolian fashion. Tagtaa's mother refused to bind them when she was five years old, and since she was only a concubine's daughter, nobody pressed her on it.

"Can I tell you a secret?" she says.

Bao leans over, heart thudding. Has she suddenly realized that she loves him, too?

"My mother wouldn't bind my feet not just because she was sorry for me. She did it because she plans to marry me to one of her kinsmen's sons."

Bao understands now. No Han Chinese of good standing would marry a girl with unbound feet. This is the only way her Mongolian mother could exert some influence on her daughter's fate. And in that moment, he also realizes why his own mother permitted their childhood friendship to continue. Nobody has ever been under any illusion that Tagtaa could be a fit wife for Bao. How stupid of him! It's been right under his nose all this time, yet he never considered it, never bothered with the niceties of clothes and fashion, and the secret signals they confer.

"Will they send you away?"

"Perhaps. My father was angry when he realized, but it was too late to change. So Mother is happy. Also, the First Wife in our house is happy, too. I'll never compete with her children."

"Then how will I see you?"

"You won't. You and I likely will never meet again."

Tagtaa gazes at him with her clear eyes, and Bao sees sorrow mingled with a strange excitement. Perhaps it's the drama of it all, the thrill of something happening to her. His eyes burn; his heart thumps unsteadily. "No!"

"What can we do?"

This is his moment to lean forward and grasp her hand. Later, he imagines that he drags her with him to his father's study, where he demands that they become engaged. *I promise I'll score the highest in the Imperial exams*, he declares, *if you let me marry Tagtaa.*

But what actually happens is that Bao gasps wordlessly.

"Next spring, I'll probably go back to my mother's people. Of course I'll miss you," she says, glancing quickly at him, "but it's been many years since we went to visit them."

"When you saw the fox god."

Abruptly, Tagtaa blushes. Her small face reddens like a peony. Observing her, his own chest constricting with confused yearning, Bao begins to understand.

"You still think about him? That black fox?"

"It's odd how I've never forgotten. His face is still clear to me." She pauses. "Maybe it's silly, but I have a feeling that one day I'll meet him again."

"Perhaps you were bewitched." Bao bites his lip. "It doesn't mean that your fiancé will look like the fox god, even if you go to Inner Mongolia."

"I know," she says. "But a girl can hope. What else do I have?"

She gives him a sad smile. It's disconcertingly adult, and Bao realizes that nothing he says, despite his best efforts to sound coolheaded and rational, will change the horrible reality unfolding in front of him: all these years, while Bao's crush has slowly bloomed, Tagtaa has been nursing the memory of a handsome stranger. Oh! It's almost too much to bear.

And yet there are no lies coming from her lips.

21

Of course I wasn't happy to see Black again. Or to give him his Japanese name, Kuro. If we hadn't all been pressed together at that railing, I'd have smacked Shiro so hard that he fell into the ocean. But since I was holding my mistress's second-best quilted jacket, I did nothing of the sort. Though I did fantasize the large splash as Shiro's imaginary body plummeted to a watery death.

"Look, Ah San!" said my mistress, eyes shining. "Aren't the buildings fine? And there are so many people."

My heart softened at her enthusiasm; I mustn't give her nightmares by causing an accident. So I stuck to my mistress, securing her personal possessions and taking her arm protectively as we descended the slippery gangplank.

After our party had disembarked, Shiro said to Bohai, "I'd like to introduce you to a friend of mine, Kurosaki."

This surname is written with "*kuro*" as the character for "black," together with "*saki*," meaning "peninsula." Knowing what to expect, I kept my face deliberately blank.

"Ah, this is the friend you mentioned earlier," Bohai said.

"Kurosaki speaks excellent Chinese, also Manchurian and Mongolian," said Shiro.

Bohai turned to us. "Grandmother, this is Shirakawa's friend, the one whose house we'll be staying at."

House? I'd carefully avoided looking at Kuro, as though I were only a peasant who didn't understand men's business, but at the mention of a house, I couldn't help raising my eyebrows in disbelief. Kuro, who has never shown any interest in an abode, owning a house? It was laughable.

"It's not really my house," he said, turning to us. "It belongs to a mentor of mine, but I'm delighted to make it available to you."

Kuro's voice, once so familiar to me, was painful to hear. That quiet, dark voice with its sober undertone. My mistress stiffened. She was staring at Kuro with a surprised expression, so I couldn't help glancing at him myself.

I was shocked, too. A scar ran across his face, slashing from the left eyebrow down to the cheekbone. It was a conspicuous injury, having narrowly missed the eye. This was a fatal marking for a fox.

We make our living beguiling people, disappearing when society becomes too suspicious of us. In the old days, one's likeness was only captured by brush and ink, and we all know how unreliable that is. Now there are photographs, which I fear will cause us trouble, but that was nothing compared to the scar on Kuro's face. When subject to official punishment, foxes will ask to be beaten on the soles of the feet or the back, whatever place is less conspicuous. We're all so very careful not to injure our faces if possible.

Kuro's expression didn't change. Perhaps he was used to people gaping at his face. He didn't look directly at me either, but at my mistress.

"Welcome to Moji," he said to her. "I hope your journey was pleasant."

With a start, she remembered her manners. What with getting all the luggage together, it took a while to gather ourselves, but eventually our little party was bumping its way over the roads (nice and straight near the port, then less so farther on).

Moji is a picturesque, tidily bustling port. "Modern," meaning European, with an imposing redbrick customhouse, a waterfront with fine views, and even a horse-watering fountain on the cobbled promontory. It's situated near the narrow Kanmon Straits, separating the islands of Honshu and Kyushu. Those straits have a long and checkered history, including the drowning of the child emperor Antoku at the Battle of Dan-no-Ura. A sad story, I thought, as we trundled along in a rickshaw.

My old lady seemed preoccupied. I was, too, but I've learned to hide my feelings. In fact, sometimes I think it best not to have any. Old wounds should remain closed, lest they fester.

"Did you not think that Shirakawa's friend is strange?" she said.

"You mean Kurosaki? He seems like a perfectly ordinary person," I said, lying through my teeth. Of course Kuro doesn't look ordinary. None of us do. And three of us gathered in such a small group was bound to attract attention, even from random passersby. It was simply reckless. I added another mental chalk mark on the post of Shiro's sins.

"Is that so?" she said, falling silent.

THE HOUSE WE were staying at was up against a hill, in an old neighborhood with lovely cedar trees and broad white roads. I inhaled deeply. The sunlight glancing off the sea, the scent of trees, and even the roadside weeds filled me with a deep sense of nostalgia. The lush growth was a different green than that of arid northern China.

I was dying to know what detailed arrangements Shiro had made and if there were other, unsaid reasons why we weren't going on to Tokyo, where Bohai, Chen, and Lu were all supposed to attend medical school. What sort of detour was this, and why did the young men appear excited? I sincerely hoped we weren't here to join some anti-Imperial revolutionary group, but I wouldn't put it past Shiro. As we alighted, I caught his amused glance. Meaningfully, he glanced over at Chen. *Remember to get close to him.* If I wanted Shiro to send for Bektu, then I'd better play along.

The house was built in the traditional Japanese way, which is different from yet familiar to Chinese architecture. There was the gated entryway, the sensation of passing into private territory, though everything was made of wood rather than stone. Long shaded wooden verandas, or *engawa*, with hanging reed screens. Narrow passages with sliding doors, and tatami rooms. An old house, dark with wood and shadows, dappled by the leaves of the camellia bushes in the inner gardens, and smelling of cedar and the musty indefinable scent of secrets.

We were assigned rooms in an annex by the housekeeper, an older woman, while the young manservant fetched our luggage. Apparently, this house belonged to a writer who'd let it to Kuro, hence the minimal staff for a bachelor household.

Frowning, the housekeeper beckoned me to help. The seclusion of the house and the feeling of secrets in the air made my nose twitch as I hurried after her.

"If the old master knew how many foreigners are here, he'd surely regret leasing his house out," she muttered.

Naturally, she'd no idea that I understood her as I obeyed her curt, pantomimed instructions to help prepare tea and refreshments for the guests, in the kitchen with its tiled modern sink and charcoal stove. Well, I couldn't entirely blame the housekeeper for being sour—it was an increase in work from taking care of one bachelor to an entire household of visitors. Under the Tokugawa shogunate, Japan had been closed to foreigners for a few hundred years, though that has never stopped my kind from coming and going. Despite the Meiji government's recent opening to outside influence, foreigners were still somewhat rare.

After my mistress had unpacked and bathed, I served her an early supper of rice, pickles, miso soup, and grilled fish.

"I'll rest tonight," she said. "Did you tell Bohai that I won't join them, and to give my regards to our host?"

I nodded, kneeling at the low table I'd brought in for her meal.

"Ah San," she said softly, "don't leave yet. This house gives me the most peculiar feeling."

Of course, it was a house with three foxes under its roof tonight. That would be enough to drive most people crazy, but I judiciously avoided the subject.

"*Tai furen*, shall I tell you a story?"

"Is it a story about you, Ah San?"

"Did you want to hear about me?" I was amused. She'd never asked before, being considerate of my feelings as a supposed orphan from Qiqihar. I felt a twinge of conscience.

"Yes, I would. Also about the grasslands." She smiled.

Dusk had descended on this wooden house with its shadowed eaves. Outside, irises were growing in the garden. Still light enough to walk without a lantern, but too dark to identify someone's features. It's the time of day that we foxes like the best.

"Not all parts of the grasslands are alike. The grass itself varies, from sheep fescue to feather grass, couch grass and wormwood. If you live there, you'll understand how they grow to sustain the Five Snouts."

"The Five Snouts?"

"Horses, sheep, goats, camels, and yaks," I said promptly. "The Five Jewels, if you prefer."

"Oh yes!" My mistress laughed, eyes bright. "I haven't heard that term since my childhood. Go on, please."

I could have spent the entire evening talking about the different kinds of steppe and taiga. She'd asked for a story, after all, and this is what we teach cubs. How to sniff the wind, which plants to chew when you have a stomachache, how to survive the long, icy winter when the dead grass is pressed down with snow. Yet as I spoke, I felt shadows lengthening around me.

Shadows of the past. Of nursing my child while lying contentedly in the grass. Sunlight dappling her sweet face. The more I talked, the sadder I felt. With a start, I realized my mistress was gazing at me patiently, and that I'd completely halted my narrative.

"Ah, where was I? Don't fall in love on the grasslands," I said lightly. "It only leads to sorrow."

"Why do you say that? Is it because of your husband?"

I'd forgotten I'd mentioned my marriage before, so I nodded.

"Did you love him?"

"Yes. A love like madness." I thought of the wind blowing through the grass and sighed.

Ever considerate, she said, "I didn't mean to pry. Yet there's something romantic about the steppe. I myself . . ." She trailed off.

"Did you meet your husband in Inner Mongolia?" I asked.

"Oh no. It was an arranged marriage."

"I thought you might have known each other from childhood."

She smiled. "I did have a friend, a neighboring boy who I grew up with. But I don't believe he was ever interested in me.

We were playmates, and he was destined to be a great scholar. I wonder what happened to him in the end?"

"Tell me more"—*about your stepson, and the people with no shadows*, but I didn't say that aloud. She was bound to tell me secrets. It was that sort of evening, when one is tired in a strange country and feeling nostalgic.

"When I was five years old, my mother took me to visit her relatives, and that was when I first saw the grasslands." She paused, as though about to say more. "Then, when I was fourteen, my mother sent me back again to her kinsfolk, hoping to make a match for me. I was only a concubine's daughter, so had no great hopes. My mother refused to bind my feet, you see."

"Did your mother find you a Mongolian husband?"

"She tried. They had a distant cousin in mind, a boy four years older. But when we finally met, I hated him." My mistress gave me a rueful smile. "For months before, they'd talked up what a good match it would be. But he was needlessly cruel. The first time I met him, he had just skinned a sheep alive for knocking him down."

I shuddered. It is an old Mongolian torture, to flay a living man.

"The older men stopped him before he was done. They were angry, and rightly so. And I, dressed in my best clothes, hoping to meet my prospective groom, vomited."

Poor girl, sent to distant relatives, only to discover that she'd been promised to a monster.

"I didn't want to disappoint my mother. She'd tried, hoping for a good match, and of course nobody had told her much about him. He was healthy, cunning, and a good horseman, but no local girl would marry him. I wouldn't either, though my uncle slapped me for it. It was a shock to me, having been raised with affection by my mother."

"What happened?"

"After months of crying, cajoling, and pressure, they sent me back when I threatened to kill myself. If I wouldn't marry that boy, there'd be no other match for me, they said. On days when I thought I'd suffocate from the uncertainty, I'd go out and gaze at the endless sea of grass, hoping that someone would save me, like he had once before."

"Who had?"

"A stranger, when I was young." She fell silent. "Ah San, do you believe that there are people who don't age?"

"Everyone grows older," I said warily.

"I'm talking about people who look the same after sixty years."

My scalp prickled as I recalled the look my mistress had given me when she'd first interviewed me. The delighted half recognition that had made me wonder if she'd met one of us before.

"Some people look exactly like their ancestors," I said. "I knew a boy who was the spitting image of his grandfather, so everyone said. Ha ha!" Hastily, I cleared the dishes off the table.

"You're probably right," she sighed.

TROTTING BACK FROM the annex with her tray, I passed the junction with the main house. The corridor was open on one side to the garden and its fresh green scent. I paused, alert. Then I spotted a piece of paper dropped on dark floorboards, tied in a knot the way that hand-delivered letters used to be.

Written in Manchu, that vertical, scrolling script that most Han Chinese couldn't read, it was from Shiro: *Chen will take a walk alone after dinner.* Shiro wasn't shy about promoting his agenda. Since I needed his help to summon Bektu Nikan, I'd better get on with it.

When my mistress had retired for the evening, I went out to the garden. It was dark, but pleasantly so. I sniffed the lingering aroma of grilled fish. From afar, I heard laughter—the young men were finishing up dinner and moving on to rice wine. They might even recite some poetry, feeling adrift in a foreign land. Quietly, I took off my plaited straw shoes and left them behind a stone lantern. Then I climbed over the garden wall. There were many things I intended to do that night.

22

"My wife has been possessed by a fox."

These are the first words Mr. Wang utters when Bao arrives for their meeting. Bao is taken aback, but perhaps this is how the wealthy behave—as though everyone should be aware of their problems.

Mr. Wang is in his forties, narrow-shouldered with a paunch. The high collar of his Manchu jacket emphasizes his sallow features and thin eyes. Birds sing in the birch trees of this villa. Not the client's, as has been carefully emphasized, but a friend's. Bao wonders why Mr. Wang has taken such pains to keep this meeting secret from his own household. The mansion is built in the style of southern China, with white walls pierced with windows and cunningly designed courtyards. A pattern of gray and black swirls in the marble floor echoes the ink-on-silk painting of clouds on the wall, and tall wooden doors are flung open to enjoy the view of a lotus pond. It's early spring, but despite the watery sunlight, Bao feels cold.

"What do you mean, 'possessed by a fox'?"

"I'm talking about my wife-to-be." Producing Bao's business card, the same one that he handed to the maid at the villa, Mr. Wang places it on the table between them. "I heard you're discreet and have an excellent reputation. And I want someone who takes such creatures seriously."

These are most unlikely words to issue from Mr. Wang's lips. It feels as though time has spun backwards a thousand years, and he and Bao are two gentlemen sitting in a forest, discussing omens and portents.

To be "possessed by a fox" could mean his wife is having an affair. There are many such tales, of a wife seduced by a strangely attractive man who comes and goes from her bedchamber despite all doors being locked. Such women are said to become disorderly, wanton, and out of their minds. Because of course, thinks Bao ironically, only madness would cause a dutiful wife to yearn after a handsome young lover. He's careful to keep his face blank, despite his own curiosity. "You mean she's associating with a . . . stranger?"

Mr. Wang shakes his head. "Nothing like that. She believes herself to be someone else."

"Have you had her examined by a doctor?"

"Of course. But she's very clever and no one besides me suspects a thing."

"Forgive me, but don't you think that this is more of a spiritual matter for a monk or an exorcist?"

Mr. Wang glances out beyond the carved screened doors. The sky is a faint blue, exactly the shade of a priceless porcelain wine cup. "She's gone. I want you to find her."

This is about the woman who escaped from the secret courtyard. Bao, too, wants to know about her. "Do you want me to look into her background?" If so, he suspects she might have appeared in Wu Village two years ago, looking for a fox cub. His heart skips a beat; how strange that he's personally so taken with this case, that he'd pursue it even if nobody paid him.

But Mr. Wang brushes off the suggestion. "Her past isn't important—in fact, you must be discreet so that word doesn't get back to my official wives."

"When did she run away?"

"A month ago, though I don't know why. I made sure she wanted for nothing. I'd ordered new furniture, a wedding trousseau." He sounds aggrieved.

"Can you describe her?"

"Middle height. Clear complexion. She's very attractive. There's no way you'll mistake her."

"Do you have a picture of her?"

Reluctantly, Mr. Wang takes out a black-and-white photograph from his pocket. The subject is a young woman, simply dressed. Not what one would expect from a rich man's wife, who should have her hair done up in an elaborate stiff confection, high and flat, that echoes the dying Manchu styles of the ruling dynasty. The light in the photograph suggests snow, which lends it a mysterious, radiant air. Her eyebrows are straight and dark, her clear gaze angled to the left of the camera. It's a beguiling portrait.

Bao examines it carefully, heart racing. Perhaps this picture was taken by the photographer linked to both the restaurant and Wu Village. He flips it over casually to see if there's a stamp. Yes. *Bektu Nikan.*

"May I?" he says, motioning to put the photograph in his pocket.

Frown. Mr. Wang doesn't want to let it go but realizes he must. "I want it back though. When you find her."

The meeting lurches forward in the same awkward, secretive manner. Not only has the client refused to allow him to examine the household from which this woman has fled, but he has also apparently failed to notify the authorities. When pressed, he turns his gaze sideways and gives only halting answers:

1. She disappeared from a secure courtyard.
2. When last seen, she was well-dressed, in a light blue *changyi*, or tunic, embroidered with birds and flowers, and loose dark trousers.
3. No, Bao cannot interview the servants at his house.

Bao would have liked to formally question the whole household. There's so much that a servant knows, especially any hint of indiscretion. At the same time, it spares him the difficulty of explaining his earlier incognito expedition to the villa.

"Given her light clothing, could she have been kidnapped?"

Silence. Mr. Wang appears to be struggling with some emotion. A thin film of sweat beads his forehead; his pallid cheek twitches. Bao wonders if Mr. Wang is unwell and recalls the words of the maid at the villa. *The master hasn't been himself for a while.* Perhaps it's Mr. Wang who needs help, not the lady who vanished.

Bao thinks of Feng, also known as Chunhua, whose frozen body was discovered on a doorstep two miles away. Impulsively, he says, "May I ask about a party that you hosted at a teahouse more than a month ago? I believe a courtesan went missing partway through."

Mr. Wang looks blank. When Bao provides more details, he shrugs. "Oh, that. I heard from the establishment afterwards. It was quite inconvenient that she left, as we were short one girl to pour drinks, though they refunded the expense."

"Were there any handsome young gentlemen in your party?"

"No. It was a business dinner, though the private room next door was booked by some medical students. I knew a few of them—the sons of acquaintances, who stopped by to greet me. If you're looking for a young man, he might have come from that party."

Mr. Wang is disinterested, his thoughts focused only on the lady who escaped his villa. He doesn't ask Bao other questions like a normal person would, but behaves like an addict, eyes full of unexpected hunger. When a servant enters the room, Mr. Wang glances up, as though the woman he seeks might miraculously appear. The skin on his sallow cheekbones tightens.

"About my wife-to-be," he says. Bao notes the possessiveness as his hands clench and unclench. "I want her back."

"Why do you think she's possessed by a fox?" Bao asks again.

"There's no other reason for her disappearance. I gave her everything she could possibly want. Also, she was unusually interested in such creatures—she asked many questions about the photographer who'd bought a fox cub." His voice drops to a mutter. "At twilight, her eyes would glitter strangely, and I felt my heart contract with fear and desire. My steward thinks I'm bewitched; the servants murmur and turn their faces away."

Taken aback by this sudden outpouring, Bao blinks twice. Mr. Wang laughs abruptly. A stilted look shutters his face as he says, "Tell me if you find her."

AFTER TAKING HIS leave, Bao goes for a walk to gather his thoughts. Mukden has outgrown its original city walls, which have fallen into disrepair. People have been systematically removing the bricks to shore up their own houses. As Bao walks beneath the looming shadow of the massive, crumbling wall, he considers his new client and what darkness might be haunting him. Thin eyes and scant brows, pale complexion like wax kept from the sun. A man like that is full of secrets.

The fluid emotional language Mr. Wang used at the end of their interview reminds him of Ah Yan, and how her speech also quickened when she described the fox lady. It's as though a deep emotion wells out of them, urgent as an overflowing spring. Sometimes Bao wonders if his gift for hearing lies has displaced part of himself: if the fox god, having healed him (why can't he remember what his old nanny said, *I asked the fox god to take away your . . . ?*), has left a space that others rush to fill with their complaints and desires.

Bao pauses under a willow tree to examine the photograph again, wondering just how crazy Mr. Wang might be. His words, *My wife has been possessed by a fox*, held a faint deceptive buzz, but they weren't an outright lie either. Is it because he used the term "wife," which Bao knows to be false, or is it the "fox" part? He can't puzzle it out; the question gnaws away at him, just as the fox spirits of old were said to dine on human livers.

Perhaps this woman is a medium, one of those who claims to be possessed by a fox spirit. There's a disreputable air about such practitioners, not being gods themselves but merely their self-styled interpreters. Most mediums are from lowly backgrounds; the majority are women who defy their husbands and families by claiming spiritual powers. Who dares to discipline a willful daughter-in-law who speaks for a god? Their only distinction is their claim to channel fox spirits, healing the sick by means of charms written on strips of yellow paper, and prophesying.

Overall, they strike him as charlatans.

BAO ONCE INVESTIGATED such a case for a client who suspected his son was being swindled by a fox medium. "I want to know if she's a fake," he'd said. Intrigued, Bao agreed. His old nanny never mentioned mediums. For her, the fox god in his silent shrine was enough. No need to go through someone else.

On a fine autumn morning, Bao and his client Zhang paid a visit to the fox medium. The house was in a poverty-stricken neighborhood, yet the medium's front yard displayed a row of costly glazed flowerpots. While they waited, Zhang explained that the medium was said to have been possessed by a fox shortly after her marriage. Tearing at her clothes, she had run around shrieking, half naked. Her husband had beaten her soundly, but she'd ignored the pain, thus convincing onlookers that she must be possessed. Finally, she'd announced in a deep voice that a fox was her lover.

They'd scarcely finished this murmured exchange when a boy of eight or nine with a dirty face ushered them in. From the child's sharp looks, Bao suspected he was routinely sent to eavesdrop on clients' conversations.

Beckoning in a friendly manner, Bao said, "Are you related to the medium?"

Suspicious, the boy nodded.

"Is she possessed by a fox?"

"Why ask?" his client said. "He won't tell you anything."

Ignoring him, Bao waited patiently, hoping the boy would speak. All this head-nodding would do him no good if he couldn't hear his voice.

"Yes," said the boy, turning hastily away. "She is."

Ah, thought Bao.

The medium's sanctuary consisted of a red curtain draped across the small room, stuffy with the smell of incense and wine. Hard-boiled eggs were displayed on a platter, as well as bottles of liquor. These were apparently customary offerings to the fox spirit. In preparation, his client produced an expensive bottle of Moutai and placed it on the table. They waited in silence. Bao thought he heard some movement behind the curtain.

It's just the medium, he told himself. Yet the silence continued. As they stood there, Bao was gradually aware that his scalp was prickling, the skin of his face had tightened, and his palms were sweating. He had the unbearable sensation that something was studying him intently from a hole in the dirty red curtain.

With an effort, Bao wrenched his gaze away. The red curtain was drawn abruptly aside. A woman emerged with tightly combed-back hair and beetle-bright eyes.

Zhang introduced them as goldsmiths, a scenario they'd prepared to test the medium's abilities. "Recently, some gold was stolen from our shop. We suspect one of the employees, but we don't know who."

The medium gestured, and the boy who'd led them in said, "Put what's in your pockets on the altar."

Zhang put a piece of silver on the table, next to the boiled eggs. A fly, buzzing around the enclosed room, settled on the red curtain. Just when Bao felt as though he was going to suffocate from the smell of the burning incense, the medium began to rock to and fro. In a strained, deep voice, she shouted, "Liar! You still have money in your pocket!"

Shaken, Zhang hurriedly placed one more piece of silver on the table. The medium continued in the same unnatural voice, "To discover the thief, burn this paper and make all the apprentices in your shop drink the ashes in a cup of wine. After that, one will confess."

Zhang seemed overcome by the medium's bold manner, her little black eyes like dried beans, and her ability to berate him. Even Bao was impressed. Normally no woman of low birth would dare to order a wealthy merchant around.

"I had a childhood friend who was sent to Inner Mongolia to be married. Will I meet her again?" he asked.

The medium's glance swept over him. "Yes."

A shiver slithered down Bao's spine, but he kept his face expressionless as he placed one more coin on the table. "My last question is—are you truly a fox?"

He half expected to be greeted with laughter or anger, but instead, the woman said very seriously, "Of course."

Blinking, they'd stumbled out into the bright sunshine.

Bao was slightly light-headed from the incense. "Well?" said his client eagerly. "Is she a fake?"

"Her first answer about the missing gold was a calculated guess. A guilty apprentice forced to drink ashes and swear upon a spirit might confess. She also guessed correctly that you had more money in your pocket. But she didn't realize we'd made up the whole story. As for the last question—"

Zhang nodded impatiently. "Yes, is she a fox?"

"No. That I can tell you for sure."

Bao had been certain this medium was a fake, from the moment when the boy who ushered them in had assured them that she was possessed by a fox.

Yes, she is, he'd said, turning away, and Bao had instantly heard the child's lie. Could have seen it anyway, in his averted face. When the medium had spoken confidently about catching the thief with a charm, he'd heard the lie in her voice as well, despite her pretense of speaking in a lower voice. Finally, when questioned, *Are you truly a fox?*, her answer was also a lie.

Yet there'd been two moments of disquiet. When they'd stood, waiting before that shabby red curtain, and Bao had an uneasy feeling of being watched. And again, when he'd asked his question about a childhood friend. He'd thrown that in because it seemed timely to ask some innocuous question from the past. Her answer had surprised him. That *yes*, he would meet Tagtaa again. That had the ring of truth to it.

RECALLING THIS ENCOUNTER, Bao sighs. The woman who took the fox cub away in Wu Village was likely such a trickster. Perhaps she went on to deceive Mr. Wang, though he feels a wobble of uncertainty about that. He reminds himself that there's a difference between a medium and an actual fox. The former are human interpreters. The latter, he's unsure of. Are they gods, spirits, or parasites that prey on humans? The very idea of an animal that can mimic a human is both captivating and terrifying.

Perhaps he's been searching his whole life for an experience like Tagtaa's, when she told him about the black fox that returned as a man. How he'd have liked to see the fox god himself! But fate is fickle; those who don't seek the gods may encounter them unknowingly.

23

The note I'd picked up in the corridor had said, *Chen will take a walk alone after dinner*. Clearly, it was an invitation to action. Shiro had promised to write a letter summoning Bektu Nikan to Moji. In return, I was to get close to Chen.

After scrambling over the garden wall, I ran off to waylay him outside the front gate. Rounding the corner too fast, I actually collided with Chen. We staggered apart as I apologized, making excuses about running an errand.

"It's late, so let me accompany you," said he.

Keeping my head down demurely, I let him take the lead. The moon was rising as we walked along the road, dappled with shadows and dreams. After a while, Chen said, "I heard from Bohai that you're not really a servant. Are you employed by Shirakawa?"

"I'm just here to keep an eye on him for his grandmother's sake," I said vaguely.

"I see." Pause. "I've never met a professional investigator before."

Neither had I, for that matter. In the old days, we just called them fixers, agents, or maybe spies. Freelance operatives working just for you.

"If you pay for it, you can get almost any kind of service," I said.

"Is that why you wouldn't take the job I offered you earlier in Dalian—because you were already hired? It was a serious offer, you know." He turned red. "I was sure you would please my aunt." *And you, too*, I thought grimly.

We'd stopped under a large pine tree. From here, the road sloped down towards the harbor and its faint tang of salt. Chen cleared his throat, embarrassed. "My family is very demanding—I chose to study in Japan to get away from my father. My aunt is just like him; she even made me investigate her husband, a man by the name of Wang. There were some disturbing rumors about him and their garden villa outside Mukden."

I inhaled sharply. Hadn't Lu mentioned, at that very first dinner before Shiro came in and derailed everything, that Bektu Nikan had known Chen's uncle in Mukden? I made an inspired guess. "A garden villa in the Willow neighborhood whose owner has a penchant for opera singers?"

"Yes, did Shirakawa tell you? My aunt, who's his First Wife, was suspicious about the private business parties that her husband held there and told me to attend one last summer, to check if he was keeping other women. His collection of rare plants was being photographed, which gave Bohai and Lu an excuse to come, too."

"What did you find?"

"Well, he'd certainly been keeping women. On and off, the servants said, in a little courtyard," Chen said dismissively. To him, an extra woman or two wasn't news. I really wanted to grill him on this, preferably by tying him to the pine tree and lighting a fire under the soles of his feet, but I restrained myself.

"I reported to my aunt that the courtyard was empty when we checked. The house party lasted a few days. The three of us, Bohai, Lu, and I, were hoping for some excitement, but it was the usual—people viewing flowers and making back-room deals."

"Did you make any deals?"

"Not me. Lu might have. His family lost money in recent speculations, and he's been anxious about it. The only interesting event was a poetry reading, where people shared tales of ghosts and foxes. The photographer, Bektu Nikan, scoffed he wasn't afraid of such creatures."

I stifled a hiss. "What an interesting man."

"Yes," said Chen. "It might have been better if we'd never met him. In fact, I regret what happened next."

"Go on," I said encouragingly. Perhaps too much so, for Chen drew near again.

"But why do you want to know about him? This isn't a good place for us to talk. Let's go back to my room." He seized my arm not-quite-so-playfully.

We were standing at the edge of the road, where the hill-side of brush separating two wooded estates dropped away below us. A good hard shove would send Chen slithering down the slope. I considered this, but Chen mistook my hesitation for maidenly shyness.

"I have some good wine," he said, tugging my hand. "We'll be very quiet, and nobody will ever know."

I dug my heels in, like a donkey. "How about that bush over there instead?"

"That bush?"

"Yes." The large bush slightly lower down the slope would be a wonderful place to tie him up. I could extract all the information I wanted about Bektu and leave him there for a couple of days if he was gagged. People almost never check inside bushes. I don't know why. I always do.

Chen looked dubious. Likely no girl had ever responded to his advances in such an uncouth fashion. As I loosened the cloth belt around my waist, thinking that it would be handy for tying him up, his eyes lit up. "Well, it would be a first for me," he said.

"Really?" Reaching down, I picked up a stone. It was a good shape and size, fitting exactly into the palm of my hand.

Chen had decided that this was going to be a great story to tell his friends and, despite initial misgivings, began to pick his way down the crumbling slope. I was following suit when I heard the crunch of approaching footsteps.

The moon had risen, and its cold radiance was bright enough that the slope below us turned white. A figure appeared at the top of the hill, where the road was. It was Kuro. I could have picked out his silhouette across a plain, no matter how dark the night. That lithe, broad-shouldered stance with the right leg turned out a little. Chen had noticed, too, and began hastily making his way back.

"Ah, Kurosaki!" he said, somewhat out of breath. "We—I mean, I was just going for a walk."

"Am I interrupting something?"

"Not at all." Chen reached the top of the slope first, over-taking me hurriedly as though we had no acquaintance at all. Beneath his hasty small talk, I sensed a deep embarrassment. I kept quiet, but when I reached the top, Kuro reached down and pulled me up without a word. Then he silently removed the stone from my other hand.

THE GOOD THING about Kuro is that he doesn't ask questions. The bad thing is that you never know what he's thinking. But that was all right; I didn't need to know. He'd promised in the past to stay out of my way, and was, I reminded myself, generally good about keeping promises (*except one time*, though I didn't wish to remember it; no, I would not think of it).

The next morning, my mistress was up early. When I went in to help her dress, she was already looking at the garden. "Bohai came by earlier. He wants to borrow you because you can speak Japanese." She gave me a worried look. "He said you were to go with Shirakawa. What is going on?"

I didn't know either, but I had a nasty suspicion. I hadn't been able to conclude my conversation with Chen last night. What did he know about Bektu Nikan—and, perhaps more importantly, what did he regret?

I'd been instructed to go to the eight-mat room where the young gentlemen were lounging yesterday, and so I did, tapping politely on the sliding door. I took a quick look around: Shiro, Bohai, and Lu. An expensive set of kimono was folded and set out in the middle of the room. I raised my eyebrows.

"Yes, it's exactly what you think!" Shiro looked pleased. "I'd like you to wear that. We have an appointment today."

"Why?" I glared at him.

"It's ridiculous," said Lu, pulling his long, camel-like lip. "You can't dress up a maid and pretend she's a young lady. Let's hire a courtesan from the pleasure district instead."

"This isn't a large town," said Shiro. "Bringing in a stranger is better. I guarantee she'll pass muster."

"What about the housekeeper and the boy who helps here?"

"They won't talk either." Shiro looked at me. "We're raising money from a wealthy industrialist here in Moji. However, he's under the impression that a young lady will be accompanying the talks."

"Accompanying?"

"I told him if he'd make time for us today, I'd bring my beautiful cousin to entertain him."

Reckless, reckless. This was so like Shiro, to have several pots on the fire. Such overreach is also why we are sometimes discovered, decapitated, or boiled to death in bottles.

I must have looked mulish because Shiro murmured in my ear, "If you do this, I'll use the money to pay for Bektu's passage here."

With considerable irritation, I took the clothes and retired to my little room. It's not easy to wear kimono. In fact, compared to Manchu dress, it's far more complicated. Most young ladies of good family can hardly get dressed by themselves, which is why Shiro sent the housekeeper after me. Looking uncomfortable, she addressed me politely in Japanese.

"Mr. Shirakawa says that you're actually not a servant," she said formally.

I wondered what new tale Shiro had spun, but I was glad of her help. To look the part of a wealthy young lady required all sorts of adjustments, particularly since kimono are made to the same size. You have to fold and tuck, with extra sashes, ties, and undergarments, to achieve a good fit.

The kimono Shiro had handed me was just the sort of thing a young lady of good family might wear. It was late spring, so it had a pattern of wisteria blossoms and leaves, with a violet obi and dark purple sash cord. Shiro has always had good taste. The housekeeper also mentioned that a professional hairdresser would be stopping by to put my hair up before our appointment. This I was grateful for, for a proper lady's hairstyle, in which long hair is oiled and put up elaborately, would be impossible to manage alone.

I should point out that, of course, these are the clothes and mannerisms of the upper class. The women of the rowhouse tenements wind their hair into rough buns, and wear kimono made of coarse blue cotton, fastened with string instead of obi. Some country women even use a piece of straw rope, which is all they have. A fine kimono, such as Shiro had given me, would be beyond their dreams.

The housekeeper was now forced to use polite speech with me, given my sudden change in status. Despite that, she proved less frosty than yesterday. "I'm not surprised, seeing as how Mr. Kurosaki's profession is what it is," she said. "But I wish I'd been told from the start that you were one of his people. I apologize again for any rudeness."

"What is his profession?" I asked, wondering why she'd accepted all the odd events of the morning.

"Why, he's a novelist. A very famous one."

Kuro, a novelist? That must be a joke.

"Kurosaki-*sensei* writes under a pseudonym, of course. But a year ago he wrote a short novel that won several prizes. It was highly praised in literary circles."

"What was it about?"

"It was a book of ghost stories. Set in northern China, which is where you're all from, I hear. I read it myself—it was quite wonderful."

An expression of utmost disbelief was reflected back to me in the mirror I was gazing at, so I made sure to close my mouth properly.

24

Bao became a detective by chance. He'd begun his career as a scholar, taking the Imperial exams, and recalls the individual exam cells where scholars were walled up for days, writing and commenting on texts. The sour taste of nerves, the awkward nods of fellow examinees as they waited to enter. The sound of a fly buzzing and crawling over the paper.

Halfway through the exam, he'd fallen sick. Chills coursed through his body, his eyes burned, and he'd collapsed with a high fever. Later, he was told that the porter who helped him out of the examinations reported that Bao had asked for his mother. "Poor young man, he must miss her terribly."

Bao thought the porter must have been mistaken. He would never have called for his mother. Still, he's felt her shadow. What would she say now, observing him pore over the trail of a missing woman?

Probably nothing.

Bao smiles wryly, remembering his mother's tight-lipped grimace. He only became a detective once his mother and then his wife died. It's not a profession that officially exists, as far as he knows. But he started finding lost objects, ferreting out the truth, and acting as an intermediary until his services were well-known enough that he felt he could charge for them.

Bao understands his appeal lies partly in his cultured demeanor. A former scholar from a good family who can recite poetry and fathom the secrets of a treacherous heart— this reassures his upper-class clientele. He ponders Mr. Wang's commission. Finding a missing person isn't the same as recovering stolen property, let alone a woman who apparently thinks she's a fox. Some might wonder who is crazed— this woman or Mr. Wang himself? Compared to an indigent woman of uncertain background, Mr. Wang is well-connected and wealthy. The imbalance of power between them is so great as to be laughable. Yet Mr. Wang's eyes were greedily fixed on an unattainable goal. Bao thinks of Tagtaa and the giddy sparkle in her eyes when she told him about the black fox that returned as a man. Who—or what—could ever compete with that?

THE SPRING THAT Tagtaa turned fourteen, she was indeed sent to her mother's relatives in Inner Mongolia. In Bao's memories, that morning is still vivid: a spring day with a blue sky so high and wide that the wispy clouds can barely span it.

Strangely, Bao wakes with a feeling of happiness. His father has offered to take him to look at horses. Magistrate Yu is selling a string of polo ponies, and it promises to be an interesting day out. Perhaps he'll buy a stick of candied fruit for Tagtaa, though he's vaguely aware that it's a childish gift.

As Bao stands outside the main gate, waiting for his father, he hears shouts and the clatter of wooden wheels on the road.

"What's happening at the neighbor's house?" he asks the gatekeeper.

"Oh, the young miss is leaving today. Didn't you know?"

"Do you mean Tagtaa?"

"Yes, she's leaving for Inner Mongolia. To get married, they say."

Disregarding the gatekeeper's pitying look, Bao hurtles down the street. Chest bursting, feet slamming against the road. He runs as though a flame is scorching the hem of his jacket all the way to Tagtaa's house. Panting and winded, he pauses. A mule cart is being loaded with a wooden chest and rolls of cloth. They look ominously like a bridal trousseau. The gate is partly open, and he races in, heedless of the gatekeeper, who raises a shout.

"Where is she?" he cries. They all know him by sight, the second son of a county official. An older servant stops him.

"If you mean Tagtaa, the concubine's daughter," she says, "she's gone ahead in another mule cart. If you run, you can catch them at the main road."

So Bao runs. He runs till his sides ache and his lungs burn, ignoring the stares and pointed fingers. He's making a scene, the kind that his father will discipline him for that night. At the crossroads, waiting in the heavier traffic of oxen and handcarts piled high with firewood, he spies the mule cart. In it is a small, upright figure. "Tagtaa!" he shouts.

She's wearing a pink blouse that's familiar from special occasions; he can't see her expression clearly at that distance. Tagtaa raises her hand when she sees him. Perhaps she even calls his name. Then the driver jogs his mules and they're off again, the gap between them too far for Bao to close, though he tries. There's too much traffic between them, and though he dodges frantically between handcarts and rickshaws on the packed main road, he can't possibly catch up. The mule cart, trotting faster, recedes like Bao's hopes. Eventually, gasping, he walks home. The day—no, the rest of his life—is ruined. There's a hole in his chest the size of an inkstone. Folded over on himself, arms crossed, Bao bears his father's chastisement later that night.

His father rarely hits him, which Bao is grateful for. But his long-winded reprimand on how a gentleman, especially one from this household, shouldn't run shouting in the streets after a mule cart is especially painful, because beneath his father's irritation, Bao hears pity. They all pity him, even his mother, though this outcome is what she expected. Everyone knows about his partiality for Tagtaa, the concubine's daughter, and now he's made a fool of himself in such a cheap, melodramatic fashion. So when plans are made to send him to study in another town, Bao isn't surprised. It's a relief to escape the shame of whispered laughter in their neighborhood.

Still, the question haunts him: Why didn't Tagtaa, at least, tell him she was leaving that day?

BAO SIGHS. It's been half a century since he ran down that street, choking with despair, yet it's etched sharply in his memory. The clotted mule dung fouling his new felt boots, the sinking terror of being too late.

Over the years, Bao has searched for her. Their families fell out of touch when his father was reassigned to another county. Tagtaa herself, as a concubine's daughter, hardly warranted an entry into any official records. "Tagtaa" was a childhood nickname given by her Mongolian mother; he has no idea of her formal Chinese name. He hopes she's happily married, though each time he's investigated a missing woman sold into the red-light district, Bao wonders. The powerlessness he felt that day still haunts him, leading him to do favors for those like Qiulan at the Phoenix Pavilion. Feng, frozen on the doorstep, is another lost woman he's tried to help.

After Tagtaa left, Bao experienced agonies, imagining her paired off with a handsome stranger or the victim of a wicked old man. Both scenarios were horrific. There was nobody Bao could talk to. He'd made himself the laughingstock of their neighborhood. Tagtaa's family would have nothing to do with him either. The whole episode suggested impropriety, as though a daughter of their house (even if her mother was a concubine) had crossed the line. And Bao, mortified and desperately sad, tried his best to forget.

Yet the memory of Tagtaa's pink blouse in the distance lingered. For years, he was drawn to girls wearing pink. In fact, it influenced the first glimpse of his own future wife. The matchmaker had said that during the Duanwu, or Dragon Boat Festival, she'd arrange for his potential bride to view the flowers near a bridge—accompanied, of course, by a chaperone. Bao, realizing what a favor this was (many only saw their spouse's face after the wedding ceremony), had jumped at the chance. His marriage had been arranged by his mother. Bao was twenty-two at the time, having passed the preliminary county exams, and, despite failing the provincial level once, was still considered a good prospect.

The day of the meeting, Bao arrived at the bridge an hour early. Three of his friends accompanied him under the pretext of sightseeing. The actual meeting had been hardly more than a glimpse. There were crowds milling under the willow trees, with vendors selling whistles shaped like birds and *zongzi*, dumplings wrapped in bamboo leaves. The young lady in question had a thin, meek face with eyebrows drawn a little higher, as was the fashion at the time. But she wore a high-collared pink blouse, and something had leaped inside Bao.

Of course she wasn't Tagtaa. And the blouse she was wearing wasn't the same shade of pink that Tagtaa had worn that last day. But Bao had gone home and written his answer to the matchmaker right away: *Yes, I accept.*

His friends made much of this story in later years, telling his wife that Bao had fallen in love with her at first sight. "Across a bridge!" they said. "He decided right away!" And there was general laughter. His wife's lean cheeks had colored with pride. To the end of her days, she believed this story, and Bao was too kind to ever contradict it. Why should he? She was a nervous woman, and when she died, she'd been worried about Bao living alone without her.

"How will you manage?" she'd murmured as he pressed her hand. She'd even tried to find him a concubine; some women felt it better to choose their own successors. Towards the end of his wife's illness, she'd sent for a girl from the countryside through her own family connections. Returning home one day, Bao found the girl waiting awkwardly, and instantly understood his wife's intentions.

The girl she'd selected was sturdy and slow-witted. Bao had felt terribly sorry, both for his wife (clearly, nobody was to outshine her position as mistress, even after death) and for the girl. He'd heard enough lies to know that no woman young enough to be his daughter would want to marry him, and had said so, firmly.

"I'll live by myself."

There'd been some tears, likely of relief on his wife's part. "What if you fall for some young hussy?"

"I won't fall in love with a young woman," he said.

And that was the truth.

Bao arranged for the girl to find a suitable husband, a poultry dealer she seemed to like well enough. At least her gratitude held no lies. And in the end, that had pleased his wife. After her death, Bao had shut up their small house, given up his teaching position, and, with no other claims on his time, become a full-time detective.

NOW BAO BREWS tea in a porcelain teapot with a lotus painted on it. The pink petals remind him of Tagtaa, lost to him so long ago, and he wonders if the emotion that Mr. Wang feels for his runaway fiancée is anything like the grief Tagtaa's departure caused him. Fourteen-year-old Bao had little expectation of being heard and no means of finding Tagtaa, while Mr. Wang's agitation is fueled with money. Yet there's an urgent, sad secrecy that Bao recognizes in his client.

Both Mr. Wang and the maid at the villa mentioned that the lady asked incessantly about Bektu Nikan. If he finds the photographer, perhaps he'll locate her as well. Setting down his teacup, Bao rubs his chest. That sharp, sudden ache is occurring more frequently, as though a rip has opened in his lung. He wonders if time is running out for the lady, or perhaps himself.

25

After the hairdresser had come and put my hair up in a maidenly *yuiwata* hairstyle, a lower, flat chignon tied with a band, I reluctantly presented myself at the house entrance. There are at least a hundred traditional hairstyles for women, with different variations announcing age and status. Unfortunately, they all involve pulling and pinning your hair so tightly that you want to scream.

Shiro, Bohai, and Chen were waiting at the house entrance when I showed up, walking with the correct pigeon-toed gait to suit kimono. "Perfect!" said Shiro. "You look just like a proper young lady."

"Don't you think this is rather old-fashioned?" said Bohai to Shiro. "A lot of girls wear Western clothing now."

Of course it was old-fashioned. Shiro's ideas of appropriate women's clothes probably dated from when they were wearing layered robes and receiving lovers behind reed screens, but there was nothing for it but to go along. Two rickshaws waited outside the front gate. Shiro helped me into one and climbed in afterwards. Chen and Bohai followed behind. Lu had been dispatched on some banking business.

"So," I said. "What's this all about?"

"It's time to spread a little goodwill in order to get funding."

"Funding for what?" When I raised my eyebrows, my scalp ached from my tightly dressed hair.

"Bohai, Chen, and Lu believe we're raising money for revolutionary purposes. Takeda, the man we're going to visit, is a financier with ties to Northeast China, but he thinks it's for commercial investment."

"And what do you intend it for?"

"Money is so useful, isn't it?" said Shiro, examining his nails idly. "As I mentioned, Takeda is a wealthy man. I met him last year in Mukden." He showed his teeth at my sudden interest. "Yes, I know you've been asking Chen about a certain garden villa. Ah! Let go!"

Infuriated, I'd seized him by the collar, pressing the sharp tip of a skewer against his throat.

"Shiro," I said, "I don't wish to be involved in your plans unless there's a good reason."

I nudged the point under his jaw. It was a short, slim metal skewer, the length of my hand—the kind used to grill fish. I'd picked it up from the kitchen yesterday. You never know when these things might be handy.

"Chen said he'd met Takeda at a house party. The same villa where Bektu Nikan took photographs. You should stop getting involved with other people's problems. It's making you overly emotional." With a swift movement, Shiro grabbed my wrist and pulled it away from his neck. "That's better."

My heart was racing, my breath coming in gasps. *Calm down*, I told myself. *Become colder.* Like ice dripping from the eaves of a faraway village, buried under the snow. Where my child was hidden from me, in a box with her legs broken, a young girl caring for her. Grief continually amazed me with its ability to resurface at inconvenient moments. Whether I was sleeping in the grass or walking beside railway tracks by myself, the wind blowing and the lonely sun shining down, it always found me.

"You said you wanted revenge," said Shiro, still grasping my wrist. "But you won't tell me what happened. Does Kuro know what you're after?" This sudden change of subject unnerved me.

"Of course not," I said. "It's none of his business."

"Such a delicate hand," he said, running a finger across my palm. "So much rage and sorrow. At least I have some hope since you haven't told Kuro about whatever you're doing."

I yanked my hand away.

Shiro said, "Takeda is at an age where life has started to become dull for him. Wife in Japan, second wife in Manchuria. Business stagnating, fears of losing his hair. Fancies himself an art connoisseur, though he has scarcely more taste than a pig."

"Pigs are very intelligent," I pointed out. Shiro ignored this.

"In short, he's bored and greedy enough to risk capital. Last summer he was in Northeast China for business and got himself invited to a certain house party in the countryside. The owner of the villa, a man named Wang, is fond of collecting beautiful objects. His collection of bonsai is unrivaled. I personally have never seen it." A lopsided smile slid across Shiro's face. "Though I suspect that you have."

I ignored this obvious fishing for information because I was thinking furiously. Shiro's surmise that I was familiar with that garden villa was indeed correct.

WHEN I'D ARRIVED in Wu Village searching for my child, I met a girl digging up pickles in the snow. Overcome with despair, I'd scarcely processed the tale she'd told me about the photographer who'd commissioned a fox to stuff and mount. It was only much later, after I'd buried my child in the cold earth, that I'd recalled every detail.

After I could finally bear to leave her sad little grave, I set out to search for Bektu Nikan. It took me far longer than I'd expected. In my grief and hopelessness, I drove everyone away; a fog of madness swallowed me. I gave up everything, including the thousand-year journey towards enlightenment I'd once pursued. By living a virtuous life and avoiding sin, certain animals, plants, and even rocks may attain a higher level of being. At least, that's the hope of those of us who aspire to greater meaning, though in my bitterness, I'd abandoned my scruples. How could I continue on the Way if my heart was filled with bleak fury?

Going from village to village, I asked if anyone had heard of a photographer named Bektu Nikan. In an inn on the main road to the city, I heard that he had caught pneumonia and died. So I returned to the grasslands and dwelled in my sorrow for another year.

And there I might have stayed if not for chance. On the eve of the Qingming grave-sweeping festival, I went to a night market to buy a pinwheel to put on my child's grave. The scent of roasting pork crackling made my mouth water, though I'd only a few copper *fen* to spend. The stall awnings were lit with flickering oil lamps, and crowds of people pressed past, buying steamed rice cakes and candied hawthorn fruit. While examining some painted bamboo pinwheels, I overheard two men discussing a photographer. "So he didn't die of a chill? That must have been a handy rumor for Bektu. He owes me money."

I knew right away who they were talking about, though my hurried questioning yielded scant results. The men knew only that Bektu Nikan was alive, though not to be found at his lodgings in the city. He'd taken a commission at a rich man's villa where debt collectors couldn't trouble him.

"Why do you ask—does Bektu owe you, too?" The men's eyes glinted in the flickering light. I was in no frame of mind to handle two of them, so I did what any sensible fox does and ran away.

I never bought that pinwheel. Grief and rage boiled up in me like scalding oil, so I could scarcely think straight. My hands were numb, my head spun. As soon as I could, I set off to find a certain garden villa on the outskirts of Mukden. It was well guarded, with unusually high walls that I couldn't scale without a ladder. My ragged clothes only added to my difficulties. It had taken me longer than expected to gain entry to that house, with its parties and well-connected visitors. Now, as the rickshaw jogged us ever closer to our destination, I wondered if there was a chance Takeda had been a guest during that time. And if he'd possibly seen my face before.

Shiro swung his leg, enjoying my discomfort.

"Remind me again why you're bringing me along."

"Why, for your distracting company. Keep him in a good mood until he agrees to give us the money, and you may discover something to your advantage." He smiled. "By the way, Kuro was opposed to this. In fact, he was quite angry with me, in as far as he ever shows his anger."

I had nothing to say about this. In fact, the less information I gave Shiro, the better, so our journey finished in chilly silence.

TAKEDA'S MANSION WAS built in the newly fashionable European style. Ornate, with stained glass windows, dark wood floors, and carpets. We were shown into an attached conservatory made of glass and filled with flowers and ferns. Meiji-era Japan was enthralled with European modes of dress, transport, and arms; it was a complete departure from the secluded land of Yamato that I recalled.

A white-gloved manservant dressed in black showed us in. Presently, the master of the house arrived. Takeda was a large, florid-faced man in a stiff dress shirt buttoned up to his neck. I felt immediate relief. No, we'd never met before, though I wondered what he'd been doing at Wang's garden villa and if he'd met Bektu Nikan there as well.

Compliments and niceties were exchanged. Takeda looked bored until his eyes lighted on me. "And this is?" he said to Shiro.

"My cousin. The one I told you about."

I bowed demurely. Women weren't expected to speak much; indeed, in a traditional setting, I wouldn't be introduced to men like this, but these were new times. Tea was served in delicate china cups with slices of lemon, milk, and sugar. Puzzled, I put lemon slices into the milk but was corrected as Shiro deftly swapped my cup for his. The men glanced at one another and chuckled indulgently. *Look at this poor little woman*, the thought danced between them, admitting them to a club I'd never belong to.

I could only nod and smile, cursing Shiro inwardly. *Distract him*, he'd said. But I needn't have worried. Takeda turned to me, mustache trembling over a wet mouth. "You came from Dalian? The seafood there is wonderful."

"I love oysters—and sea cucumbers, too." Oysters and sea cucumbers are well-known aphrodisiacs. Taken aback, Takeda wondered whether I'd really meant the innuendo. I gave him my most innocent smile.

Shiro said, "I was wondering if we could discuss the terms of the loan you were thinking of giving us."

The conversation focused on business matters with no mention of any revolution. Instead, they discussed establishing a sugar mill on the island of Formosa. None of the young men had any background in this, but they did their best to appear expert. Bohai's egg-shaped face was particularly suited to monologues about profitability. Takeda looked bored and in danger of losing interest, but I managed to catch his eye over the rim of my teacup.

Selecting a large piece of seed cake, I demolished it in two swift bites. Takeda's eyes widened. *Snip snap!* A plate of scones disappeared as Bohai droned on about sugar-refining machinery. Fascinated, Takeda passed me a heaping platter of finger sandwiches. By this time, Shiro had noticed with a withering glare. An eating contestant wasn't the role he'd brought me to play, but who cared? Takeda was enthralled.

"And so, if you advance us the capital required, we're sure to turn a profit within two fiscal years," Bohai concluded triumphantly.

"Yes. Yes, I agree completely," said Takeda. His eyes were still glued on me as I silently swallowed the last sandwich and dabbed my mouth primly.

"I shall submit the paperwork to the bank today. We look forward to our partnership," Shiro said jubilantly.

Smiles all around, though I wondered if Takeda had paid any attention to what he'd agreed to. "Please send my regards to your uncle Mr. Wang," he said to Chen. "I enjoyed my stay at his villa, despite the sad incident that occurred. Was it true there were photographs? Did they have anything to do with that man Bektu Nikan?"

Alert, I glanced from one to the other. What were they talking about? Chen mumbled, "I'm not sure about the rumors."

Seizing matters into my own hands, I asked Takeda if he'd give me a personal tour of his greenhouse. "Do tell me more about this photographer you mentioned," I said as we lingered over a rare fern. "What happened at that villa last summer?"

"Oh, it's nothing to worry about. A student made a scene at the gates."

I touched Takeda's arm. "That sounds terrible."

"Yes, I happened to witness it," he said. "He was distraught. It was odd though—" Takeda broke off sheepishly. "Perhaps I've been reading too many mysteries. I understand you're staying with Kurosaki, the author? I'm a great admirer of his and have often thought of writing something myself. In fact, I've lent your cousin several detective novels."

I recalled the book I'd discovered while snooping in Shiro's ship cabin. Doubtless, he'd been cultivating Takeda's friendship. Well, two could play at that game.

"Won't you write down your recollections of what happened at that house party for me?" I said enthusiastically. "Since I'm staying at Kurosaki-*sensei*'s house, I could even ask him to take a look at them."

Takeda was ridiculously delighted with this idea. As we said goodbye, he pressed my hand. "I'll send you my written notes soon. It was quite a dramatic incident."

26

Bao draws two converging lines in his notebook. One is labeled *fox lady*, the other *Bektu Nikan*. Between them lies *Mr. Wang's villa*, which he crosses out. Though he hasn't a good explanation for how she escaped from a locked suite of rooms, and the window seems impossibly high, Bao thinks prosaically that perhaps a door was left unlocked, or someone was bribed to let her out.

Mr. Wang's secret courtyard reminds Bao of unsettling tales of wives or concubines who have been walled up and forgotten. Fed through a slot by uncaring servants for years, they wither away like discarded cicada husks.

Bao once investigated such a case, concerning a house that a client had inherited from a distant uncle. "Every night during the hour of the rat,* we'd wake up because of a sound like this." The client drummed the top of the table with his nails. "One evening, my son stayed up and discovered the tapping came from a wall at the end of a corridor. The next day I got some workmen to knock a hole in it, thinking it might be rats or even a fox. When the workmen broke the wall, they discovered a tiny room that had been bricked up. Inside was a corpse. We were shocked! I'd like to know what happened, since I'm living in this house."

Bao had gone to the house to inspect what was left. The poor remains had already been hastily buried, but the client was able to describe the items discovered with the body: a metal pan and faded rags, the remnants of a woman's dress. Pitifully, there were also cloth bandages used to wrap bound feet. Possibly a minor wife or concubine, Bao thought. According to the workmen, the corpse itself had shriveled to resemble a large monkey with long hair.

"Looked like a woman," said the plasterer. "She must have died and then they bricked her up."

Bao peered into the dusty, darkened cell, barely four by

*Chinese zodiac time, corresponding to between 11 p.m. and 1 a.m.

eight feet. The presence of the metal pan hinted ominously at imprisonment. The style of the clothes dated from fifty or sixty years ago. By patient questioning, Bao had tracked down an old man who'd been a bricklayer's apprentice at the time.

"There was one job my master went to do, late one evening," the old man had said, sucking appreciatively on a plum. Bao had brought some fruit as a courtesy. "He never said what it was, but I had to mix the mortar for him, and he used a barrow-load of bricks."

"Enough to fill a doorway?" Bao had asked.

"That's right," the old man said. "There were rumors that the owner had locked up his third wife for adultery. For years and years, they said, until she was an old woman. None of the servants saw her for decades. Whether she died before he did, or if he ordered her bricked up as his last revenge, we'll never know. But it was likely her they found."

The client had the proper ceremonies performed and demolished that wing of the house. But gossip seeped through the neighborhood like water from a cracked cistern, and eventually he sold the property at a loss.

RECALLING THIS, BAO feels uneasy. Retrieving a runaway woman doesn't sit well with him, but he was dazzled by the photograph, just as its original subject has clearly enthralled Mr. Wang. Is it selfish that Bao also wants to find this woman, who's said to be either possessed by or an actual fox spirit? In the years he's spent searching for traces of the fox god, his only face-to-face encounter has been the fake medium. He's getting older; the pain in his chest is starting to worry him, yet his yearning has intensified like a flame.

Bao makes inquiries in the country neighborhood near Mr. Wang's villa. His legs ache, but late in the afternoon, an old man pulling up radishes in a field claims he's seen her. "She was hungry. I gave her a roasted sweet potato."

"This woman?" He shows the photograph again. There's something magical about that picture; the peasants around here have never seen one. Every time he produces the photograph, people gather, wanting to touch it.

"Yes, that's her," the old man says stubbornly, wiping his hands on his trousers. Dirt has caked in the deep wrinkles on his face beneath his woven bamboo hat.

"Was she wearing a light blue *changyi* embroidered with birds and roses?"

No, she'd been dressed like a peasant, carrying a bundle. Bao rubs his nose. This doesn't match Mr. Wang's description of the outfit she disappeared in. The old man is offended that the detective appears to doubt his eyesight. Scowling, he turns his back, ragged trousers held up with a piece of frayed rope. He only comes round when Bao presses a coin into his hand, saying she caught a lift to Mukden from a bullock cart. "She asked the driver if he was going near the pleasure district."

The pleasure district is an odd destination for a runaway. The maid at the villa mentioned the lady had come from a high-class establishment. Another thought is that Bektu Nikan's rented lodgings were close to the red-light district, as was Gu's restaurant. Bao has the sudden, urgent sensation that this elusive woman has moved faster and farther than expected.

27

I dislike being taken home by men. It's usually a losing proposition, especially when your arm is seized in a firm grip. I could tell that Shiro wanted to ride in the same rickshaw again, but I shook him off briskly and climbed in with Chen, who looked pleased.

"Shirakawa was right to bring you along," he said. "Takeda has as good as guaranteed the funds."

"Why do you need them?" I asked. "Isn't your family wealthy?"

"Yes, but it isn't my money."

"Tell me, are you really opening a sugar factory in Formosa, or is the money for a revolution against the Qing government?"

Chen was momentarily taken aback, but I've found that men don't really count what they tell women like me, who occupy a dubious position in society. "Are you also part of our movement?"

"I'm against emperors and monarchies. So what is it—sugar factory or revolution?" I pressed.

"Shirakawa says we should try both. And if the Qing government comes looking for us, Formosa is far enough away."

Shiro was probably hedging his bets, leading these gullible young men along by the nose. I sighed. "I want to hear the rest of the story you were telling me last night, about that photographer and why you regretted meeting him."

"Oh, that." Chen's cheeks flushed. He'd the grace to feel embarrassed after his hasty disavowal of me when Kuro had come upon us on the slope. "He offered to take a photograph for us."

"What sort of photograph?"

Chen hesitated. "A group portrait to commemorate our friendship, that's all."

I didn't press him further because I was busy slapping his wandering hand off my knee. But if he'd told me then what I later found out, perhaps things might have turned out differently for both of us.

We returned to Kuro's house, where, with great relief, I changed back into my old clothes. To my surprise, my mistress was nowhere to be found in her quarters, and I was forced to ask the housekeeper where she'd gone.

"She's with *sensei*," she said, using the polite term for "author."

That must mean Kuro. While her back was turned, I swapped the metal skewer I'd borrowed for a sharp paring knife. I needed one if Bektu Nikan was really on his way here. Then I set off to find my mistress.

The sliding door to the famous writer's study was slightly ajar, enough to peek in. Normally I'm careful not to do this. Not only is it undignified to be caught gluing one's eye to a crack, but you can also suffer horrendous wounds. A one-eyed fox cautioned me against it. Today, however, there was no helping it.

From within the study, a six-tatami-mat room with half-glass sliding doors opening onto the *engawa*, or covered veranda, came the low murmur of voices. My old lady was talking to Kuro, and shockingly, Kuro was chatting away with her. They were speaking of foxes.

I told you earlier that the first rule of foxes is *don't talk about foxes*. The second rule is *don't fall in love with foxes*. I don't know who made them up, but in most situations, following either one of those rules would avert a great deal of trouble.

"So you mean there's a difference between what we call *huxian* and *hujing*?" my mistress asked. "I've never understood the distinction between them."

"To be honest, those are only names made up by people," Kuro replied. His quiet, dark voice sent an involuntary shudder up my spine. "*Hujing* is just a fox spirit, while *huxian* hints at the transcendental. There are as many kinds of foxes as there are types of people. Some are criminals. Others hope to escape this world by refining themselves."

"You sound as though you know them."

Unlike Shiro's crooked grin, Kuro's smile has always had a tinge of melancholy. More so now than ever before, because of the scar on his face. "Is that so?"

"Do you believe in the fox god?" My mistress sounded nervous yet eager.

"By that, do you mean a deity who answers prayers?" Kuro shook his head gently. "I think people expect too much. And then they're disappointed."

"I know. They hunt foxes and they also worship them. But I've always, always longed to meet one." She hesitated. "When I was five years old, I was saved by a fox. For years afterwards, I questioned whether I was dreaming or had a hallucination. Yet the memory is still fresh, as though it were burned into my mind."

At this point, I would have leaped in and derailed the conversation with chatter about how she must have been mistaken, but Kuro said nothing. He simply waited.

"I got lost in the grasslands when we were visiting relatives. A black fox led me back to my mother."

"What makes you think it was one of the *huxian* and not an ordinary beast?"

"Because . . . the fox went away, then came back as a man. I know it sounds foolish. I only ever told one person, my childhood friend, and I'm not sure even he believed me."

Kuro was silent for a while. Dust motes hung in the sunshine, and in the afternoon stillness, I heard the rhythmic *clack* of the bamboo deer-scarer in the garden.

"How old were you again?" he asked suddenly.

"Five. It was almost sixty years ago," she said with an embarrassed smile.

"And where did this occur?"

"Somewhere in the grasslands near Horqin. Do you know that area?"

"Yes, I do. Quite well, actually."

"Shirakawa told my grandson that your Chinese and Mongolian are very good. In fact, speaking to you like this, I find it hard to believe it's not your native tongue. Are you a linguist?"

"No. But I've learned to speak a number of languages."

"Forgive me. I'm an old woman, and I can't help remembering my childhood with nostalgia." My mistress seemed abashed at having divulged her secret, though it explained a great deal about her. No wonder she'd been well-disposed towards me from the very beginning!

"It's interesting you remember that encounter so clearly. I would have thought a child of five would have forgotten it."

"I could never forget it. It was a magical experience."

Kuro tilted his head quizzically. "Why?"

"I was so frightened. Terrified, even. Being alone in the vastness of the grass was something I'd never experienced before. I fell and sprained my ankle, and looking up at the wide white sky, I started to feel ill, as though I would die alone. Until the fox came. I think it was watching me for a while. It led me onwards, and when I couldn't walk anymore, it came back as a man and gave me a piggyback ride."

At this, Kuro laughed. He laughs so seldom that it's quite a shock to hear, but like Shiro's (and all our laughter), it is very pleasant. Perhaps more so because Kuro's laugh is genuine.

"You have an amazing memory," he said. "A piggyback ride must have been just the thing then."

"You don't believe me?" my old lady said, though she was smiling, too.

"Whoever it was who helped you, I am glad that you were saved that day."

"Actually, the reason I brought it up is because you remind me of him," she said in a rush. "Of that fox. I was struck by the resemblance as soon as I saw you."

"Did he have this?" said Kuro, touching the scar on his face.

"Oh no! I'm sorry, I didn't mean it as an insult. In fact, when I was little, I thought he was the very handsomest man I'd ever seen."

Kuro said quietly, "I'm sure no harm was intended. And please, don't let my face disturb you."

"It doesn't bother me at all. May I ask, how did it happen?"

That was what I was burning to know, too. As well as what had occurred sixty years ago. I pressed closer to the gap between the sliding doors, my heart beating uncomfortably fast.

"It was an incident with a hunting knife."

"Did someone else . . . ?" My mistress opened her mouth as though she wanted to ask more, then closed it out of politeness.

"The other party unfortunately did not survive, so I'm grateful this was my only souvenir."

Pause. Conversations with Kuro are filled with silence. He's very patient and will wear you down. That's why I can't deal with him.

"I wished to talk to you today, not just to thank you for your hospitality, but to ask if you have any relatives in Mongolia. You look so much like that fox of my childhood that I started wondering last night whether I'd been mistaken, and perhaps your grandfather or another relative might have saved me instead."

"So now you've decided that you were saved by a person after all." Kuro smiled. "What if I told you that my grandfather had a pet fox?"

My mistress's small, wrinkled face made a positive O of astonishment. In that instant, it was easy to imagine her as a little girl of five, lost in the tall grass.

"I'm joking," said Kuro quickly. "My grandfather didn't have a pet, but it's true that our family has traveled through the northeast for generations."

It was a clever answer. A kind one, too, plausible enough to cloud her memories. My old lady started to laugh. "I suppose I'll never know," she said. "But I've always been on the lookout for foxes. My dearest wish has been to meet one again before I die."

"Be careful. Not all foxes mean well."

"But are they not gods, or at least spirits?"

"It depends on what you want to believe. What's important is the ability to tell truth from lies," said Kuro. "Or perhaps truth from what's merely hope."

Crouching in the polished corridor, I frowned. Hope, of course, is the most painful thing in the universe. Clinging to a thin strand is the most agonizing way to live. I know this too well. No wonder my heart was racing.

"Don't trust those who claim to speak for the gods," said Kuro seriously. "They are charlatans."

"What about families blessed with money from foxes?"

"Those stories are more concerned with the relationships between foxes and people. The money is secondary."

My mistress sat up straighter. "I've been collecting tales about foxes for years. In fact, the best documented one I heard was from a friend in Beijing. May I ask your opinion?"

"Please." Kuro inclined his head courteously. I pressed my ear closer. We foxes always pay attention to the latest gossip about us. It saves being run out of town by dogs.

"A Manchu family in a northern suburb of Beijing reported that for three years, bricks were mysteriously tossed into their yard. Eventually, there were enough bricks that they built a low wall around the yard. When this was done, a voice spoke, claiming to be a fox from Jiangsu. The family said they had many conversations with it, though the fox remained invisible, and what the fox liked best was cooking. In fact, its principal joy was to prepare food for the family's guests, taking money from a locked cashbox. If there wasn't enough money in the box, the fox would pawn the family's clothing and leave the pawn ticket on the table! When questioned, the pawnshop owner always said it was the same short old man who did so. Do you think this is a false account?"

"Oh no," said Kuro. "That one is probably true."

I covered my mouth to keep from bursting into laughter. I knew that old fox. He wasn't from Jiangsu at all, but from Jinan. To think that old Fatty was still cooking and spending other people's money! But Kuro was explaining it, very gravely, to my mistress.

"The fox in that instance was lonely. Cooking for guests was both his hobby and a way to keep himself part of their family."

"Do foxes get lonely?"

"Yes."

Do you? was the unspoken question that hung in the air.

Part of me wanted her to press him. Loneliness had been increasingly on my mind, a numb ache that I tried to ignore. But my mistress didn't voice it. Mindful of the time, she said, "I'm sorry to bother you with so many questions. You seem very knowledgeable for a young man. I'd love to read your novel, though I can't understand Japanese."

Kuro gave a faint, melancholy smile. "It's really nothing. A book of old tales and ghost stories. I was quite surprised that anyone wanted to read it at all."

"May I come and talk to you again?"

"Of course."

I sprang up as she opened the sliding door, just in time to retreat backwards around the corner. Like many old Japanese houses, it was full of shadows and strange creaks, the corners dim as though a perennial dusk lurked in them. Don't play hide-and-seek in a house like that. You may find someone extra in your party—that's all I can say. At least that was my first horrified thought when I collided with another person. I bit my tongue to avoid crying out, in case my mistress heard me, but she was still politely taking her leave.

The other person slid his hands, overly familiarly, around my waist. Elegant, long-fingered hands that lingered on the small of my back. He smelled of expensive clothes, cabbage dumplings, and hair pomade.

"Go away, Shiro," I hissed, elbowing him.

"I'd have thought you'd be more . . . grateful, since there's news you might want to hear."

Sometimes I think Shiro has spent too much time romancing rich, bored women, because he talks like a second-rate gigolo. With a practiced move, he pinned me against the wall with one arm. I was alarmed. Despite his smooth words, it hadn't escaped me that he'd been increasingly invading my physical space. It's a hunting tactic: herding the prey into close quarters, be it sheep or young ladies. One way or another, I'd no intention of being eaten by Shiro.

Pressing his mouth against my neck, he murmured, "I wondered if you could stay away from Kuro, but I suppose things never change."

"I came looking for my mistress." Tensing up, I hoped that she wouldn't come this way and run into us. I felt the sharp edge of Shiro's teeth against my skin, testing it. "I told you I'd help you with Takeda! And I did, so let me go."

He did, but not without biting me, hard, first. I was so enraged that I headbutted Shiro violently enough that he gave a yelp of surprise. Then I ran away.

It was only later that I stopped to wonder what he'd meant by "news you might want to hear."

28

The old man pulling radishes said the lady hitched a cart ride towards the city. More specifically, the pleasure quarters. As Bao recalls, Bektu Nikan's lodgings were also near that district. Now that he has the photograph, he'll check if Bektu's landlord has seen her. Perhaps she, too, came looking for him.

The narrow tenement alley, or *hutong*, is lined with cramped stone courtyard houses and smells like fried fish and boiling laundry. The house where Bektu rented rooms is shuttered, its door locked with a heavy chain. As Bao knocks fruitlessly, a woman emerges from the opposite house. He tells her that he's looking for the owner. "Is anyone home?"

"They went on a religious pilgrimage." She stares at him curiously. Though young, she's missing her front teeth and places a self-conscious hand before her mouth

Introducing himself, Bao says, "Do you know his former tenant Bektu Nikan?"

"He left a month ago."

"Did this woman come looking for him?" Bao produces the photograph.

"No, I'd have remembered someone like her. I'm here all day, weaving." She points across the narrow alley, and Bao sees a loom through the open door. The faded door curtain is looped back, so she has a good view of the opposite house.

"Did Bektu have any strange visitors?"

"There were a few university students. Looked like political activists, the way they talked." She pauses. "If you're asking about anyone unusual, there was a gentleman who visited before he left. Somehow, he reminded me of that picture."

Bao's thoughts fly to the little boy's tale of the night that Feng, also known as Chunhua, disappeared from the restaurant. She'd been seen walking down a snowy street, arm in arm with a stranger said to be a fox.

"Was he good-looking?"

A flush suffuses the woman's face. She gives a quick nod. "It was a late-winter afternoon when he came. The light was dim, yet I could see his features very clearly, though maybe it was the reflection off the snow. He looked so elegant, like a nobleman from ancient tales. Bektu came out of the opposite house and handed him a package, grumbling about being a deliveryman. The gentleman smiled and looked across the alley, to where I was standing behind the door curtain. Such a sharp glance that made my heart flutter—and me, a married woman!" She laughs self-consciously.

"When was this?"

"Two days before Bektu left. I remember the date because of the missing person incident in the next *hutong*."

Bao's eyes widen. Another disappearance. He hasn't forgotten about Feng's mysterious death. Despite his official role in her case being concluded, her frozen body in the doorway sits uncomfortably at the edge of his consciousness.

"Was it a young woman who vanished?"

"No, it was the pork butcher's wife. She went missing the same evening that the gentleman came to our *hutong*. I heard she went out to buy fried tofu and didn't return. It was snowing, so everyone was worried."

Glancing round, Bao pictures the scene. A lavender dusk is falling in the tightly packed alleys. The curved-tile roofs and cracked gray stone walls are thickly blanketed in white. Anyone who doesn't return all night may freeze to death in this northern city. "Was she reported missing?"

"Oh no! She was found the next morning under the eaves of the secondhand bookstore around the corner. When she came to, she couldn't remember anything. They said she must have taken ill because there were no visible injuries, but she's not been the same since."

"How so?" Bao can hardly contain his excitement. This sounds remarkably like Feng's situation, except nobody found her before she froze to death.

"There's no life in her anymore; she used to be energetic, laughing and helping at the butcher shop. Now she stares out of the window as though waiting for someone to return. I saw her yesterday; she gave me the oddest feeling, like a maiden in love. Whenever I see her, I remember the gentleman who visited Bektu, because of the date."

Bao scratches his head. "Why did he remind you of this photograph?"

"You know how people from a certain region have a look? That's how he struck me, like he was a traveler from the same country as this lady." She gazes at the photograph again with fascinated eyes.

A traveler from the same country. That's a picturesque way of putting it, Bao thinks. "Has anyone seen a fox in this neighborhood?"

"Foxes? Never. I don't believe in them, do you?" The woman looks askance at Bao, as though he belongs to a cult. Which is fair enough, since those who pray to the fox gods are often seen as charlatans or country bumpkins.

UPON LEAVING, BAO walks through the jostling crowd that fills the streets, quilted cotton jackets bundled against the cold. This working-class neighborhood is filled with drab indigos and grays. A handsome, well-dressed stranger would stand out here. Bao has no evidence linking this man to any crime, just the uneasy coincidence of his being nearby when people vanish. The woman this time was found in an altered state—this is why people ascribe such uncanny happenings to foxes and ghosts. Bao can't quite bring himself to embrace such superstition, yet neither can he abandon it. At the edge of his raging curiosity lurks the possibility of the divine, an unknown veil that Bao longs to pierce.

There's one more place to check: the pleasure house that the maid at Mr. Wang's villa mentioned the lady might have come from. It has a select clientele and won't admit him through the front unless he's a paying guest. Instead, he passes a note to the doorkeeper, asking to speak to their cook and saying he'll wait at the back door.

The rear, accessed through a maze of back alleys, is shabby compared to the elegant frontage. Each establishment employs cooks, servants, and doormen. They jealously guard their women, who are apt to run or commit suicide. The back court-yard door is small, a tightly compressed mouth that refuses to give up its secrets. After knocking fruitlessly, he decides to wait in the alley. The back door is bound to open at some point. A skinny cat hisses its disapproval at him. Leaning against the wall, Bao closes his eyes.

Bright images chase across his mind: foxes, deer, and snow—that's what the maid at the villa said Mr. Wang talked about. It was snowing, too, in Wu Village when a mysteri-ous woman came to collect a fox cub. Soft, muffling snow piling up in drifts over buried jars of pickled vegetables. Bao remembers the snow of his own youth limning the delicate branches of the plum trees. Plum blossom was his mother's favorite flower. Also Tagtaa's.

A memory from his childhood: Tagtaa sits on her haunches, making a snow rabbit to put in a snow cave. From time to time, her glance flits, longingly, to the plum tree in front of Bao's father's study. The children are forbidden to break off blossom-ing twigs; his mother has reserved all the cuttings for her salon, where she hosts gatherings to admire the flowers and write poetry. Years later, Bao will find a notebook of his mother's poems and be surprised to discover that they're quite good. A couple of them are even brilliant. How strange to realize that his mother has another life, apart from the one in which she, self-servingly, complains that she's done everything for her sons!

That winter day, Bao is determined to acquire a branch of plum blossoms. It will delight Tagtaa (whom he wants to impress) and declare his independence from his mother's rules. Borrowing his older brother's clasp knife, he attempts to saw off a branch. The knife is blunt and slips on the wet branch, the fragile flowers scattering. With a crack, it snaps into an ugly jagged tear. Panting and filled with shame, Bao clutches his illegal prize. No longer beautiful, the branch resembles an amputated limb. He thinks of throwing it over the neighbor's wall so nobody will discover his crime. The neighbor's house, the one where the fox shrine is.

"What are you doing?" Tagtaa's small, anxious face appears. "Did you cut this off?"

He nods.

"Don't throw it over the wall! Give it to your mother. If you say you meant it for her, she'll forgive you."

No, that's *exactly the wrong point,* he wants to say, but Tagtaa is too quick. Deftly, she removes the branch from his numb hands and trims off the damaged twigs. "Give it to your mother before anyone reports it," she says.

But I meant it for you, Bao thinks.

The scene is so real that he can hear her voice in his head. Bao blinks blearily. He's fallen asleep outside the back door that he's been watching. How did that happen? Still, the scene is so vivid that he's tempted to close his eyes and return to that time. A time when his intentions towards Tagtaa were consistently misunderstood. He should have said to her, *The one I want is you.* The flower that bloomed in his own court-yard and was given to another.

A knot forms in his stomach; he almost wants to cry except it's ridiculous, an old man like him, squatting in an alley on a stakeout. If anyone should see him, they'll think he's either drunk or an opium addict.

With a sharp click, the door opens.

That's what has woken him up. Not the breaking of a branch in his dream, but the sound of someone behind that door, struggling with its stiff lock. Time, which compressed itself while he was sleeping, has started to move again. Bao scrambles to his feet as the door lurches open.

A little girl comes out. She's about nine years old, dressed as a page in a fairy costume with trailing sleeves and loose trousers. Someone has dusted her pointed face with rice powder and painted a tiny red diamond, like a Tang dynasty beauty mark, on her forehead. "Uncle," she says politely, "are you the one who wants to speak to our cook?"

Bao follows the child, guessing that she's costumed for a themed dinner. Such entertainments are common; wealthy patrons are easily bored, and dressing up the courtesans and staff as characters from famous operas adds excitement and color.

The girl, noting Bao's concerned expression, says, "You needn't worry, I don't work here normally. I'm the bookkeeper's granddaughter."

She's a sharp little creature and already understands that this isn't a reputable place for women, no matter how lavish the decor. She leads him across the back courtyard and into a kitchen.

"He's here," says the child, and looks at Bao expectantly. He hands her a sweet, a jujube boiled in syrup wrapped in waxed paper, from his pocket, and she takes it with a little sigh of disappointment.

"That one will go far," says the cook as she scampers off. He's about Bao's age, and a passing acquaintance. "How can I help you?"

"I'm looking for this woman." Bao produces the photograph.

The cook examines it. "Never seen her before."

"Are you sure?" A flat sense of depression hits Bao.

"Yes," says the cook. He, too, looks at Bao expectantly, and Bao gives him most of his coins. The little girl appears again to escort him out.

"Can I see that picture, Uncle?" she says when they're in the courtyard. Bao produces it, and her eyes widen with excitement. "Oh, that's the fox lady."

"The fox lady?" Bao can hardly believe his ears. "You saw her?"

"Yes." The child's face is rapt. "Twice, in fact. She came back afterwards."

29

There was a bite mark on my neck. Though to be fair, I'd pressed a skewer to Shiro's throat that very morning. I once knew a professor who insisted that every action results in an equal or opposite reaction. But he was a scientist and Shiro is nothing of the sort, so I could only conclude that he bit me out of pure spite and irritation.

Well, I didn't care what Shiro thought as long as he kept out of my business. And my business, right now, was with my mistress. By cutting across the garden and squeezing through a bamboo hedge (bamboo comes in all sizes, and the miniature type is particularly charming, although my passage through it left a hole), I managed to arrive at our quarters before she did. Placing a large cotton kerchief around my neck to hide the bite mark, I tidied up the room like a good servant. There wasn't much cleaning to do, since my old lady was very neat. A few times I'd even caught her mopping and wiping.

Soon, I heard her soft, slow footsteps, then a rattle as the shoji doors slid open. "You're back already. How was the visit?"

"They just needed an extra pair of hands," I said noncommittally.

"Bohai said it was to help with an investor, but I don't want them to force you into anything."

Poor old lady, she had little idea of what her grandson was up to. Young gentlemen and maidservants have always been a volatile mix, but I could hardly tell her that her grandson was starry-eyed about revolution, not me. Fortunately, my mistress seemed distracted and proposed that we go for a walk.

I'd discovered a side gate while squeezing through the bamboo hedge earlier. "Are you sure it's all right to go through?" She looked doubtfully at the small wooden door. I assured her it was perfectly fine, though I'd no idea where it led. It opened to a hilly slope. My mistress gave me a mischievous glance. "I feel like we're on an adventure."

It was only a back lane, but she seemed so excited that I couldn't help smiling. In Dalian, she couldn't leave the house without giving an account to her son and the chief clerk. The soft spring air was pleasant; birch catkins dangled like striped caterpillars overhead. As we trudged along the deserted path, my mistress said, "I was talking to our host, Mr. Kurosaki, just now." Her cheeks were faintly pink, either from excitement or the fact that we were walking uphill.

"What sort of person is he?" Never mind that I'd just been eavesdropping on her conversation; I was curious to know what she thought of Kuro.

"A most unusual man. In fact, he resembles someone from my childhood so much that it's uncanny. I almost wonder if I'm dreaming. But you're here with me." She squeezed my hand. "Ever since I met you, my life has been more vivid than it's felt for years. And talking to Mr. Kurosaki today felt like destiny. Almost like meeting a spirit or a god."

"A god?" I ran my finger along a leaf. "That's quite a description. Does he strike you as divine?"

"It's his eyes. The expression in them is so clear, like a dog's eyes. That was what I remembered from my childhood. Not a god, but not quite human."

"He is certainly a very striking-looking person," I said.

"Striking" was a mild way to put it. That scar across Kuro's face now marked him forever. Likely, he wouldn't survive long like this. I felt a deep melancholy. What had he been up to, to receive a wound like that? But it was none of my business, I told myself. "Have you felt the same way about other people, like Shirakawa, for example?"

"I'm not sure if one can fully trust Shirakawa. He's almost too persuasive; it's unnatural."

As I'd suspected, she really did have a certain sense about foxes. I wondered whether it was due to her childhood experience, and if the fox she'd met had actually been Kuro. I wouldn't put it past him to rescue someone and not mention it. And his remark, *A piggyback ride must have been just the thing*, reminded me that Kuro has always been good with children. I gritted my teeth. But my mistress was still talking, almost to herself.

"Of course it's impossible. Maybe the person I met was his grandfather. But for years afterwards, we made offerings to the fox god in my friend's garden."

"Your friend had a fox shrine?" These always interest me. Sometimes people leave offerings like fried tofu (my favorite) or dumplings. It used to be that every neighborhood had a household shrine or two, but lately they've been disappearing, which is a great disappointment.

My mistress smiled. "It wasn't a real shrine. We made it ourselves out of pieces of wood and stones. My dearest friend was the second son of our neighbor. His father was a county magistrate, and his mother, though she insisted that I come over, somehow disliked me."

"Perhaps she was afraid the two of you would form a romantic attachment."

"The servants teased, asking what I thought of the young master. It was mortifying. So I was extremely careful to show him that we were only friends."

"Did you like him?" We were walking steadily away from the houses, following the curved lane as it began to climb through lightly wooded slopes.

"As to like—I don't think I really understood myself at the time. Besides, he wasn't my idea of handsome." Her eyes crinkled. "But later, after I'd married a husband so much older than myself, I often thought of Bao. I missed him tremendously. He was an unusual boy. He never told lies."

"Never?" A righteous fox must abstain from lying, though it's one of the most difficult injunctions for us. I'd been trying to be good, not just for myself but for my child. Even now, the memory of cradling her on my chest in the prickly warm grass made my heart constrict.

"I cannot recall a single one. In fact, he was honest to the point of folly. Once, he broke the branch off a plum tree and made a mess of it. We were terrified because the gardeners were told to keep the plum blossoms for his mother. Bao wanted to throw the branch over the neighbor's wall to hide it, but I told him to pretend he'd broken it off for his mother as a gift. That would soften her up. But he said he wouldn't lie. It made him sick. So I did it for him." Her face wrinkles ruefully.

"When you said lying made him sick, do you mean physically ill?" I'd never heard of this before. If more humans suffered from it, society might be better off.

"Yes. He'd have this peculiar expression sometimes. Like this." She closed her eyes and rubbed her mouth. "Bao was the only person I trusted to be completely honest with me, even more than my mother, who sometimes got ahead of herself, like the time she tried to make a marriage for me in Inner Mongolia. When I was pregnant, with no friends save my young stepson, I thought of Bao. You remember what I said about my marriage?"

"You were married at seventeen, the fourth wife to the medicine shop," I said. My old lady seemed touched that I'd remembered.

"It was after I came back in disgrace, having refused a marriage to that distant cousin. I was so relieved to be sent home, I told myself it didn't matter if my half-brothers made remarks about my unbound feet, but of course eventually I did feel miserable again. Young girls are fickle."

"What of your childhood friend?"

"When I returned, he'd been sent away to study. Shortly after, his father was reassigned to a different county. Likely he's forgotten me, but I still remember the games we played when we were young. I played them with my little stepson after I got married. Those were the happiest times, when I could forget about being in a strange house, with servants who whispered behind my back that I wouldn't last very long. When I got pregnant, that was the first time I heard about them. The people with no shadows."

The lane petered out as we went farther up the hill. Wild mugwort and *fuki*, the bitter buds of butterbur, grew by the path, and we stopped to gather some.

"Was the child you had Bohai's father?"

"Yes. He was the second son of the house. The midwife called me a fool to cry when he was born, when a son guaranteed my position. But I wept because of my young stepson, and how he'd said that if I gave birth to a daughter, they'd drown her since he already had a sister by a previous stepmother. But if I had a son, he himself would die.

"He was only nine years old, and I seventeen. Sometimes he forgot and called me Sister, instead of Mother, as he was supposed to. The two of us were closer than I was to my husband, who hardly ever spoke to me. I was grateful though. My husband was far better than that cruel boy in the Horqin grasslands, whom I'd refused to marry.

"At first, I thought my stepson, being young and frightened, had imagined the idea of people with no shadows. I asked him to point them out to me, but I couldn't tell because it was usually in a crowd. I even mentioned it to my husband, who dismissed it, looking uncomfortable.

"There's a tradition of one month's postnatal confinement, so after my son was born, I wasn't allowed to go out or wash my hair. I barely saw my stepson, though he visited to look at the baby. He was pale by then and had lost weight. I wanted him to stay longer, but the servants fussed. He wasn't to disturb me, they said. And I was to eat well and become plump, to nurse the baby. The new heir, though nobody said so. They all knew what to expect—the tradition in that family being that the first son would die, though nobody knew when.

"I hated being confined and couldn't wait for the month to be over. I told my stepson that we'd fly kites together before autumn began. He was happy then, holding his new brother carefully on his lap. Smiling shyly, he promised to make a toy for the baby out of bamboo.

"Two days later, my stepson fell from a bridge while reaching to cut bamboo for a child's whistle and died."

I halted. My mistress bowed her head.

"If only I'd told him not to make a toy, perhaps he wouldn't have slipped! If only, if only. The servants gossiped that I'd sent my little stepson out on a capricious whim, and that my tears were due to guilt. I was indeed guilty, I thought. By bringing a son into the world, I'd doomed him. Though grieved, my husband seemed unsurprised. He even told me to stop weeping so much because it made people talk more."

She was silent for a while.

"Well, that's all there is. It was such a difficult birth that the midwife said I'd have no more children. The house was so forlorn without my stepson that I begged my husband to bring back the little girl born of his third wife, so I could raise her. She'd been sent away to be nursed when he married me. I suppose they'd thought it a courtesy at the time. That's my daughter, as I call her, and she calls herself. She's married now, but those were her clothes I lent you back in Dalian. Eventually I took over running the business when my husband died. Though I had no medical background, luckily we had excellent master pharmacists who stayed on. I was determined not to pass on the practice of restricting children—as you know, Bohai has four sisters. And I never heard about people without shadows again until late last year."

"Why is that?"

"Because Bohai is the oldest son of the house now."

"Does he have a younger brother?"

"He may have one soon."

I recalled the odd conversation she'd had with Bohai's father before we'd left for Japan, and everything fell into place, including her decision to accompany Bohai to Japan. A child was about to be born to Bohai's father's mistress. That also explained the master's harried, nervous looks. There'd be a lot of screaming and (well-deserved) fury in that house.

SPRING DUSK WAS descending; it was time to return. Though if I'd been alone, I might have gone on walking deeper into the woods. Far away from people, trotting onwards and never returning. It never ends, the pain of living in this world.

"*Tai furen*, do you still pray to the fox god?" I asked.

"Sometimes. I'd been praying for a good companion if I needed to travel with Bohai. And here you are!"

"So you prayed to the fox god, and he sent me?" I was amused. "Shouldn't you be afraid of me? Some say that foxes are unlucky."

We'd left the path as we gathered the curling fronds of

fiddlehead ferns. My old lady and I, busily harvesting as we discovered more plants, looked like two peasant women in a grove.

She said, "In ancient times, black or white foxes were said to be omens of good fortune. When Emperor Yu, the founder of the Xia dynasty, was still unmarried in his thirtieth year, a white fox with nine tails appeared to him. The emperor said, 'White is my color, and nine tails is a sign of prosperity and a good wife,' so he took a wife from that region. Some say that he even married the fox."

"Oh, that's not true," I said. "He married a perfectly ordinary woman from Tushan."

My mistress paused. "The way you said that was exactly the same way Mr. Kurosaki spoke earlier today! How do you know?"

"My grandmother told me," I said. That was no lie.

"I thought you grew up in an orphanage."

"Ah—yes, but I still remember my grandmother. Like you, she was very interested in foxes."

"Really?" That was enough to distract my old lady. Thank goodness she was so enamored with the subject. "Then can foxes and humans marry each other?"

"Seldom, and then it's often a marriage only in name. There are no children born of such unions."

"But what about all the stories of people who claim to be descended from foxes?"

"Foxes aren't prolific. Even in nature, the *hujing* rarely produce children with each other, which is why they're so precious. In those tales of fox children, the human has been fooled. A man who believes his fox woman has given birth to a son has no idea that she likely has a male fox as her lover."*

Astonished, my mistress opened her mouth to ask more questions, and I realized I'd overstepped myself. That's the problem of getting too comfortable with people. "How shall we bring all this home?" I said hastily.

Between the two of us, we'd gathered a large heap of wild spring greens. "I could hold them in my skirt," said my mistress. "I'm an old lady and nobody will pay attention to me."

*People like the famous Heian astrologer and exorcist Abe no Seimei, who claimed descent from a fox woman, were simply foxes themselves. Adding a human "father" made them more palatable to society.

I unfastened the large cotton kerchief from my neck. The light was fading, and hopefully the bite mark on the side of my neck wasn't noticeable. "Here we go!" I said cheerfully. Piling the greens into it, I tied the corners together like rabbit ears. Then we turned to go.

"But where is the path?" said my mistress.

This was the stupidest mistake I'd made in a long time. There's a reason so many stories begin with *Late one evening, a woodcutter was lost*, because it's easy to get confused at dusk, with the stars hidden by trees.

But I wasn't too worried—yet. We'd left the house an hour or more ago, and I was certain I could find my way back. My mistress, however, looked tired. There was a chilly nip in the air and we had no lantern. Giving her my arm, we set off, though first, I used the paring knife from the kitchen to cut a strip of bark off the nearest tree. One tends to walk in circles in the woods, and it's best to make a mark. Twilight had fallen in a dim curtain. The trees seemed larger, their branches reaching darkly upwards.

My old lady clutched my arm tighter. "Is that a light?"

A faint, bobbing radiance had appeared in the distance. To be honest, I'd noticed it earlier, but I'd had a bad feeling about it. My instinct was to hide and wait till it had gone by.

Thin, wispy lights that show up in the woods are seldom good news.

30

"You saw her twice?"

Bao is astonished at the child's assertion. Upon closer inspection, she's not so little—ten or possibly eleven, although her slight build makes her look younger. She has a pointed chin and, as he'd suspected, is a sharp creature.

"Uncle, what will you give me if I tell you about her?"

Bao recalls her sigh of disappointment when he'd handed her a sweet earlier. There are two coins left in his pocket, and he takes out one to show her. "But you have to tell me the truth," he says.

The girl's eyes flick from the coin in his hand to his face, that sturdy, plain face that has served Bao for more than sixty years, and she nods—"I wouldn't lie"—though that itself is a lie. Bao smiles to himself. She's young, and her duplicity is artless, though he imagines she'll grow up to be a formidable woman.

"The first time was soon after she came. Grandfather is the bookkeeper, so I help him out. Sometimes he pays me."

"Do you like to be paid?"

"Money is very important. If you don't have any money, you get sold." She says this matter-of-factly, and Bao's heart breaks a little. But just a little, because he has the feeling that this girl would manage anywhere.

"Are most of the girls sold into this house?"

"Yes. They're brought in by men. Mostly good-looking ones who buy women from rural areas. That's why I don't plan on marrying a handsome husband."

Bao is impressed.

"But the woman in that picture arrived by herself. It was snowing heavily, so I accompanied Grandfather to make sure he didn't slip. The fox lady came knocking on the front door early in the morning before we'd opened." A look of admiration flits across her face. "She asked to see the owner. The real one, not the Madam."

Although the day-to-day running of such establishments is usually left to women proprietors, the actual money and muscle behind them are controlled by men. Many of whom have underworld connections.

"They went off for a long talk upstairs. At the end of it, he told us she was going to join us for a bit. I've no idea what she said to him; he's not easy to deal with usually. Also, the door-keeper and my grandfather were sworn not to say anything. That's why the cook didn't recognize your picture—he never saw her.

"She specifically asked to join the next party at Mr. Wang's garden villa. The Madam wasn't happy at all, but the owner overruled her. That's why Madam was suspicious. She said, 'That woman is a vixen!'" The girl announces this with relish, reliving the excitement.

"Is that why you called her the fox lady?" Bao asks.

"Yes. There's a cupboard upstairs that's right next to Madam's private room. If you press your ear against the knothole in the back, you can hear almost everything."

The child looks triumphant, and Bao can't help smiling. "Though eavesdropping isn't right," he says reprovingly, recalling his previous career as a teacher. And now he himself is paying a child to gossip. A vague sense of shame suffuses him.

"But I'm not lying! Didn't you say it was all right as long as I didn't lie?" she says, opening her eyes wide. Bao scratches his head.

Pleased at her victory, she continues, "The owner didn't have any good reasons; he just kept repeating it was to be a onetime thing. That made Madam jealous. Because she and the owner are like this." She holds out her hand with two fingers pressed together, indicating a relationship. Bao reflects that even if she doesn't actually live in the brothel, this child has learned far too much about human nature.

"When I came out of the cupboard, I ran into the fox lady myself. She was standing in the upper corridor that opens onto the courtyard. It was snowing, and bits of fluffy white drifted onto her shoulders and hair. Her cheeks were pink, and her eyes were so bright, as though she was more real than anyone else here. When I told Grandfather, he said she must have too much *qi* for a woman. According to him, women like that devour men and must be subdued. I knew that she knew I'd been eavesdropping, but instead of looking embarrassed, she just smiled.

"Then she asked me to lend her clothes. We both knew the Madam wouldn't give her anything good. The house has special costumes, like this one I'm wearing, when there are entertainments." She indicates her fairy costume with pride. Bao says, obediently, that she looks very nice.

"So I took her to the storeroom. At that time in the morning, the women were all sleeping. They work late at night, so they're always tired and ill-humored in the mornings. She asked me the same question you did, whether I'd been sold here. I told her about Grandfather being the bookkeeper, but she looked very fierce and said that I mustn't ever be sold.

"I told her not to worry because I was saving money. I've quite a lot hidden away at home. We picked out a dress for her, and she promised to return it. I had to go home after that. But later, when I heard about the trouble, I figured she really was a fox."

Bao inhales. Sometimes he wonders whether a collective insanity has descended upon everyone involved in this case.

"What trouble?"

"Mr. Wang asked if he could buy out her contract, so the owner was forced to pretend that he knew all about her background. Madam was furious." She sucks contemplatively on the sweet in her mouth. "And then she ran away from them."

Bao straightens up. "You said you saw her twice."

"A few weeks later, I heard a thump in this courtyard, right over there. When I opened the back door, she'd just climbed over the wall." The girl looks impressed, and Bao is, too. The brick wall is higher than his head.

"When she saw me, she said, 'I've come to return the clothes.' She didn't want me to get into trouble. Nobody has ever kept a promise like that for me, for free."

The look on the girl's face is almost worshipful.

"Most things have a price for you?" asks Bao.

"Grandfather said so. He used to be a chief clerk in a merchant's store, but he gambled too much. That's how he ended up keeping the books here."

At Bao's sympathetic look, the child flushes. "He makes quite a decent living now."

Bao says quietly, "I'm sorry, I meant no offence."

The tips of her ears turn pink, but she nods gruffly to indicate he's forgiven. The gesture reminds Bao of another girl, long ago. Tagtaa's words, *You are the only boy who says sorry to me*, ring in his ears, and for an instant, he closes his eyes. This case is dangerous. It keeps dredging up memories and reminders of his first, lost love.

"She asked if there was any leftover food. I told her to wait in a storeroom while I put some steamed buns and cold chicken on a tray, just like I make for Grandfather. He's my responsibility. If Grandfather should get sick or die, our family won't have any income. That's why I always accompany him so that he doesn't fall."

That explains her irregular hours, her curious mixture of adult sharpness and childish enthusiasm. "When I asked how Wang's villa was, she made a face. 'What an annoying man,' she said. Mr. Wang is one of our best clients, so I was dying to hear more. While she was eating, she said she'd been searching for someone, but he'd escaped her.

"I asked why she'd left, since Mr. Wang is rich and wanted to marry her, but she said she'd been married before. It didn't seem like it had gone well from her expression. I was burning with curiosity about her husband. Was he handsome? At that she looked serious and warned me to beware of unusually attractive men or women who approached alone. 'Don't follow them.' Then she sighed and said there weren't many left anyway. I didn't really understand that."

Bao thinks immediately of the elegant gentleman who seems to have abandoned at least two women in the snow. Did he lead them away, quietly at dusk, and was the lady talking about him or giving a general warning about predators? He listens intently.

"She was in an awful hurry. I've never seen anyone eat so

fast, or so much. The plates were licked clean. While she was eating, I suddenly realized it wasn't normal to eat off the floor like that."

"Off the floor?"

"I brought the food on a tray, but there wasn't a table. It was dark and shadowy in the storeroom. The snow was falling softly like feathers, and the storeroom smelled like dried leaves and wet earth. Suddenly, I had the strangest feeling, like we weren't in the right time anymore. And for a moment, I didn't even know what year it was."

Bao is fascinated. He recalls his own conversation with Mr. Wang, when, for an instant, he felt that the two of them were two gentlemen in a forest, conversing about foxes, deer, and snow. "I see. How very odd," he says aloud, more to himself than to the child, but she brightens.

"She finished the food, but I didn't want her to go. 'I'm very sorry,' she said, 'but I made a promise to someone else.' 'What about me?' I said. Then she laughed and said that I was to grow up well." The girl's eyes sparkle. "She was going to Dalian, because that's where the man she was chasing had gone."

Bao's heart leaps. "You're sure she said Dalian?"

"Yes, she was going right away. I felt like crying, though I didn't know why. Just that I'd had a chance to see something special and it wasn't ever going to come back again."

"Thank you," he says. "You've been very helpful."

"Uncle, what are you going to do if you find her?"

Belatedly, both of them realize that Bao hasn't given his reasons. The girl is suddenly anxious. She bites her lip and twists her forehead in a frightened scowl.

Bao says honestly, "I'm not sure."

He reaches into his pocket for the promised coin, but she says, "I don't want to be paid like that. If you meet the fox lady, won't you let her go? Tell her I'll be waiting for her."

WALKING HOME IN the dark, Bao tucks his chin against the cold as he listens to the watchman's wooden clapper and the occasional burst of drunken merriment. It's been a day of surprises and useful information. Yet he feels a thin haze of melancholy. Perhaps it's because the red-light district always depresses him, no matter how luxurious the establishment.

There's a likely explanation for this woman—the fox lady, as the child called her. In fact, as soon she'd described how she'd scaled the wall, he'd had some immediate thoughts:

1. Chinese opera schools select children from orphanages, training them in acrobatics. If she is an actress, that would explain her unconventional charm.
2. But why is she looking for Bektu—is it because of the fox cub? Even if she's a fake medium or a pet owner, surely nobody in their right mind would go so far for a wild animal.

Bao struggles to think rationally; there's a gnawing feeling in his chest. He's surprised to realize it's envy. Envy for the wonder glimpsed in the girl's eyes just now, like Tagtaa's long-ago gaze. The delight they expressed for an encounter that he has no way to participate in.

As he hurries on in the dark, he thinks, *Who, or what, are you?*

31

Through the sparse trees, the faint, bobbing light continued to draw closer. My mistress gripped my arm hopefully. Before I could stop her, she shouted, "Hellooo! We're lost!" Never mind that we were now in Japan and nobody was likely to understand her. It was too late anyway; whoever was carrying the light was approaching rapidly.

I didn't like that. Generally, a lone peasant will make a timid approach. Sudden advancement usually indicates confidence in numbers or purpose. And here we were, two women alone in a deserted area. I feared my mistress was too trusting.

"We are saved!" she cried, in great relief.

The light resolved itself into a paper lantern carried on a stick. A lean figure appeared behind it. But I didn't need the lantern glow to pick out his features; from the stride, I knew it was Kuro.

"It's getting late," he said. "I came to bring you home."

He offered his arm to my mistress, who was delighted to see him. "How did you know to find us?"

"If I were to go for a walk, I'd likely climb this hill, too."

"This is the second time you've saved me," said my old lady. "Or perhaps I should say, someone like you has come to my rescue, since we don't know about the first time." She was in much brighter spirits, even making jokes. I kept quiet. How had Kuro unerringly come right up to us? Or perhaps I was more predictable than I'd thought.

Kuro turned to me. "Let me carry your bundle."

"There's no need," I said brusquely.

"We were picking wild greens," said my old lady, puzzled by my unfriendliness, "and got lost."

"Did *you* get lost?" he said to me.

"Yes."

I bristled defensively, but he merely said, "Be careful in these woods." The light from the lantern shone on my face and he paused. Self-consciously, I placed my hand over the bite mark on my neck. It wouldn't do to have my mistress notice it. Kuro said nothing, but he started walking again a little too fast.

The smell of damp leaves and fresh earth rose around us, the night scent of the forest. Trotting behind the swinging lantern light, I heard Kuro and my old lady talking.

"Could you slow down, Mr. Kurosaki?" she said. "I'm afraid my old legs can't keep up with you."

"I'm sorry," he said. "Do you want a ride?" Crouching down, he offered her his back.

"Oh, I couldn't."

"Please," he said. "The ground is uneven, and you look tired. We're at least a mile from home."

"I'll carry the lantern," I said as he hefted her up easily. If Kuro had indeed saved her as a child, this would be the second time he'd given her a piggyback ride. The thought gave me an odd pang that she might never know it. Since I was now holding the light, I was forced to walk by Kuro's side. It was a sensation both familiar and painful.

My old lady looked no bigger than a child as she clung awkwardly to his back. Embarrassed, she said, "Now I really am a burden to you, besides being a guest. You're very kind. Do you have a family?"

"No."

Only Kuro could reply in such a polite, flat manner. Quickening my pace, I walked a few steps ahead. I didn't know who I was angrier with—Shiro, for setting this whole stupid connection up; myself, for following along; or Kuro, for just being himself.

"May I ask how you know Shirakawa?" asked my mistress.

"We're childhood friends," said Kuro. "We grew up in the same region, and our families knew each other."

"I see," she said. "I'm worried about my grandson, Bohai. Ever since he met Shirakawa, he will hardly listen to anyone else. For instance, I can't understand why he and his friends have stopped here in Moji rather than continuing to Tokyo for their studies."

"And what did your grandson tell you?"

"He put me off with one story after another, and now he's proposed starting a business with Shirakawa—a sugar factory in Formosa."

My poor old lady sounded so forlorn that a rush of guilt swept over me. Especially since I knew very well what Bohai was up to. She hesitated. "Do you think he's trustworthy?"

"Shirakawa has always been clever," said Kuro. "Even among us, as children, he was noted for his nimble mind."

I couldn't help snorting. As I mentioned, Shiro has been responsible for at least five small wars.

Kuro paused. "He's good company, but he mostly looks after himself."

"That sounds like a warning," said my mistress. I wondered exactly who his words were directed at.

I didn't like walking in front of Kuro. In fact, I'd rather be far away from him, preferably in another country, but there was no helping it as I was the one carrying the lantern. As we walked, I had the uneasy feeling that his gaze was burning into me. Well, let him look. If all he had to remember after this was my back, marching away, that was all right with me.

WE ARRIVED BACK at the house faster than I'd expected. No sooner had the main door opened than Bohai popped out.

"Where have you been?" he said to his grandmother. In the lamplight, his complexion had an ivory tinge, like old teeth dug up from a burial mound.

"We got lost," she said. "Is anything the matter?"

Bohai blinked nervously. "I couldn't find you, and then Kurosaki and Shirakawa went out separately."

"There's nothing to worry about since we're all back safely." She looked sharply at him. "Did you see anything unusual?"

Untying the bundle of wild greens, I crouched over, listening. In the shadowed hallway, Bohai sounded young and uncertain. "I was worried since it was getting late, so I went to the front gate to wait. And then I saw . . ." Averting his face, he muttered something in an undertone. My old lady's back stiffened.

"Thank you so much for bringing us home," she said to Kuro. "I'll take Bohai to his room. Ah San, no need to wait up for me."

She led Bohai away, though he was much taller than she was. I stared after them.

"'Ah San'—is that what she calls you?"

In my absorption, I'd forgotten that Kuro was standing next to me. Or perhaps, to be honest, I'd fallen back into old habits. His height, the breadth of his shoulders, and the reach of his arms were all insidiously familiar. Kuro turned his face towards me. From this side, you could hardly see the scar across his cheekbones.

"Yes," I replied stiffly. "That's the name they gave me right now."

"I see. You always did like the number three."

"Should I have chosen four instead?" The number "four" is the Chinese homophone for "death," while "three" sounds like "life."

Kuro smiled faintly. "I'm glad you are 'three' and not 'four.'"

Meaning, presumably, that he was glad I was alive. I couldn't say the same, however. There'd been a time when I'd wished him and myself both dead.

Silence. If he meant to ask about my life for the past couple of years, I'd no intention of answering, but Kuro said, "There's something wrong with that young man."

"Bohai?"

"Yes." Kuro frowned. "He looks haunted."

I wondered if I should ask further. As unpleasant as it was to be under the same roof as Kuro, he's an excellent judge of character. It was for my mistress's sake, I decided as I opened my mouth. Besides, I was very curious about the people with no shadows, having never come across them before.

"What do you mean by that?"

"He's frightened. Doubtless that's why he crossed the sea, likely on Shiro's advice."

"Are you talking about ghosts?"

"You know as well as I do that the mere suggestion of such things is enough to kill a man. Who is it who wants Bohai dead?"

That was a new thought to me. Wrapped up as I'd been with my mistress's concerns, I'd never considered that Bohai's terrors might have an earthly origin.

"I don't know. But you've clearly been spending far too much time writing ghost stories," I said, stooping to gather my bundle.

Kuro said quietly, "Have you read my book?"

"No, though your housekeeper has been singing its praises."

"I never expected it to be published. But please don't read it. It's of no concern to you."

OF COURSE, BEING told not to do something is like salt herring left out to dry for foxes. An almost irresistible bait. I couldn't decide whether Kuro was being sincere or merely coy as I hurried off to the kitchen. My face was burning. From indignation, I told myself, though I knew deep down that it was from Kuro's voice. That low, dark voice that has haunted my dreams and nightmares, and that I never wished to hear again.

I carried my bundle of greens to the kitchen, where the housekeeper was none too pleased to be presented with extra work. "I'll wash them right now," I offered. As I reached for a woven bamboo colander, the housekeeper noticed the bite mark on my neck. With a house full of young men, her frown deepened.

"Kurosaki-*sensei* has an excellent reputation around here," she said stiffly. "I hope you understand that."

I had to stop myself from retorting that I'd had nothing to do with this—Shiro seemed bent on tormenting me for his own amusement. "I was nipped by a dog."

"On the neck?"

"While I was crouched over picking herbs." Never mind that the bite was human shaped, but to my surprise, she blanched.

"It might have been a fox. There are rumors that foxes live on that hill, which is why nobody goes to those woods."

"But Kurosaki said he goes there all the time."

"I've warned *sensei* not to walk there. You're very lucky that he went to find you this evening; otherwise you might never have come home."

"What is it that the foxes do on that hill?"

"In my grandfather's time, a little hut was said to appear from time to time. Those who wandered from the path through the woods would be greeted by either an old man or a beautiful woman."

"Hm," I said, "I think I've heard this story. Was the traveler given a meal and a soft bed?"

"Why, yes. But the next morning all that was left were dead leaves, rotting food, and excrement. Foxes are terrible creatures."

"Perhaps that was all the fox had to offer. Maybe it was sleeping on dead leaves and eating rotting food itself," I said.

The housekeeper drew herself up. "The wickedness of foxes lies in their deceptive natures. Also, they degrade humans."

"Is that right?" Shiro had appeared silently behind me.

"Oh, Mr. Shirakawa!" said the housekeeper. "I was just warning her about the foxes on that hill. She seems to have been bitten by one."

"It was a nasty little cur," I said.

Shiro's eyes, the color of Shaoxing wine, slid to my neck. "How unfortunate. You should be treated right away in case infection sets in."

He went out into the courtyard, and I followed grudgingly, carrying the wild greens in a colander. As I primed the water pump to rinse them, Shiro perched on a stool.

"The more I see of you, the more I wonder why we haven't kept up over the years," he said musingly.

"Please get to the point. You said there was news I should hear."

"Bektu Nikan has arrived."

"Already? You said you were going to write to him." How much had Shiro hidden from me? My stomach clenched.

"Actually, I wrote to him before we left Dalian, just to let him know."

"Yet you made me help you with Takeda, saying you needed funds to buy him passage from Yokohama!" I glared at him.

"One always needs more money," said Shiro smoothly.

"Where is he?"

"He's lodging in town, in an inn near the harbor. However, I must insist that you don't pay him a visit right away. I have an assignment for him—after that, you may do as you please. Though I suspect you've already been doing that. Running off to some hill this evening was really very careless of you. Were you, by any chance, planning to leave me?"

The implication that Shiro and I were a team was uncomfortable. We were nothing of the sort; in fact, his assertion rather surprised me.

I dislike surprises.

I also dislike being told what to do, so the next morning, after my mistress had risen (pensive, rather quiet after her talk with Bohai last night, of which she said not a word to me), I volunteered to go into town on an errand.

For this, I needed regular clothes, not the fancy kimono provided by Shiro the other day, which would draw too much attention. Fortunately, I'd discovered a light blue kimono with a *hanakago*, or flower basket, pattern while rummaging around in the cupboard. In fact, there were several sets of clothes, all modestly suited for a young woman. I wondered who she was and whether she'd been a guest of Kuro's.

To my mistress, I explained the borrowed clothes as a way to avoid attention as a foreigner. She nodded absently, looking worried. "Bohai seems nervous when Shirakawa isn't with him. I wonder why."

"Do you want to know where Shirakawa went last night?" I was certain he'd met up with Bektu. And all without bothering to tell me!

"Is it possible to find out?" She looked so hopeful that I felt guilty. "I wonder if this trip was a mistake. If Bohai is unwell, it might be better managed at home."

"I can find out what Shirakawa has been up to," I said.

"You're a good girl, Ah San."

I am not a good girl at all. But I said nothing as she pressed my hand gratefully. My thoughts were already set on Bektu Nikan.

32

D alian, that port city to the south, is the first solid lead on where the mysterious lady went after leaving Wang's villa. Early the next morning, Bao heads to the railway station. There's no better way to get from Mukden to Dalian, and this woman doesn't seem like a fool.

The Fengtian, or Mukden, railway station has been taken over by the South Manchuria Railway Company, or Mantetsu. It's Japanese-run, a semiprivate company that has begun the process of replacing the railway gauge to a standard size, all the way up to Kuanchengzi, the last remaining Russian-held station. Many of the steam locomotives, as well as the rails and signaling equipment, come from America, which lends the whole affair an oddly cosmopolitan air. But Bao isn't here to admire modern progress. How would a lone woman get herself onto a train? If she had money, she'd presumably buy a ticket, though the little girl at the brothel had commented that she'd been wearing poor clothing when she returned.

The grand, brick-fronted station is abuzz with activity. Horse-drawn trams stop on the wide street, disgorging swarms of passengers. Bao despairs of finding a clue, though he patiently shows the photograph to every ticket seller and porter. *No, no*. Nobody remembers her buying a ticket.

Bao eats lunch at a noodle shop near the station. It's cheap, and the noodles come with a free side of *paocai*, the pickled cabbage that's a staple of Northeast China. Swirling the last dregs of tea in his earthenware cup, he shows the stall keeper the photograph. The man scratches his head. "She might have been picked up by one of the pimps. Good-looking girl like that. Come to think of it, I did hear from Shorty Jin about an uncanny incident a month ago. He picked up a girl who insisted on going to Dalian."

Bao leans forward, exhaling slowly. "What happened?"

"He was planning to sell her, but during the journey he blacked out and found himself lying by the railway tracks. The woman was gone—likely to Dalian by herself. Says he can't remember a thing."

Bao finds this intriguing. *If I were a fox*, he thinks, *I'd try to have people forget the details about me.*

IF I WERE a fox, what would I do? The words skitter inside Bao's head, like drops of water on a hot pan. It's an absurd suggestion, but Bao goes along with it. First of all, if he were a fox, he wouldn't ever come to the city. The air is hazy with smoke, and he buries his face in his scarf, sidestepping a puddle of horse urine. But perhaps there isn't enough to eat in the countryside. He admits to himself that his knowledge of foxes is patchy and limited.

Where did his old nanny learn about foxes, anyway? He recalls her rough, warm hand, her certainty that the fox god would listen to her petitions. And what had she said, in the very beginning before he fell ill and she was sent away? She'd said, *I prayed that the fox god would take away your . . .*

No matter how hard he's tried to remember that phrase, the blankness remains: an unsolved mystery of his childhood. It couldn't have been the jaundice that triggered her dismissal. That happened after the first visit to the shrine. What ailed him, as a child, that his nanny took him secretly to the fox god? There's no one left to ask; his parents have long since passed, and he doubts that his older brother would remember. Tagtaa wouldn't know either. She came after his nanny, and anyway, she, too, has been lost to him.

A bicyclist swerves past him with an angry shout, and Bao begins walking again. The word "uncanny" reminds him of the pimp's encounter with a strange woman. Perhaps all gifts from the fox god are similarly marked. Even foxes in stories bear this trait: at first mistaken for humans, sooner or later they betray themselves by a bushy tail glimpsed under a trailing hem. Unnatural, frightening beauty. At twilight or in dark places, it's said, their faces shine faintly.

BAO BUYS A railway ticket for Dalian. He's certain this is the same woman. Heady excitement fills him, the thrill of the hunt. How long has it been since he's felt this young?

His own mother outlived his father by more than fifteen years, growing older, with her mouth pursed like a tightly sewn pouch, in his brother's house. Filial piety meant living with the oldest son. Bao's wife had reported the details to him, nervous yet eager. She was terrified of his mother yet loved to dissect her dealings.

When Bao was first married, he'd been surprised at his wife's timidity. The slightest decision sent her into a tizzy: a casual remark that he preferred green mung beans to red beans led to tears and much hand-wringing over her house-keeping ability. "I don't mind either," he'd said mildly.

"But you like green beans, don't you? Green is better then," she'd insisted, plucking at the hem of her blouse long after the beans were gone.

Having grown up surrounded by assertive women (his mother, his nanny, and even Tagtaa), Bao was taken aback by his new wife's hesitancy. He had to guess what she wanted; her weakness became his chains. His friends made fun of him. "You must love your wife very much," they said, recalling the story of how he'd agreed to the arranged marriage at first sight. Bao only smiled.

"Still," they'd said, "you shouldn't listen to her so much. You spoil your wife." By then, everyone knew that Bao's wife would scarcely do anything without consulting him. Every trivial detail must be rehashed. Bao wondered whether children would have given her more confidence. It was a lack that she constantly felt—yet another inferiority that she must suffer, that surely caused others to look down on her. Bao sighs as he walks home from the railway station. Children might have sent his late wife into even greater agitations. *Poor children*, he thinks wryly. *Poor me.*

When he looks back over his life, Bao doesn't feel particularly sorry for himself. Sorry should be saved for the bodies that he sees by the side of the road like pitiable bundles of rags—the corpses of peasants who have come from the countryside and died of starvation. The saddest are the skeletal children, clutched to their mother's breasts. Passersby quicken their steps, averting their eyes. The empire is falling apart; last year's Jiangsu famine had long teeth.

No, Bao shouldn't be sorry for himself. He's had a mediocre career but no great hardships. A long marriage with little love but a great deal of faithfulness. And now he's free to take on jobs as he pleases, with no one to dissolve into nervous tears if he comes home late. Bao presses a hand to his chest. Lately, when he coughs, the sharp pain in his lung flares up worryingly. He ought to use his time well.

33

It wasn't hard to find Bektu Nikan. A foreigner draws attention, even in a port town like Moji, and Shiro had said he was lodging at an inn near the harbor.

Dressed in the light blue kimono that I'd found in the back room, I'd made my way out of the house, only to be stopped by the housekeeper. She regarded me with disapproval. "Where did you get that kimono?"

"From Kurosaki-*sensei*"—though I'd asked for no such permission.

The housekeeper's lips tightened. "I heard that you're Shirakawa's cousin," she said, "but don't you think it's too much to borrow Miss Yukiko's clothes without asking?"

"Miss Yukiko?"

"She's the granddaughter of the owner of this house. Kurosaki-*sensei* is only renting it. She comes to visit quite often, as *sensei* is very fond of her."

"I'm very sorry," I said hastily. "I must have misunderstood."

Clothes are a sensitive item, particularly for women. I gave the housekeeper my most penitent look. Ears down, dark eyes peeking up.

"Well," she said, softening, "I suppose you didn't know any better. And it's not like she wears this often."

"Who is Miss Yukiko, and how do you write her name?" Usually "*yuki*" in Japanese uses the Chinese character for "snow," which is my own name. Somehow, I didn't like that.

"It's written as 'happiness,' not 'snow,'" said the housekeeper. "Like I said, she's the owner's granddaughter."

"How old is she?"

"Twenty-nine—she's a widow, poor lady. To be honest, I think that the owner would like Kurosaki-*sensei* to marry his granddaughter, especially since *sensei* has a rising reputation in the literary world."

"She comes here often?"

"Yes, this is her childhood home after all, even though the owner has several houses. She returned to her family after her husband died. Don't you know anything?"

"No," I said, looking very meek. "I suppose I'd better find other clothes, in case Miss Yukiko comes back."

"Since you're dressed already, never mind." The house-keeper was clearly excited by this bit of gossip. I couldn't blame her—the house was full of foreigners, not to mention three foxes. As I said, that was enough to drive most people a little crazy.

I set off, having asked the houseboy, a stocky youth of about fourteen, to hail me a rickshaw. Fortunately, I'd changed some money earlier. The thick wallet that I'd taken off the pimp on that train from Mukden had been converted to yen at a ruinous exchange rate through a money changer in Dalian. I couldn't well refuse, as there hadn't been many options for me. As it was, the man had given me several doubtful glances. An unaccompanied young woman with money always raises questions; I'd have to be careful since, short of robbing someone again, I didn't see how I was going to acquire more. Instead, I thought about this Miss Yukiko. Why was the sound of her name, so similar to mine, irritating?

"A Manchurian?" replied the maid at the second inn I inquired at. "Yes. He arrived yesterday."

She indicated a hat hanging on a peg in the hallway. That must be Bektu's, I guessed. It had a well-worn, greasy brim that matched the faded decor of the inn. A grandfather clock with a brass face stood in the foyer, ticking softly. Assessing my appearance (modestly respectable), the maid said he might be sleeping right now. "He told us not to disturb him," she said apologetically.

"If that's the case, I'll come back later," I said. "No need to trouble him."

Naturally, I had no intention of doing anything of the sort.

I trotted around the corner and waited. From the maid's involuntary glance, I was fairly certain that Bektu was in one of the upstairs rooms on the left side of the inn. After a while, I peeked back inside. All was quiet.

Upstairs was a long narrow corridor, fronted with sliding doors. To the left were three rooms that could have housed Bektu. One of the doors was open, revealing a vacancy. Another was shut, but so still that I was certain there was no one inside. The last, the corner room, held the sound of someone breathing heavily.

Putting my hand on the door, I gently opened it. This kind of sliding door often doesn't lock. It was a small six-tatami-mat room, most of it taken up by a futon. Bektu's large, muscular frame, which was going to fat, sprawled across it. Catching him asleep was an unexpected bonus, and one that I ought not pass up.

As I stared at him, I thought of my child again.

THE ONE TIME I'd laid eyes on Bektu Nikan had been at that garden villa on the outskirts of Mukden. Winter's chill seeped through the elaborately carved dark rosewood screens. I had agreed to have my portrait taken—a necessary evil to meet the photographer who had ordered the death of my child. It had taken longer than expected to find him, until I managed to enter Wang's villa.

That villa had reminded me of gardens in the south with their rare plants and winding walkways, particularly in Hangzhou around the West Lake. I'd said as much to Wang while making small talk. "How did you know?" he'd said, running a thick finger along my neck. I didn't mention that I'd been to Hangzhou when it was young and green. Instead, I'd tilted my head and asked about a certain photographer.

Wang was eager for me to sit for a portrait. Preferably wearing one of the ridiculous opera costumes he'd collected. I'd said no to that (and several other things—keeping his hands off me involved increasingly elaborate pretexts of wanting to be married properly, etc.). Fortunately, he turned out to be one of those particularly susceptible to foxes. Unfortunately, he also behaved erratically, which causes other problems. A hundred years ago, the family might have called in an exorcist and then I might really have been in trouble, but as it was, his steward could only regard me with nervous suspicion.

Sometimes I wonder if having my photograph taken that day will come back to haunt me. We are so very careful, after all, not to preserve an accurate likeness. But there was no helping it. On an overcast winter morning, I waited in that long, cold room for Bektu Nikan. I'd hoped to be left alone with him, but that wasn't to be. Wang, accompanied by the steward and two maids, insisted on staying.

My first impression of Bektu was of a wide face, thick arms, and hungry eyes. I felt a surge of fury that I struggled to conceal.

"So this is the new girl," he'd said.

Briskly, Bektu set up his equipment: a bulky wooden box camera with heavy glass lens and slides, a hood of velvet to block out the light. Sharp scent of chemicals. The damp breeze blew in through the carved wooden lattice, recalling grass growing on graves. A single spray of winter-blooming narcissus nodded on the table. White is the color of the dead.

Bektu had been silent and workmanlike. It was difficult to gauge his vulnerability to foxes as his eyes were hidden behind the camera most of the time. Since Wang and his retainers wouldn't leave, I decided to observe Bektu first. If he was a frequent visitor, as the servants claimed, there'd surely be another chance for me to get him alone. However, I'd been wrong. And in the end, I'd had to chase him all the way to Moji.

Now, AS I stared at him sleeping in front of me, I wondered if the hunt had been worth it. Asleep, his face was lax and empty as a child's. Once, he, too, had had a mother. But now wasn't the time to hesitate. Reminding myself that he'd stolen all the future years of my child's life, I gritted my teeth.

Very quietly, I took out a length of rope from my sleeve.

Good rope is hard to come by. You want it to be strong, yet thin enough to hide. Also, it should hold a knot well. Just as I was about to slip it over him, there were footsteps in the corridor. The maid tapped on the door. "Excuse me, sir, are you awake? There was a visitor looking for you."

I froze. Bektu's eyes flickered open. Hastily I stuffed the rope back into my sleeve and slid back on my haunches so that I was sitting in front of the closed door. With a lurch, he sat up blearily. "What are you—?"

"Sir?" said the maid from the hallway.

I did my best impression of a blushing maiden. Eyes down, hand delicately over my mouth in a gesture of silence. If the maid hadn't disturbed us, I would have trussed him up like a hairy crab, a famous Shanghainese delicacy. Now things would be far more troublesome.

"It's all right," he called to the maid.

Blink. His little eyes were wary. "Aren't you Mr. Wang's latest mistress?" He'd recognized me faster than I'd expected.

"Why, yes. I'd hoped to see you again in Mukden, but I didn't realize that you'd left town right after our photo session."

This wasn't a great story, but I hoped he was still too sleepy to process it. Bektu rubbed his face. "Didn't Mr. Wang tell you that I'd relocated?"

"No," I said coquettishly. "He didn't tell me anything about you."

Which was true. I'd been sadly misled by that waxy-faced Mr. Wang, leading me to waste an additional week in that villa waiting for the photographer to come back.

"Is Wang here then?" Bektu heaved himself upright. The stale smell of sweat and alcohol wafted towards me.

"I have a new patron—Shirakawa." The nervousness in my voice was only part pretend. Despite Bektu's flabby appearance, I'd heard he'd been a wrestler in his youth. And there was something about him that made me uneasy.

"So you're Shirakawa's woman now?" He looked suspicious.

Rapidly, I improvised, "He and I are madly in love and wish to take photographs together."

"What sort of pictures did you have in mind?" His eyes narrowed.

"Private photographs," I said, pausing for emphasis. Tensed forward, weight on my knees and my toes braced against the floor. The knife was palmed behind my back. If I was fast enough, I might get his throat, though a better plan might be to stab him in the leg and cut the femoral artery.

"Shirakawa never mentioned you when I saw him last night."

He rose abruptly, closing the distance between us. Faster than I'd anticipated. Many of my kind have met their deaths at the hands of Manchurians like Bektu, and I leaped back, off my haunches, so we were standing face-to-face. The hair on the back of my neck stood up.

"Don't you know that Shirakawa has never permitted any-one to take his picture?" he said softly. "It makes me wonder why you're asking about 'private photographs'—or if you have other motives."

"I've no idea what you're talking about." I willed him to pause, soften his gaze. Alarm bells were beginning to ring in my head.

"Your eyes are filled with rage." He grinned suddenly.

He was too close now. Close enough to grab me if I went for him. And I realized that I'd made a fatal mistake.

This man was highly resistant to foxes.

34

After alerting his landlord of his impending trip to Dalian, Bao visits his older brother. There's no real need to, but Bao dutifully updates him. These little check-ins, brief yet cordial, perpetuate the illusion that they're close. Bao learned long ago that frequency is a good substitute for intimacy. Besides, they're both getting on in years.

Bao's older brother has retired from his official career, but the walls and bookshelves of his private study are still decorated with commemorative wishes and poems from colleagues. Bao sits in his usual seat, opposite his brother's carved rosewood desk. The chair is a little lower than his brother's chair, a detail he's often noted with secret amusement. No doubt it's meant to set the proper tone, and he wonders who else has sat in its wide, low seat. His brother's children, colleagues, supplicants asking for favors. Himself, of course. In the Chinese hierarchy of family, Bao will never outrank his older brother. The four years between them is a gap that a lifetime hasn't closed, though from time to time he's reminded of his boyhood tutor's words, overheard speaking to his mother. *The younger one has more talent*, he'd said. And his mother's eyes closed in a hooded blink.

What did talent matter if Bao was unable to gain office? At least he'd become a teacher, though the spectacle he'd made of himself at fourteen, running after Tagtaa's mule wagon through the streets, followed his family in whispers. His older brother's official appointment was dogged by sniggers of *Yes, but the younger brother* . . . Even his late wife heard rumors. She'd asked him when they were first married if he'd had another lover.

"Of course not," he'd said.

It was true. At fourteen, he'd barely held Tagtaa's hand, let alone exchanged words of love with her. His wife had been satisfied. Still, Bao sometimes wonders what his older brother thought of this.

"You're going to Dalian, then?"

"Yes, for a client."

Bao gives no details, and his brother asks for none. The conversation drifts to how the trains are running and a reminder to be careful.

Changing the topic, Bao says, "Do you remember our old nanny—the one Mother sent away after I got jaundice?"

His brother's forehead creases. "She was more your nanny than mine. She came when you were born."

"Really?"

"Yes, I had a different nursemaid who left to be married. Mother liked her better, but Father sent for your nanny from his home village, so she couldn't say no."

"Why did he send for her?"

"It was Grandmother's suggestion." His brother shrugs, uninterested, although this sheds new light on his mother's animosity towards Bao's old nanny: a rural woman sent by her mother-in-law, doubtless in response to some long-ago grudge. "You were very attached to her. She took you every-where, including the wet market. Mother didn't like that either. She said you'd get a disease from the peasants. You were often sick when you were young."

"Was I?" The only illness that Bao remembers is the jaun-dice that afflicted him after his visit to the fox shrine.

"Yes. You didn't have much energy and your hands were always cold." His brother laughs.

Bao smiles, too. "I must have been troublesome."

"Not really. I should have been better to you."

"You were busy studying." Bao harbors no ill feelings. His older brother was the one who was drilled to memorize the classics, who stood stiffly in front of their father to recite poems, and whose every friendship was scrutinized.

"Why so many questions about your old nanny, anyway?"

"She took me to the fox shrine in our neighbor's back garden."

"I never went," says his brother. "I was too frightened to go."

"Really?" Bao is surprised. In his memories, his older brother is always confident.

"The servants said occasionally an aged gentleman would appear in that bamboo grove. Some said it was the old master of the house who'd died, and others that it was a fox who had assumed his form. That's why nobody went there."

Bao recalls the rustling of the bamboo leaves and the wooden shrine where his nanny devoutly prayed. It had seemed ancient to him, but then again, so had his nanny's bent back and lined face.

"She said something to me when I was a child: 'I prayed to the fox god to take away your . . .' But I can't remember what she asked for. For years I've wondered. Do you happen to know?"

To his utter surprise, his brother nods. "Yes, I remember. She asked the fox god to take away your shadow."

Of all requests, this is nothing that Bao could have conceived of. He's at a loss for words. His brother says, "It was supposed to be a secret. I'm sure Father would have been furious."

Their father had no patience with folk religion, speaking with ghosts, or the manipulation of *qi* in the body. He would, indeed, have been apoplectic. "But why?" Bao asks.

"The doctor said your body was unbalanced with too much *yin*. That's why you had cold hands, lethargy, and no appetite."

Yin is negative, cold energy, as opposed to *yang*, which is bright and hot. The two are complementary opposites and constantly in flux.

"Perhaps that's why your nanny asked the fox god to remove your shadow. To take some of the *yin* away from you."

Both of them know it's an absurd request. Traditional Chinese medicine strives for a delicate balance between cold and heat, damp and dryness, *yin* and *yang*. No learned practitioner would be so reckless.

"Anyway," his brother continues, "I never told Mother what your nanny said; I didn't think it would work anyway."

"I still have a shadow," Bao says. *Or at least I think I do.* He moves his arm experimentally, but it's hard to tell indoors.

"Maybe she asked the fox god to remove part of it. When you came back from the shrine, I used to watch you. Just to see if it had worked. That's why I wouldn't let you into my room for a while. You frightened me."

Bao is fascinated by this previously unknown history. The gap of four years between them meant their relationship during childhood was neither distant nor intimate. His brother's superiority in age, diligence, and family expectations has maintained that space, like two railway tracks forever separated by wooden sleepers. "I thought you wouldn't let me into your room because I'd borrowed some of your books and got them wet."

"That, too." An amused grimace.

"So, you think the visit to the fox god didn't work then?"

"It had some effect," says his brother. "Weren't you very ill afterwards?"

At this moment, his sister-in-law enters the study to announce another visitor. Bao takes his leave, promising to bring back a souvenir for her from Dalian. As he hurries home, scarf pulled up against the biting wind, he considers his brother's words. *Weren't you very ill afterwards?*

Jaundice—the childhood illness that turned his skin and eyes yellow, alarming his parents and leading to the dismissal of his old nanny—is said by traditional Chinese medicine to be of two kinds: *yang* type, which is acute and caused by an excess of heat, and *yin* type, which is chronic and enfeebling. From what Bao remembers, he suffered from the *yang* version, an illness that came on with sudden ferocity. That made sense if his body had become unbalanced by losing too much *yin*, or shadow.

But it's ridiculous to consult a fox to meddle with a child's constitution. Only an illiterate peasant, a devotee of folk religion, would think of doing so. As he walks, Bao studies the shadows around him. His own shadow seems faint to him, though perhaps he's just being critical. It's never occurred to him to observe it carefully before. Flattened, it slides from the street up to the wall, then around a corner. Yet it lacks a certain crispness and substance that other shadows possess. A trick of the light, he decides uneasily.

Does the lack of shadow translate to his own peculiar

relationship with the truth? A more accurate description of his condition is that Bao is allergic to lies. He scratches his head. Perhaps it's good that he's never told his brother about this. He never even got to tell his nanny, as she was sent away abruptly.

The bent back of his old nanny rises in his memory, her forlorn little figure stumping away from him. Even at the age of seven, he'd felt she was only slightly bigger than himself. The injustice of it brings a pang to his heart. His mother should have been more merciful, for his nanny loved him—he's sure of it. And if she accidentally caused other problems, he's long since forgiven her.

At least, that's what he tells himself.

On a crisp morning with gusty winds, Bao boards the train from Mukden to Dalian. Spring is coming, but it will be late, as it always is in this corner of the world. The Manchu bannermen on the train wear hats trimmed with otter fur and thick quilted jackets. As the train passes flat fields of sorghum and poplar trees under a white sky, he's lulled to sleep by the rocking carriage.

He's in the familiar backyard of his childhood, staring over the wall at the neighbor's bamboo grove. Bao pushes open the wooden back gate. In his dream, his hand is that of a young man, not a child, but that's impossible because they left that house when Bao was fourteen. He's never been back since, but the dream doesn't care. It rolls onwards as the gate opens. The wood is weathered gray, the iron hinges silent. A path leads through courtyards, white plaster walls, gray curved roofs dappled with sunshine. Bao keeps walking, and there it is, the bamboo grove of his memories. He halts suddenly.

Someone is waiting for him in front of the fox shrine. Is it his old nanny, long lost to him? Or his mother, or his wife? It occurs to him suddenly that all three women are dead. Whoever it is faces the shrine, her back towards him. The rustling leaves warn him that he's approaching a mystery, different from the fox shrine. His tongue sticks to the roof of his mouth. The figure turns. Is it the fox lady who he's been pursuing?

No, it's Tagtaa.

"I want to tell you something," she says, eyes alight. "I found him! I met the black fox again."

Why is she still talking about that fox, even though Bao is here in front of her? But he, too, is searching for a fox. "You did?"

"Yes, though I had to cross the sea."

The breeze overhead whips the tops of the bamboo so it bows and creaks. He strains to hear her. "What about me?" he says. "Why did you leave without ever telling me?"

The wind is now blowing so hard that the bamboo bends like a green sea they're drowning in. Tagtaa's eyes shine. "I've always, always wanted to meet a fox again."

A HARD JOLT. The train has crawled to a halt at a station. People push by, jostling their packages and baskets down from the overhead racks. Disconcerted, Bao opens his eyes. What a strange dream, like a fevered fragment.

A drowsy, sad heaviness settles on Bao. He's a sentimental old fool, thinking across half a century of a girl who left him behind. But the emotion of the dream lingers. *It's because of foxes*, he thinks. Bao sits up groggily. Pickpockets are rife, and he should be careful about falling asleep. When the train lurches out of the station, he stands in the end corridor looking out. The rails, shiny with use, pass rapidly beneath the open carriage work.

Did the fox lady also leave the train when the pimp did? Bao suspects not. In his mind, she continued her journey to Dalian. A woman like that, so fiercely set on a goal, would hardly turn aside. As he inhales the scent of cut grass, cleared from the tracks, Bao wonders if she's found Bektu Nikan yet.

35

It's terrible to discover that someone is immune to foxes.

Especially when they're larger, stronger, and standing too close to you. The little knife in my hand wouldn't save me at this range. At best I'd stab Bektu and drive him into a frothing rage, during which he might break my neck. I'd been far too emotional and reckless, as Shiro had pointed out. I ought to have considered that there are always some people who cannot be fooled by us.

The last time this happened to me was in Luoyang, when I was caught by a Jurchen soldier. Despite my pleas, I was locked up within a palace of echoing corridors and screens of carved wood pasted over with fine white mulberry paper. There were women's quarters, and a bronze cage for me. I only got out of it by biting my tongue until blood ran out of my mouth and pretending to be dead. Since then, I've been careful to steer away from anyone who displays immunity.

So when I realized my error with Bektu, I froze.

"You're asking a lot of questions about private photographs. Did someone send you?" Seizing my left arm, Bektu twisted it backwards. My back pressed against the door; I shifted my grip on the knife.

"You're frightening me," I said plaintively.

I cry very prettily. It's an art I've practiced over many years. Of course I've cried genuine tears of anguish before—heartrending screams and rivers of grief—and they never got me anywhere. So I've learned to use whatever I must.

Indecision flickered in his stare. Jaw clenched, I stared at the pulse in Bektu's neck. Right where it throbbed beneath the skin. His head jerked sideways; in that instant, a speck of an opening hung in the air. But I hesitated, pulse racing.

I, too, had heard the rattle of approaching footsteps.

"Sir, there's another visitor for you downstairs."

It was the maid again. I felt her presence behind the thin

door, the huff of her indignant breath, annoyed that this foreign guest had so many callers in the morning.

"Excuse me, I just need to—" With a rattle, the maid pulled open the sliding door. She gave a shriek as I fell out. "Oh! I didn't realize you had company!"

The moment had vanished. My moment, which I'd planned and agonized over. Which I'd waited two years for. I'd told myself I was prepared, but in the end, I'd missed it. I felt like drowning in silent, numb misery.

"Excuse me," I said, ducking and bowing. Then I was off, walking swiftly down the worn corridor.

SUNK IN GLOOM, I arrived back at the house after completing several trivial errands for my mistress. My skirmish with Bektu had ended in defeat. His arrogant little eyes and stale breath haunted me. If I hadn't hesitated when I'd entered the room, I could have slit his throat in his sleep. Was I losing my nerve? I tried to console myself that I'd learned something interesting: he seemed to believe I was after some private photographs. Also, that Bektu was, by pure bad luck, one of those highly resistant to foxes.

Which led me to the burning question: Why hadn't Shiro mentioned that to me?

I don't expect much help from others of my kind, but a warning would have been well within reason. I could only conclude that Shiro had purposely withheld it, though I needed to figure out why. I reminded myself that only one in ten hunting forays succeed when you're working alone, but it didn't dissipate the bitter cloud of frustration that settled over me, like a cloud of ink poured into a basin of water.

THE YOUNG MANSERVANT at Kuro's house was waiting for me at the front entrance. It was a sunny, bright afternoon, and the bamboo planted in front of the house made a pattern of shadows across his face. He blinked shyly.

"This letter came for you," he said. It was addressed to

"Shirakawa Yuki," since Shiro had informed everyone I was his cousin, and was from Takeda, the rich man we'd visited yesterday. Apparently, he'd made good on his promise to write an account of the incident at Wang's garden villa last summer.

"Thank you," I said, tucking it into my sash and smiling, despite the urge to run away somewhere and scream. What a failure that morning had been! And now Bektu was likely to be on guard against me.

A flush appeared on the boy's tanned face as he said, "By the way, Miss Yukiko is visiting right now."

"The owner's granddaughter?"

"Yes." From his flustered glance, he'd overheard the house-keeper exclaiming over my borrowed kimono earlier and was now giving me a warning. I was grateful; there's nothing so embarrassing as appearing in somebody else's clothing.

"Does she come often?"

"Every week, to see *sensei*. Sometimes more." The boy shifted uneasily from one foot to the other. "She's in *sensei*'s study right now."

"I see. I'd better give them space then."

MY MISTRESS WAS resting, so I went into the garden, feeling depressed. Lately, I was slipping up. We foxes live on the edge of shadows, one heartbeat away from being trapped and skinned. The wiliest old fox I knew was beaten to death by a drunk peasant on a country road during the New Year's cele-brations in Heilongjiang. It makes you wonder whether every living creature has its allotted span of years. Either that, or fate is a capricious master.

I was unlikely to get another chance at Bektu—not a good one, like that. Enlisting Shiro's help was the easiest way, though I didn't like that at all. I comforted myself with fan-tasies that when this was all over, I would tie a large stone around Shiro's neck and roll him off a cliff.

The sun was warm on the wicker chair I'd curled up in,

tucked against a large bush. Spring was in the air. Across the grasslands, a silent symphony of wildflowers must be blooming. Cranes and wild goats were on the move, and in ponds fed by melting snow, fish were rising. Thoughts of my home brought tears to my eyes. My child was already lost to me. Why was I here, so far away, on this bitter mission?

As I sat there, wiping my eyes on my borrowed kimono sleeves (one never has a handkerchief when one needs one), I heard approaching footsteps. I froze. A man and a woman, walking in a garden on a spring afternoon, will have many things to talk about. Particularly if the man is good-looking and the woman charming. Or maybe that was just my cynicism, eavesdropping on their conversation.

"I enjoyed the poems you recommended," said the lady as they stopped on the other side of my leafy screen. This must be Miss Yukiko, I decided: the landlord's widowed granddaughter. "I read them in one night."

She had a pretty voice, light yet warm. I could only see her feet, paused in exactly the right feminine pigeon-toed formation. "If you have any new stories, I'd be happy to give you feedback."

"Thank you," said Kuro. "But I haven't written anything new."

"You should write a children's book. My nephews were thrilled when you visited. They still ask after you."

"They're good boys. I enjoyed playing with them." A smile in his voice.

"You're very patient. My late husband was never interested in children."

"And you?"

"I'd love a baby of my own. But my husband was ill since his youth, and it didn't happen for us. Nursing him was like caring for a child sometimes. He was often frustrated and angry. Who could blame him?" She sighed.

"I'm sorry. It must have been difficult for you."

"Don't be. It's over, and I'm grateful for every day I have now."

She sounded terribly sincere. If it were Shiro she was talking to, I'd burst out of the bush to warn her, but since it was Kuro, it was unlikely he'd toy with her feelings. No, Kuro has always been deadly serious. They must be quite intimate for her to be confiding in him. The thought gave me a peculiar twinge.

Pause. One of those long pauses when Kuro says nothing. I know them well and could imagine the lady's delicate hesitation as she continued, "Have you given any thought to my grandfather's proposal?"

"I cannot give you a reply right now. But I will sincerely consider it."

This seemed to please her because she started talking of other matters, like his guests. "I'm sorry to have missed them today."

"Yes, the young men went to the harbor with Shirakawa."

Hugging my knees, I noticed he didn't mention my mistress or myself.

"You look tired. Is anything troubling you?" she said.

By peering up through the bush, I found I could see their faces. Miss Yukiko was plainer than I'd expected from her girlish voice, but still attractive, like a porcelain doll with a pleasing old-fashioned quality. The crease in her collar was impeccable, and her face was lightly touched with powder and rouge. But none of that mattered because she was obviously in love, which makes any woman radiant. Her eyes shone as she gazed up at Kuro. I didn't want to look at him at all.

"Sometimes I can't sleep," he said. "You may say it is my guilty conscience."

"The past is ever with us. But it doesn't have to be. I hope that one day you will be free of it."

A flame burned my cheeks. I could feel the blood rushing to my head, my pulse raced erratically. Just how much had Kuro confided in her? From her gentle sympathy, it could be nothing or everything. I bit my lip. Besides, I was wearing her clothes. How much more awkward could that be? Very quietly, I picked up my wooden clogs. I had just begun to sneak off when the veranda door opened and Lu came out.

He stopped short when he saw me, clogs in hand. "What are you doing?"

I waved my hand frantically to indicate silence, but it was too late. Drawn by his raised voice, Kuro and Miss Yukiko came around the bush. I'd no chance to slip inside because Lu's lanky body was blocking the door.

"You're back already?" said Kuro.

Since I was stuck on the veranda, I did my best to pretend that I'd just come out with Lu, who said obliviously, "Yes, we had some business at the bank."

The requisite introductions were made. Miss Yukiko greeted Lu charmingly, saying any friend of Kurosaki-*sensei* was most welcome. I felt her curious glance on me. If only she wouldn't recognize her own clothing! That was obviously too much to hope for, because she addressed me indirectly.

"And who is this pretty lady next to you, Mr. Lu?"

Lu vacillated, his long lip trembling. I opened my mouth, but before I said a word, Kuro stepped in.

"This is Shirakawa's cousin," he said quietly. "Another old friend of mine."

Trapped, I stood politely as Lu kept talking. I resisted the urge to rub my face. Doing so would only draw attention to the tearstains from my earlier bout of crying. Miss Yukiko's gaze rested on my clothing. Kuro's description of me as an old friend had probably inflamed her curiosity—how like him to not notice that!

"I love the pattern of your kimono," she said at last. "I have one very similar that I wore before my marriage."

"I think this is yours," I said, finally raising my eyes. "I'm very sorry, but I found this in a drawer. My apologies for borrowing it without permission."

It was a moment of supreme awkwardness. The conversation ground to a halt, as even the two men realized it.

"Oh, please don't feel bad!" A blush stained her cheeks. "I still have clothes in this house, so borrow them as you wish.

Are you also staying here?" Her eyes darted from myself to Kuro and back again.

"Only temporarily," I said. "I'll make sure to wash this and return it to you." With that and other polite excuses, I managed to escape into the house.

A FOX WHO lives for more than a hundred years will be tested with catastrophe. Some say that is heaven's way of eliminating creatures who live too long. At one hundred years of age, it's said, lightning strikes from heaven. At two hundred, an earthquake will try to swallow you. At three hundred, a raging ball of fire appears. Naturally, foxes who die have never passed on the exact details. All we know is that we will each face trials; if you can survive for a thousand years, you may reach enlightenment.

Or so they say.

I had tried to be good, but the last two years of sorrow had undone me. Humiliations like wearing another woman's clothing and being outmaneuvered by Bektu filled me with further doubts. Well, there was no use licking my wounds, so I trailed off despondently to my little room. Changing my clothes, I felt the crisp rustle of Takeda's letter tucked into my sash, so I opened it, wondering if he'd remembered anything interesting that I could use against Bektu.

Takeda turned out to have surprisingly beautiful handwriting. As I feared, however, he was long-winded. Skipping past the requisite niceties, I got to this part:

And so on a beautiful late-summer day I arrived at the vast estate of Wang, a renowned collector of bonsai. I'd been trying to get an invitation to view this gentleman's private collection and was only able to do so through my connection with a certain Mr. Lu's family.

Lu was a common-enough name, but it made me wonder whether the Lu who was part of our party might also have a connection to the Wang household. The wealthy have their own circles; just as Chen's aunt was married to Wang, Lu's family likely knew them as well. Frowning, I continued reading Takeda's letter, which he'd written in the florid style of a detective novel, starring himself.

It was a grand house party in the old Chinese style. Outside, the empire might be crumbling, but within those high walls and delightful courtyards, it was as though we were still dining and exchanging poetry in the Ming or Song dynasty. In the evening, dozens of paper lanterns were lit in every corridor, hanging from the curved eaves and reflecting in the lotus ponds. It was a marvelous extravagance of candles.

I reflected sourly that the empire might not be falling if people like Wang stopped wasting candles while peasants were starving in the street, but humans are always like this. They don't realize that an uprising is coming until the watchtowers burn down. As for lamps, one or two is good enough to read by at night. Wrinkling my nose, I continued reading.

And now I must tell you about the curious incident I referred to at our last meeting.

I sat up. This might be useful.

36

The train hisses to a stop in Dalian's station. Plumes of steam announce its arrival as the engine exhales like a great iron beast. It's a minor miracle that nobody has died or been exploded. As Bao exits the crowded station, he muses that his childhood self would have been amazed at today's train ride. He's living in an age of fables—riding an iron horse in search of a beauty who might be a fox. It's best to keep quiet about such fancies, however. If his older brother knew, he'd worry that Bao had lost his mind.

What is it that connects foxes with madness? Upon arriving at his lodgings (recommended by a former client, worn but clean, no visible bedbugs), Bao sits on the narrow wooden bed and considers the symptoms induced by both the lady and the strange gentleman who led two women to be abandoned in the snow: excitability, euphoria, and forgetfulness. They're too vague to attribute to a particular toxin. Opium, for example, gives users vivid dreams but also sluggishness. Besides, opium addiction is sadly common, and Bao hasn't seen any evidence of pinprick pupils or slurred speech in the people he's interviewed.

Foxes are said to beguile people. Charming tricksters, they will carry off your gold wine cups as well as your heart. The worst ones devour your vitality. Yet they seem oddly vulnerable. Easily killed or maimed, they lose paws, tails, and their own lives in gruesome ways. Overall, it seems to Bao that they're weaker than humans and only survive by their wits.

After depositing his luggage, he returns to the station and shows the photograph around. Nobody, however, has any recollection of her, and Bao feels discouraged. To make matters worse, a steady drizzle begins and his shoes fill with water. Perhaps this is the end of the trail. Having eaten a desultory supper and noted that food tastes worse when traveling alone, Bao lies in bed and stares at the darkened ceiling. He exhales carefully. If he takes shallow breaths, the sharp pain in his left lung dissipates slightly, though its persistence worries him. The fatty gray pork that he ate for dinner rises in his throat, and Bao wonders if he has food poisoning.

DURING THE NIGHT, Bao's fears materialize. Dawn finds him hollow-eyed from retching over the enamel chamber pot. It's horrible to have food poisoning, especially when traveling. If he were home, his landlady would make him broth, but here he must ring for the porter to empty the slops and refill the teapot with hot water. The man looks askance; there are rumors of bubonic plague in the north. People are dying of fever, with swollen lymph nodes in the groin and armpit, after eating raw marmot liver.

"Is there a medicine shop nearby?" Bao asks, tipping the man generously.

Yes, there's a famous medicine hall a little farther away.

"Give me whatever they have for food poisoning," says Bao, grimacing.

The porter returns with a paper packet of bitter pills, which lull Bao into uneasy slumber after swallowing them. The day passes in fitful sleep and waking. Illness reminds him of his age, the ache in his knees, and how nobody knows that he's alone in a far city.

When he opens his eyes again, it's morning. The sun is rising in a blaze of orange against the white plaster wall of his room. Bao sits up slowly. The wrenching pain in his intestines has subsided, and amazingly, he feels hungry. The porter downstairs is unsurprised at Bao's recovery, attributing it to the medicine shop.

"It used to be managed by the previous owner's widow," he says. "A very clever lady. She was the fourth wife—all the other ones died. Too bad she's not in charge of business decisions anymore."

"What happened?" Bao watches as the man sketches a map of the area, marking the photography shops for him.

"Some say the daughter-in-law, Madam Huang, sent her to live in the back of the house, but likely she simply retired."

THERE ARE TWO photographers that the porter knows of. Studying the hand-drawn map, Bao notes that one of the shops is nearby. His legs feel shaky, but his stomach is more settled. If he should drop dead of food poisoning here, it would be most inconvenient for his older brother.

He has no luck at the nearest photographer's shop, which is closed. It's run by a Japanese man named Oda. Perhaps later. People mill in the wide city streets, packed with new businesses and the fresh faces of country laborers.

The second shop is run by a Han Chinese who has no patience for him. "I don't answer questions about clients." He waves the photograph away suspiciously without a glance. "I've never heard of Bektu Nikan either. Why are you asking?"

Bao explains he's looking for a missing woman, and the man averts his eyes. "If you're looking for scandal, try the Japanese photographer, Oda."

"Why's that?"

"Some of his clients have vanished."

Bao takes a wild stab in the dark. "Is this anything to do with foxes?"

"Foxes? Funny you should say that. Oda has a friend staying with him—a very handsome man. It's said that whoever goes out drinking with him disappears. Married women also flock to get their pictures taken at Oda's studio. At least one divorce is pending where the husband said his wife was bewitched."

"Is this man a photographer, too?"

"No, just a friend of his. But I don't think it's fair that Oda has been drumming up business using a gigolo."

Bao's eyebrows rise. The word "bewitched" sets off alarm bells. He's just come from Mukden, where at least two women have been found abandoned in alleyways. Is it possible that it's the same person?

"Rich young people are going to parties with too much

opium and drinking. There's even a rumor going around that a fox has been eating people's livers. That's why I won't have anything to do with them. Our business is very respectable." The man draws himself up, pressing his lips together. He looks as though he regrets talking too much, but Bao's heart thumps uncomfortably. His chest tightens; his blood pressure rises.

Foxes, foxes.

And now someone is accused of eating livers.

37

*I*must tell you about the curious incident I referred to at our last
meeting. These words made me sit up and read Takeda's
letter closely.

*The truth is that people die at very inconvenient times. Nobody
knows exactly when his last hour on earth will come* . . . blah
blah—I skipped over Takeda's long-winded philosophizing.

*The morning after I arrived at Wang's villa, I rose early for a
stroll in the garden. None of the guests were about, having drunk
too much the night before, so I was surprised to hear raised voices
nearby. Pushing my way through a thicket, I discovered two
people talking through a side gate. It was bolted, but the top part
had a metal grille through which they conversed. The man on the
inside was a thickset fellow who reminded me of an ex-wrestler.
The young man on the outside looked like a university student.
He seemed highly agitated.*

*"I sold my mother's jewelry and have nothing left. You prom-
ised me the photographs in return!"*

"If you don't pay in full, I shall send them to your grandfather."

"Have you no mercy?"

*I didn't hear the other man's reply, for with a sudden cry of
despair, the young man dashed his head against the gate. Blood
spurted from his forehead as he collapsed in sobs. The other man
observed him coolly for a few minutes, then said, "You must
come up with the payment. I, too, desperately need money."*

*At that the young man staggered away down the side path.
I didn't know who to follow, the man on the inside, who'd
walked swiftly back to the main house, or the student. From
their dress, neither appeared to be servants. After wavering, I
unbolted the side gate and ventured out, but unfortunately lost
sight of the young man.*

*I returned to the villa wondering who the other man was.
If he was a guest, I never saw him again, despite my discreet*

inquiries. The next day, I heard from a servant that a university student had thrown himself off a nearby bridge and drowned.

"Had he a wound on his head?" I asked.

The servant was much astonished at my perception. "Why, yes, he did."

I therefore deduced that he must have been the same young man who'd been blackmailed. I found this incident both disturbing and intriguing. Who was the other party and where did he disappear to?

I sighed and put the letter down without reading his further theories and exposition. What a tragedy! Despite Takeda's florid, rhetorical account, I could easily solve his little mystery: the man on the inside must have been Bektu Nikan. None of the other guests, nor Mr. Wang, recognized this description because Bektu wasn't a guest. He occupied a nebulous position in the household in which he came and went at odd times. Mr. Wang barely thought of him unless his services were required, and it didn't sound like Takeda had done a good job questioning people anyway.

I wished I'd known earlier that Bektu had a side business in blackmail. Now I understood his hostility when I'd tried to stall him by babbling about "private photographs." No wonder he'd been so suspicious! I'd really made a mess of things today; it could hardly get worse.

A FOOTFALL IN the corridor recalled me to the present. I stuffed Takeda's letter into a drawer and jumped up, expecting my mistress. But it was none other than Shiro.

Closing the sliding doors behind him, he murmured, "You've really outdone yourself. After I specifically told you not to go after Bektu until my other business was settled."

We knelt on the tatami, facing each other warily.

"Why didn't you tell me that Bektu was resistant to foxes?"

"I thought you knew. After all, you're the one who's been chasing him. If you'd bothered to share your secrets, we wouldn't have such misunderstandings."

I raised an eyebrow. It's an art I've perfected over the years, telegraphing disdain at a distance. But hostility wasn't getting me anywhere, so I said, "I shall need your help. Are you willing?"

Shiro smiled. In the afternoon sunlight, his tea-colored eyes glinted. It was a very pretty effect. "Of course. What do you want?"

"I want to get rid of him."

"Painfully? Quietly? Painfully *and* quietly?"

What would best avenge my child? Was I really doing this for her, or for myself? My motives were becoming hazy, unraveling like a purplish-black fog and confusing me with creeping tendrils of doubt. This bargain might bind me to more than I'd expected. As if reading my mind, Shiro said, "Of course we must discuss the price."

"Which is?"

"Ten years," he said. "That's rather cheap for a man's life, don't you think?"

"Ten years—are you crazy? I could go out and hire someone to cut his throat tomorrow."

"How about a year then?"

"No."

"One night. That's my best offer."

I considered this carefully. What project did Shiro require me to embark on for one night? Foxes sometimes aid each other; we are comrades, after all. Shiro is so fickle that a night's work could range from robbing a bank to slaughtering all the geese on a lake.

"One night of what?"

"Of passion."

"With whom?"

He looked hurt. "With me, of course. Can't you tell how I've pined for you?"

"No, no, no." I leaped up, but he was faster, catching me in an embrace. We tumbled over, breathless, on the floor. The more I struggled, the more disheveled my clothes became, riding up over my legs, so I stopped abruptly to tug them down. I could feel the thump of his heart. Strangely, it was beating wildly, as though he was nervous or happy.

That was another warning. I don't like it when Shiro is too pleased.

The warm weight of his body seeped into me, a pure animal comfort. It had been a long time since anyone had held me in their arms, and for some reason it made me feel like crying. Shiro held me tight. Not grabbing as I'd expected, but almost tenderly. With one hand, he smoothed the loose hair from my face. "It's a good deal. You won't regret it."

"Rubbish," I said, closing my eyes. They snapped open an instant later when I felt the heat of his mouth, the soft pressure of his lips. I bit down so hard that I tasted blood, though it wasn't mine. He let me go then, wiping his lip. The bright red smear reminded me of what I'd set out to do that morning, and I shuddered. I really had no stomach for blood anymore.

Shiro said, "Will you ask Kuro, then?"

I shook my head vehemently. That was even less of a possibility.

"He's busy with his own affairs," said Shiro. "Very busy indeed. My poor Snow, when will you learn?" He gave a sharp, bright smile. The blood running down his mouth made him look slightly crazed, yet lethal—no doubt some foolish girl would fall for it. He wiped it away delicately; his other arm tightened around my shoulders. "I'm much more efficient than most people. Besides, I'm tired of being alone."

Loneliness. I'd lived with it for almost two years, that aching void when the snow fell like an endless soft curtain. Dark nights, alone. Freezing dawns, also alone. No mewling chirp to greet me, no sweet child to nuzzle into my warmth. There was a prickling in my chest as though my breasts were swelling with milk again. A burning flush rose in my cheeks. Perhaps it was the presence of another fox, or maybe Shiro was simply exerting every bit of his charm, but I was overcome by a frightening wave of emotion.

"Shiro," I said, "you are going to kill me."

"How absurd. I try not to leave a trail." He bent his head close. Iron scent of blood on his lips. I shivered. "Do you want another child?"

The spell broke. I leaped up, kneeing him in the thigh.

"Don't speak to me of children!" Seizing a vase from a nearby table, I hurled it at his head. It shattered against the wall, and I heard the distant alarmed sound of doors opening and footsteps approaching.

"I don't need your help getting rid of Bektu Nikan!"

Instead of becoming angry, Shiro gave me a wry look. "Think about it. Not many can give you what you desire."

I WILL SPARE you the ignominious spectacle as the housekeeper, my old lady, and even Chen showed up to gawk. It was obvious that we'd been fighting. No amount of distraction or polite words was going to erase my rumpled clothes, the bite mark from yesterday on my neck, and the blood running from Shiro's lip. He didn't even bother to pretend. "A lovers' quarrel," he declared airily. Beyond him, I saw the silent shape of Kuro and even Miss Yukiko. She covered her face delicately, embarrassed for me.

I wanted to sink into a pit or, failing that, burn the entire house down. I looked like a cheap woman; I could see it in the curl of Chen's lip, recalling, no doubt, how I'd suggested a rendezvous in a bush. Nobody, I noted, cast judgmental eyes on Shiro as he exited triumphantly. It was my mistress who closed the doors on them.

"Now," she said, straightening my clothes, "what happened to you?"

I expected to be fired. That's the usual human reaction to scandal. Recklessness, fighting, lasciviousness—foxes embody the animal traits that humans abhor, though they practice them all. But my old lady looked at me with sad eyes. Dazed, I sat down. I could still smell Shiro's faint musk on me—the scent of a male fox in his prime.

"Is he the one?" she said. "I think you know each other from before."

At my surprised glance, she said, "I saw you talking on the ship's deck, but I didn't want to pry."

"Shirakawa and I are old acquaintances," I said. It reminded me of Kuro's careful response to my mistress when she'd asked if Shiro was trustworthy. Only Kuro had delivered it calmly, and I was a mess, with tearstains on my face from crying in the garden earlier. In the last few days, I was steadily unraveling. Nothing was going right.

"The two—no, the three of you are very alike," she said.

"Who?"

"You, Shirakawa, and Kurosaki." I was alarmed at this insight, but my mistress merely looked dreamy. "So much emotion. Perhaps your fates are bound together."

Fate is whatever you make of it, I wanted to shout. The mark of a fox is to disrupt order. But I didn't have the heart to tell her that.

"I don't think Kurosaki is emotional at all," I said stiffly. "He's a block of wood."

"Oh no!" she said, and I remembered what a big fan of Kuro's she was (along with the housekeeper and Miss Yukiko). "I think he's someone who feels things intensely. Forever, probably."

I sighed. Shiro has his way of getting under people's skin, and so does Kuro. It's a different way, but they end up with the same results. Namely, I always get burned.

"Let me clean up," I said penitently, mindful that my mistress shouldn't be sweeping up broken porcelain. She seemed genuinely fond of me, though sometimes I wondered whether that was because she was crazy about foxes.*

"I'm getting old—few things surprise me. But throwing vases at Mr. Shirakawa crosses the line, especially since this isn't my house."

I assured her that I'd make it up.

"Are you sure you don't want to get married again?" she said. "Being single makes you a target. When we return to Dalian, I'll try to make you a good match."

"What's a good match to you?" To me, a good match is— well, I won't go into details here, but I've been sorely disappointed in the past.

"A steady man who doesn't drink or smoke opium. A good

*People who love foxes too much can also be a burden, especially if it is romantic love—an obsessive attachment that often leads to one of the parties dying.

livelihood, with no debts. Oh, and an easygoing mother-in-law." She listed these qualities gravely.

"What about love?" After all, she'd described her own marriage in bleakly practical terms.

"I never had that chance myself."

"Are you thinking of your childhood friend—the one you told about the black fox?"

"I wonder . . ." She folded and unfolded the damp cloth she'd used to blot the spilled water. "Through the long years of my marriage, when my husband had little to say to me, I sometimes pretended that I was talking to my dear friend. But he was surely married long ago. His mother had many plans for him." Her face wrinkled mischievously. "None of which included me."

38

Bao is alarmed yet intrigued by this mention of someone eating livers. When pressed, the man clams up, claiming not to know the details other than that two people have been found dead. They were wealthy dilettantes; likely their families paid to cover up the scandal.

In any case, Bao isn't here to investigate other unexplained deaths. He's hunting his mysterious fox lady, with the increasing certainty that he's drawing nearer. The words that spill from people's lips have the clear tone of truth, like fine white jade. When Bao's wife died, she requested that he bury every necklace, ring, and bracelet that he ever bought for her in her grave. It was an odd request, but Bao understood it was because his wife was afraid he would remarry.

None of it was to go to a second wife or concubine.

She dared not make him promise. That would be unbecoming, as a faithful wife should seek her husband's interests. Many arranged for concubines or maids to take over after their deaths, but by the end of her long illness, Bao's wife was no longer willing to pretend such selfless devotion. He was to be hers for always, and Bao, taking pity on her emaciated arms, too thin to bear the weight of the jade bangles, understood.

"Tell me again how you saw me across the bridge, wearing that pink blouse," she said. "And how you decided right then that you'd marry me."

Bao obediently repeated his plainspoken tale. He knew his wife longed for embellishments, but that wasn't his way. At the end, she pressed his hand. "Am I your first love?"

Because she was dying, her lips pale and sunken over her teeth, Bao hesitated. Yet it was precisely because she was dying that he couldn't bring himself to have the last words she heard be lies. Instead, he simply squeezed her hand back.

"Don't give anyone my jewelry," she said. "Don't give them anything that was mine."

BAO PAUSES OUTSIDE a store selling roast duck, recalling his wife's words. His relatives had been dismissive. In life, they'd never particularly liked her, not even his mother, who'd arranged the match in the beginning. Strange how that turned out.

His mother had interviewed his prospective wife, meeting her informally at mahjong parties and invitations to write poetry and drink tea. "The third daughter of the Liang family is soft-spoken and learned," she said. "And her bound feet are very small."

"How many inches?" his aunt asked.

"I'm told three and a half," said his mother. "Though they seemed larger than that to me."

Bao, sitting with them in his mother's salon, said nothing. The size of a woman's foot was said to indicate her virtue and her willingness to endure pain for her husband's pleasure. He preferred Tagtaa's feet, sturdy enough to kick a ball. The scent of white narcissus in the porcelain bowl next to him was sweetly cloying.

"What do you think, Bao?" His aunt peered at him.

"I will do what Mother wishes," he said.

Yet in the end, his mother had been displeased with his wife. Her extreme timidity, her nervousness, her frail physique that bore no children were all disappointments. In an unguarded moment, he overheard his mother say, "I should have let Bao take that Mongolian concubine's daughter as a second wife. She was strong-minded and didn't cry all the time. At this rate, we shall have no grandchildren from him."

Bao, pausing outside his father's study, had grimaced, wondering whether to laugh or be angry. In the end, he had simply walked on.

Decades have passed since then. Enough time for his mother and wife to leave this world. He imagines them meeting each other in some hall of the afterlife, criticizing his new choice of career. It's an uncomfortable thought and Bao glances behind him. But there's no one, only the pale flicker of his shadow. Does it seem even fainter than when he first examined it, in his brother's study? He wonders, suddenly and irrationally, if the fading of his shadow might be connected to the increasing pain in his chest, as though his life is seeping away.

He's been standing outside the roast duck shop for so long that the proprietor comes out to eye him. Embarrassed, Bao buys a portion of braised goose and rice. It's too rich for him to eat, coming off his food poisoning, and he wonders what possessed him. Not having anything better to do, he walks to a nearby park to pass the time before trying the Japanese photographer's shop again.

Men have brought birds in cages to the park, swinging them to make them flutter. There are women, too, walking with companions. Compared to his youth, fewer girls have bound feet, and Bao is glad. Tagtaa would have approved.

I didn't give away what was yours, he thinks ruefully to his departed wife. *Tagtaa had a portion of my heart from before.*

Bao shakes his head. What an old fool he is. Rising creakily to his feet, he places the opened packet of braised goose neatly under a bush. It's an offering to the foxes, though there are probably none in this city. Perhaps a stray cat will eat it instead. He bows his head briefly and makes a wish.

RETURNING TO ODA's photography shop, Bao is disappointed that the shutters are still drawn. Someone else, however, is waiting outside: a woman, her clothes a fashionable mix of European and Manchu dress, with a fur pelisse draped over her shoulders. As Bao approaches, she turns expectantly. She has an expensively powdered complexion and strong features; her eyes flick away from his in disappointment.

Since she obviously doesn't want to talk to him, Bao keeps quiet. Another five minutes pass while the lady keeps checking her slender gold wristwatch. Finally, a thin figure with a concave chest and sleekly parted hair appears. He gives a start when he sees the woman and almost turns around, but she's too quick.

"Oda!" she calls out. "Have you had any news?"

"No, I haven't heard from Shirakawa."

"Are you sure?" Her hands twist the slim leather strap of her handbag.

"You know he's gone to Japan. I've no idea when he'll come back."

The lady's rouged mouth opens, but Oda, seeing Bao, says hastily, "Excuse me, I must attend to this customer."

Unlocking the door, he ushers Bao into the shop. The woman follows stubbornly. From Oda's anguished glance, Bao guesses that she's come before. Bao says quietly, "Please excuse us, madam. I'm here for a private conversation."

She hesitates, then turns to go. Oda says with relief, "How may I help you?"

Bao produces the photograph. "Have you seen her?"

Oda's eyes dart sideways. "Oh yes. She's . . . Shirakawa's friend."

"Who's Shirakawa?" Bao sounds like somebody's grandfather, and Oda blanches, assuming he's a relative. Afraid that he'll clam up, Bao puts on his saddest, most trustworthy face. "I just want to know if she's all right."

"Shirakawa is an acquaintance of mine. As you saw, he has a lot of friends."

Meaning, no doubt, the lady waiting outside earlier. Bao wonders if Shirakawa is related to the disappearances hinted at by the other shop owner. "Friend" has many connotations, and in this case, it sounds suspicious. "How do you know Shirakawa, if I may ask?"

Confusion clouds Oda's face. "Let's see, how did I meet him? He's an old friend from . . ." His voice drifts off. "How strange, I can't recall right now. He even stayed with me for a while. But I don't know how he's acquainted with your granddaughter. She came by the shop before, with the young master from the medicine shop and his grandmother. And later, I ran into her when Shirakawa brought her to the house." He wipes his forehead, and Bao wonders why he looks so rattled. "Anyway, he's not here anymore. He sailed to Moji and won't return anytime soon."

"I see." Bao frowns. He doesn't see, not at all. "Would you say they were well acquainted?"

"They seemed to know each other. Your granddaughter speaks excellent Japanese. Are you by any chance also fluent?"

"Not at all." Now this is really surprising.

Regaining his composure, Oda clamps his lips into a tight smile. "I don't know any more than that. I'm very sorry, I thought perhaps you might have a Japanese connection as well."

And that's all that Bao can get out of him.

THE SHARP SUNSHINE outdoors makes Bao squint. Leaving the shop, he starts walking. Soon, he hears her. Swift clip-clop of shoes, then she passes him in a waft of expensive foreign perfume. Drops back, glancing at Bao. Now she's the one who wants to strike up a conversation.

Ladies of good family, no matter how fashionable or modern, don't roam around waiting outside photographer's shops and accosting strange men. She's neither young nor old, handsome enough, though flashily dressed. To Bao, she looks like the mistress of a Russian financier.

"Excuse me," she says. "Can I have a moment of your time?"

"Of course."

Reassured by Bao's age and respectability, she suggests they go to a nearby restaurant. It smells of stale cooking oil and there are grease stains on the table. The lack of clientele suggests the food isn't very good, but the lady sits down as though she doesn't care. It's simply a convenient place to interrogate him. Two cups of indifferent tea appear in front of them, and Bao orders a bowl of noodles with pickled mustard greens. She doesn't order anything.

"Were you asking about Shirakawa?" she says.

"I'm looking for someone who might be connected to him."

"Is it a woman?"

Bao takes out the photograph of the fox lady. A red flush suffuses her face and her eyes well up. Alarmed, he proffers his handkerchief, but she fishes out her own. Dabbing at her eyes, she says dully, "So that's why he's gone."

"I'm afraid I don't understand," says Bao. "Have you seen her before?"

The noodles arrive, steaming hot and topped generously with pickled greens.

"I saw her when he was leaving," she says. "I went to the harbor to say goodbye to Shirakawa. There were a few others. It was awkward." She looks up at him suddenly. "Silly, isn't it? I don't even know why I'm talking to you now."

Bao knows why. It's because he's a stranger who's also looking for someone. And because of his sympathetic gaze. He feels guilty about exploiting this.

"What did Oda say?" she asks.

Briefly, Bao recounts their conversation. He calculates that telling her he's an investigator will get him further. Perhaps it's her boldness, her bitten mouth tinted with rouge so dark it's almost purple. Her businesslike tenacity that reminds him of Qiulan from the brothel. It's better to talk as one professional to another.

Bao says, "How do you know Shirakawa?"

"I met him at a flower-arranging club. The instructor brought him to demonstrate a technique for bending branches by wiring them. I don't remember much about the lesson; I ended up watching his hands, not the flowers. Such beautiful, elegant hands. Afterwards, I stayed behind, as did half the class. I felt like I'd spent the last hour in another century." She colors unexpectedly. "He's like the person of your dreams. I'm not excusing myself. You know, I have a patron, and he'd be very angry to find out about this."

So Bao was right. She's indeed somebody's pampered mistress. *The person of your dreams* reminds him of something, a faint ringing in the back of his head, though he can't think of it just yet.

"My family was from ancient nobility, descended from the Duke of Zhou, but nowadays we've nothing left but pride. My relationships have been strictly pragmatic. I knew perfectly well what Shirakawa was up to; I told myself to be careful, even as I watched other women lose their heads over him."

She pulls her pelisse a little tighter around her shoulders, although it's warm inside the noodle shop, with the steam billowing off the soup vats and the acrid scent of burning charcoal. "It's all right to talk here," she says to his unspoken question. "My patron never goes to places like this, and if any-one sees us, I'll say you're my uncle."

"Was Shirakawa supported financially by women?"

"Of course. He'd no money—he said so himself. That's part of his charm. If you ask, he'll tell you. I don't know whether that was intentional, or if he was simply careless. I rather liked that; it made me feel alive." Her eyes shine.

Bao feels sorry for this middle-aged lady with the heart of a young girl. Whoever Shirakawa is, he must be trouble. "How old would you say he was?"

"I never asked; he looked younger than me. Between twenty-five and thirty-five, I'd guess. My pride didn't want to know. Sometimes he gave me advice that felt as though he were much older. Yet he was also childish. Once I surprised him by buying an entire roast duck and leaving it on his bed as a joke. He was so delighted that you'd have thought I'd given him a bag of gold. Though he liked money, too," she says wryly.

The image of this well-dressed woman playing a prank with a roast duck is so unexpected that Bao can't help but think of the braised goose and rice that he left under a bush. A present for the foxes. His companion continues, "Everyone who met him was charmed. I even introduced Shirakawa to my patron once, about a business venture. I was nervous, though nothing came of it in the end. He wasn't afraid to take risks."

"Do you think he might have been an actor?"

"I did wonder that myself. I tried to look him up once, by hiring someone like you."

So this is why she's happy to talk to an investigator. "Did you find anything?"

"I'd lent him a large sum of money, and one of my girl-friends said I should make sure he wasn't spending it on other women. So I hired a man to follow him, but Shirakawa found out right away—I don't know how he knew. And he was so angry." She shivers. "I promised I'd never do it again. Still, though he has a Japanese name, he struck me as being local. He spoke several dialects of Chinese as well as Korean. I even heard someone once address him as Mr. Kim."

Bao thinks of Feng, frozen on a snowy night on a back doorstep. "Did he ever go to Mukden?"

"Yes, he traveled a great deal around the northeast."

Things are beginning to line up in an interesting way. "You mentioned seeing this woman at the harbor with Shirakawa. Did they know each other?"

As expected, this dampens the conversation, returning to the unhappy fact that Shirakawa boarded a steamship and left her.

"At the time, I didn't consider it." The droop of her eyelids expresses her disappointment. "I noticed her though; she was accompanying the grandmother of that famous medicine hall."

"What was your impression?"

"At first, I thought Shirakawa was staring at the grandmother and wondered if he'd borrowed money from her."

"Really?" says Bao.

She lets out a sad snort of laughter. "Yes, really. I wouldn't put anything past him. Yet I still care for him madly. Then I realized he was watching her servant. Fierce yet pleased. Like he was going to eat her one day.

"She didn't pay him much attention. In fact, I rather thought she disliked him." Compressing her lips, she rummages in her handbag and produces a slim cigarette. A worldly, modern woman, yet she's sitting here in a dingy noodle shop, obsessing over Shirakawa. The arch of her plucked brows expresses discontent at herself, though she has a bitter sense of humor.

"When I took a good look at her, I understood—well, you've seen her photograph. Good complexion, the kind you don't see in the city, only in the countryside. I'm surprised that old grandmother dared hire her. Letting her into the house would be like opening the door to a fox."

That word again. *Fox.* "And she wasn't friendly to him?"

"No. You'd think they'd have nothing in common, a servant like her and a gentleman, as Shirakawa claims to be, yet they were alike. As I glanced at each of them, I felt more and more disturbed. My heart started racing and I felt dizzy, as though I were being pulled in two different directions."

"Did Shirakawa give you any medicine or perfume?"

"Was I drugged, you mean? I don't see how. Though I've wondered before whether Shirakawa was drugging me." She sinks her chin into her hands. "When I'm with him, I can't think of anything else. The way he tilts his head when the wind's blowing, and how he smiles out of the corners of his eyes. I really feel almost crazy. When he's gone, I recover myself. I can read novels again, see my friends for lunch. Buy new clothes, though there's a yawning emptiness in my heart, and I search frantically for him. Believe me, when he said he was going to Japan, part of me was actually relieved."

"How so?"

"I told you, my family's very proud. You could say I'm the same. My patron has a Russian wife in Vladivostok, but I'm the one who hosts his parties and helped him make connections here. Since I met Shirakawa, I've lost my independence; I pine desperately. When I can't see him, I behave like all the irrational women I've despised in the past, the ones who secretly snip locks of their lover's hair and cry all night. He's a terrible man."

The words spill from her mouth, reminding Bao of his bout of vomiting from food poisoning. "Are there others like you?"

"There are certainly other women, like the widow of the dry goods store. I ran into her last week. When I asked if she'd any news about Shirakawa, she looked at me as though she didn't know who I was talking about. Can you imagine that?"

Bao recalls Oda's peculiar vagueness about the man he said had lived in his house for a while.

"I had to remind her that we'd taken flower-arranging classes together. It was so odd that I wondered if she was playing a joke on me. After all, she's the one who rented out an entire restaurant to celebrate Shirakawa's birthday. How could she say she didn't know him?" The lady bites her nails, as though the doubts in her mind have nibbled away at them like mice.

"I heard rumors about people going missing," says Bao. Could the strange alleyway disappearances in Mukden and here in Dalian have the same perpetrator? He mustn't jump to conclusions, yet his heart is hammering.

"Maybe." Her mood darkens. "Shirakawa socialized with dilettantes, the younger sons of wealthy families. There were a few disappearances, though it's rumored that some students who study abroad become revolutionaries. Maybe they vanished, if there were spies within their ranks. Politics isn't something I want to get involved in."

"What about the talk of livers being eaten?"

She blinks, unsettled. "One person was discovered in an alleyway; wild animals might have got at the body." But her face has turned pale. Even her lips, beneath their coat of rouge, look white. Her eyes are imploring, yet angry. *Save me from myself*, they seem to say.

Bao says, "I'm sorry to upset you."

She recovers her composure. What a strange, furtive conversation they've had, almost like old friends meeting up except all she's done is talk about this mysterious Shirakawa. It's like one of those dreams where you meet peculiar people and talk in a dark space, steam rising around them from the giant bamboo steamers filled with dumplings and steamed buns. The emptiness of the restaurant, the sticky floor. The sensation of being displaced from the normal flow of time and circumstances, discussing the secrets of an unknown world that lies parallel to theirs. She hasn't lied, though there are slanted omissions. Especially the last bit, about disappearing people.

"I hope you find the woman you're looking for," she says. "If you meet Shirakawa, tell him I'm waiting for him."

It's only after she's gone, in a final waft of foreign perfume, that Bao realizes that he doesn't know her name. Running after her, he presses his business card into her hand. She takes her own calling card out. It's printed on thick cardstock; her name is Zhou Yuling. "Yuling" means "jade bell," and Bao is suddenly and illogically reminded of his wife's injunction to bury her jewelry in her grave. He wonders what other secrets this lady is hiding in her heart, though she seems more concerned with unearthing Shirakawa's.

"Let me know if you hear of him. You seem trustworthy. And I need a friend."

What an odd thing to say. Surely a woman like her wouldn't need a friend, but there's no lie in her words. Bao returns to his soggy noodles and the glare of the shopkeeper, who was afraid Bao was planning to eat and run. The whole conversation reminds him uncomfortably of another one: a little girl in the back courtyard of a brothel, telling him, *If you meet the fox lady, tell her I'll be waiting for her.*

39

After my mistress was settled for the night, I took a bath. I'd waited till all the servants were done. My ambiguous status made them uneasy, so I'd eaten dinner gloomily by myself, sitting on the back step with salt-grilled fish, two rice balls, and a pickled plum.

The moon was shrouded by wisps of cloud. Nights like this are good for prowling, though I wouldn't be doing any sneaking around tonight. Bektu Nikan would be on his guard—I'd even announced my intentions, loudly, to half the household this afternoon during my fight with Shiro. Too many mistakes are dangerous for a fox.

Picking up my bundle of clothes, I headed over to the bathhouse, a small, detached building with a cast-iron tub heated from the outside by firewood. After scrubbing and rinsing yourself thoroughly outside the tub, to keep the water clean for others, you stepped on a floating wooden tub lid when you entered. The weight of your body pressed the wood down to the bottom to avoid your feet being burned by the heated iron tub. Children were too light to do this by themselves, and thus must go in with an adult.

I found that I could think about children quite calmly again, though the ache in my heart would never vanish. At one point, I'd clung to the pain as a reminder that my child had existed, but I was beginning to let her go. I wondered if that was a betrayal.

Sitting in the warm bath (now rapidly cooling), I considered my options. I could hire someone to slit Bektu's throat, but that wasn't the way debts were paid, at least not in the old days. A proper blood debt was repaid face-to-face, ideally with a recounting of sins—I'm a stickler for old traditions. While I was soaking, I heard the clunk of firewood being added to the bath furnace outside, then the steady pump of bellows.

"Thank you," I called through the bathhouse's small, high

window, assuming at first it was the young manservant. But the steps were too heavy and deliberate. What if someone decided to stoke the fire up enough to boil me? Alarmed, I splashed upright in a wave of water.

"Don't get out. It's me."

He spoke quietly, yet I knew his voice. Kuro continued to add wood to the fire, carefully and methodically. Sinking back under the water, I listened to his movements outside.

"Are you all right?" he said at last. "You didn't look well today."

Of course not. Today had been an utter failure. I said, "I'm fine."

"What happened with Shiro?"

I let the water idly run down one arm as I thought of a suitable reply. "I asked him for help. His price was too high."

"Help with what? With whoever Bektu Nikan is?"

Not being able to see Kuro made this conversation easier, yet unbearable. Easier because I didn't have the urge to stab him, but dreadful because his voice filled me with sadness. There were so many questions I had, including where the scar on his face had come from; I laced my fingers tightly to stop myself. "You promised not to interfere."

I thought I heard him sigh, or perhaps it was the flames hissing in the cold air. "I will do it for you. Whatever you want."

"I told you, I don't want to talk to you anymore."

Silence. One of those long silences in which I could hear the leaves rustle in the night breeze.

"You and I agreed a long time ago to walk a better path," he said. "It is not yet lost for you. Let me be the one to soil my hands instead."

"This has nothing to do with you." I splashed angrily. "Did you hear me? I forbid it!"

No answer, only the faint crackling pop of the fire.

I HATE IT when people make decisions for me. Especially when it's done in a noble and valiant way, the way Kuro goes through life. You know those heroes of old, the ones willing to throw themselves over a battlement to save a besieged citadel? Well, I don't know any of them either—at least not living ones. They all end up dead, and who's left to bury their mutilated bodies and write mournful poems to their starving families? The rest of us, that's who.

This is why I can't stand Kuro, because he makes me cry.

He also drives me crazy, though in a different way from Shiro. I got out of the bathwater, despite its being nicely heated, and hastily dressed, but when I rushed out, there was nobody there. Only the frosty stars above, shining in their uncaring way. A thousand years might pass, during which dynasties could rise and fall and a fox could attain sainthood, yet their faint, malicious sparkle wouldn't change. It was almost enough to make me give up.

Almost.

I still had to take care of my old lady; I'd promised to serve her for a while, and didn't want to add abandonment to my sins, so I crawled into bed. While I slept, I dreamed of a really good plan. One that would avenge my child and wipe out Bektu Nikan without requiring outside help. I was just getting to the best part, where I was triumphantly returning to Dalian on a boat laden with rice dumplings and fried pork chops, when a noise woke me up.

A creaking sound, as though someone was priming the pump for water, then sloshing. It was so still in the early dawn, the edge of the sky turning light, that it carried clearly across the kitchen yard. Rolled up in my cotton futon like a pill bug, I debated getting up to investigate. It was chilly, however, and I'd had an exhausting and disappointing day, so I burrowed deeper into my pillow (stuffed pleasantly with buckwheat hulls) and went back to sleep.

Later, I was to regret this.

MORNING ARRIVED. FIRES were stoked, amid the usual clatter of getting food on the table in a large household. I accompanied my mistress to breakfast. Bohai was sitting alone in the large room where they all dined. Usually, he slept in, so I was surprised at his appearance.

"Grandmother," he said as I placed trays of rice, miso soup, grilled sardines, and pickled eggplants in front of them, "I want you to get ready to leave."

"But we've hardly been here a week," she said.

He lowered his voice. "Keep this a secret from the others, but I think we should return to Dalian. I'm going to buy steamer tickets this morning."

My old lady looked worried. "Has something happened?"

"I shouldn't have let you come with us."

"Bohai!" she said sternly. "You must tell me what's going on."

There was an invisible struggle of wills, and she won. Of course she did. She'd been running the medicine shop since he was crawling on the floor; there was no way he could refuse her. In a low voice, he said, "I think there's an informer in our organization."

So, he'd told her about his revolutionary activities after all, likely the night we'd returned from picking herbs on the hillside. Many Chinese studying in Japan had anti-Imperial sentiments, yet among them were also spies recruited by the Qing government. It was a dangerous activity.

Bohai gnawed his lip. "If we leave now, I'll say I was merely accompanying my grandmother on a trip, and we had nothing to do with any of this."

She nodded. "Very well. You get the tickets, I'll be ready."

They stopped talking because Lu and Chen appeared for breakfast. I noticed that they, like Bohai, looked worried. Some news had arrived either late last night or early this morning, from their uneasy glances. After my mistress took her leave, I lingered in the corridor to listen.

"Should we leave?"

"The photographer Bektu Nikan is in town."

This last was of particular interest, reminding me of Takeda's note. What business did Bektu have with these young men? Strain as I might, however, I couldn't hear anything further.

Bohai and the other young men took turns going in and out on business to town. Their irritable, nervous glances reminded me of dogs penned up together. The path to rebellion is always surrounded with treachery; without knowing where their orders came from or which faction they'd allied with, I didn't give them much of a chance. Three wealthy, idealistic young men were prime targets for exploitation, even if it wasn't by Shiro.

"I HOPE BOHAI manages to buy tickets!" There was an anxious expression on my old lady's face. "If I'd known he was dabbling with revolution, I'd never have agreed to let him come to Japan to study. All that talk about sugar factories in Formosa was just a blind!"

"It could still be a viable business," I said. "And you coming along gives him an excuse to return home, so your presence here is a good thing."

She patted my hand. "You always make me feel better. It reminds me of how Bohai is so attached to Shirakawa."

Being compared with Shiro is no compliment; I hadn't seen a whisker of either him or Kuro all day either, which made me nervous. The tense atmosphere had even spread to the housekeeper, who muttered something about an unlucky day. According to *rokuyo*, the old Japanese system of six-day rotations, certain days were more or less fortunate than others. Today was apparently *butsumetsu*, a supremely unlucky day.

"The foxes on that hill must be active again," said the housekeeper. "That's why there are no houses built there, despite the good view. My grandmother said so, but people always forget."

I'd seen no sign of any other foxes in the area. Still, I couldn't shake my unease, as though a baby spider were walking delicately over my skin. To prepare for our return, I hung the laundry to dry on bamboo poles in the back courtyard, noting that the handle of the water pump had a red-brown stain, as though someone's hands had left a smear of blood. Perhaps the housekeeper had been rinsing fish or meat.

THAT AFTERNOON, THERE was a commotion at the front door. Everyone gathered hastily. The houseboy had returned from an errand and was bursting with news. "A man has been killed in town!"

"Who was it?" asked Chen.

"A Manchurian photographer who was staying at an inn near the harbor. I heard the police want to interview all the foreigners in the area who might have contacted him."

I gasped silently. My throat knotted, a rope drawn tight, tight.

So Bektu was dead.

Someone had got to him before me. My limbs felt heavy, my head thick and muffled. Dumbstruck, I froze, heart thudding uneasily. The young men gathered in the entryway looked fearful. A police investigation into foreigners in the area was bad news, particularly if they already had suspicions that their movement had been infiltrated by an informer. Nervousness rippled through them, like sheep in a meadow lifting their heads at a predator.

In the sudden hush, Shiro said languidly, "Dear me, how distressing. How did he die?"

The houseboy, eyes wide with this sensational news, said, "He was stabbed in his room. The maid found him in the morning, covered with blood."

There was a muffled shriek as the housekeeper pressed her hands to her face. "It's foxes," she moaned. "The foxes on the hill have started killing people again."

In the ensuing uproar, I wasn't sure how to feel—anger, relief, or perhaps both? I stared at Shiro. He has an excellent gambling face; it was hard to tell if he was shocked or even upset, which is why he's survived so many purges and wars. When he saw my eyes narrow, he gave a little shrug. "That's too bad, but it's nothing to do with us." Cool words, calculatingly reassuring.

Bohai said, "Shirakawa, what shall we do?"

"If the police wish to interview us, I'll be happy to talk to them."

A collective sigh of relief. The housekeeper was revived, though she kept babbling about foxes, a dangerous precedent.

Such rumors quickly spiral into frightened mobs. Even more worrying, where was Kuro? I didn't see him anywhere.

MY EXPERIENCE WITH police is that they're predictably xenophobic. A house full of strangers, who'd gone around raising money from rich men like Takeda, stuck out like the lone pine tree on a lightning-prone hill. If I were the local police, I'd swoop in and arrest Bohai and his friends simply for the crime of being foreigners.

Beyond that, who had killed Bektu, and why now? Bektu had been a photographer with dubious interests. I wondered if the maid at the inn would remember me—after all, an unknown woman who'd gone to his room the day before would be highly suspicious.

The more I considered this, the more I wanted to rush out and search Bektu's room myself. Confirm his death with my own nose and eyes, and howl with rage and confusion. But I had to refrain from this rash impulse; many a fox has walked into a trap out of sheer curiosity. Besides, if I waited long enough, it was likely that the police would come to us.

Sadly, I was right.

40

Zhou Yuling's perfume clings to the card that she's given Bao, a musky foreign scent. Bao watches as she disappears into the busy crowd. The expression on her face is determined; he wonders if her yearning for Shirakawa will disappear one day, just like the memories of his other acquaintances. Oddly, she seems a little more resistant than them.

After paying the bill, Bao returns to his hotel. Opening his notebook, he writes the name *Shirakawa* in it.

Despite his suspicions, there's no evidence that Shirakawa is the same handsome gentleman who abandoned two women in the snow in Mukden, or that he's deeply connected to the lady he's looking for. Bao is simply jumping to conclusions, seeing a fox behind every shadow. It would be ironic if he, too, were to succumb to a kind of mania about foxes.

Eating livers doesn't match the previous cases either. Perhaps, as Zhou Yuling said, one of the bodies was scavenged afterwards. The thought makes him shudder. Eating livers is an ancient atrocity that foxes are suspected of. When Bao was a child, he witnessed a mob tear the hair and clothes of a peddler accused of this crime, and still recalls the screaming, ferocious rush and the sour smell of terror, as though the people had all turned into beasts.

It's more likely that Shirakawa and the fox lady are fellow actors from an opera troupe. They share an aptitude for living on the fringes of society, are fluent in various languages, and have a knack for reading their audience. Bao should go to the medicine shop to inquire if she's still working there, or to the steamship ticket office to find out who boarded that ship, but exhaustion hits him. He's overtaxed himself, first with food poisoning and then by walking all over Dalian interviewing photographers and lovelorn mistresses.

Closing his eyes, Bao thinks of sloe-eyed women and gentlemen with elegant hands. People dying mysteriously.

41

The police arrived wearing smart uniforms and uncomfortable-looking hats. There were two of them, standing in the entryway and glancing around curiously. The older one had grown out his whiskers in the style of the Meiji emperor. Puffing them pompously, he announced, "A foreigner was murdered this morning. We've reason to believe he might have been connected to this household."

A shuffling of feet. It was almost comical how the young men placed themselves behind Shiro, so they formed a triangle with him at its point. At any moment, I half expected Bohai, Chen, and Lu to burst out in song, like a bad musical comedy. Of course they did nothing of the sort. Instead, their eyes swiveled to Shiro.

"Please come in. As you can see, my companions are students from good families. We've nothing to hide."

Shiro oozed courtliness and nobility. I don't know what the police were expecting, but they seemed taken aback. In fact, I was rather worried that Shiro had overdone things. This was, after all, a private home and not a palace waiting room.

I didn't realize I'd been gritting my teeth until Kuro came quietly in from the garden. I'd no idea where he'd been all day, but he'd likely been fetched by the housekeeper in a frenzy of anxiety. Dressed in a dark gray kimono of subtle weave, he looked sober and distinguished. "Gentlemen," he said.

"Ah, Kurosaki-*sensei*!" The senior police officer looked relieved. "I'm glad to see you."

They followed Kuro and Shiro into the receiving room, and the doors slid closed behind them. Bohai, Lu, and Chen stood uncertainly in the corridor, like schoolboys wondering what to do. Alarmed, I ran up and pressed my ear against the door. The young men hastily followed suit.

I heard the first officer say, "The man who died was a Manchurian photographer. From a letter found in his luggage—a letter originating from this address—it appears that he was instructed to come to Moji."

"That's right," said Shiro smoothly. "I asked him to take photographs of rare plants for Mr. Takeda. How shocking to hear of his demise! What happened?"

At the mention of Takeda, a rich financier, the police softened. Either that, or Shiro was doing his very best to sway them. I couldn't see what was going on in the room, but I heard the conciliatory shift in their tone.

"The maid discovered him dead in his room. He was stabbed late at night or very early this morning."

"Were there signs of a struggle?"

"No, but the inn is busy. It's also easy to get over the back wall," the younger policeman chimed in. "The body was lying on his futon, as though he'd been stabbed in his sleep. Likely with a common kitchen knife."

"Was it a robbery?"

"The maid mentioned he had a leather folio case that he warned her not to touch when she was cleaning. She said it had contained photographs, but it was empty when we examined it."

The police were being far too compliant. They must be susceptible to foxes, and I could only imagine that the combination of Shiro and Kuro in a private room was overpowering them. Really, they ought to be more careful. At this rate, I feared there'd be other wild rumors.

"Did anyone visit him before his death?"

"Quite a few people did, including an unknown woman the day before."

"Did you find her?" Kuro spoke for the first time.

"Not yet, though the maidservant said she wore a blue kimono with a *hanakago* design. There were also a couple of male visitors, but nobody saw their faces."

"So it could have been a simple robbery," said Shiro, exerting every bit of his charm.

"Yes . . ."

"And you don't need to interview anyone else in this household."

"No." Said with a faint air of surprise, as though the policeman was just realizing this. "Thank you for your time."

I jumped back from the door before they could slide it open. Bohai, Chen, and Lu were astonished and hugely relieved. Bursting with questions, their mouths hung open though nobody said anything as the police were shown out. The two officers appeared vaguely stunned, which concerned me. One should never overdo things because that sometimes backfires.

I've told you before that every action has an equal and opposite reaction. Those of us who can't control this balance inevitably end up dead—which is likely why Kuro said almost nothing during that brief interview.

I GAVE MY mistress an update on the police visit. She was agitated, and so was I, though for different reasons.

"I fear that Bohai went out last night," she said, twisting her hands. She'd been busy packing, ready to leave at dawn. "Last night, I woke up to use the facilities and thought I saw a figure cross the courtyard. I didn't think much of it, but now you tell me that photographer died, it makes me so uneasy."

"Perhaps whoever you saw last night couldn't sleep either."

"It was a man's figure, though I do hope it wasn't Bohai. Can you tell him I want to talk to him?"

I hurried off. Beyond the veranda, the moon rose, a slender crescent in the velvet sky. The shadows lingering in the corners seemed thicker, as though the darkness was gathering like soft black feathers or piles of inky soot. Bohai, Chen, and Lu were sitting together after dinner, drinking warmed bottles of sake against the spring chill, and eating roasted dried squid. Nobody looked happy.

"Your grandmother would like to see you," I told Bohai.

Chen glanced at me. "Please join us."

I was surprised and rather suspicious at this request. But I slid the door shut behind me.

"Since you're not a regular servant, but seem previously acquainted with Shirakawa, perhaps you can answer a few questions." Chen drew himself up, gravely pompous, as though he'd never propositioned me in the moonlight on top of a hilly slope.

Lu frowned. I'd noticed that he was the least likely to look me in the eye, as he addressed his remark to Chen and not me: "How do we know that's even true? She could have fed you a load of lies."

Bohai looked mulish. "I can vouch for her. Tell us more about Shirakawa. How was he able to persuade the police to leave like that?" The specter of an informant in their ranks, combined with Shiro's uncanny dismissal of the police, had clearly rattled them.

"I've no idea," I said. "Perhaps he was just very persuasive. Though if you have doubts, maybe you should go home."

There. I'd said I wouldn't meddle with humans anymore, but their callow faces elicited pity. These young men, sons of wealthy merchants playing at politics with their soft hands, had abandoned their studies in the service of revolution. They had no idea how torture could twist limbs and break spirits.

"Do you think Shirakawa was involved with Bektu's death?" Chen said to the others. My ears tingled.

"Why?" said Bohai.

"Because the police behaved so strangely this evening, almost as though they were reporting to him. They even mentioned a missing folio." Chen's eyes were shadowed. "If my father hears about this, he'll be furious."

Bohai shifted uneasily. "As long as he doesn't hear rumors of certain photographs . . ." His voice trailed off. "What if they arrest us after all?"

In the lamplight, their faces turned yellow as parchment. "We'd better leave as soon as possible," said Lu, his long face stiff with alarm.

"I'm going to look in on my grandmother." Bohai signaled me to follow him into the corridor.

As soon as we were alone, I said, "What did you mean by 'rumors of certain photographs'?"

Bohai hesitated, probably calculating that his grandmother would find out anyway and it was better to have me on his side. At the veranda, he indicated that we should talk in the garden. We walked in silence towards a decorative pond, surrounded by irises. He looked nervous.

"Bektu wasn't just a photographer. He was a courier for our revolutionary movement, though some said we shouldn't trust him because he was half Manchurian himself. As a photographer, he went to all sorts of places for work, so he was useful. I was concerned he was a risk, especially with his unsavory side business—he might sell us out to the Qing government."

"Did Shirakawa know that he was working for your organization?"

"Yes. He assured me that he'd handle Bektu if he got troublesome."

Bohai sounded as though he was trying to convince himself, but I was so furious that the roots of my hair stood up. My head blazed with rage, like a lit match.

So! Shiro had been keeping secrets from me as well.

His relationship with Bektu Nikan was more complicated than he'd let on. Shiro is flexible and opportunistic. Upon discovering I was hunting for Bektu, he'd likely decided that it would be convenient if I eliminated him, especially if Bektu's blackmailing habits were becoming a liability. Was he keeping me, even now, as a potential scapegoat?

Bohai said, "Why do you look so angry?"

In the dark, he seemed young and timid, a student who'd been swept up over his head. Who knew if this so-called revolutionary cell that he'd joined even existed? I wouldn't put it past Shiro to have invented the whole affair, ensnaring this trio of rich merchants' sons to milk them for funds. My mind was exploding with various possibilities, though my chief emotion—as Bohai nervously pointed out—was rage.

Controlling myself, I said, "I was just thinking how unfair this is to you."

Nod, nod, from Bohai. Yes, it was indeed terrible that he, a young master, should be embroiled in scandals like this.

I continued: "Why didn't you tell me earlier?"

"I just heard that there might be an informant. Also, I

thought you were working for Shirakawa. Though when I heard you arguing with him yesterday, I figured you'd be looking out for my grandmother, not him."

At least my fight with Shiro had come in handy.

"Don't mistake me," he added. "I want to believe in him—he's my good friend. If Bektu was indeed an informant, then perhaps Shirakawa was trying to save us." (I concealed a snort at this.) "Or maybe his death was just a robbery. I've been having doubts about this whole venture anyway, and I need to take care of my grandmother. Chen and Lu have lost their nerve as well."

I suppressed a sigh. This generation of young men was none too hardy. True zealots, the sort who can topple a dynasty, would think nothing of trekking day and night across the steppe, surviving on mare's milk and horse blood. That's the kind I'm talking about. But perhaps it was best to retreat before the strange goodwill of the police evaporated.

I STILL WASN'T sure whether to feel relieved or cheated that Bektu had died. To be honest, deep inside I'd known that hunting Bektu down wasn't right, but another part of me, the bitter knife-edged part, didn't care. What was the point of struggling on to complete a thousand years without my child? Numbly nauseated, I felt I was drowning in a sticky miasma of unease. His death hadn't resolved anything; I wasn't miraculously happier. Instead, it raised all sorts of painful sensations, a gnawing recognition that no further blood spilled would ever console me for the loss of my child.

For now, I buried my feelings deep in an imaginary hole on the frozen steppe. The way foxes cache extra food under the snow. Bektu Nikan was dead. Mentally, I added a large pile of rocks on top for good measure.

Bohai had been lucky to secure tickets, as a ship was setting out for Dalian tomorrow. It was empty enough that Chen and Lu, galvanized by Bohai's decision, had also bought passage, and since they seemed either too distracted or depressed to pack their own belongings, my mistress helped them. Meaning I was dispatched as well.

Approaching their quarters with a stack of folded clothes, I glimpsed Lu sullenly drumming his fingers on the windowsill and looking out. "Since Takeda has transferred the money, maybe we should really go to Formosa and open a sugar factory," he said.

"I don't want to go home either," said Chen. "You know what my father's like. I wish we'd asked more questions when we heard that student committed suicide near my uncle's villa. We might have discovered Bektu's liabilities earlier."

"You're overreacting—how were we to know?"

At my approach, they both shut their mouths abruptly. As I helped Chen pack his trunk, he fussed around nervously, complaining that I didn't know how to handle books and even removing a package to repack himself. I had to bite back the indignant retort that I'd once helped a monk cache some priceless Buddhist scrolls in a cave near Dunhuang (they may still be there to this day). Lu, too, seemed deeply uncomfortable, though I couldn't tell whether he was agitated with Chen, myself, or the police investigation.

THE NEXT DAY (a hasty day, rising early and securing all the luggage), we took our leave. Unlike our arrival, which had been filled with hope and adventure, it was an ignominious departure. Now the young men were anxious, glancing at every strange face for fear of being arrested. It was windy and warm, with sneezy clouds of pollen that dusted our clothes yellow.

I was sorrier than expected to be leaving Moji. The scent of the sea and the fluffy white clouds, the sunlight on the dark pine trees near the house, were all evocative of this land of earthquakes. They made me nostalgic; I'd expected a longer journey on to Tokyo with my mistress and was surprised at the disappointment and grief that welled up in my chest.

It had nothing to do with Kuro, I told myself. I'd said goodbye to that part of my life before and mustn't be sentimental. The whole day that we were preparing our departure, he hadn't come by once. My mistress had passed the closed door of his study several times, expressing timidly that she wished to thank our host.

"He's been called away on business," said Bohai. "I'll write him a letter."

"I wanted to see him one more time," she said.

"Grandmother, why are you so fond of Kurosaki?"

"He reminds me of my childhood. Also, I feel less worried when he's around."

I hated to admit it, but I, too, had felt better knowing Kuro was there that night the police came. Though another part of me, the dark, bitter despair that I tried so hard to bury, also feared what he might have done. Had he gone out into that chill starry night, after our talk through the bathhouse window, and killed a man on my behalf?

A busy inn, an easy wall to climb in the back. Bloodied hands. The sound of the water pump in the back courtyard in the silent hour before dawn.

If he had, it didn't make me happy at all.

42

Bao's food poisoning resurges almost triumphantly, as though his intestines are punishing him for neglecting them. *Walking around a strange city and interviewing photographers and mistresses was clearly the wrong choice*, they seem to say as they squeeze unrelentingly. Dull pangs rack him; he should have stayed quietly in bed.

Dozing fitfully, Bao dreams of foxes. A white one and a black one. They appear over the crest of a grassy knoll, trotting side by side. They have black noses: the white one is a true white fox, not an albino. The two foxes stop to look at him. The white one has dark eyes and a playful, winsome air. *A pretty vixen*, he thinks. The black fox is larger, a male with a white-tipped tail and an inscrutable gaze.

Something about the scene makes Bao think that it's from the past. Perhaps it's the light that fills the open sky, brilliantly clear sunlight on the fresh grass, such as his eyes, now cloudier than in his youth, haven't seen for years. Bao has never gone to such a wild and faraway place in his life, yet it's so vivid that he feels like weeping. Far away, a speck approaches in the sea of waving grass. The foxes tense; the hackles on the male's neck rise. And then Bao sees it. A third fox, as white as the vixen but larger, with amber-colored eyes.

Three foxes! Bao can hardly believe it. Even in his dream, it seems uncanny, and he wonders if it's a sign of fortune or something more ominous.

The third fox—another dog fox—emerges, straight-legged and wary. The foxes circle one another. Are they playing, conferring, or preparing to hunt? As though they've suddenly made up their minds, all three foxes lope away through the grass. The foxes break apart: two go one way; the third goes another. Bao wants to know which fox went where, and with whom, but it's impossible to tell in the long grass.

His eyes snap open. Bao is back in his hotel bed in Dalian. It's dark now, and after washing his face in the basin, he crawls back into bed. His dream of foxes was so vivid that he wants to return to that time again, when he himself was a child. It's nonsense, of course—sixty years ago, who knows if three foxes met in the grasslands—but seems real enough in the dimness of his room.

His stomach pains have subsided. Unable to sleep, Bao dresses and goes downstairs. At this time of night, there's no clerk. Bao pushes the front door open with the faint sensation of trespassing. The street outside is deserted, with the stillness that only the middle of the night holds. Chill air rushes around Bao's bare ankles, stuffed hastily into his felt boots. As he pokes his head out to gaze at the sky, the full moon is dimmed by shreds of racing clouds.

A shadow moves down the dark street; an animal, sniffing around. Too large to be a cat, he thinks it might be a stray dog. Or a fox. Boldly, they come in from the countryside, scavenging food and digging dens under people's houses. Bao wonders whether the packet of braised goose he left under a hedge in the park, as an offering to the fox god, has been accepted. Bringing his hands together, he murmurs a brief prayer. "Please let me finish well."

He walks out into the street, pulling his quilted jacket around him. Inhaling sharply, he feels the familiar ache in his chest. That, at least, hasn't gone away. If anything, it seems sharper, as though a rip in the balloon of his left lung is enlarging. There's nobody around, not even a night watchman. As his eyes become accustomed to the darkness, the whole street comes into focus, as though the shadows and moonlight are shifting in a mysterious realignment.

On such a night like this, ghosts can be seen, and bargains made with spirits—or so they say. His old nanny always cautioned him to stay indoors when the night wind was blowing.

Don't go out at night, she'd said, looking particularly at Bao and not his older brother. At the time, he'd dismissed it as babying him again. Up and down the street, cloth awnings and banners whip in the wind, shadows dancing in the shivery moonlight. As Bao turns to go back inside, he freezes.

He has no shadow.

43

The morning of our departure from Moji was bright and breezy. Spring had advanced in the brief time we'd been here, and the peony buds were plump knots of promise. The housekeeper looked relieved that we were leaving, but the young manservant had a disappointed air; likely the old house hadn't seen so much company in years.

My mistress was sad. There was no other way to describe her forlorn gaze at the house as our rickshaw rattled off on the white dusty road. "I wished to say goodbye to him," she said quietly.

Despite my own misgivings, I, too, had looked for Kuro, but neither he nor Shiro was anywhere to be seen. The young men had written elaborately polite thank-yous and goodbyes, not mentioning that they were running away from a possible police inquiry. Nervous, they could hardly wait to leave and boarded the ship as soon as passengers were permitted.

Only my mistress lingered. I'd taken care of her luggage, and as I walked back down the slippery gangway, I saw her small figure still standing there. It looked melancholy, despite the sunshine sparkling off the waves reflected against the painted port warehouses. As I watched, she raised her hand to wave at someone. It was Shiro. Following behind were Kuro and Miss Yukiko, no doubt to send him off.

"I didn't know you were joining us, Shirakawa!" said my mistress.

"I thought I might have to stay to wrap up business, but as it happens, everything worked out nicely," he said, with his crooked, charming grin.

Shiro had probably realized he'd overdone it with the police and had better disappear before they came to their senses. But I was looking at Kuro. In the bright sunlight, he looked deathly tired. I'd no idea where he'd been, but Kuro is not the kind of person to run around without reason. When he saw my old lady, he smiled faintly and offered her his hand.

She took it eagerly. "I'm glad to see you! It seemed churlish to leave without saying goodbye."

At that moment, I wished irrationally that I were the one standing there, holding Kuro's hand. It was a pain that pierced like an arrow, unnerving me—how often had he extended that steady grip in the past, once saving me from falling off a barge on Hangzhou's West Lake. If you'd told me a month ago that I'd meet Kuro again and long to touch him, I'd have snorted in your face, but now I was filled with a disturbing churn of emotions. I clenched my hands. I, too, would have liked to say goodbye properly, but that was not to be. Unnoticed, I stayed quietly a few paces away in the shadow of the ship.

Kuro said, "I found your letter on my desk when I returned. The housekeeper said you'd all bought passage on this ship."

"I must apologize for our sudden departure."

"There's no need to apologize. In fact, the imposition is mine. I am joining you today."

My old lady's face lit up; you'd have thought that she'd won a prize pony at a polo match. Glancing at her, Shiro raised one eyebrow humorously.

"So you're happier with Kurosaki than with me!" he said.

"Oh no, not at all," she protested. While they were smiling and laughing, I noticed someone else in great distress. Miss Yukiko, face pale and eyes swollen, could hardly hold back her tears. She'd been standing a little behind Kuro, the way women do with the men they love, and now I saw her delicate hand pluck his sleeve. Bending his head, he turned. I couldn't see his face, but her words carried to me on the wind, clear and imploring.

". . . is that why you talked to Grandfather yesterday?"

Realizing the awkward situation, my mistress and Shiro moved farther away.

"I gave him my answer," said Kuro.

"No!" she said. Then, controlling herself, "Must you go? Grandfather was disappointed. And I, too . . ."

"I'm very sorry. I gave it a great deal of thought, but it's an honor I must decline."

"You didn't think about it," she said, quietly and desperately. "You didn't think long at all. You made up your mind right away, when *they* came."

By "they," she presumably meant us—Shiro and the whole crowd of foreigners he'd brought from China. I felt terribly sorry for her, yet conflicted. It isn't pleasant to witness heartbreak; she was trying so hard not to cry, the tears spilling silently from her eyes. *How she must love him*, I thought. My heart gave a painful lurch.

"Will you write to me?" she said at last. "Just to let me know you're safe. Promise me."

After a long pause, he nodded. "Yes."

"I know you'll keep your promise." Then, as if she couldn't help herself, she buried her face in his chest. It felt wrong to watch them, as though I were a thief. Turning, I went up the gangway silently.

BOHAI HAD BOUGHT the tickets in such a hurry that we were all in second-class cabins. Either that, or steerage was full, but I didn't complain. My mistress and I were to share one, Bohai was alone, and Chen and Lu apparently also had separate cabins. A tense atmosphere had descended upon the three young men since Bektu's murder. As for Shiro and Kuro, I'd no idea where they were; my thoughts were in disarray as I sat on my narrow twin bed, sorting my mistress's clothes.

"It's good they're coming with us. Bohai is likely relieved," she said.

I wasn't so sure about that. When Shiro had joined our onboard party, I'd seen a brief flicker of panic in Bohai's eyes. Had he tried to break free of Shiro's influence? It happens sometimes that a human begins to suspect they've been fooled by foxes. That's what leads to all those tales of disillusionment and discovering yourself naked, covered with fleas and eating rotting meat in an abandoned grave. Of course that exact scenario seldom happens, but it's a good metaphor for how people feel when they discover they've been duped. That's why a careful fox refrains from unduly influencing others.

As far as I could tell, Shiro had been completely reckless. I wouldn't put it past him to have killed Bektu as well. Yes, that was the most likely option, I told myself. Much better than other possibilities.

This ship wasn't as modern or luxurious as the *Shinano-maru* had been. The cabins were cramped and dark, with damp bed linens. The porthole windows refused to open, and my seasickness soon resurfaced.

"You'd better lie down," said my mistress worriedly. "I'll bring you some food."

It was a short voyage, I reminded myself. An overnight trip. Still, a wave of nausea seized me, worsened by the mildewed smell in the cabin. Trying the window again, I managed to crank it open enough to stick my head out. As I closed my eyes, wishing the sea would stop heaving around, I heard voices from the next open window.

That was Bohai's cabin. By the sound of it, Chen and Lu were with him. It wasn't hard to hear them because they were in the middle of an argument.

"What about our plans to build a better society?" That was Lu. "If you leave, how do we know you won't report us?"

Chen said angrily, "Perhaps you're the informer who's secretly sold us out for your own immunity!"

"I never would! Besides, I'm not the one who's acting suspiciously about Bektu Nikan's death. Don't you find it strange that he should have died so conveniently?" Bohai's voice rose in agitation.

Chen said, "I went to see him the day before he died. He was hostile, asked whether I'd sent someone after him. Apparently, that very morning, a woman from my uncle Wang's household came to question him about private photographs."

My ears were freezing in the sea wind. The woman referred to was obviously me—they hadn't put it together yet, but my appearance had rattled Bektu for reasons I hadn't fully understood at the time. And I remembered how, when the maid had interrupted us, she'd said there was another visitor for him.

"I told him I'd no idea what he was talking about. Bektu said if we didn't pay up, he still had the negative, and wouldn't it be a shame if copies began to circulate? Then he showed me the commemorative photograph taken when we wrote that banner against the Imperial government. We're all in it."

Silence. An angry silence that filled the cabin. I strained my ears.

Chen said bitterly, "You needn't worry. I bought it from Bektu. I paid him in silver the day before he died."

"Including the negative?"

"Yes. But you can't leave us like this."

"Are you blackmailing me?" Bohai's voice rose in indignation. "I thought we were friends!"

"So did I, until you planned to sneak off by yourself!"

"Let's be honest, Bektu contacted each of us, asking for more money when he arrived in Moji, didn't he?" Bohai's voice cracked under strain. "But unlike you, I didn't go to see him."

They started shouting over one another then. I couldn't hear more because there was a click as my own cabin door opened and my mistress came in. I'd barely time to pull my head in from the window and compose myself.

"I forgot my shawl." From her worried expression, she'd heard the disturbance next door. "I meant to ask Bohai to come with me, but he seems busy."

"Busy" was a nice way to put it. Their argument, though muffled, ended with a crash as the door banged shut and people stamped away angrily.

"I'd better go and check on him"—but instead of leaving, she sat down on her bed, looking at her hands. The sun shone brightly in through the porthole.

"Your shadow is so solid," she said to me.

I glanced down at my feet, where it puddled darkly. "Is Bohai still worried about the people with no shadows?"

"It's what made him join this whole misadventure in the first place." She looked old and small. "He's always been anxious, and it got worse after he found out about how the first son dies young in this family. He decided he'd leave Dalian and study in Japan. I thought it was a good idea. Especially when, last year, Bohai started talking about seeing strange things." She paused. "When you first came to me, you said you weren't afraid of ghosts."

I nodded. Foxes aren't afraid of ghosts; some of us even doubt their existence, particularly since our own antics are often mistaken for specters. But fear of ghosts can drive people to great lengths. "What has he seen lately?"

"A peddler in Moji. Bohai said they're hard to tell from ordinary humans, but he feels cold and nauseated in their presence. He believes he won't live long, which is why he threw in his lot for revolution."

Privately, I'd long suspected that Bohai was vulnerable to all sorts of nervous fantasies. No doubt helped along by Shiro, to extract more money from him. My mistress stared at the wall. "Ah San, do you think it's wrong to kill a ghost?"

"Aren't they already dead?"

"Bohai says that if the people with no shadows come for him, he'll stab them first. I'm very worried about him. It's best that we go home as soon as possible."

ALL THIS TALK about stabbing reminded me of how Bektu had died. I wondered if my old lady was entertaining the same fears. It was quite amazing how many people might have wanted Bektu Nikan dead. Enough to make one dizzy. Feeling restless, I went up on the deck after she'd gone to look for Bohai. The brisk salt air cleared my head and blew away my seasickness. There weren't many passengers on this ship, so I spotted Chen before he saw me. He was holding the railing in one hand, and I realized as he drew near that he'd been drinking.

"It's a bit early to be in your cups," I said.

Forced smile, though he looked miserable. "I don't have any more friends, so who cares?"

"Why don't you have any friends?" I asked, though I'd a fairly good idea from eavesdropping.

"Lu and Bohai ought to be grateful. I'm the one who bought that photograph from Bektu. And the negative. They should be thanking me! Instead of talking about blackmail and backstabbing . . ." His voice trailed off as he hung despondently over the railing.

"Be careful, you might fall in."

"If I do, will you go with me?"

There's a tradition of lovers' suicide. Drowning is the favorite method, usually by tying their arms and legs together, and weighting their clothes with stones. I'd no intention to accompany Chen to a watery grave, but he was persistent, seizing my hand and running his fingers over the palm.

"You and I never got together, as promised the other time." He was referring to the rendezvous on the hillside that Kuro had interrupted. "In Dalian, likely I won't see you anymore. My father's very strict. Won't you come to my cabin tonight?"

"No." I was done with Chen. Whatever troubles he'd got himself into, he ought to face them himself instead of peevishly demanding comfort from someone else. I resisted the impulse to slap him.

Chen's mouth drooped; he looked aggrieved, the way men do when you rebuff them. "Don't look at me like that. You were willing enough to suggest a bush the other night. Or are you only Shirakawa's slut?"

This time I did slap him. Hard enough that his head jerked back, and he stumbled, catching himself on the railing. My palm stung. Now I'd really done it.

Chen lunged forward and grabbed me by the throat. I don't know why men do this. They seem to instinctively want to strangle a woman. My vision blurred; my arms flailed wildly. There was a terrible pressure on my neck. Dimly, I realized my tongue was swelling, filling my mouth. So this was how I was going to die, throttled in a fit of rage in the middle of the ocean.

The pressure vanished abruptly; he released me, looking horrified. Or perhaps it was because Chen was being restrained. There were a lot of people screaming, including Bohai and my mistress. They must have come up on deck just in time. Coughing and retching, I dropped to my knees on the damp planks.

"I didn't mean to," Chen said. "The devil got into me through her eyes."

Shocked, he stared at his trembling hands. Lu and Bohai were shouting at him. My old lady wept as she helped me up. "Are you all right?"

I nodded, gasping. The sudden attack had taken me off guard. When I finally spoke, my voice was hoarse and cracked. "Where's Kuro—I mean Kurosaki?"

"I don't know. I haven't seen Shirakawa either."

I breathed a sigh of relief. Neither of them was about. I'd been reckless, overly emotional. Usually, I'm careful to avoid a physical confrontation. Today, I didn't know what got into me. Neither did Chen, it seemed. His face turned the dull, meaty red of horsemeat. Dropping his head, he muttered apologies before leaving abruptly. Everyone was sunk in gloom, nervously eyeing one another. The police investigation, our hasty withdrawal, and the suspicions the three friends held against one another had raised tensions to a dangerous simmer.

MY MISTRESS, AGITATED, made me lie down back in our cabin while she dipped a handkerchief in cold water to make a compress. She, poor old lady, could scarcely hide her distress. "Why did he do such a thing?" she said repeatedly. "I'm going to complain to his family!" Given her trembling hands, I feared she might faint or have a stroke.

When she turned away, I palpated my throat carefully, examining it with a small hand mirror. Swallowing was painful, though I'd been lucky he'd been yanked off almost immediately. A little longer and he might have grievously injured me, though I'd instinctively tucked my chin and raised my shoulders. The bruises on my throat, together with Shiro's fading bite mark, were a warning that I'd been taking too many risks.

We all went to bed early, retiring to our respective cabins. Despite my seasickness, I slept like the dead. So it wasn't until the sun was high in the sky and the ship was drawing near to Dalian that I realized there'd been a great commotion.

In the night, Chen had disappeared.

44

B ao doesn't recall how he returned to bed that night. All he sees is himself standing in the street, staring at the ground. It's night, a windy black night where the full moon illuminates the racing clouds and the wild dance of cloth awnings. Everything has a shadow. Every single thing except Bao.

Under his feet is nothing but moonlight. Bao shifts his weight back and forth, waggles his hands. Nothing. It's as though he doesn't exist. He's a ghost, the silvery light passing straight through him. Bao walks down the deserted street looking for his shadow, but no matter where he stands, there is none for him. What does it mean? His chest aches suddenly, with that pain in his lung that has recently and ominously worsened.

I must be dreaming. Or going crazy. That's a sure sign of foxes. Bao recalls his offering of braised goose and has a spasm of regret. What did he pray for again? It's so late now, with a strange mood in the wind whipping through his clothes, that he can hardly think straight. *I should go to bed.*

And so he does.

MORNING ARRIVES. WHEN he opens his eyes, Bao lies motionless for a while, with the sensation that a momentous event happened last night. Like an earthquake, or the destruction of a city by fire. Something has altered inside him, invisible to others; a sea change that has seeped through every capillary in his body. He imagines that his blood has turned deep purple or perhaps green. That kind of change.

Cautiously, he raises his hand above the thin cotton blanket to where the sunlight spills in. He still has a shadow, a very faint, hand-shaped likeness. Relief floods him. Last night was a dream, a hallucination born of food poisoning and too much time thinking about foxes. Bao doesn't want to think about how alarmingly muted the shadow of his hand looks, compared to even yesterday. Lilac gray, it pools timidly on his stomach. Was the dream a warning that his lifespan is running out, or an indication of some internal deterioration? He tells himself that it's a trick of the light, even though other shadows in the room are distinctly darker.

In the speckled mirror above the enamel washbasin, his reflection looks about the same. The street outside is innocuous in the daytime; a mule harnessed to a cart relieves itself while a dog trots by. He must have dreamed last night.

Bao heads to the medicine shop where his prescription came from, and where the mysterious fox lady seems to have connected with the young master and his grandmother. The shop itself is a famous establishment, with a grandly imposing entrance. The back is given over to private family quarters, and from the high wall that runs around it, Bao estimates it's a sizeable property.

Inside is dim and scented with bitter herbs. Earthenware pots bubble on charcoal braziers, and serving counters run around the double-height hall, screened in dark rosewood with an upper gallery hung with dusty red lanterns. Bao approaches one of the many clerks totting up figures on a black-beaded abacus and asks to speak to the young master.

"Young Master Bohai went to Japan to study," says the clerk.

"What about his grandmother?"

"The old mistress? Why do you want to see her?"

Bao hesitates, thinking of a plausible story. "She's an acquaintance of mine from Mukden."

To Bao's shock, the lie that passes his lips doesn't buzz. Did last night's mysterious episode really change something in his body? The clerk, mistaking Bao's look of surprise, says, "The old mistress isn't here either. Are you a friend of her husband, the late master?"

Bao smiles. "Something like that." This time the lie registers its familiar numbing twinge.

"She'll be sorry she missed you; they're all actually returning today. We just got an unexpected telegram. If you come tomorrow, she'll be here."

"I see. That's good news," says Bao. "By any chance, did she bring her maid with her?"

"You mean the girl from Qiqihar, Ah San?"

"Her family asked after her." Bao produces the photograph diffidently, as if he's just an old man running an errand. "They sent this photograph." All lies, as he's reminded from the unpleasant tingle on his tongue. There's nothing wrong with his ability after all.

"Yes, that's her. I thought she was an orphan." The clerk flushes. "Can I keep this picture? I'll give it to Ah San when she returns."

"I'm afraid I can't leave this with you, but I'll call again," says Bao.

In the meantime, he'll go to the harbor to see if he can spot her disembarking. It won't be too hard to find out which vessels are arriving from Japan later today.

45

Chen disappeared in the night. His bed was unslept in, the thin shipboard blanket and sheets still sharply tucked in by the steward. His clothes were still packed in their steamer trunk, although the trunk itself was unlocked.

I'd come with my mistress, drawn by Bohai's alert. We were approaching Dalian, near enough that land was a dark smudge on the horizon. Nobody had seen Chen since yesterday after dinner; he'd been sullen and out of sorts, and they'd presumed he'd slept in this morning. As the hour advanced, however, Lu had gone looking for him. His cabin was unlocked. But no one was inside.

A ship-wide search ensued, despite reassurances that he was likely sleeping in a deck chair somewhere. After everyone had left, I lingered in his cabin. I'd wound a soft cotton scarf around my neck; my voice was hoarse, but I was lucky Chen had only grabbed me briefly before he'd been pulled off. Also, he clearly wasn't used to physical fights. If it had been Bektu Nikan, he'd likely have broken my neck. But Bektu was dead, stabbed in Moji. And Chen was nowhere to be found.

I had a bad feeling that no one would ever see him again. The same sensation you get when you sniff a burrow and know that it's empty, all the way down in the darkness. Chen's presence was gone from this ship, no matter how diligently they searched. No clothes were hung up on any hooks in the cabin, nor toiletries unpacked by the washbasin. It was as though he'd barely been in this room at all. Quietly, I opened the lid of his trunk and stared at the neatly folded clothes.

I'd helped Chen pack that trunk the day before, when we were rushing to leave. He'd done a horrible job, throwing a jumble of shirts, trousers, and books together with loose toiletries, so I'd repacked neatly for him. Books on the bottom, folded clothes on top. Everything looked much as I recalled, except for a gap between the clothes and the side of the trunk, as though someone had thrust a hasty arm down it. I started digging. Was anything missing?

The door clicked open.

I almost leaped into the air. It was too late to hide what I'd been doing—how could I possibly explain my search of Chen's belongings? Then I saw who it was.

"Oh, it's you. And you."

Foxes are naturally drawn to trouble. Some say that's because we are the cause of it, but the truth is that chaos is always interesting and often profitable. I shouldn't have been surprised that both Shiro and Kuro would turn up at the news that Chen had disappeared.

"What are you looking for?" said Shiro. His eyes slid around the room, considering its dimensions. "Don't worry, everyone is still searching the ship for him."

Kuro said nothing, but he locked the cabin door behind him. My pulse began to hammer. I don't like being trapped in a small space. Kuro shook his head very briefly. His eyes looked sad. "Are you all right? At dinner, Lu mentioned you'd had a disagreement with Chen on deck."

The last thing I wanted was to show him my bruises, so I said briskly, "It didn't go well. But he said he'd bought some photographs and a negative off Bektu. Since Chen's now missing, I want to know what happened to them."

The best thing about other foxes is that you don't have to explain—at least not right away. Shiro and Kuro immediately began to search the room, ransacking every possible hiding place.

"A photograph could be hidden anywhere. But a negative is a rectangular glass plate," Shiro explained as he emptied out Chen's other luggage. I hadn't known that. Shiro looked amused. "What, you mean you were just blindly searching?"

I didn't bother to respond because I was thinking quickly. A glass plate. There'd been a slim, flat package of two pieces of cardboard wrapped carefully in brown paper and string that Chen had taken from me, saying he'd handle it himself. It might easily have held a glass plate negative and a few photographs. He'd put it carefully away into the steamer trunk, wrapped in one of his shirts, so I started unfolding the clothes. Meanwhile, Shiro and Kuro took apart the rest of the cabin, lifting the mattress and checking the lining of Chen's jacket.

Nothing.

"Put it all back!" I hissed, mindful of passing footsteps in the corridor. We were running out of time. In a perfect frenzy, we folded and repacked everything. If anything, we were almost too efficient. The cabin looked frighteningly pristine. Then, after listening carefully to make sure the corridor was clear, we scuttled out.

"Let's talk," said Shiro, seizing me by the hand. "Come to our cabin."

I hadn't known that Kuro and Shiro were bunking together—well, I hadn't even known they'd be on this ship until the last minute. With everyone hunting for Chen, I supposed there was no help for it, so I followed along.

"Here we are," he said, five doors down.

He opened the door. Kuro was behind us; just then someone called out, "Mr. Kurosaki?"

It was my mistress's voice, coming down the corridor. Shiro yanked me into the cabin and closed the door before she could see me. I shook his hand off mine. Their cabin was exactly the same as all the others. Same twin beds bolted to the floor. Same dingy decor. The only difference was that neither Shiro nor Kuro appeared to have much luggage at all. I supposed they'd left in a hurry. Outside, I could hear my old lady talking to Kuro and his low voice answering her. I turned to Shiro.

"You owe me an apology—you tried to use me in Moji to get rid of Bektu Nikan!"

"My dear Snow, I simply allowed you to exact your revenge. I see you managed quite well without me."

"You think I killed him?"

"Didn't you ask me for help? I would have, but you moved too fast. I rather like that in a woman. Now, I wonder where that photograph went?"

So he didn't know who'd murdered Bektu either. "Why do you want it?"

"As insurance, of course. I didn't ask those young men to

sit for a photograph under a handwritten banner proclaiming *Death to the Emperor*. But I didn't stop them either." Shiro's smile was insidiously sharp. "Bektu was probably trying to blackmail them. A useful man, but greedy."

I sighed. "You must stop leading people on like this. It's incredibly reckless."

He looked momentarily cross, then started to laugh. "Well said! Forget about the photograph. Takeda's transferred the money and we've left Moji."

"What about Bohai and Lu? And why is Chen missing?"

"Give them a few months and they'll find another worthy cause to enlist in. As for Chen, both you and I can guess he won't be found today."

"Shiro, you are very wicked." My thoughts were racing. If he hadn't killed Bektu Nikan, who had? And was Shiro insinuating that I'd got rid of Chen?

I stared out of the porthole. The white foam in the ship's wake, as it plowed steadily onwards, looked like froth on a cup of milk. Like snow swirling on a mountain pass. Shiro dropped his voice. "Yes, I am. Very wicked indeed."

If that was all he had to say, I was going back, but he took my hand and pressed it against his face. Gently now, no grabbing. "Snow, won't you stay with me? When we're together, I needn't play these stupid games."

"That's your own choice. I told you—*we* told you—not to do so a long time ago."

A dangerous gleam in his eye. "But there is no *we* anymore, is there? As you've seen, Kuro has been busy. Miss Yukiko is an earnest young woman. Just the kind he likes. Tragic background." Shiro put his mouth against my ear. "Needs saving."

I flinched.

"Poor Snow," he said. "Don't you know that most males want to take care of a pretty woman? And here you are, marching along doggedly by yourself. It's heartbreaking to watch you. But I like you just the way you are." His amber gaze was honeyed in the sunlight, enough to make most women weak at the knees. Even I had difficulty turning away as Shiro slid his arm around my waist.

We must have looked like a pair of lovers. At least the startled expression on Kuro's face, as he opened the cabin door abruptly, seemed to imply that. His eyes lit upon my neck, and I realized that the kerchief wrapped around it had slipped.

"What did my old lady say?" I said, quickly recovering.

"That Chen can't be found anywhere." Pause. "Your voice is hoarse."

Before I could deny it, Shiro pulled off my scarf. A sharp hiss escaped his lips as he and Kuro stared at the purpling bruises. I knew it looked horrible. You could even see the outline of Chen's thick fingers, where they'd pressed in. Though I'd done nothing wrong, a burning shame suffused my cheeks. With trembling fingers, I retied the kerchief around my neck.

"Well," said Shiro. "That's even worse than we thought. It's a good thing that Chen is now at the bottom of the ocean."

A meaningful glance passed between him and Kuro. I felt an icy shiver trickle, like black seawater, down my back. "How do you know?"

Shiro shrugged. "If a man vanishes on a ship at night, there's only one place he could have gone."

"He asked me to commit double suicide with him." I recalled Chen's words, though I'd thought him merely drunk at the time.

Kuro's jaw tightened. "Don't mention that to anyone."

"I already told my mistress. There were others on deck, too—it's possible someone else heard him." Exhaustion rolled over me in a numbing wave; I wanted to close my eyes and let it drown my consciousness. Being in this enclosed space with both Kuro and Shiro was making my head tight, or perhaps I hadn't fully recovered from the shock of being choked yesterday. "I'm going back."

Despite my protests, Kuro escorted me. Wordlessly, loyally, as he'd always done in the past. Shiro moved to follow, but Kuro had been swifter, blocking him as we left. It was so casually done that I wondered if I'd read too much into mere politeness. My throat ached. Sometimes I felt as though I were living in a dream and could no longer tell what was real or a nightmare. At the turn in the corridor, I was seized by dizziness and stumbled. His hand steadied my elbow, but I shook him off.

"It's just seasickness," I said with a grimace.

Kuro said, "We all suffer from it. You more so than others."

At that moment, I felt like weeping. I was tired, I told myself. Kuro's words were no more than his usual grave courtesy. I'd lie low for a bit and rest. For surely trouble was coming.

When the ship docked in Dalian, Chen's disappearance became official. We waited for hours as authorities were notified, and a police report made. My poor old lady was eventually allowed to go home, myself accompanying her, while the young men remained to answer questions about their companion. To the best of everyone's knowledge, it was a tragic accident. Chen had continued drinking through dinner, and even the stewards had reported him as morose. Perhaps he'd fallen over the railing.

Nobody said anything about suicide.

Or murder.

46

When Bao arrives at the harbor, it's long past lunch. He stops at a roadside stall to eat *roujiamo*, braised pork belly with fresh green cilantro, wrapped in a homemade flatbread. As he suspected, it's not difficult to find a steamship from Moji. She's docked already, and longshoremen are busy unloading her cargo. Talking to a porter, Bao learns that though most of the passengers disembarked, a few have been detained.

"A passenger vanished on the ship, so they're searching again," says the porter.

Is it a coincidence that the same ship carrying the fox lady and this unknown Shirakawa should suffer a mysterious disappearance? Alert, Bao heads to the shipping office to see what he can find out.

The atmosphere in the office, desks piled with ledgers and hard benches lined with people, is tense. Nobody has time for him, but from what he's overheard, they're questioning some of the passengers again on the ship. Bao settles himself against a wall to wait. The windows are closed, and the air is stale with garlicky breath and the scent of unwashed hair. After a while, Bao notices a stringy, harried-looking man glancing at him. There's a familiar air about him, and Bao wonders where he's seen him before. The man must have come to the same conclusion, for he approaches, an apologetic smile on his face.

"Teacher Bao, we've met before, haven't we? In Mukden—I'm Hong, the deputy headmaster's cousin."

Bao recalls him now, a young instructor at a private boys' school who was accused of theft. Bao had still been teaching when a colleague had asked him to intervene in his cousin's case: a new teacher who'd disciplined one of the popular boys and consequently been framed for the theft of student funds. The crude, malicious setup was solved by Bao and his ability to hear lies. It's been fifteen years, yet the man still looks timid.

"Have you been well?"

"Yes, thanks to you. I've never forgotten your help back then. I heard from my cousin that you've now become a professional investigator."

Bao makes a few embarrassed noises, but Hong is delighted. "I left teaching after that incident and am now working for the Chen family. Have you heard of them?"

The Chen family is extremely wealthy, and Bao is aware of their far-reaching influence. He congratulates Hong, who says, "I'm only an undersecretary. However—" He pauses. "Are you by any chance here in a professional capacity?"

"I'm just checking if a lady has left the ship."

"All the women passengers have already disembarked. But would you be interested in taking on another case? I believe the Chen family could use your help."

Leaving the stuffy shipping office, they walk along the docks. Seagulls wheel overhead as the lowering sun turns the sea to beaten copper. There's a cloud on the horizon, exactly the shape of Mount Tai, until the wind flattens it out. Hong runs a finger under his high collar. "It's been a terrible day. The third son of the Chen family, Chen Jianyi, was supposed to return from Moji on this steamship, but it seems he vanished overboard last night. The family is talking to officials right now, but as you can imagine, everyone is extremely upset. If you have a moment, may I introduce you to my employer?"

And so it is that Bao finds himself informally involved with the Chen family. He's worked with one of their subsidiaries before on a Mukden embezzlement case, though the connection likely doesn't register with Hong's employer, the father of the missing young man. A florid man with a fierce, anguished expression, he's so distracted that he barely registers Bao's presence other than to nod. Hong, however, is enthusiastic, seeing this meeting with Bao as a chance to bolster his own reputation with his employer.

The facts are simple: Chen, a medical student, abandoned his studies and returned suddenly from Moji. After drinking heavily, he either fell overboard or committed suicide. Bao doesn't see what there is to argue about, other than the Chen family's natural grief.

"My son would never commit suicide." Mr. Chen's eyes are red with unshed tears, mouth twisted with fury. "It must have been an accident. The shipping company is liable, or one of his companions, for not watching him carefully."

That's his pronouncement. Grief has swiftly been channeled into rage and blame. There's no body to recover, an affront to Confucian rituals. How can they properly mourn this young man, fearing him lost at sea and doomed to become a wandering ghost?

"I don't know what I can do for the family," says Bao privately after Mr. Chen has turned away. "Unless there's further information, it looks like an accident."

Death can't be commanded to yield its secrets, no matter how stricken the family. Hong looks unhappy. "Would you at least listen to the accounts of Chen Jianyi's traveling companions? I remember you have a knack for discerning truth."

Bao shifts uncomfortably. "Did you mention this to Mr. Chen, your employer?"

Hong drops his eyes. "I told him that you could sort thieves from honest men, and that you were an excellent judge of character. He said to bring you tomorrow morning when they interview his traveling companions."

It's hard for Bao to refuse this request in the face of bereavement, so despite his reservations, he agrees.

47

The worst part about Chen's disappearance was his anxious, waiting family. I didn't know how the official channels handled it, but my mistress was sadly distressed. "That poor young man! His parents will be so upset."

"Do you know them?"

"No, but I'm sure they'll want to question everyone."

I, too, wanted answers. If a treasonous photograph of all three young men, pledging revolutionary zeal against the Qing Empire, had vanished, who was likely to have taken it? Or in the darkness, leaning out over a railing, had Kuro or Shiro lent a hand? I imagined a brief struggle, then a splash. No one would hear his cries as the ship steamed on into the night. Nobody can cheat death in the end, even those of us who embark on the thousand-year journey. That's a different sort of reckoning, just as frightening and transformative—or so they say. Yet right now, I could only think of Chen. Despite my dislike of him, it must have been terrible to die alone in the freezing black water.

And so we'd returned to the medicine shop, with its prosperous, comfortable rooms. My mistress was relieved as we entered to the familiar scent of bitter medicine and the welcome of family and servants, who seemed overjoyed to have their old mistress back. She was careful, reminding them that she was now retired, and the formal mistress of the shop was Madam Huang, her daughter-in-law. That lady with her pouched mouth, who'd hired me off the streets with my geese, also looked relieved to see her. I wondered if there'd been trouble between her and the master of the medicine shop while we were gone.

The elm tree in the rear had small new leaves, and my mistress's quarters in the little back courtyard were aired and the bedding freshly washed. I'd never expected to set foot in this house again, thinking only of hunting down Bektu Nikan.

Fate has a strange way of biting you in the buttocks when you least expect it.

Madam Huang said, "Mother, perhaps you should move back into the main house." She had a strained look on her face.

"No, that's all right," said my old lady. "I'm used to the back now."

It seemed that Madam Huang had got wind of her husband's mistress and the impending pregnancy that threatened Bohai's status as the only heir. Now it would be better for her to get her mother-in-law on her side.

My mistress said, "Let me rest first. We'll talk tomorrow when things are more settled."

Yet there was hardly any time for family politicking, for the very next morning, Chen's family sent for Bohai and his grandmother to give a personal accounting for the loss of their son.

"You needn't go."

That was the first thing that Bohai's father said upon receiving the message. I was standing outside his study, once again pretending to water the plants. The azaleas under his window were my favorites because you could hear everything. "The way the message was delivered was very rude. If you go, they're bound to blame us for their son's death."

"We can't refuse," said his mother. "They're grieved and distressed. Of course we must offer our condolences. I'd have gone anyway, even without this summons."

"But it's the way that they've phrased it. Like a criminal investigation!"

Bohai finally spoke. Stricken by the loss of his friend, his tone was muted. "I'll go. Grandmother can stay at home. Chen always said his family was intimidating, but yesterday they were obviously in shock."

In the end, it was decided that all three of them, including the master of the medicine hall, would offer their condolences and apologies. I stayed at home, avoiding the questions of the other servants, who were agog with curiosity. At the poultry pen, I noted the geese I had brought were still waddling arrogantly around. The cook mentioned they'd grown so aggressive that they hadn't been eaten yet. Leaning my chin on the gate, I watched them pensively.

Time for me to go, indeed.

A vague sensation of sorrow and unease filled me. The cool spring breeze rustled the leaves, but I'd no stirring to see the stars in the north again. Instead, I wanted to curl up somewhere safe and hide. When I'd lost my child, I'd fallen into a deep well of misery. I heard and saw and felt nothing except the screaming void of her absence. Yet time had passed inexorably, and I, too, had changed like the grass. When I'd faced Bektu Nikan in his hotel room, I couldn't summon enough rage to put a knife through his eye directly. Instead I'd wavered, overtaken by doubts. If I were truly honest, being with Kuro and Shiro had shaken me. The easy familiarity of their presence—how swiftly all three of us had fallen back into old behaviors—was deeply unsettling to me.

Shiro had asked me to stay by his side. Kuro had said nothing (of course!), but his silent gaze undermined my best resolutions. If I wished to break cleanly with the past, I ought to leave now. Yet I hesitated, wanting to say farewell properly to my old lady. It wouldn't do to vanish one late-spring morning, leaving her forever wondering.

Half an hour had barely passed before another delegation arrived from the Chen family. The chief clerk explained to them that the master, his mother, and Bohai had already left for the Chen family residence. That was no matter, said the man in charge, a thickset fellow. The Chen family had particularly requested the young woman who had accompanied my mistress on the ship.

"That must be Ah San," said the chief clerk, calling me over.

When I saw the men standing together at the entrance to the family quarters, I froze. These were no mere errand boys, sent as an afterthought to fetch an extra pair of hands.

They were private security.

48

Early next morning, Hong is at Bao's hotel with a waiting rickshaw. As they rattle along, Hong updates him.

On the ship, young Chen was traveling with Lu Dong, son of another prominent family, and Huang Bohai, the son of the medicine hall. All three were medical students, so his family was surprised to discover that they'd gone to Moji, rather than heading straight to Yokohama.

"He wrote that he and his friends were putting their studies on hold to start a sugar factory in Formosa. They had financial backing from a Japanese sponsor, but they suddenly abandoned this plan and returned to Dalian."

Bao has a personal interest in Bohai, the young master of the medicine hall, but he doesn't mention it. "How were their relations?"

"Good. Lu was a childhood friend, and Bohai met Chen when they were fellow students. Last year, however, the family was concerned that Chen was associating with a shady crowd, including student revolutionaries. Though, of course, he never participated in such activities."

Bao wonders how Hong can say this with a straight face. He likely has no idea what the third young master of the Chen family was up to before his abrupt demise.

Hong hesitates. "There was another associate of Chen's onboard: a man named Shirakawa. Mr. Chen would like you to ascertain if he'd anything to do with his son's disappearance."

Ah. "Is it because of the rumors around Shirakawa?"

"So you've heard them, too? Nothing gets past you, Teacher Bao!" Hong looks impressed, and Bao hopes that this doesn't turn into hero worship.

THE CHEN FAMILY'S mansion is palatial, with beams of precious wood and exquisitely tiled floors, but Bao feels no joy or pleasure. Death hangs over everything, from the hasty mourning clothing worn by retainers to the white paper funerary lanterns hung at the massive gates. Hurrying servants have a strained, anxious expression. Bao notes the number of private guards, enough for a security force.

Bao isn't a guest, so he's led past echoing reception parlors to a garden deeper in. Tortoiseshell bamboo, with its elegant, short leaves, is planted along the path, together with dwarf pine; Bao understands these plants signify entering a scholarly male domain. The meeting room has carved rosewood doors that open to the garden, a stone-tiled floor, and expensive scroll paintings, including a landscape by the famous Ming dynasty painter Shen Zhou. Bao would like to examine it but can only gaze from a distance.

Chen is a landowner and banker, a man accustomed to power. Yet death and uncertainty have invaded his sanctuary; no amount of disbelief can will away the sad fact of his third son's disappearance. Bao is greeted with a curt nod. "Stay and listen. Notify me if you notice anything odd."

Hong sets a couple of chairs against the back wall, apologizing for Mr. Chen's abruptness, but Bao says gently, "He's lost a son. There's no need to apologize."

Indeed, the man looks ill, mouth grim and eyes blearily red. Most people would retreat to nurse their grief. Bao, however, understands Chen's desire to control the situation; perhaps it's the only way to channel his feelings about his wayward third son.

A tall young man with a lantern jaw and sloping shoulders enters. Though his expression is mulish, Bao guesses that's more habit than actual feeling, for he goes straight to Mr. Chen to pay his respects. This is Lu, one of the travelers. At the sight of his son's friend, Mr. Chen looks deeply pained and turns away for a moment.

"I'm very sorry," says Lu. "I spent the whole morning searching the ship for him."

"I heard." The elder Mr. Chen places a heavy hand on Lu's shoulder. "But what I want to know is if my son was upset the night before he disappeared. Do you think—?"

The word "suicide" hangs in the air, unspoken.

"He was in good spirits. It must have been an accident."

But Bao has heard his first lie: *He was in good spirits.* Studying Lu, he discerns no change in his wooden expression. So this young man can lie easily. But why?

"One of the stewards reported my son had an argument with a woman on the ship's deck earlier. Do you know anything about that?"

"He reprimanded one of the servants."

"What was their relationship?" Two vertical lines appear between Mr. Chen's thick eyebrows.

Lu takes a deep breath. "She works for Bohai's grandmother."

Bao leans forward. Who else could this be but his elusive fox lady?

"I want to see her." This sounds ominous.

"You'd better ask her mistress. Or maybe Shirakawa. I believe they have a connection." Lu clears his throat uneasily. Mr. Chen's grief and fury hover over the room like a tiger. Even the servants cringe.

"I asked you to bring Shirakawa with you today. Is he here?"

"Yes, he's coming. About the young woman," says Lu diffidently, "it's possible that Jianyi was in love with her. I know he went out of his way to talk to her several times."

A tendon tightens in Mr. Chen's neck. He motions Hong over abruptly, his eyes stabbing a question.

"Sir, the old lady and Bohai have already been requested. They should be on their way here," says Hong.

"Dispatch two guards to bring the servant as well."

Hong hurries off. Left alone, Bao gazes around. How many fortunes have been made and lost, what bargains have been struck in this private meeting room? Now it's the Chen family who's in agony. As if hearing his thoughts, Mr. Chen raises his head. His eyes meet Bao's; is it his imagination, or does a brief understanding pass between them? An acknowledgment by the two older men of death's casual cruelty.

Lu looks up as a shadow falls on the raised stone lintel, overlaying the delicate patterned shade of leaves.

"Ah, Shirakawa," he says in greeting.

Bao's first thought is that Shirakawa ought to have been an actor. Or maybe he is one, for such theatrical good looks cannot go unnoticed. In fact, it's almost frightening how his features adhere to popular taste. Narrow-eyed and slim-hipped, he moves like a predator, with cheekbones that would make even a matron stammer. He's dressed formally in a dark European suit, sober enough to convey the depth of his emotion, but it doesn't really matter what he wears. Bao notices that everyone, even Mr. Chen himself, seems bewildered, as though Shirakawa's entrance has changed the temperature of the room to make it either hotter or colder.

The more Bao gazes at Shirakawa, the more shaken he feels, as though he's not looking at a real person but rather the fantasy of one. Zhou Yuling's words, *He's like the person of your dreams*, echo in his head. He discovers that his own pulse has quickened and, glancing over, sees a nearby retainer's eyes dilated in a glassy stare.

Shirakawa advances. His mouth opens, and all the right words come out. Heartfelt condolences, sincere reflections. If Bao closes his eyes, he can't believe that this is supposedly a foreigner speaking. The tone, the accent, the polite nuances are all perfect—almost too much, as though an aristocrat from the capital is addressing them. It takes a while for Bao to separate the meaning of Shirakawa's words from the melodious sound of his voice, and when he does, his mouth drops open.

For almost everything that Shirakawa says is a lie.

"Chen Jianyi was a distinguished and intelligent young man. The world of medicine and letters has lost a light, and I, too, a dear companion."

Lies, all lies.

The retainers nod along, but Mr. Chen is resistant. A frown darkens his face. "I want to hear about my son's last hours. Did he seem well to you?"

"He was cheerful, though I believe he felt seasick and spent most of the afternoon leaning over the railing."

A numbing hum fills Bao's ears. He shakes his head, drawing Mr. Chen's glance. Scowling, Mr. Chen says, "My son never suffered from seasickness in his life! If you're suggesting that he fell overboard because of that, that's nonsense."

A faint expression of annoyance creases Shirakawa's elegant brows as he turns to regard Bao. His irises are surprisingly light, like the yellow eyes of an animal, and when his lean, hungry gaze rests on him, Bao feels deeply uneasy.

Shirakawa's eyes open wide for an instant, as though he's astonished by Bao. A flicker—is it alarm, amusement, or a mixture of both? It vanishes so fast that Bao wonders if he imagined it. Then Shirakawa's head snaps up.

"My apologies, I must have been mistaken."

He seems eager to leave suddenly, but the guards at the door block him.

Mr. Chen says, "What is your relation to the young woman servant on the trip?"

Bao, too, would like to know.

49

The men sent by the Chen family bundled me into a mule cart without ceremony. I'd no chance to speak to them; one jumped into the front with the driver, and the other was so silent that I guessed he was a deaf-mute. An interesting choice—I hadn't seen the use of such guards in years, though in the past they were often favored for palace intrigue. Briefly, I considered throwing myself out of the cart but decided not to. If I ran away, what would happen to my old lady? Besides, I was curious about the Chen family.

Most people only think about how to remove foxes from houses. They rarely consider how we enter in the first place. All I can say is you ought to be careful who you let in. Particularly if your home is a mansion. The grand front gates were for guests, so we went around to a back entrance where I was unceremoniously frog-marched through various passageways. A household of this size had many servants, none of whom gave me more than a passing glance. I guessed that either they'd been trained not to ask questions or they were used to strange women being dragged in, neither of which boded well for me.

The first guard said, "You're to wait in this room until further notice."

"Why?"

But he wouldn't say more, hastily locking the door behind him. The waiting room was small, with two rosewood chairs and a mother-of-pearl inlaid table. More importantly, there was a small window. Hip height and framed with wooden shutters, it looked out into a camellia bush with furled buds.

As soon as their footsteps had died away, I stuck my head out of the window. By wedging my shoulders sideways, I managed to squeeze out onto a paved courtyard. It was quiet and sunny; on the low tiled eaves, amorous pigeons strutted and cooed.

Fortunately, I was dressed like a servant in a household teeming with them. To further this disguise, as I passed a room filled with rare porcelain, I placed two teacups (celadon, likely Song dynasty) from a display shelf onto a tray and carried them as though I'd been called to serve. An appetizing whiff of roast duck indicated the kitchens, so I avoided that direction. The master of the house would never have his study near them. Trying the other wing, I wandered the endless corridors. At the entrance to a courtyard garden, I paused. Dwarf pines and tortoiseshell bamboo, symbols of masculine scholarship, lined the path. They might as well have screamed, *Here is the master of the house. Come and rob him!*

I walked swiftly down the winding, shaded path to a private pavilion. From within came the sound of raised voices. Stowing the tray with teacups behind a rock, I looked for a window. I had to crawl through a shrub but was rewarded with a good view into the meeting room.

Bohai's father was giving an apologetic speech, blaming himself and his entire family for not taking better care of young Chen on this trip. Speeches like this are usually rhetorical, since the other party is supposed to lament their own carelessness, but I noticed that Mr. Chen (who must be the furious-looking gentleman at the head of the room) didn't say a word. That in itself was very rude, implying that Bohai's family was indeed to blame. In fact, the entire room was arranged like a tribunal. The penitents—my mistress, Bohai, and his father—sat in a neat row in front of Mr. Chen. Bohai's complexion was fish-belly white. My old lady looked calm, her eyes cast down, but I noticed her wrinkled hands trembled slightly.

There were a number of other people in attendance, including Shiro. He was seated near the front, legs crossed elegantly. From time to time, he touched his left eyebrow with one hand. I know Shiro well enough to recognize that tic (he has never quite recovered from almost being branded on the forehead by a Khitan soldier), and I wondered what had made him skittish. Following his line of sight, the object of his unease appeared to be a short, sturdy-looking older man seated among the ranks of Chen's retainers.

He had the sort of face that you see in honest peasant farmers, the type who dutifully notifies the local warlord that this year's harvest will be short and then gets killed for his pains. I wondered why Shiro should be nervous of him when the poor man was clearly fixated on my mistress, her face angled away from him as she endured Mr. Chen's glare. He had the air of a professional observer and likely wasn't part of Chen's regular household because he wore traveling clothes, a thick quilted jacket, and felt boots, as though he'd come from the north. Perhaps he was hunting foxes. I drew back from the opening with a hiss.

No, no. I reminded myself that Daoist exorcists capable of handling us have become increasingly rare. Besides, this man was staring at my old lady, not Shiro. When she finally spoke, he leaned forward eagerly.

"I'm deeply sorry about your son," she said. "It was a tremendous shock to all of us. I don't believe that it could have been any more than a tragic accident."

Her sincerity touched a nerve in Mr. Chen, for he looked away for a pained instant. Then he said, "What about your servant? I heard that she might have been involved with my son. In fact, Lu informed me that he first met her at a dinner hosted by your family."

"Yes, she spilled soup on a guest."

"Where did she come from?"

"From Qiqihar, I'm told—a decent, hardworking young woman."

"Was she involved in an improper relationship with my son?"

"No. The day after the dinner party, your son offered to employ her. I discussed it with Ah San, and she refused."

Mr. Chen's eyebrows rose. "Are you absolutely sure your servant was never alone with my son?"

My mistress bit her lip. "She wasn't."

The short old man dressed like a traveler gave a start. Likely, nobody else noticed it, just me and Shiro (who was stealthily observing him from behind a paper fan). And Mr. Chen.

"She had nothing to do with your son," my old lady repeated defensively.

Again, that telltale flicker across the old man's face. He passed a hand over his jaw. Very quietly, I began to back out of my hiding place. I couldn't see any good ending to this farce. If I were to run away right now, what would happen to my poor mistress and Bohai's family? Perhaps Chen's family would drop the matter.

Or not.

Long ago, someone told me that I really shouldn't get attached to humans. Nothing good comes of it since they detest our kind and kill us when they can. Yet I've always found it hard to leave. In any case, I was past calculating exactly where my soul lay in the grand scheme of things, when I heard the uneven thump of running footsteps. I peeked back inside. The guards who'd fetched me from the medicine shop had just discovered my absence.

"Sir," said the first one, "I beg your pardon, but . . ." He whispered into Mr. Chen's ear. His face was a thundercloud.

"What do you mean, missing?" Turning to Bohai's father, he said, "Apparently your maidservant has escaped from my custody."

"Why was she even in your custody?" was Bohai's indignant protest, while his father complained at this treatment of his household servants. My mistress, however, turned white. She understood right away that when a woman is not in her place, men can get very angry. Pressing myself against the window, I made eye contact with Shiro. It was the merest blink, but I knew he'd spied me peeking through the leaves.

Shiro stood up abruptly. "May I use the facilities?"

A servant was dispatched to accompany him as everyone continued to argue. Hardly more than a minute had passed before I felt a sharp yank on my ankle. I turned with a snarl. It was Shiro, crouched down half into the bush—he'd managed to find me after all.

"Where's Kuro?" I asked.

"I gave him the slip this morning. Didn't tell him the Chen family wanted to see us." He smiled. "Shouldn't I get a reward for that?"

I ignored the last bit. "Good. Don't tell him."

The last thing I wanted was for Kuro to be involved. Heaven knows what he might have already done on my behalf. No—I mustn't think of it.

"Anyway," said Shiro, "I came to warn you. Don't say I don't love you."

I ignored this latter, too. "About what?"

"See the short old fellow?"

"The one who looks like a traveler?"

"Yes. Stay away from him."

"Why?"

An odd expression flitted over Shiro's face as he tilted his head. "He can distinguish lies from truth."

I burst out laughing. Not a very clever thing to do when you're hiding under a bush, but Shiro looked absurdly serious. "Please. There's no such ability except among the saints."

"I'm telling you he's definitely been tampered with. Most likely by one of us. You wouldn't know since you never paid attention to refining such arts."

"Are you saying he isn't susceptible? That's nothing new. Even Bektu was resistant to foxes."

"It's not the same thing. He's susceptible, just not the way you'd think. In fact, I find him dangerous. And not just him. Chen's father is on a rampage. If I'd known he came from such a troublesome family, I'd have cut ties with him earlier."

This was a ridiculous conversation to have in the middle of a bush. Shiro's rear end stuck out as he was talking to me. At any moment, a guard would discover us, as indeed, one did.

"Sir!"

"I dropped my fan," said Shiro, backing out carefully. But not before hissing, "You should leave now."

INSIDE THE MEETING room, the conversation had devolved into a heated exchange. Bohai's father said (barely politely) that he'd suffered enough insult, and that the Chens had no right to lock up members of his household. Mr. Chen turned red, then white, then red again. I thought he might have a stroke if this kept up. My old lady put her hands over her face. Enter Shiro, who announced blandly that he was leaving.

"No one is going to leave until I find this servant!"

Mr. Chen had evidently decided that I must be the key to his son's death. Poor man. Losing a child is a pain that is almost unbearable, a grief that drives sense out of one's head. For that reason alone, I decided I ought to answer his questions. Scrambling out of my hiding place, I hurried to the carved doors. The guard, seeing my drab clothes, shooed me off, saying that the master was in a meeting.

"He sent for me." Here I was, willingly walking into a trap and being turned away. I decided that if he didn't let me in, then I was fated to be released that day (though generally I'm not a great believer in fate) when he suddenly relented.

So it was that I opened the doors and tripped meekly in.

50

It has been a troublesome morning of short arguments, punctuated by long stretches of waiting for people to arrive. Bao feels increasingly uneasy; he wishes that he never ran into Hong at the shipping office. If he hadn't, he'd have likely filed his final report to Mr. Wang, saying that the woman in the photograph took a ship to Japan. Instead, he's been roped into what seems to be a private trial.

Rich men set their own rules, and Mr. Chen demands accountability for his son's death. He refuses to believe it was suicide or even a careless accident. If his son is gone, it's due to malicious agency, and someone must be punished.

The other reason Bao feels uncomfortable is Shirakawa, who lies so effortlessly. If Bao gazes at him too long, he feels that he can't breathe. A darkness emanates from Shirakawa's elegant figure. When he tilts his head to observe Bao, as he does from time to time, Bao feels as though every hair on his head is tingling in a cloud of apprehension. It's a sensation he's experienced a few times in his life. Once, when he was a child in a bamboo grove. And another time, when the grubby red curtain at the fox medium's house had twitched from an unseen hand.

Nonsense, Bao tells himself. Indeed, his earlier suspicions that Shirakawa might be involved with the frozen women in Mukden feel hazy, as though smeared with ink. No matter what the rumors are about Shirakawa (seeing him in person, Bao understands just how tongues might wag), he's only a man. He has a shadow, and he's wearing proper clothes and sitting in a civilized manner. He's nothing like a beast.

So when Shirakawa gives a roundabout nonanswer about his relationship with this servant, Bao stares out of the side window and pretends he's unconcerned.

He drops this act when the Huang family, from the medicine hall, arrives.

They comprise three generations: the current master (stocky, bald, worried), his son (quivering like a block of tofu), and the grandmother. A little woman, she walks with an alert, birdlike step. Her somber clothing indicates she's a widow. Bao catches only a glimpse of her face before she's guided to her seat in front of Mr. Chen. Expensive rosewood chairs, arranged unpleasantly for an interrogation. The grandmother sits down, and her neat posture makes Bao catch his breath. She resembles a small animal sitting on its haunches.

Bao shifts, angling for a closer look. He wonders who she reminds him of, and if he's met her before. Mr. Chen is quick on the uptake; his red-rimmed eyes have noted Bao's every headshake, and he clearly agrees that Shirakawa is not to be trusted. Now he's listening to the master of the medicine hall's apologies with an impatient air. By the time the conversation pivots to the missing maid, his complexion has turned an ominous beef-liver purple.

Bao finds himself hoping that the fox lady (if she's indeed the missing servant) has run far, far away. Because nobody can help her if she falls into the clutches of a rich man like this, with his own private guards. Bao knows, more than others, the extent to which disgraced wives and concubines have been walled up or forced to commit suicide. Outside these thick walls, famine and disease stalk the streets, and families sell their own children for lack of food. A missing servant will hardly elicit a raised eyebrow—unless someone else wants her. Unbidden, Mr. Wang's yellow face, like a wax death mask, appears in Bao's mind.

The grandmother from the medicine hall is answering questions now, and the careful, measured tone of her voice makes Bao's pulse quicken. Her accent is from the north, the accent of his childhood. His hands grip the smooth turned arms of his chair as he leans forward. The interrogation goes steadily downhill as it's clear these are the wrong answers. A vein pops out in Mr. Chen's scrawny neck, extended like an angry rooster.

"No one is going to leave until I find this servant!" he declares. It's like a horrible play, a Chinese opera where the plot is going wrong and the general is about to be beheaded. And then the door at the front of the meeting room opens—slowly, because it's heavy and carved of expensive wood, just as everything in this pavilion is worth more than the life-wages of twenty peasants—and *she* comes in.

BAO RECOGNIZES HER at once, though the real woman is different from a black-and-white photograph. Those large, bright eyes; that slender, strong frame, lithe as the branches of a slim tree with green sap running through it. There's no doubt she could scale a wall, as the little girl at the brothel described. And most of all, that mischievous, charming face. Never mind the rough clothes or the carefully downcast eyes, trying to look penitent. This is a bewitching creature. Everything else in the room—furniture, sunlight dappled on the stone floor—fades, as though the color has bled away. Only Shirakawa remains in focus, his suave profile drawn into an irritated frown.

Approaching Mr. Chen with proper courtesy, she folds her arms into her sleeves and bows. The gesture reminds Bao of ancient rites illustrated in old silk paintings. Between her and Shirakawa, he's beginning to feel disoriented. Her voice is low and charming.

"I'm truly sorry for the passing of your son. Losing a child is a fate worse than death."

Unlike Shirakawa, there's no lie in her words. She really does feel pain for Mr. Chen. He sees it in her clear eyes filled with sorrow. Their limpid darkness has a guileless opacity that reminds him of an animal.

Mr. Chen is taken aback but recovers himself faster than any of the retainers around him. Bao has noticed he's not easily swayed. "Who are you?"

"I am known as Ah San, the servant of this honored lady," she says. "Hearing that I'd been summoned, I came as soon as I could."

Her speech is exquisitely polite. This is an educated woman, though Bao doesn't know what to make of her servant's clothes. Clearing his throat, Mr. Chen says, "Is 'Ah San' your real name?"

"Of course not," she says, demurely.

Flummoxed, Mr. Chen doesn't know how to treat her, and neither does Bao; all he knows is that she still hasn't lied.

"Did you have a relationship with my son?"

"I don't wish to speak ill of him, but we were barely acquainted."

"Yet you quarreled with him aboard the ship, before he died."

"Yes. I struck him on the face."

A faint gasp from the grandmother of the medicine shop; she puts a hand over her mouth.

"Why?"

"He asked me to visit his cabin that night. When I refused, he tried to strangle me." She lifts the scarf around her neck to show bruises, fading but still vivid. "Fortunately, I was saved by this gentleman and my mistress."

And now she looks directly at Lu, who turns pale. Mr. Chen pins him with an accusatory, stabbing glance. Clearly, this is news to him. Unlike Shirakawa's sweet words, this woman is disruptive in a completely different way. Bao now understands why Mr. Wang, his original client, was so taken with her, and also why his household said she was nothing but trouble.

"That was the last interaction we had."

A freezing silence descends on the room. Mr. Chen's glare flicks to Bao, to see if she's been lying. *She's telling the truth,* Bao telegraphs with his brows, but the man is too angry now.

"Do you mean to say that you never saw my son again?"

"Yes."

Is that pity in her eyes? It's the worst possible emotion to show a man like Mr. Chen, who's used to being in control, and whose womenfolk are all properly sequestered in high-walled quarters. Jumping up abruptly, he shouts, "You're lying! Take her away."

Bao desperately shakes his head, but Mr. Chen won't look at him. His rage and grief have no bounds, even as the room explodes. Amid the uproar, Shirakawa stares at this woman who's dared to talk back to Mr. Chen. An unspoken communication dances between them as he shrugs his shoulders.

Yet it's over soon. Almost too quickly, but perhaps that's not surprising. Nobody pretends this is a gathering of equals. They're in Mr. Chen's house, surrounded by his private guards. If the master of the medicine shop and his family should vanish, that might cause some problems, but they're not the ones detained. It's the young woman who's swiftly removed by the guard whom Bao suspects is a deaf-mute, as he responds only to Mr. Chen's hand signals. Before anyone can object, she's gone.

Once her presence is removed, Mr. Chen regains control. Through nostrils still pinched white with anger, like the dents in soft pastry, he announces coldly, "In view of my son's death, surely you can lend your servant to me for a few days?" He makes it sound entirely reasonable, and the family from the medicine shop is cowed into silence and hastily escorted out. Even Shirakawa leaves without protest.

Bao stands up as well. Hong snatches at his sleeve. "Teacher Bao," he whispers, "what do you think?"

"Please excuse me," Bao says. "I must ask them a few questions."

Hong releases him reluctantly. "Very well, but Mr. Chen will want to hear from you."

Mr. Chen's small, pouched eyes, opaque as fermented black beans, fix on Bao. Accusing, yet also terribly sad. Bowing, Bao makes a hasty exit.

As he hurries through the mazelike mansion, Bao asks a passing servant how to find the main gate. He's looking for the family from the medicine shop. They can't have gone too far. In the broad street outside, lined with plane trees, he spots them about to climb into a rickshaw.

"Wait!" he gasps, running after them. He's too old for gestures like this, but he ignores the ache in his chest, the twinge in his weak knee. They turn, and as he gazes at the small woman, he suddenly knows who she is. "Tagtaa!"

Immediately, he regrets this. Strange men shouldn't run after respectable widows on the street, shouting their personal names. The master of the medicine shop frowns, tugging his mother's arm to get her away. But she says with delighted astonishment, "Bao?"

"Yes, it's me!" He steps forward into the brilliant sunshine, out of the shadow of the buildings.

As he does, her grandson gives him a look of absolute horror, as though Bao is a ghost or some undead creature.

51

I ought to have kept my mouth shut as soon as the questioning began. But flippancy is the reverse side of my courage. I cannot change my nature. I've been dangled over city walls for my defiance, so I hoped that Mr. Chen (extremely purple in the face now) had no such plans.

Perhaps this might be the end.

There'd been many times since I'd lost my child that such thoughts had occurred to me. Why should I still go on? Bektu was dead and young Chen drowned. If screaming and yelling at me made his father feel slightly better, then that was all right by me. So I didn't resist when they dragged me off.

Take her away had been Mr. Chen's instruction, accompanied by a hand signal. Not being able to speak to the guard meant I had limited influence over him. Indeed, this is one reason why such servants were in great demand in the past. A fox's voice is one of its chief weapons. Many a nobleman or -woman has been seduced by sweet nothings whispered through a crack in the wall. If Mr. Chen had been at all reasonable, he'd have realized that locking me up wouldn't bring back his son, but I understood his grief.

If I were honest, had I truly only thought of avenging my child, or had hunting Bektu been an outlet for my own rage? Though I hadn't managed to kill Bektu myself, I'd the uneasy feeling that I might have led someone else to do it. Which complicated matters on a moral plane. While I was trying to puzzle out exactly where my guilt began and ended, we arrived at my prison.

I say "prison" because that's obviously what it was. A little stone room, standing in a barren high-walled courtyard. No windows save a narrow grating on the door. Whoever built it had some experience in confining people, since there was a convenient slot for sliding food under the door. Inside was a bucket for night soil and, more ominously, an iron ring fixed into the wall. My sympathies for Mr. Chen as a bereaved parent drained away as I beheld this. Clearly, the man was a professional jailer.

Normally, rich financiers do not maintain private prisons. I was beginning to feel alarmed. If they chained me to the wall, I'd be in serious trouble, but the guard merely shoved me in and closed the door. I heard the jingle of keys, then the clink of a dropped bolt. The cell smelled of dried mouse urine and despair. As there was nothing else to do, I curled up on the dusty floor and went to sleep.

When trapped, it's best to conserve energy until the time is right. As I drifted off, I had two realizations: First, I didn't actually want to die. At least not at the hands of the Chen family, in this terrible stone room without even a proper privy. Second, if I were killed here, Kuro might go crazy. That worried me. Shiro has his moments (including burning down half a town after being cheated at gambling), but Kuro is a lot more methodical. And I really didn't wish to add to his sins. I already had a horrible suspicion about both Bektu's and Chen's deaths.

I consoled myself that Kuro would have no idea what had happened this morning if Shiro kept his mouth shut. Besides, the specter of Miss Yukiko's soft hands wound around Kuro's arm rose in my mind. He had no reason to look for me anymore. Nobody did. Feeling rather sorry for myself, I squeezed my eyes shut.

I WOKE FROM my nap with a start. The door opened slowly. A sad, faded-looking woman put a tray of food on the ground. It seemed nobody had given her proper instructions on how to deal with prisoners. You should never open the door if they're unchained, like I was. That's what the meal slot was for. She'd also tucked the keys roughly into her pocket, so a child could remove them. But she was curious; her wondering gaze rested on my face. I obliged by looking tearful.

"*Ah jie,*" I said, calling her older sister, politely. "Why am I locked up here?"

She said, "Aren't you the Third Young Master's lover?"

"How could that be? I'm a virtuous woman. I've been married, and I even had a child." Strangely, I now began to weep real tears. If my child were still alive, I'd make sure that no man ever locked her up in a room like this.

"I'm sure they'll only keep you for a day. The master's so upset that he had to lie down."

"How should I explain this to my husband? I never had anything to do with young Chen." Tears ran down my face, mixed with snot. Now I was really howling, not just for show, but for all the grief and loneliness I'd endured over the past two years.

Feeling sorry, the woman brought over a jug of water. "Here, drink this." While she bent over, I slipped the key out of her pocket and up my sleeve.

"I can't stay here. It's haunted."

At this, she gave a start. "Did anyone say so to you?"

"No, but I can sense it. There's something in this room." Looking up, I pointed vaguely at the ceiling, guessing that this little prison had its own share of grim rumors. "Like a person with long black hair."

The effect was quite satisfactory. The poor woman blanched.

"It's hanging there right now. Please let me out!"

"I can't." Rising swiftly to her feet, she backed away.

"There's black hair in the corners, too," I said softly. "Hanks of human hair."

For some reason, humans dislike cut hair, perhaps because hair and bones are the last substances to decompose in a grave. The servant ran out of my prison with a clatter. She was so rattled that she let the thin metal bolt drop down into place without locking the door with the key: the same key that was now up my sleeve.

Now all I had to do was lift the bolt. But first, I sat down and ate the plain *mantou*, or bun, she'd brought and drank all the water. Then I took out the paring knife from Moji. It was a good thing that nobody had bothered to search me because the blade fit neatly into the door crack. Carefully, I levered the bolt up off its slot.

* * *

THIS WAS THE second time in one day that I'd escaped within the Chen compound. They were really very careless, I thought as I locked the door behind me and put the bolt in place. It would take a while to discover my absence, and that locked door would cause no end of speculation. And now what should I do? I could run away, though that might cause problems. Instead, I decided to pay Mr. Chen a personal visit.

Foxes are incurably nosy. That's why you'll often find us at festivals, riots, and other people's birthday parties. I'm not saying this is a good thing—many a fox has been killed for trespassing—but who am I to deny our nature? I couldn't resist peeking into every room that I trotted past. Mr. Wang's garden villa had been filled with rare bonsai. Mr. Chen's house was stuffed with antique porcelain and paintings. I reflected on this coincidence; when you've more money than could be used in a single lifetime, people start to get grandiose.

Unlike Mr. Wang's deserted garden villa, this mansion was filled with people. If I had to choose, crowds are better. An intruder is less likely to be noticed when people are clomping down hallways and chattering loudly. I searched methodically for Mr. Chen; he'd struck me as somewhat resistant to foxes, although I'd not been able to test him one-on-one. Though the very skilled among us can sway crowds, most foxes have trouble with more than three people at a time. But one person, in a quiet room, is a different matter.*

When I found Mr. Chen, however, he wasn't alone.

He was resting in a private study that opened onto a court-yard. Large vases of Ming blue porcelain stood tastefully here and there, the walls were hung with paintings of landscapes and clouds, and precious scrolls were piled on side tables. The whole room looked like an arsonist's dream. Mr. Chen was propped up on a daybed inlaid with mother-of-pearl. Seated at a respectful distance was Lu.

I recalled that Lu and Chen were childhood friends, which explained the scolding he was getting from Chen's father.

"Why didn't you tell me about my son and that woman? To think that he would go so far as to strangle her!" Mr. Chen's face was mottled, his voice hoarse.

*People like Bektu Nikan who are completely immune to us are very rare.

"I didn't wish to trouble you." Lu shifted uneasily, his camel lip pursed. "It's all her fault. She tried to seduce him from the beginning."

It's never pleasant to eavesdrop, especially when people are lying about you. Gritting my teeth, I inched closer.

"Was she the reason why he took a leave of absence from his studies? I hope for your family's sake—and mine—that none of you were involved in some foolish revolution."

Lu kept his eyes down. "I'd never dream of it."

"I heard that there was trouble with a photographer in Moji who ended up dead. Was he the one rumored to be a blackmailer?"

"How did you know?" Lu's lantern-jawed profile went rigid.

"I have my sources. Last summer a student threw himself off a bridge because he was blackmailed over some salacious photographs. I said nothing at the time as indiscretions with women aren't my concern, but treason is another matter. Talk of revolution could sink this family. And yours, too. Don't forget that I'm helping your father with his debts."

Mr. Chen's hard stare was unnerving. "Was my son being pressured by him? You'd better tell the truth."

Lu's eyes darted around the room. "Of course not. You told me to keep an eye on him, and I did."

"Like you didn't tell me about him strangling that servant on the ship?"

"That . . . that wasn't important. I wished to spare you pain."

Mr. Chen fixed him with a piercing glare. "Well, you didn't. That girl is trouble. And I just received word that someone else is coming this afternoon, apparently concerning that woman again. I received a card from this man." He tossed over a calling card and a note. "He's a Russian financier. I don't know him well, but I'd better see him."

Lu looked shocked, and so did I. As far as I knew, I had no connections to Russian financiers.

52

It's really Tagtaa. She stands before Bao, smiling with delight. The longer he gazes at her, the more he sees the little girl who played with him in the heart of a rhododendron bush. She takes a step towards him, hands out, as though they're still children, then stops herself.

"Mother," says the master of the medicine shop, "who is this?"

Bao introduces himself, noting the flicker of unease in her son's eyes. A childhood friend who works for Mr. Chen? Bao hastily assures them that it isn't the case; he happened to be dragged into it by Hong's enthusiasm and their fleeting past connection.

"Let's not stand in the street," says Tagtaa. "Come to our house. It's been a long time."

She suggests that her grandson accompany Bao in a rickshaw while she and her son ride another one. This proposal is met with great reluctance from the young man. He turns ashen, glances away, and seems almost terrified of Bao. Tagtaa is too excited to notice this, but Bao is taken aback.

In the narrow rickshaw, the young man scoots into the corner. His fingers tremble, and Bao wonders if he's an opium addict. But the pupils of his eyes are normal, and the sweat on his brow seems more like nerves.

"Thank you for accompanying me today," says Bao politely.

After a long pause, Bohai breaks his silence. "Does my grandmother know you well?"

"We were childhood friends."

"I see." He turns stiffly away. From time to time, the young man reaches into his pocket nervously. Bao wonders if he's carrying a knife. But that's nonsense. Still, his discomfort unsettles Bao, so he's glad when they finally disembark, the rickshaw swaying violently as Bohai springs out in relief, as though he can't bear to sit next to Bao for one moment longer.

Back at the medicine hall, the chief clerk greets them anxiously. "How did it go, *tai furen?*" Bao notes that he asks Tagtaa, not the master of the medicine shop.

"Not so well. They kept Ah San." Her face falls.

What has Tagtaa been doing, all these years? The last day and a half have been filled with strange occurrences, as though a lifetime's worth of coincidence is spinning them together, or perhaps it's the fate of a fox god that has reunited them.

Finally, they're alone. Not really alone, of course. How could a respectable widow receive a man by herself? But the servants who set down clinking teacups in the salon aren't particularly interested in Bao, an old man visiting an old lady. Tagtaa's son has excused himself on business matters, and Bohai has disappeared. Seated at a round marble table, its cool stone surface traced with veins of gray, Bao feels a flutter in his chest as Tagtaa pours tea. The light color reminds him of Shirakawa's eyes.

"How did you know it was me?" she says.

"I just knew. And you?"

"Nobody else calls me Tagtaa." When she smiles, the lines around her eyes crinkle.

"Not even your husband?"

"He's been gone for more than thirty years."

To hide his guilty gladness, Bao shares an abbreviated sketch of his own life. Catching Tagtaa's eye, he feels a warmth spreading in his chest. *Have you been happy?* he wants to ask, but that would be too forward. Instead, he says, "Is your family all right? Today must have been difficult."

Unlike her son and grandson, Tagtaa harbors no suspicion towards him. "I'm worried about my servant."

The fox lady, as Bao calls her in his mind. Should he tell Tagtaa that he's been sent looking for her? As he hesitates, she says, "I can't believe Mr. Chen detained her. Can you help?"

"I'll try. Though I barely know Mr. Chen," he warns.

"He trusts you. I saw how he glanced at you. You still have that habit of grimacing when people lie."

"You remember that?" Bao is embarrassed yet delighted.

"Of course. You're the only person who always tells the truth. Please help her—she's a good girl."

A good girl. That's not exactly how Bao would describe the fox lady, who in the flesh is more winsome and delicately insolent than he ever imagined. In fact, whenever he thinks of her, he starts to feel dizzy, the same way Shirakawa affected him. Surreptitiously, he checks under the table. His shadow is still there, attached to his feet though it's as worrisomely faint as it was after he awakened from his strange dream.

"Have you heard any rumors about foxes?" he asks.

It's an odd question to ask in that quiet room with an imported brass clock ticking in the corner, but he knows he can ask Tagtaa. Her eyes light up and she clasps his hand. "I've been waiting and wanting to tell someone about this, and for you to come today is almost too wonderful."

"What do you mean by that?" And now Bao's heart thumps unevenly, like a youth of fourteen. Her hand is warm and feels as though she's seized his heart.

"About foxes! Do you think we met again today because of the fox god?"

"I made an offering the other day," he confesses. "I put some goose meat and rice under a bush." *Crazy talk*, he thinks. But Tagtaa looks delighted; the years have melted away and they're together again, telling each other their secrets.

"I have something to tell you." Will she say that she's thought of Bao over the years? But Tagtaa whispers, "I met the black fox."

"You did?"

"I think so. Or his grandson." Her cheeks flush and Bao's stomach drops. Anyone listening to them would think they're insane. Maybe they both are. Bao opens his mouth, trying to think of what to say, as a shadow falls over them. They spring apart like guilty children to meet Bohai's accusing eyes.

"Grandmother," he says, "why are you holding this man's hand?"

Embarrassed, she drops Bao's hand. "I'm sorry, I forgot myself."

Bao apologizes, too, but the young man's eyes narrow. He stares at Bao so insistently that he half rises. "Perhaps I should be going."

"So soon? Where are you staying, Bao?"

Hearing his grandmother address him so familiarly, Bohai twitches a hand towards his pocket, and Bao has that presentiment of danger again. He gives the address of his hotel. Gazing at Tagtaa's face, old but still sweet, like the last plum left to wrinkle in a corner of the storehouse, he can only think, *I liked you when we were fourteen and I still like you now.*

"May I call on you again tomorrow?"

"Yes, we have so much to talk about!"

Bohai frowns. Bao takes his cue and leaves. Somehow this young man dislikes him intensely, or is it merely protectiveness towards his grandmother? Bao reflects that he's behaved improperly, holding her hand and speaking so familiarly. The idea is amusing at their age, but a woman, even a beloved matriarch, is never completely free to do as she wishes.

On his way out, Bao passes the master of the medicine shop. He looks worried yet excited, standing in the open passageway between the family's private quarters and the medicine shop. From the letter clutched in his hand, a messenger has just left. Bao makes his polite goodbyes. "Thank you, it was wonderful to meet an old friend again."

"My mother was very happy to see you."

The man looks so distracted that Bao asks if he's all right.

"Ah, yes. I just heard that I'm about to become a father again. The baby is due either tonight or tomorrow." His smile is sheepishly proud.

Bao congratulates him. "I wish your wife a safe childbirth."

The master of the medicine shop scratches his eyebrow. "It's not my wife, but my concubine. She's at a different house." A concubine installed in a separate household usually means relations are strained with the first wife. Bao wonders whether the child about to be born is a boy or a girl. If it's another son, perhaps that would explain Bohai's nervousness. But why would that displace him? He looks to be in his early twenties, old enough to get married and have children himself. A much younger half-brother will have little impact.

Or so Bao thinks. After all, every family has its own secrets.

53

I couldn't think of a single reason why Mr. Chen should be visited by a Russian financier with an interest in me. The last time I'd been in Vladivostok was years ago, when it was a new Imperial naval base; at the time I'd decided it was punishingly cold. Besides, Russians are a little too fond of fox fur.

The sound of approaching voices. Could this Russian be arriving right now? I'd been standing just inside the door, out of Lu and Mr. Chen's line of sight, and had no choice but to scuttle farther in. Fortunately, there was an enormous porcelain jar in the corner, as large as a man, that I squeezed behind.

Tramp, tramp went the footsteps. Four people entered the room. A retainer, who announced the others and then exited; an expensive-looking woman with a fur stole; Shiro; and then (*No, please no*) Kuro. There was no sign of any Russians.

Mr. Chen looked surprised. "I thought Mr. Turgenev was coming. Where is he?"

The woman, who'd introduced herself as Zhou Yuling, said, "I'm afraid that I'm the one who sent his card. I'm his wife."

At least that was the word she used. We all knew that she was likely his official mistress in Dalian, but I was rather impressed with her. In her mid-thirties with a strong jaw and wide face, she looked vaguely familiar. Apparently, she came from an impoverished patrician family. Mr. Chen asked after her father, though he seemed puzzled as to why she was here now. Frankly I was, too, until I saw her steal a quick glance at Shiro.

Oh, I see. Shiro was the cause of this. I had to admire his nerve, as I suddenly realized that Zhou Yuling had been one of the ladies who'd seen him off at the docks, when we'd departed from Dalian. Why had he called in this woman, who was clearly madly in love with him? I could see it in the way her eyes drifted hungrily, back and forth, as though she were starving, and Shiro's flesh was the only meat and drink that would sate her. I would have warned him that she was getting to the dangerous stage. Why hadn't Kuro stopped him?

But I refused to look at him. I didn't want Kuro involved at all.

"Mr. Chen," said the lady (such an expensively dressed lady, as though she'd armored herself in her patron's money), "I'm here to retrieve my friend's servant."

"You mean the maid from the medicine hall." He was no fool, was Mr. Chen.

"That's right. Her mistress wants her back."

"I think not. I told the old lady I would keep her servant."

Zhou Yuling's painted lips trembled. She'd been very bold, using her patron's name to get in and hoping that it would open doors. Which it had, but only up to here.

Mr. Chen's mouth tightened dismissively. "I'll send her back after I've questioned her. After all, you say you're doing this for a friend"—here, he cut his eyes knowingly at Shiro—"but in light of my son's loss, I'm sure you understand my claim is greater."

Kuro made a slight movement, a shifting of his shoulders. It meant he'd come to a decision, one that he'd carry through fire and ruin. I really can't stand it when people decide things for me. Besides, I was tired of crouching behind the vase, so I made my appearance. The effect was ruined by stumbling over a potted plant, but still quite satisfactory. Mr. Chen's face turned purple. At this rate, he might keel over if I kept reappearing without being summoned.

"You!" he exclaimed. An inelegant greeting, but we foxes are used to it. "How did you get out again?"

I ignored this. "Did you not wish to question me, Mr. Chen?"

Flick, flick went his eyes, like a lizard on a wall. The tension made my ears ring. It's not good to have too many foxes in one room, particularly if they're each exerting their will. I almost expected to see fur fly, so electric was the atmosphere. I focused my will on Mr. Chen; I only had to get one person to agree with me. Mentally, I hoped everyone else would stay out of it.

At last, he said in a strangled voice, "Yes."

I took a quick gauge of the room. Neither Lu (still frozen in his seat) nor Mr. Chen was particularly susceptible to foxes. As for the woman, Zhou Yuling, who'd bought Shiro and Kuro entry to this house through her relationship with a Russian financier—well, she was an unpredictable quantity.

My heart was pounding. It had been a long time since I'd done anything like this, with so many in attendance. "If I grant your request, will you agree to mine?"

You must always outline the contract clearly, whether it's between you and your fishmonger, or the emperor's favorite general.

"Yes."

My eyes glittered. I know it's a little unseemly, but I always feel like this when I make a formal bargain, though I try to avoid them if possible. The air in the room turned chilly, as though a breeze from the north had slipped into the room. The hair on the men's necks was standing up.

"What do you wish to know from me? What is your heart's desire right now?"

A shudder ran through Mr. Chen. Clearly, he wasn't used to being questioned by a woman.

"My son," he said at last. "I heard he was involved with you. I want to know if you're possibly carrying his child."

And now I finally understood what he'd been driving at and why he'd insisted on bringing me to this house. How terribly, terribly sad. I know what it's like to cling to shreds of hope, long after a soul has left this earth.

"It's not true. I had no such relationship with him."

Mr. Chen closed his eyes. "But you said my heart's desire! You haven't given it to me yet."

Oh no. I'd assumed his heart's desire was to question me. I'd been careless with the wording. Shiro's eyes rolled in alarm, and as for Kuro—well, I didn't want to know. I took a deep breath, feeling the room quiver in agitation. It must be done swiftly, before I lost everyone's attention.

"I answered your question. Now my request is that you leave the Huang family alone."

Before he could answer, Kuro's voice cut through the room like a dark knife. "Don't listen to her. Mr. Chen, do not accept such a bargain."

As soon as he spoke, the thin vibrating tug of everyone's attention broke in a hundred spider-thin lines. Their thoughts scattered, like marbles rolling across the floor. The delicate balance that I'd been building toppled.

"What?" I cried indignantly. This was dangerous and no fox should do this to another, not when you're making a proper contract.

"Exactly! I'll be taking her home now." Shiro seized my wrist.

There was an agonized wail from Zhou Yuling. "Shira-kawa, you said she was just a servant. What's she to you?"

And Lu began to scream.

It was a high-pitched shriek, shocking from such a tall man. Some people can't deal with mental interference, particularly if they're already agitated. Lunging forward, I smacked him sharply on the forehead. That's the only way to stop people from going on to delusions like being forced to eat acorns and worms, and then going crazy and burning all the local foxes.

Lu hurled himself at me, upsetting his chair. Eyes rolling back in his head, he made horrible slavering noises as I fell on the floor. Shiro dropped my wrist as Zhou Yuling twined herself around him, weeping. Kuro seized Lu by the collar. It was as though a howling chaos had taken hold of the room and madness was seeping everywhere. An overturned incense burner spewed burning embers across a table. Mr. Chen's mouth hung open as I grabbed his knees. He recoiled in horror (perhaps nobody had dared handle him in years).

"Let go, you disrespectful woman!" he shouted.

"I haven't finished! I want you to leave the Huang family alone."

"Why should I make a bargain with you? You've no stand-ing or family—you're nobody!"

Kuro yanked Mr. Chen's chin up. His long-fingered hand gripped his face too tight; I could see it in his white knuckles.

"She is my wife," he said.

THERE WAS A moment of perfect silence, in which I could hear a bird singing in the distance. A vein stood out on Kuro's neck as he held Mr. Chen's gaze. I could feel the pressure in the room, so heavy that I couldn't breathe. Closing my eyes, I willed everyone to exhale. Lu stopped screaming. Mr. Chen looked dazed. Even Zhou Yuling, who'd been overcome by a storm of weeping, subsided. My legs trembled; my stomach heaved. But this was only a temporary reprieve.

Soon, they'd recover, riding that wave of resentment that always comes over those who realize they've been unduly influenced. That loathing that manifests in a raging desire to slaughter every fox in the area. Nobody likes to feel a fool, and the downside of playing with people's feelings is the whiplash fury of betrayal. I could almost smell the burning pyres when I realized that there really was smoke. Flames licked across the table, piled with priceless scrolls. The incense burner that Lu had knocked over had started a fire. Shouts broke out as the smoke billowed up, catching thin sheets of loose rice paper. Mr. Chen's face contorted like an opera mask as Zhou Yuling continued to wail. There was nothing for it but to run.

And run we did. I couldn't believe how quickly the room was engulfed in smoke, as flames greedily engulfed the hang-ing scrolls and the loose billowing gauze curtains to the courtyard. The sound of smashing porcelain made me wince, Song dynasty celadon destroyed by the hasty firefighting attempts of servants, who swarmed like a panicked ants' nest. We dashed through courtyards and legged it over the walls. Some were too high for me to manage, but Kuro yanked me over. Shiro came behind, gasping and panting. I hadn't seen him run so fast in years.

At the last wall, the perimeter that encircled this grand,

sprawling mansion, my stomach sank. It was too high. We'd never make it. Black smoke billowed up behind us. The urgent cries of guards echoed across the stone courts: "Catch them!" Kuro braced himself against the wall.

"Stand on my shoulders," he told me.

"What about you?"

"Don't worry about me." Those were the exact words he'd said at the Mongol siege of Kaifeng.

"Are you crazy?" I shouted.

He didn't bother to answer, just grabbed me and boosted me up. Shiro yelled, "Hurry up, you idiots!" and then I was perched at the top of the wall, looking down at the other side. It was so very high, but I'd no time to hesitate as Shiro ascended next, scrabbling over Kuro's shoulders. Gripping my hands, he lowered me over the wall, my feet dangling for a heart-freezing moment. Then he let go and I fell, dropping into a crouch. Shiro followed after. From behind the wall, I heard shouts.

"What about Kuro?" I cried, even as Shiro hauled me to my feet.

Seizing me by the elbow, he dragged me along. "If we get caught now, it will be for naught. Come on!"

People poured into street, drawn by the billowing smoke and shouts. Our faces were blackened with smoke, the hem of my dress ripped, and Shiro's jacket had split down the back. We looked frightful, and I might have laughed if I hadn't been so worried about Kuro.

"We should wait for him."

"Don't be silly. He'll get out—hurry up!"

I didn't know Dalian well, but Shiro clearly did as we turned down one alleyway after another until we arrived in Oda's backyard. It looked smaller and shabbier in the daylight, though the wisteria vine that led up to the second floor was now in full bloom. Shiro unlocked the back door.

The stairs to the second floor creaked as we tiptoed up. It was dim, the light from the windows green from the wisteria outside, and smelled like chemicals from the darkroom below. Shiro's room under the eaves was much as it had been the night I'd visited. Bare, save for a rumpled bed and unpacked trunks. There was a pitcher and basin on a washstand, and fresh water. While I was cleaning the scratches on my hands, Shiro stripped off his torn shirt.

I was too tired to say anything to him, so I turned my back and continued washing my face. "Is Kuro going to meet us here?" I asked.

He came up behind me. Not touching, but close enough that I could feel the heat of his bare chest, the tickle of his breath against my ear. "We shouldn't wait here. Mr. Chen is bound to come looking."

"But what about Kuro? Did you agree on a meeting place?" Shiro is very slippery, a master of the nonanswer, and you must pin him down.

"This is all because of you," he said. "Kuro requested—actually he insisted—that we go to the Chen mansion, even though I told him it was a bad idea."

"So you asked your mistress, Zhou Yuling?" A thought struck me. "We left her behind! What's she going to do?" I'd completely forgotten about that poor woman, who'd been wailing maniacally when the fire started.

"She'll be all right."

"How do you know?" I swung around. "And you shouldn't have used her. It won't take much to push her over the edge; she'll be completely uncontrollable."*

He shrugged. "It wasn't my choice. If I get stabbed one of these days, it will be your fault."

I didn't have the heart to argue. None of this was going to bring consolation to Chen's father in that burning mansion, nor would it return my child to me.

"The problem with you and Kuro is that you're both so half-hearted." Shiro elbowed me aside so he could wash his face as well.

I glared at his lean back. "That's because we have something called a conscience."

"Conscience is overrated. Sainthood is also overrated. I never thought about embarking on the thousand-year journey."

"Shiro, you need to break it off with that woman properly."

*Certain people develop immunity and mania if over-exposed to foxes. That's why we try to limit relations with humans. Think of us as a drug that should be taken only in small doses.

"Believe me, I tried. I even got on a ship to get rid of her."

"You know you shouldn't make contracts lightly."

His eyes opened wide in mock horror. "You're one to talk! You just offered Mr. Chen his heart's desire. It's a good thing Kuro stopped you."

"I wasn't thinking. I haven't done anything like this for a long time."

Shiro sighed. "You're making too many mistakes. And Kuro is probably finished."

"How could you say that?" Enraged, I hurled the towel at his head.

Shiro dodged neatly. "Obviously, because of the scar on his face. You know he won't survive long like that. He's too recognizable."

I hung my head. A wrenching sadness filled me.

"Are you crying, Snow? Funny, I thought you never wanted to see him again."

Sometimes I can't tell if Shiro is being malicious, or trying, in his own warped way, to do me a favor. Shaking him off, I went and curled up on the bed. Shiro continued changing his clothes. When he was done, he started packing up. "Aren't you going to ask where I'm going?"

"I don't care."

"Don't tell me that you're planning to go back to the Chen mansion to look for Kuro. That's the stupidest thing you could do. And he wouldn't want it." Shiro knelt, resting his chin on the bed. He looked tired and rather angelic, as though he was waiting to have his ears patted, but that wasn't going to fool me. "I've said this before, but stop being so moralistic."

"I'm trying to do less damage. Which is more than can be said about you! You never did explain whether you had anything to do with those people Oda said were found in alleyways."

"You can't expect me to recall every meal I've had. Besides, I don't believe any of them were dead when we parted—they were all having a delightful time. One courtesan practically dragged me out of a teahouse in Mukden, saying she'd rather spend the evening walking in the snow with me. It's a natural cycle. We prey on humans, and they kill us whenever they find us. There's no more regret than a shark taking a bite out of a man's leg."

"Shiro, you know very well there are other ways to live."

"Ah, but then I wouldn't be a beast, as they say." Shiro showed his teeth briefly. "Why struggle against your nature? You should enjoy life."

He smiled. "Preferably with me."

54

Bao walks back towards his hotel. There's a tight giddiness in his chest that he hasn't experienced for years. He feels as though he's seventeen again. Or maybe even younger, that magical age when the world is bright with possibilities. It's because of Tagtaa, of course. She's aged but hasn't changed. Over the years he's observed this phenomenon in his old friends—though their bodies have weathered, stretched, or shrunk, the same soul peeks out from within.

Tagtaa is a respectable widow, and Bao should really be attending to other matters, including the elusive woman who he's finally met. Bao's recollections of being in Mr. Chen's meeting room with her and Shirakawa are strangely foggy. When he tries to focus, he starts to feel feverish, as though his body temperature is rising and falling erratically.

The fox lady is now locked up in Mr. Chen's mansion. That worries him, not to mention that Tagtaa is distressed. As he walks, he inhales slowly, feeling the increasing pain in his left lung. Back in his hotel, Bao tells himself he'll lie down for a moment. Enough to calm his racing heart and decide what to do.

Closing his eyes, Bao slips out of consciousness into a dream world of mansions and gardens, princely courtyards that lead to crooked bridges. He's running low to the ground on all fours. *I must be a fox*, he thinks without surprise, *or maybe a dog*. His neat paws trot along winding paths, looking for something, or is it someone? At the foot of a stone bridge, curved like a turtle's back, he finds her. A pretty white fox stands there, head tilted.

"Everything is burning." Her eyes are dark and serious, so different from the flippantly defiant woman he met at Chen's mansion. Yet they're the same. *Is this your true form?* he wants to ask, but the sense of destruction—of pavilions and towers burning, silk curtains catching fire, and sparks flying in the air—overwhelms him. He's seeing an ancient city burn, Chang'an, or perhaps the fabled Kaifeng through her eyes.

"Are you looking for Shirakawa?"

"He's not the one."

She turns and starts to run. Why do the foxes avoid him? Why do they run away each time? Embers and half-burnt fragments of paper drift past him like a soot snowstorm. The smell of burning grows stronger, until Bao wakes up, gasping.

THROUGH THE OPEN window, he sees a faint column of smoke in the distance. A building really is burning somewhere. Bao ought to go to Mr. Chen's mansion to give an update, though he hasn't been formally engaged. It will reflect badly on Hong if he never comes back. Sitting up, Bao grimaces. His head feels clouded, the same disorienting vagueness that Bao recalls from childhood after that bad bout of jaundice when his nanny prayed to the fox god. He's running low on stomach medicine and decides to buy some on his way to Mr. Chen's mansion.

As he passes the side gate of the medicine shop, it opens unexpectedly. A head pops out—one of the servants who served tea to Bao and Tagtaa earlier. Recognizing Bao, she looks confused. "Are you here to see my mistress again?"

"Ah, no, I forgot to buy some stomach medicine," Bao says with embarrassment.

"If you're *tai furen*'s guest, there's no need to go to the storefront." Before Bao can stop her, she's called out to someone inside the courtyard. "Young Master, there's a guest here."

The person who comes to the side gate is Tagtaa's grandson. Bohai's mouth drops open and the whites of his eyes show upon seeing Bao. It's such an extreme reaction that Bao wonders if the young man has suddenly been taken ill or seen a ghost. Glancing behind, Bao sees nobody else on the side street. There's only himself, outlined by the late-afternoon sun.

"I didn't mean to bother you," says Bao hastily. "I was passing by on other business."

Bohai's gaze is drawn to the ground, staring so intensely

that Bao, too, looks down. Though faint, his shadow is still there. Or is it? Suddenly dizzy, Bao clutches the side of the gate. It's the same disembodied sensation that he had upon waking from his nap. The young man freezes as though approaching a dangerous beast.

"What other business?"

"I'm on my way to Mr. Chen's mansion."

"So am I. My grandmother asked me to go and check on her servant Ah San." Bohai immediately looks like he regrets blurting that out. He's nervous; his hands tremble, and Bao wonders again if this young man is right in the head.

"Shall we go together?" Bao asks awkwardly, since they've both declared their intentions.

Bohai glances around, gnawing his lip. He appears to have nerved himself up for a confrontation. After some hesitation, they head off reluctantly together. They hail a rickshaw, and once again, Bohai sits as far away as possible. As they rattle along, he clears his throat.

"Sir," he says formally, with none of that pretend-relative familiarity, "you're not an ordinary man, are you?"

Did Tagtaa tell her grandson about his odd knack of hearing lies? When faced with uncertainty, Bao falls back on the truth. "Yes, you could say there's something strange about me."

The young man gives a terrified twitch. "I knew it," he mumbles. "So you admit that you're one of them."

"One of what?"

"People without shadows."

Bao is speechless. How does this young man know about his dreams? Or about his nanny asking the fox god to take away his shadow? He's only discovered her request recently himself, and doesn't know how to reply. The smell of burning has been steadily getting stronger as they turn a corner.

"Looks like a fire up ahead!" says the rickshaw man.

Distracted, Bao peers out. Could it be the Chen mansion? Smoke pours out from behind high walls as stray dogs bark hysterically and people shout. Unable to go farther, the rickshaw man halts. Bao alights to pay him, but Bohai crouches in the corner, sweating and trembling.

"Have you come for me?" His small eyes are wide with fear.

"Come down," Bao says kindly. "I won't hurt you."

"If I'm not the one you're after, who is it?"

His words make no sense to Bao. At that moment, there's a deafening rumble and roaring sound. Part of a building behind the high walls has fallen. The crowd gives a collective gasp; screams break out. Some retreat, while others press forward eagerly. If a rich man's house burns, there may be looting. Emboldened, the crowd rushes forward, creating a shoving tide of push and pull. Bao thinks they'd better get away on foot, rather than be stranded in a rickshaw, and holds out his hand again.

"Are you after my grandmother then?" Bohai's lip trembles.

What can Bao say to that? "It's true that your grandmother interests me."

Bohai blanches, then, with a sudden jerk, launches himself out of the rickshaw. The young man stumbles into the road, casting around wildly as if all his nightmares have come to life. "Don't touch me!"

He flings himself into the crowd, now roaring in excitement as sparks fly and roof tiles crack. The blaze is rising in the inner courtyards; someone shouts that the house is full of priceless porcelain, and people surge forward, even as guards struggle to keep the gates closed. The heavy gate flies open, and in the frenzied press, a dark shape emerges from the mansion.

Bohai's eyes fix on it in desperate recognition. "Kurosaki!" he shrieks, even as he plunges out of Bao's grasp. "Kurosaki, help me!"

Who is this Kurosaki? The figure hesitates, then turns towards Bohai's frenzied cries, fighting the mob that eagerly strains forward. If her grandson is injured in a riot, Tagtaa will never forgive him. Bao tries to keep up with Bohai—is he having a fit? Flames lick up from behind the walls, and the crowd heaves dangerously again. People have been crushed to death in such stampedes.

Heart hammering, Bao reaches Bohai first and grabs his arm. "Come with me."

"Let go!" At the touch of his hand, Bohai's terror explodes. He tries to shake him off, but Bao hangs on grimly. If Bohai disappears into the crowd, who knows what will happen to him? "I won't go with you! Never!"

Bohai reaches into his pocket, the same pocket that he's been fingering, but there's too many people pressing against them and Bao can't see what he's pulling out until it's too late, there's a flash of metal. A searing pain as the knife plunges into Bao's side. More than anything, he's shocked. Bohai, grimacing in terror, waves his arm wildly. The knife blade is red. A spatter of blood hits Bao's face as Bohai lunges forward, slashing in reckless frenzy. The other man has reached them. Lean arms, strong back. Throwing himself forward, he shields Bao as he staggers under the attack.

Bohai flings the knife away, white-eyed and babbling. "Kurosaki! I didn't mean to hurt you! He has no shadow." His trembling finger points at Bao.

The man named Kurosaki turns to look at Bao.

It would be a memorable face, even if it weren't ruined by a scar. Bao thinks disjointedly that this man had better never find himself on a wanted poster because there's no mistaking such a mark. His head swims. A roaring fills his ears, or is it the howling crowd? Doubled over, Bao presses his side. Blood wells over his hands as he topples forward. Kurosaki's eyes gaze deep into Bao's. Dark as a bottomless pool, like a lake under moonlight. Bao is falling, sinking. Images flicker past: Ears lifted and a sharp muzzle across endless waves of grass. A lonely shape trotting down a mountain. Blink and he's back, staring into the eyes of this stranger. Unreadable eyes, grave yet inhuman. They pierce Bao to the depths of his soul, or perhaps that's the knife wound in his side.

Tagtaa, Bao thinks with utter surprise, *I've met the black fox.*

55

Of course I didn't stay in Shiro's room. How could I linger, in that bolt-hole under the eaves, with the light coming in green and dappled from the leaves outside? I said I would to shake Shiro off, but I wasn't sure if he believed me. After changing his clothes, Shiro looked the respectable gentleman. We usually pretend to be foreigners of some sort, and he'd clearly prepared for this.

"I think I shall be Mr. Kim, a traveling Korean merchant," he said. "Are you sure you don't want to be Mrs. Kim? I hear that Jeju Island is beautiful in spring."

In answer, I merely snarled at him.

"Oh, I forgot. You're already married." Shiro's eyes narrowed, mouth sliding into a lopsided smile. "Though you left him once already, Kuro doesn't seem to have changed his mind about your mutual status."

"Why are you still propositioning me—don't you feel any loyalty to him?"

He sighed. "For the longest time, I've been Kuro's friend. And I've also desired you. That hasn't changed." For once, Shiro looked absolutely serious. "It's the tragedy of my life."

I was almost taken in by his earnestness. Then I remembered that sympathy from women is something that Shiro cultivates in spades—also, all his fiancées have mysteriously ended up dead. "Go away, Shiro."

"I've often pondered where the three of us will end up," he mused. "Do you want to hear my predictions? I shall have a fairly entertaining life unless I'm poisoned. You're likely to be executed for insolence."

"How dare you!"

"Nobody talks back like you. If anyone completes the thousand-year path to sainthood, that would be Kuro. But I wouldn't give him such good odds anymore. You know what he's done, don't you?" I drew back with a hiss, but Shiro continued, "Or at least you suspect it. From the scar on his face. You and I know that Kuro is very unlikely to sustain an injury like that in a fight unless it was rigged against him."

Shiro gazed at me. Earnestly, sincerely, with his eyes the color of yellow wine and poisoned tea. I know he's quite capable of hurting me to achieve his aims. And I also know that he wants Kuro and me to stay with him, but in a different arrangement, with me as his mate and Kuro as his best friend. Shiro always has to be the center of everything. But two can play at that game, so I closed my eyes as though I were inconsolable.

"How shall I prove I'm serious about you?" he murmured.

"Stop killing people, for a start! Not only is it immoral, but it also endangers the rest of us."

He tilted his head. "I'll consider it."

"I haven't promised you anything though," I said warningly. "That ought to be your own ethical decision."

"You'll stay here till tomorrow?"

Nod.

"Very well, I'll be back soon." With that, Shiro went off to do goodness knows what. Likely raising money from various benefactors and women. As soon as I heard the back door click shut after him, I got up and wrote a quick note to Kuro in case he came by. I stuck it to the wall above the bed with my paring knife. A bit dramatic, but there was no mistaking it. As I fingered the knife, I felt a tingle of anxiety. Getting out of a burning house shouldn't be too difficult for Kuro. Why was it taking him so long? In the past two years, I'd done my best to stifle any feelings of longing or concern towards him, but now I couldn't help but wonder if something had happened.

I left a few other notes, including one scratched on the lower side of Oda's back door. Then I set off, having tidied my smoke-blackened clothing so when I showed my face at the medicine shop again, I hoped they wouldn't be too horrified.

My plan was to bid farewell to my old lady. Shiro would doubtless say that's a sign of my attachment to this world, but I've never listened to him anyway. Trotting along, I listened to the chatter on the streets. It seemed that Mr. Chen's mansion was still burning. I'd have thought a rich man would have a better-run household with firefighting capabilities, but they'd suffered a shock with the death of his son. The thought sobered me. When my own child was lost, I'd been unable to eat or even speak from sheer grief. The fury and sorrow that had consumed me left nothing for anyone else, as though a madness had descended upon me—one that was gradually fading.

All living creatures change in response to others. Coming out of the grasslands and seeing new people and places had softened the cracked clay of my heart, though attachment creates vulnerabilities. That's why hermits and sages of old always retired to a cave on a mountain, though the ones I met were all very ill-tempered, unwashed old men.

My old lady had enough troubles on her plate, what with her son having another child by a mistress and Bohai's increasingly erratic behavior. A shiver ran down my spine. That warning again, but I ignored it.

Heading to the side gate, I banged on it to avoid the front of the shop. If Mr. Chen found out that I'd stopped by after setting his house on fire, it would only complicate things for my mistress. Surprisingly, the gate popped open almost immediately. It was Ting, Madam Huang's servant.

"Ah San, you're back! Thank goodness."

"Were you expecting someone?"

"The young master went out a while ago, so I thought it might be him returning." Ting looked nervous. "He went with *tai furen*'s old friend. The man who came to visit when they returned from the Chen house."

Who was this old friend? The quiet fellow dressed in traveling clothes at Mr. Chen's house came to mind. I didn't have to wonder long though because my old lady came rushing out in joyful relief. She ran up to me like a little girl and clasped my hands. "Are you all right? Did they hurt you? How did you get out?"

I replied, yes, no, and an ambiguous shrug. It seemed that

news of the fire hadn't made its way to her ears yet. We went into her little back courtyard.

"Today is full of wonders," she said. "Do you remember my childhood friend? I met him again for the first time in fifty years."

"You mean the one who always told the truth," I said.

So Shiro had been right about that old man, the one he thought had been meddled with by a fox. I was instantly on the alert. There's no such thing as pure coincidence; when the tides of fate move, it's usually due to man's desires.

"How did he know to find you?"

"It was chance. He says he's become a private investigator. I was surprised, though when I think about it, it makes a lot of sense."

A private investigator who'd come down from Mukden. My nose prickled. Rich men tend to share their contacts, whether it's art dealers, brothels, or personal detectives, and Mr. Wang and Mr. Chen were family friends.

"Did he want anything from you?"

"No, we were just happy to see each other." And she really did look delighted. *Hm.* A childhood friend. Perhaps a little more than that, from her pink cheeks. "Though he did ask if I'd heard any rumors about foxes."

"I see." When three or more occurrences line up like this, a wise fox knows that it's time to disappear.

"You don't look surprised at all, Ah San. But I'm glad you're all right—I was so worried. I even put out an offering to the fox god." Tugging my hand, she showed me a makeshift altar under a bush. On it was a leaf adorned with flowers and a sweet bean paste cake. Like a child's offering: very pretty, though not much to eat. My heart melted a little.

"Not only did you return to me, but also my friend Bao," she said. "When Bao and I first became close, it was because we built an altar to the fox god together. So I believe."

Now was a good time, with no other servants around. I opened my mouth to bid her farewell, but what came out instead was "What do you believe?"

We sat under the elm tree on a stone bench. "Some people

say that old age is sorrow, but I don't find it so. As the daughter of a concubine, my youth was full of uncertainty. I married a man as old as my father, lost my stepson, and struggled to run this shop as a widow. Yet I feel happier the older I've become. I don't wish to be young again."

"Why's that?" I should really go, but curiosity is the weakness of foxes.

"I still feel the same way inside. You know, when I saw Bao, my heart skipped a little." She smiled, eyes crinkling. "You must think I'm a foolish old woman."

"Love is the same, at any age."

"I'm not sure you could call that love." Embarrassed, she shuffled her feet. "But seeing his face gave me such an unexpected pang. Tell me, do you ever miss your husband?"

It was the first time she'd asked me so directly, and I couldn't think of a reason not to answer her. "Once I would have said I didn't care if we never met again. But I think I'd be sad if something happened to him."

"Is he alive then?"

I'd given her the impression that he'd died, so I simply nodded.

"Was it an arranged marriage?"

"No, I fell in love with him as soon as I met him."

How WELL I remember that day.

The wind was blowing from the west, an autumn wind that smelled of damp yellow earth and rain. The grass bowed under heavy seed heads, and in the distance, gathering clouds were pierced by shafts of bright late sunshine. I'd stood at the top of a valley watching the dusty white road below as it wended its way across the wide sweep of the hills. Sun and rain together are what people call a day for a fox's wedding, though that's just folk superstition. We get married just the way you do, by choosing a lucky day that all parties agree on. In any case, I hadn't been thinking of getting married at all.

A purge of foxes had descended on the ancient city of

Luoyang, and we were leaving. Those of us with property had sold it (sometimes it was other people's property, though a righteous fox ought not to thieve), while others left with only a bag of millet. I was young then and didn't realize that what I witnessed was the beginning of the slow dwindling of our race. For every great purge has lessened our numbers, and our children are few and precious.

There was one last straggler, so my grandmother had informed me; I'd been instructed to wait for him. A friend of Shiro's, they'd said. I was annoyed. Shiro was always causing trouble (that hasn't changed to this day), and I didn't want to wait for his acquaintance, a fox from the north with the ridiculous name of Black. That could be anyone.

Then Kuro had come trotting up the hill towards me. Young, grave, and impossibly handsome. Carrying a large sack laden with grain and turnips, the final gleanings from a storehouse in the city for the elders, he'd said. Always so serious and stupidly noble for being the last to leave and risk being caught. Not my type at all, but his gaze had burned a hole in my heart, one that has never been filled by anyone else. And of course, I made a fool of myself.

I sighed.

My old lady didn't ask any more. That was the good thing about her, she had tact. The sort of tact learned when you're a concubine's child struggling in an unfriendly household. She said, "You're planning to say goodbye to me, aren't you?"

Indeed, I was. In all my leave-takings over the years, she was the first person to anticipate it.

"I'm happy that you returned today. I don't know why Mr. Chen wished to keep you, but he's bound to come looking soon."

In the distance, I could hear faint shouts. Chen's burning mansion was likely being looted. But here, under the light shade of the elm tree, it was green and still.

"Mistress," I said, but I never got to say goodbye to her because there was a commotion from the front shop and the servants burst in.

"The young master is out in the street, and he's covered with blood!

I ALWAYS SUSPECTED that Bohai would be trouble, though now wasn't a good time to be right. We rushed to the front, where a small crowd had gathered, shouting about the blaze that continued to burn the Chen mansion and could be seen from across the city. It had gutted half the house, and fire-fighting crews were struggling to contain it. But that didn't matter to me. I stared in disbelief at three figures splattered with blood. The rickshaw puller who'd brought them was demanding to be paid. They were heavy, he said, and one of them was a madman who claimed he'd killed a ghost.

56

Bao bumps along in a rickshaw, supported on the lap of the stranger named Kurosaki. Why did he think he was a fox and not a man? It must have been the shock, driving all rational thought out of Bao's head. Crammed in the other corner, Bohai has fallen silent, frozen like a nervous hare. The rickshaw man, the one who originally brought them to the Chen mansion, is now tasked with bringing them home, though he's reluctant because of the blood and grumbles that three are too heavy for him.

"I'd help you, but I'm not in good shape." Kurosaki speaks slowly, with pained effort. Yet his words, or perhaps it's his penetrating gaze, have an effect. The rickshaw puller shivers as though he's received an unseen directive. Without further complaint he shoulders on. At one point they get stuck in the crowd and Kurosaki leans out of the rickshaw, speaking to bystanders. They move aside obediently, even helping to push the rickshaw along for a while. It's strange, yet also exhausting, because each time Kurosaki leans back, his face looks paler.

If Bao weren't so weak and feeling such pain, he'd worry about that more, but he keeps his hand pressed to his side where the knife went in. Closing his eyes, he grits his teeth. Dying is more painful than he expected. No scenes of his past flash by, only stunned surprise, as though Bao's body hasn't quite absorbed the fact that he's been stabbed. His hands are clammy and cold. The bleeding from his side is slow but steady. Sweat pours down his forehead as they jolt towards the medicine hall. Ironic that Bohai's home is the best place to bring two wounded people. Bao suspects Kurosaki has also been injured. It's the way he sits carefully, propping up Bao's head and trying not to move too much himself.

And then they've arrived. The rickshaw man drops the poles with a clatter. The spell breaks, and he bursts out shouting that Bohai is crazy, and he wants to be paid. People spill from the shop like startled ants. There are wails and cries; Bohai stumbles out of the rickshaw and stands silently, trembling. The master of the medicine shop rushes up and seizes his son by the shoulders, exclaiming at the blood on his hands. Bao thinks faintly that he doesn't want to die on Tagtaa's doorstep and give her nightmares.

Faces. Tears. A beautiful woman is weeping over Bao. A bewitching creature, one that comes straight from the pages of an ancient book, bent over him. It's the fox lady he's been chasing, the beauty who's haunted his dreams. Has his life come to an end and is this heaven's reward? No, because her pretty eyes are all swollen and she's sobbing hard in a most undignified way, all hiccups and snot that she wipes with the back of her hand. Besides, she's not crying about Bao at all, but over Kurosaki, who still sits upright, cradling Bao's head on his lap. Kurosaki's arm is cold and stiff.

"What are you doing, you idiot?" she says. "How could you get stabbed like this?"

Bao, who has an unwitting front-stage seat to this drama, wants to say that it's not the stranger's fault, but Kurosaki smiles faintly. "I'm glad to see you again. I've fulfilled my promise to you."

"What promise did you make me?" She's crying again.

"I said I wouldn't leave you until my last breath."

"I don't want that! I want you to get well. I forgive you for everything—for leaving our child alone that day and going hunting. I've forgiven you a long time ago, so please don't die now."

"Snow, you must finish the thousand years without me." The words are slow; Kurosaki's breathing is uneven, his fingers icy even as they rest on Bao's chest.

Snow. So that's her true name. They speak as though Bao doesn't exist, and indeed, he doesn't in their world. He knows, wordlessly, that he's witnessing a tragedy. The end of the opera, the death of a lover. An impossibly old yet painful story, as though a hole has been torn in the firmament of stars. Tears run out of Bao's own eyes, trickling down his neck. Their longing and grief are so palpable that his own pain is forgotten.

Bao has always been the observer, the one who sorts out truth from shadows, and now, at the end of his own life, he senses no lie in their words.

Ah, he thinks, *I am sorry.*

WHEN BAO COMES to, he's staring at an unfamiliar ceiling. Outside the tall wooden-shuttered windows, dusk has encroached. Bao lies on a bed, his side neatly bandaged. The distinctive bitter smell of herbal concoctions drifts in, and he realizes he must be in the private quarters of the medicine shop. Outside, someone is giving quiet orders. "Please pay the doctor and instruct him to return tomorrow. Has my son calmed down yet? Tell him that I'll talk to Bohai myself."

It's Tagtaa, and he's never been happier to hear her competent voice. There's no weeping here, and he recalls her reputation for running the business. The door opens.

"Bao?" she says softly, coming to sit by his side. His throat is so dry that he can't speak, but Bao turns his head. "I must apologize to you, on behalf of my family."

"It's all right." Though of course it isn't. What happened to Bohai, anyway?

In answer to his questioning look, Tagtaa says, "My grandson has been confined to his room. We're extremely ashamed of his behavior." She pauses, painfully. "I know you're within your rights to report him to the authorities, but he's never done anything like this before. If you wish to turn him in, I won't stop you though."

Her lips tremble. Bao could keep Tagtaa on a string, make her wait on him, blackmail her into being close. But if he did, he'd hear the lie in her voice every day. So instead, he shakes his head.

"The other man," he says. "Kurosaki. What happened to him?"

"Oh!" Tagtaa looks sad. "He, too, was injured."

"He saved me."

"I guessed that might be the case, though he didn't mention it."

"And the young woman—your servant? She returned."

"Yes, she came back to me. I didn't realize they were married. Though of course it all makes sense now."

None of this makes sense to Bao, including how the fox lady escaped from Mr. Chen's mansion. And who is this man Kurosaki? He has a vague memory of her tears, a strained, passionate conversation over him as he lay bleeding in the rickshaw, his head on Kurosaki's arm. Such a peculiar conversation, with references to snow and a thousand-year journey. It makes his ears burn, as though he's eavesdropped on secrets that he shouldn't have. What about the black fox that he thought he saw? His thoughts float up like colored pieces of confetti that wink out when he tries to focus on them. Glancing at Tagtaa, he sees the same bewildered blankness on her face as well.

"The black fox," he says, before he forgets. "I saw him."

"Did you?" That snaps her back into focus. "I told you I think I met his grandson."

No, no, that's wrong, Bao wants to say. *There's only one fox. Or are there more?* His head swims.

"Rest now," says Tagtaa, looking worried.

Bao closes his eyes, but visions of foxes continue to dance behind them. Black and white. It's snowing—no, it's autumn and the rains are coming. The one waiting at the top of a hill is a lovely maiden, or is she really a white fox? *I must find the truth*, he thinks before sleep overtakes him.

57

The truth is that Kuro, of course, didn't die.

I say "of course" because it only occurred to me afterwards that he shouldn't succumb to such wounds. Bohai's wild, inexperienced swings did no more than slice up Kuro's arms and back. The main fear was blood loss, and I suppose if he'd been left on a battlefield for another hour, he *might* have died. I explained that to my mistress, though she looked blank. To be honest, I was trying to reassure myself more than her.

"And of course, he's survived things like being shot with arrows and falling off Ping Yao's city wall. Though it was really touch-and-go that time."

She stared at me, surprised, and I realized in my nervousness, I'd let my tongue run on. That was no good; I'd give myself away like this. What should I do? Kuro looked very bad. His hands were icy, and the pulse jumped irregularly in his throat.

They put him in a room next door to the old man. I cleaned him up after informing everyone he was my husband. Such familiar yet painful words that hadn't crossed my lips in two years. There'd been so many shocking events today that nobody questioned me. Only Ting said, "Ah San, so you were married to a foreigner?" I'd nodded, and she'd lingered in the doorway, asking if I needed help. No. I'd manage by myself.

A doctor was brought in, using all the connections that the medicine hall had. He was trained in Japan and also spoke a little Russian, both of which he practiced on me. I hadn't noticed that my hands were shaking. There was so much blood. The image of my poor child, her legs broken, rose before me, and I felt like vomiting.

Seeing my blanched face, the doctor said that I should leave, but I refused. "I'm used to wounds and I can help." Mostly, I wanted to ensure Kuro didn't get blood poisoning. That's how many perish after a battle. Even a wound from a farmer's sickle, if smeared in dung, will deliver a fatal blow. I explained this to the doctor, and he gave me the same surprised stare that my mistress had given me.

"So you see," I continued, "I must insist that you wash your hands. And we should pour strong liquor all over his cuts."

"That will be very painful for the patient!"

"It's all right, he has a high tolerance. Maggots would also be good for cleaning wounds."

"I must protest! These are grave cuts, several of them rather deep."

He was right. I was simply in denial. I wanted Kuro to jump up and tell me that he'd just been playing dead, for fun. Though of course that's not his style. I went and sat in the corner to cry quietly, while the doctor and his assistant worked on Kuro, sewing up some of the worst slashes and using poultices and various horrible-smelling herbs. I supposed they knew what they were doing.

When he was all bandaged up, the doctor said rather kindly to me, "Mrs. Kurosaki—" I must have looked blank, for he repeated it several times before I answered.

"He's lost a lot of blood. The next few days will be critical to ensure his wounds don't get infected. Though you seem quite aware of that."

I dug my fingers into my arm. Episodes of my and Kuro's history rose before me. The way he'd recovered from pneumonia when we'd been living under a bridge in Suzhou. The time both of us almost drowned when the Yellow River flooded, and a moneylender had shoved us off his boat with a pole. Kuro has always been physically stronger than me. Surely it would be the same this time?

"You're a devoted wife," said the doctor as he took his leave. I wanted to scream that I wasn't, and that this was all my fault. Or, rather, that something had broken between us one winter's day when I'd returned to the den and found it half dug out and our child missing. Kuro, that fool, had gone on a long hunting trip, leaving her alone. I squeezed my eyes tight,

tight, but could no longer find the burning hatred I'd nursed against him. At some point, it had simply evaporated.

When everyone had gone, I sat on the cold stone floor next to Kuro's bed, trying to tell myself that this was still better than hiding in a ditch from Mongol horsemen. Those days were long gone; we were younger then and filled with optimism. But people died all the time, no matter how much you prayed, made vows, or held them tightly in your arms. When I closed my eyes, I could see my child, patiently enduring another long night of pain from her broken legs and internal injuries. She'd lingered, getting weaker and weaker, while I'd frantically tried everything in my power to nurse her. There were no doctors in that remote area for a fox child. Too young to speak or cry much, she'd nuzzled her face into my chest and finally left this life.

The stillness was what had alerted me. Her shallow breathing, the way she'd curled in on herself towards the end. And now Kuro, too, was silent. "What have you been doing?" I murmured, examining the scar on his face.

As I touched his cheek, he opened his eyes.

"How long have you been awake?" Hastily, I snatched my hand back.

"Since you told the doctor to use maggots on me."

"It's good treatment for wounds."

Instead of arguing, he said simply, "I'm very sorry to have caused you so much pain. Not just today, but also two years ago. There's no one else to blame but me."

That made me tear up again, which I hate. "Just make sure to get well then."

"Snow, I cannot complete the thousand-year journey with you. I've killed a man."

"What made you do such a thing, after we vowed not to?" If you wish to reach enlightenment, a virtuous fox must not kill, steal, lie, engage in money-laundering, or, for that matter, burn down other people's houses.

"I tracked down the hunter who took our child and killed him with my bare hands."

"You were unarmed? That doesn't count then. Anyone would say it was self-defense." I was babbling again because I didn't want to hear his words.

"I knew exactly what I was doing. I used his own knife against him."

"Is that how you got this?" I touched the scar on his face. Gently, gently, as though my heart was breaking.

"At that time, I'd already decided that I would die, too." Kuro turned his face away.

I wept bitterly then. Because I was the one who told Kuro to get out. To never come back or speak to me again. *I hope you die*, I'd said, snarling and furious. *Because you can never bring our child back.* Sometimes our wishes come back in the darkest, most twisted ways, like a thorn that pierces and grows through your flesh. A tree that drinks blood and blots out the sun. The sin was mine; I had watered it with hatred and tears of rage, and it had grown to cast a monstrous shadow.

"Don't cry. I'm already marked, and I accept heaven's judgment."

"Shiro has caused the death of countless people and he's still running around," I said. "Why must you die for repaying a blood debt? Live and make reparations another way. I'll do penance, too."

He gave a wry glance. "You mean to start the thousand years all over again? I don't think I'll survive long enough."

"Don't talk like that!" Turning my back, I took a deep breath. "You will get well. And go back to Japan, where Miss Yukiko is waiting for you."

"Why should she be waiting for me?"

"Isn't she in love with you?"

"I've no idea what you're talking about. Her grandfather offered me a job at his publishing company. I turned him down, that's all."

"How can you be so dense?" I wanted to smack him, but one must not hit invalids. Shiro pays too much attention to women. Kuro's charm lies in his willful obliviousness.

"Anyway," he said quietly, "I already have a wife. Even if you won't acknowledge it."

Silence.

I told you I'm often at a loss for words around him. It was so long and awkward that I turned around to find that Kuro had fallen asleep.

I WENT OUT into the corridor and closed the door. Evening had descended, a soft haze of twilight and lanterns. In the courtyard garden, purple wisteria hung from the eaves. I heard household chatter and the clanging of pans in the kitchen. The family was at dinner; perhaps they were even deciding what to do with Bohai.

While everyone was eating, I had a chance to interview him. Quietly, I went over to the men's side of the house. Bohai was confined in his room on the second floor, opposite the women's wing. One of the male clerks from the shop was sitting in the stairwell eating his dinner, so I went up to the upper floor of the women's quarters, climbed out of the window, and walked gingerly along the roof to Bohai's window.

The roof tiles made a crunching sound. Every so often, I paused cautiously, but there was no one around except a small bat flying wildly out from the eaves. Chinese consider bats to be good fortune, so I hoped that would work in my favor. The window to Bohai's room was ajar. From within came the faint sound of whimpering. At that moment, I felt pity for Bohai, despite his suspicious little eyes and the fact that he'd stabbed two people. Not wanting to frighten him, I tapped on the window.

There was a terrified silence. Then Bohai said in a quavering voice, "Who's there?"

"It's me, Ah San. Your grandmother's servant."

"Why are you outside? Isn't this the second story?"

Once people have trained themselves to believe that nobody enters through an upper window, they have great difficulty adjusting their expectations. "I wanted to talk to you, in case you had anything to say."

"I already told Grandmother I don't. I shall die here. My life is over." Very melodramatic, but I made all the right sympathetic noises and said he shouldn't take on so.

"Nobody is dead."

"Really? Is Kurosaki all right? They wouldn't tell me anything; my father has rushed off to see his mistress tonight."

That seemed like awkward timing. Bohai said bitterly, "His mistress is about to give birth. Everyone knows, even my mother. He'll have a son, and that will be the end of me."

Muffled sobs. I peered in. "Why will it be the end of you?"

"Everyone knows the family curse. The second son always inherits. Even Grandmother thinks so, especially since I began to see the people with no shadows."

"And when did that start?"

"Nine months ago. Right when his mistress got pregnant. So it's a sign, isn't it?" Bohai's laugh caught in his throat.

"Why did you stab Kurosaki?"

"That was an accident! I was going for the old man who claims he's Grandmother's friend." He lifted his head abruptly. "You must keep him away from her."

"I will if you tell me what happened in Moji. The real story, please. I think you know who killed Bektu Nikan."

"How did you know?"

It had been a simple process of elimination. I'd suspected Kuro, but just now he'd said he'd killed a man. Not several, just one. Kuro isn't the kind to lie, especially when he's busy giving me a deathbed goodbye, so I'd followed my hunch, all the way up to the second-floor roof.

Bohai sighed. "It makes no difference now, but I guessed it was either Chen or Lu. Most likely Lu. That's why I was in a hurry to return home. In the early hours of the morning that Bektu died, I heard one of them come back and wash his hands at the kitchen pump, then return to the room they shared. Afterwards, they were both so jumpy and suspicious of each other."

"Because of the photograph of all of you, with that treasonous banner?"

"We should never have taken that photograph, but at the time, we were stupidly fired up. When word got out that a government spy was investigating us, Chen and Lu were extremely worried. Both of them had more to lose than me.

After all, these past nine months I've known that I'm going to die. Joining a revolution seemed like a good way to go out with a bang. I don't know what came over all of us—we shouldn't have listened to Shirakawa!"

I didn't say anything as he continued to pour out his tearful regrets. "I shouldn't have taken Grandmother to Japan. That's what worried me, when Bektu decided to use the photograph as blackmail. He was short of money, but I'd thought Shirakawa was handling him before everything fell apart."

"Chen said he bought the photograph and the negative from Bektu. There was no reason to kill him after that."

"That's why I thought it was Lu. He wanted to shut Bektu up permanently because he didn't trust him not to have made copies. He's a lot more decisive than either of us. Oh, why did we ever listen to Shirakawa about becoming revolutionaries?"

Choked sobs, made more awful by the self-loathing in Bohai's voice. I'd nothing to say, except to feel both sorrow and a hearty dose of *I told you so*. You must never, ever listen to Shiro.

"When I first met him, my father had just taken a mistress. We were out drinking, and Shirakawa asked what my greatest fear was. I told him that if my father had another son, that would be the end of me. Everyone else laughed—only he took me seriously."

That's exactly the kind of information Shiro would be interested in. I sighed. "Did you start seeing the people with no shadows afterwards?"

"Yes. Since I was a child, I'd heard gossip about Grandmother's stepson and what happened to him. Of my friends, only Shirakawa believed me. I wonder whether I'm going mad."

Poor, hapless Bohai. I wouldn't have put it past Shiro to engineer the whole affair, including hallucinations of people with no shadows. Yet even as I listened, I felt a burning shame. It's one thing to know that our kind preys on people's feelings, and another to witness firsthand the betrayal and degradation of those who put their trust in foxes.

"You're very lucky you didn't murder anyone. If I were you, I'd do some repenting."

At these words, Bohai burst out wailing, "But I'm going to die! I know it."

He flung himself facedown on his bed. There was no use being sorry for him since he was so unreliable. Though what he'd said about Lu interested me.

Lu's behavior at Mr. Chen's mansion, including the way he'd unraveled under pressure, hinted that he'd had a lot on his mind. Crouched on the roof tiles, I did some rapid thinking. If he'd been decisive enough to get rid of Bektu, he might also have pushed Chen over the railing during an argument, fearing that Chen would confess their revolutionary activities to his father. Hadn't Mr. Chen mentioned he was helping Lu's family with debts? But short of tying Lu up and lighting a fire under his feet, I was unlikely to ever get a confession. In the meantime, it was getting cold on the roof.

My foot slipped on the curved tiles as I stood up. Bohai's quavering voice said, "Don't go."

"I'm going to check on Kurosaki." Mentioning Kuro made Bohai weep more in remorse. Perhaps there was still hope for him. "From now on, try to live a proper life," I said through the window.

Back in the main house, I paused outside the room that held the old man with no shadow. The carved wooden door yielded under the pressure of my palm. A frisson ran up my spine. Perhaps it was Bohai's terror of him or simply Shiro's earlier warning, but I wondered what kind of creature he was.

Foxes are naturally wary, though that's balanced by our insatiable curiosity. So as I hesitated on the threshold of this old man's room, I felt a prickle of warning. *Don't go in*, it whispered.

Of course, I did.

58

It's dark when Bao opens his eyes. A beautiful dusk that has descended in deepest purple. If this color had a sound, it would be the tolling of a low, clear bell. For some reason, he's convinced that he hears it. He even knows which one it is— the city temple bell of his youth. But that's nonsense because he hasn't been back for decades. The ringing of the bell (or is it the color of the evening?) echoes through his head, making him shiver. It fades until there's only the dusk that creeps in from outside, smelling of wisteria blossoms, bitter herbs, and an undertone of burning.

Someone is standing outside his room, a faint shadow seen through the oiled paper lining the wooden screen doors. Bao's chest seizes up. His room is dark, without a lamp. The twilit sky is the only source of light, and against the paper-screened door, he gradually discerns a woman's form.

A servant, he tells himself, for it's too slender and tall to be Tagtaa. The thought of Tagtaa, her sweet face with its wrinkled laugh lines, gives him courage. Nothing will happen to him in a house run by her. Yet his heart hammers painfully; there's a sharp pang in his left lung. Bao holds his breath, overwhelmed by the vague terror that he experienced as a feverish child.

Creak. The door opens gently, and she comes in.

Dusk is the most dangerous time, according to Bao's old nanny; the blurred gap between day and night when creatures who resemble humans appear. They exist on the very edge of society, at the tipping point of madness where dreams and nightmares come true. Bao's mouth is dry. He licks his lips nervously as the figure approaches. It's so dark now that he can barely see her features, yet her eyes glitter.

"Are you awake?" she says.

Softly, softly. A polite voice, full of concern. And instantly Bao is chagrined. What was he thinking to be so afraid of her, for isn't this the way that all stories begin? A beautiful woman taps on the door of a scholar's study and enters with the night. The dull rushing thump of blood echoes in his ears. He thinks irrationally that this tale is wrong, because Bao is an old man and he's not studying for the Imperial examinations or writing poetry by lamplight, because he's been stabbed by Tagtaa's crazy grandson. Before he realizes it, he's blurted his thoughts out loud. What's come over him?

But the tension breaks, and the woman who has entered his room bursts out laughing. "That's the best reaction I've heard in years," she says, dabbing at her eyes. "You're too old, indeed! Most men never think that of themselves."

Her laughter is so engaging that Bao can't help feeling flattered. "Aren't you Tagtaa's servant? How did you get out of Mr. Chen's mansion?"

"It was rather troublesome, but I had help climbing over the wall from Kurosaki."

"How is he?"

"He's still alive, if that's what you were wondering." Behind her light facade, he senses sadness and anxiety.

"Tagtaa told me that he's your husband."

She inclines her head gracefully.

"Yet I was told you have another husband."

"Oh?" And now she sounds wary. "Who might that be?"

"Do you know a gentleman named Wang, who owns a garden villa on the outskirts of Mukden?"

"Waxy-looking fellow, small eyes? We never had that sort of relationship. In fact, I escaped from his villa—or shall I say prison."

"He wants you back. I was sent to find you."

"Are you a detective? A real one?" Why is she suddenly so enthusiastic? Most women would be crying at this news. She draws nearer and sits on the floor near his bed. Bao's vision has adjusted to the darkness, and he can make out her features. Perhaps his eyes are playing tricks, for her face seems to shine faintly. The more he looks, the dizzier he feels. His heart races; if he were younger, he'd be mesmerized already.

To hide his embarrassment, Bao says, "I'm a bit of an amateur. But I investigate people for a living."

She tilts her head to one side. It reminds Bao of a dog, bright-eyed and curious. "That sounds either interesting or extremely tedious. Which one is it most of the time?"

"The second one." Bao is enjoying this unexpected conversation far too much.

"How much is Mr. Wang paying you to find me?"

"He's most generous. I'm on a monthly retainer."

"Would it be better if you didn't find me for a while?"

"Though the money is handy, I can do without it. In fact, I'll inform him that you left for Japan. That wasn't my idea, by the way," he adds hastily before she can thank him. "A little girl—the granddaughter of a bookkeeper in a brothel—asked me for a favor."

He wants to be strictly honest with her. After all, compared to other people he's interviewed on his long journey to find her, she hasn't told him a single lie. It's almost shocking.

"Thank you. And please thank her, if you ever see her again." She pauses. "How would you like me to repay you?"

For an instant—a mad instant—Bao wants her to stay with him always, to be his alone. A feeling of passionate possession that must have tormented Mr. Wang. But no, that's wrong. He shakes his head; the idea evaporates. Bao is too old and already has someone he loves. She watches him with a half smile that's rather sad, as though she's read his thoughts and approves of his decision.

What shall he ask for then? Bao has the feeling that this is a once-in-a-lifetime opportunity and he mustn't waste it. A breeze shivers through him. When she's silent, he feels afraid of her again, that creeping sense of unease. Perhaps it's her uncanny attractiveness, the picture of his ideal girl (no, no, his ideal woman is small and resembles a Manchurian chipmunk), and he suddenly remembers Zhou Yuling's description of Shirakawa. *He's like the person of your dreams.* It's a warning; the hair on the back of Bao's neck prickles.

"You needn't be so frightened," she says. "Honestly, I don't have much to offer. But I'll answer one question for you."

"Only one?"

"One is what most people get. But it can be a big one, like

what's the meaning of life, or is there really a rabbit on the moon, or where's the hidden grave of Genghis Khan." She wrinkles her nose, and Bao resists the urge to pat her head.

"I see." Yes, he was right to guess that he must use it well. What shall he ask? *Are you a fox?* comes to mind. It trembles on his lips, along with questions like: *And those two absurdly handsome men, are they foxes, too? Is one the black fox that Tagtaa met sixty years ago?*

Perhaps he should ask for something more selfish, like the way to win Tagtaa's heart. Or practical, such as the day of his death, so he can prepare himself. But he already knows what he wants as he opens his mouth.

"What happened to my shadow?"

Her head jerks up, but she remains silent, thinking. At length, she says, "Tell me what you know."

Bao pours out the tale of his childhood sickness and his old nanny's dedication to the fox god. He's starting to feel tired, the wound in his side sapping his strength, words slowing. "So you see, I heard from my older brother that my nanny asked the fox god to take away my shadow."

"*Hm.*" She closes her eyes. Again, Bao has the presentiment of danger, the way you feel when a wild animal draws too close for comfort. Then her eyes snap open. They're so piercing that he's momentarily frightened. "Did you develop any unusual senses after this?"

"As a matter of fact, yes." Bao decides to take a risk. "I can hear the truth when people speak."

"That must be useful in your line of work."

As expected, she's wary, though her tone remains playful. And still, she hasn't told a lie. Nor does she ask if Bao has been testing her.

"What does it sound like?"

Haltingly, he describes the numbing, buzzing sensation he feels when he hears a lie, and when one passes his own lips. Her eyes light up.

"What an interesting side effect! Do you mind raising your arm?"

Bao does so, oddly compliant. It's so dark now that he can't see any shadows. Yet he can make out her features clearly, particularly her bright eyes and teeth. Such beautiful white teeth, not at all stained like most people's. Come to think of it, Kurosaki, too, has excellent teeth with very sharp canines. Bao's mind is wandering again, perhaps because of the increasing pain in his side. Holding his arm up is an effort; cold sweat pours down his forehead.

"You can put it down now. May I take your pulse?"

Bao nods, and she places her hand on his wrist. His heart begins to race again; no matter how you look at it, he's lying in a dark room with an attractive woman holding his hand. To hide his embarrassment, Bao says, "Do you notice anything?"

"Your *qi* is unbalanced. Someone removed too much negative *yin*, then tried to patch things up by moving things around in your body. The result is a complete muddle—I'm afraid they didn't do a good job."

"What shall I do?"

"Over time, your body has adapted. The excess *yang*, or positive energy, has been leaving through your ears and mouth, which is likely why you can hear the truth."

This is such a peculiar conversation that Bao wonders if he's running a fever or dreaming. The dimness of the room makes the shapes of the furniture blurry. The hand that holds his wrist is warm, almost like a furry paw. Yet everything seems to make sense.

"I see," he says. "So I should just leave it?"

"I think that's the best solution. I'm not skilled enough to help you in this matter."

With that, she releases his wrist. Bao feels a stab of disappointment; she's going to leave now. But he's too proud to say, *Don't go*, and also has the feeling that one shouldn't ask for more favors from creatures who come at dusk. Besides, his head pounds as though he's drunk too much wine, and the wound in his side aches.

"You're not well." She looks concerned. "I'm worried about you."

For some reason, that makes Bao happy.

59

While the old man named Bao was telling me about shadows and childhood fevers, I watched him carefully. I'm no expert at disease, but any fox can take the measure of someone's *qi*. After all, that's what sustains us. Think of us as experienced fishermen who can eye a river and tell you roughly where the fish might gather.

Observation proved what Shiro had already guessed: someone had meddled with the poor man. In fact, his *qi*, which usually circulates in a regular manner through living beings, had been rerouted all over the place. *Qi* controls much more than bodily functions. It affects luck, disposition, and many other things. Despite Bao's obvious intelligence, I'd bet good money that this disturbance meant that he would fail almost any important examination.

Considering the possible outcomes, he was lucky the ability to discern truth seemed to be the only other side effect. Shiro seemed convinced that one of our kind had done it. I'm not as experienced as Shiro, since he feeds directly off other people's *qi*, a practice that both Kuro and I had forsworn except as last resort. But he was right; the sheer carelessness and optimism with which the operation had been performed indicated the meddling of another fox.

I rather liked Bao. Plain but pleasant, like an old dog with bandy legs, he rejected temptation without being overly sanctimonious. How interesting that both he and my mistress had had memorable encounters with foxes in their youth. I wondered if that was coincidence—or fate.

In the outer corridor, the chill-scented evening seeped into my bones. Today was packed with unexpected troubles. And I hadn't even checked on Kuro's condition yet. Perhaps I was afraid to. After all, I'd spent the past two years nursing my grief and resentment. It was a lot easier to consider Kuro dead to me than to deal with the pain that his presence reminded me of. I should have known better. What you bury eventually comes to light in some form or other. That's just the way the world works.

Kuro was asleep, his forehead clammy and feverish. The shadowed hollows of his face gave me such a stabbing pang that I hastened away. An injured fox must consume large amounts of *qi* to recover. My mistress had given the cook instructions to prepare tonic soup, made of chicken essence, red dates, *dang sheng*, and *bai he*. But that alone wouldn't save Kuro. Fresh blood and raw meat would be best.

At the poultry pen in the kitchen courtyard, all was quiet, other than a sleepy rustle from the henhouse. The two geese I'd brought with me when I'd first entered this house were still mine, as no one had thought to pay me for them. Entering the pen, I removed both birds while they slept, bundling them swiftly into a tablecloth. Then I headed to Kuro's sickroom. It must be done now, before he got weaker.

It's hard to open a door quietly when one is lugging two geese that are beginning to struggle, but I kicked it open with my foot, which was enough to make Kuro's eyes open.

"Wake up!" I said, trying to sound cheerful. "I got you two nice geese. And they were properly paid for by me."

I couldn't help feeling mildly triumphant. The geese were large, fat, and aggressive, which meant they were filled with *qi*. At first, Kuro was reluctant. He closed his eyes again, but I made him dispatch one. After that, the color came back into his face.

"You should eat the other goose, too," I pointed out. That would set him up properly, but he shook his head.

"Give it to the old man."

"You mean Bao?"

Nod. "His *qi* is unstable."

So he, too, like Shiro, had noticed Bao's peculiar condition.

"He said it was done by a fox that his nanny prayed to, about sixty years ago. Also that he barely has a shadow anymore," I reported.

Kuro was silent. Then he said, "I believe that man is half dead."

"What do you mean by that?"

Perhaps it was the gathering darkness, or the iron smell of blood and the fact that we were squatting on the stone floor amid the remains of a dead goose, but if anyone should walk in on us, they'd call us demons. Or animals. That's the other accusation leveled against us, which I don't find offensive since it's true we are a different species. But humans are particularly preoccupied with the distinction between themselves and what they call *beasts*.

Anyway, I didn't like Kuro talking about Bao being half dead when he himself was barely out of danger, but he went on, "Likely, Bao almost died during his childhood; even now, he's continually leaking *qi* through his left lung. No wonder he's had only half the amount of luck he should have in his life. So perhaps we should give him the other goose."

I frowned at Kuro. A fox like Shiro will feed directly off humans, but it's also possible for us to transfer *qi*. This involves passing the breath in your body back into another person and is best done in what resembles mouth-to-mouth resuscitation.*

"Are you honestly telling me to do that?" I felt insulted, especially since Kuro had just reasserted our relationship (to which I hadn't given a proper reply, anyway).

"No, I'll do it."

"You're in no shape."

"Didn't you tell me to make reparations for killing that hunter?"

Not when you're still wounded, I wanted to scream. But there was no point arguing. Kuro swiftly consumed the second goose and, as I'd predicted, it did him a great deal of good. Then he headed to Bao's room. I stayed behind to clean up the blood, feathers, and scattered bones on the floor. Dinnertime was over, and my ears twitched uncomfortably at the sounds of clinking dishes and chatter. If Kuro didn't hurry, he'd be caught in Bao's room. I wished he'd remembered to wipe the goose blood off his mouth; I'd thought of doing it myself but had been overcome by uncharacteristic shyness.

It was unsettling to be close to Kuro again. How quickly

*For this reason, foxes are often accused of being licentious.

we'd slipped back into familiarity, yet we were still guardedly cautious. At least I was. I wasn't sure what I expected out of this—a truce, or something more complicated? After all, the last two years, I'd done nothing but curse Kuro in my mind. Yet at the sound of his voice and his familiar scent, my resolutions came utterly undone.

60

That night, Bao is visited by a demon. At least that's his first thought when he opens his eyes, blurry with pain. He's been sleeping fitfully after she left him—that charming woman whose name he can no longer recall, only the wisteria-scented dusk in which she came. The wound in his side throbs, the bandages heavy with oozing blood. When he exhales, the old pain in his left lung is sharper, stabbing like a blade. Bao knows, in the way of all animals, that he's drifting closer to death.

Fear snakes around his shoulder and bites him in the chest. His heart is a drumbeat, counting off the seconds as they slip away. If only he weren't alone! He closes his eyes against the moonlight that seeps in like hoarfrost. When he opens them again, someone is at his bedside.

Whoever it is entered so silently that Bao is stricken with terror. Or did he appear, like an apparition, between one heartbeat and the next? Bao's hair freezes into needles; his tongue cleaves to the roof of his mouth. He recalls his old nanny's tales of vengeful ghosts and creatures who devour human livers. They come on moonlit nights to sit on your chest and suck out your breath.

"Please don't be afraid. I didn't knock because I thought you were asleep."

It's the voice of Kurosaki, the one who saved him from Bohai's wild slashes. The darkness of the room, the sweat pooling under his lower back, and the pain in Bao's side have a dreamlike quality. He struggles to sit up, but his weak body won't obey. Kurosaki's broad shoulders blot out the moonlight. He moves fluidly, as though he hasn't been injured. That can't be right; Bao recalls his pale, tight face only a few hours ago, the stiffness of his cold arm. He couldn't possibly have recovered so fast.

Though it's dark, he can make out Kurosaki's fine features, limned faintly with a strange light. Bao tells himself not to be frightened. Sharp brows, lean jawline, and that unmistakable scar. There's a stain around his mouth—is it blood? Perhaps this isn't Kurosaki at all, but a creature masquerading as a man. Bao gasps.

Everything goes black.

Black is the color of a woman's tresses. Of smooth-grained ebony wood, dark seas under a moonless night. The emperor's favorite horse without a single white hair; a stick of fragrant Chinese ink; the shiny wing of a crow.

It's also the color of a fox that comes at midnight.

The black fox puts its triangular face against Bao's, a fearfully nonhuman face with pointed muzzle and pricked ears. So close that it could bite off his nose and eat out his face, yet the movement is delicate. Almost considerate. He feels its breath sigh, fresh and hot like the wind across the plains, smelling like iron and blood.

THEN IT'S MORNING and a bird is singing outside.

Bao lies in bed, listening to its warbling trill. The milky sky is overcast with the scent of rain. So, he's not dead yet. Last night was filled with strange dreams and apparitions, including a long conversation with Tagtaa's servant, who is also the fox lady. And there's another vague memory, one that makes Bao even more uncomfortable, for it reminds him of the tales of demons.

Wincing, Bao sits up. His side aches from the knife wound, but nothing like yesterday's feverish throbbing. When he exhales, even the familiar pang in his left lung has faded. The visiting doctor is surprised when he examines the bandages. The wound has stopped bleeding and there's no sign of infection.

"Remarkable," he says. "Though not as much as the patient in the next room."

"Is Kurosaki all right?" For some reason, Bao recalls the

name but not the features of the man who brought him back to the medicine shop.

"He seems to have made almost a full recovery. Yesterday it was late when I saw him, so perhaps I overestimated his injuries." The doctor strokes his wispy goatee. "Either that, or I'm a much better doctor than I thought. Ha ha!"

Bao senses a hint of embarrassment, recalling the doctor's whispered warnings to Tagtaa last night. Perhaps that was just professional modesty, though there's an uneasy look in the doctor's eyes as he leaves.

Speaking of Tagtaa, he hasn't seen her at all this morning, though there's been a great deal of hurried activity in the household. Shuffling out into the open corridor, he leans on the carved railing. There's an elm tree in the courtyard, and its serrated leaves tremble in the breeze.

That's how Bao feels, as though his insides have been mysteriously mixed around during the night so that they wobble like jelly. But that's nonsense, of course. Nobody has given him any medicinal infusions (again, he tries not to think of half-remembered dreams) and he certainly hasn't suffered further accidents. As Bao stands there, he sees Tagtaa walking alone across the courtyard. Age has set her free as a woman; she can come and go without being remarked on.

Spotting him, she smiles. "I can't believe how well you look!"

"I feel much better. Thank you for your care."

"It's the least we could do." Her eyes are wet, as though she's been crying, yet she seems cheerful.

"Has something good happened?"

"Yes." Glancing around, she calls a servant to fetch tea. "You mustn't stand so long when you've been injured."

They sit at the marble-topped round table in the family salon, where servants pass by the opened screen doors. Public enough for propriety, yet allowing a private conversation.

"My son's concubine has given birth to a daughter!"

Bao is surprised by her excitement. Most people would prefer another son, not a daughter, particularly since Bohai, the heir apparent, seems to have lost his mind. Still, he makes his congratulations.

"It's a temporary reprieve," says Tagtaa, "since his mistress may have more children. But it gives Bohai time to sort himself out."

Bao has no inclination to see Bohai again but inquires after the young man anyway.

"The doctor suggested that we send him to a private sanatorium for treatment. In fact, Bohai went this morning since they had space."

That explains the hurried rush of activity earlier. Having him admitted at a private hospital, rather than sent for questioning to a magistrate for stabbing two people, is a prudent move.

Tagtaa drops her gaze shamefacedly. "I'm very sorry. He has harmed you, and perhaps it was wrong to send him away, but I believe he's not a criminal. He . . . has other problems and may not live long."

"What will you do if he stabs more people?"

Tagtaa looks him in the eye. "There's no guarantee. But he'll be confined at the sanatorium while they evaluate him. I spoke with Bohai this morning before he left. He says he accepts his fate."

Her wet eyes, mingled with relief, and flushed, apologetic face make Bao think of inappropriate things like pressing her hand to his heart. "If you visit him, may I accompany you?"

"Why?" She's horrified. "He might go crazy again if he sees you. He says you have no shadow."

Bao lifts his hand up over the table. It's an overcast midmorning and the marble table itself is gray and cloudy, which might excuse the faintness of his shadow. But it's there, and distinctively darker than the day before. He regards Tagtaa anxiously.

Her eyes widen. "You do have a shadow."

"Yes." This demonstration was a gamble for Bao; he realizes it only after he pulls his hand away. Yet there's a certainty that today, of all days, he'll be able to show his shadow. Perhaps it's the aftereffect of the dreams he had last night when someone (or something) touched their face to his.

Tagtaa says hopefully, "If Bohai sees this, perhaps he'll come to his senses."

Bao has no wish to lie, so he simply nods.

61

I didn't wait for Kuro to return from Bao's room that night. My feelings were complicated enough that it seemed inappropriate. Besides, my old lady would worry, so I hastily cleaned up the carnage. The bones and feathers were rolled up in the cloth I'd wrapped the geese in (nobody would ever use that tablecloth again), and I poured the basin of bloody water onto the azaleas. Perhaps they'd bloom especially well next year.

By the time my mistress returned from an exhausting post-dinner family discussion, I was waiting in our little back courtyard with her bedding turned down and a pot of hot chrysanthemum tea. The oil lamp was lit, and her face brightened.

"Thank you, Ah San. But don't you wish to stay by your husband's side tonight?"

I shook my head. When Kuro had shown up covered with blood, I'd explained my relationship with him briefly and persuasively. My mistress had accepted my explanation with the same blank look that everyone else had, but I was reminded that we ought to leave soon. Fortunately, she seemed burdened with worries about Bohai, and her daughter-in-law's hysteria over the impending birth.

"I thought it was him," she said sleepily as I tucked her in bed.

"Who?"

"Kurosaki—I thought the two of you were connected. I was confused."

"What makes you say that?"

"It's the way you looked at each other. Or, rather, didn't look at each other, when we were walking back from the woods in Moji."

So she was more astute than I'd thought. In any case, I

didn't want her to dwell on this; otherwise she'd have even more questions the next day.

MY HOPES FOR a quiet morning were dashed by the sudden removal of Bohai to a private sanatorium, along with tearful goodbyes from his mother and sisters. There was such a rush that various servants were dispatched on errands. I was hastily sent to buy rope and pastries, an odd but useful combination, to secure both Bohai's luggage and his sweet tooth, and had no time to check on Kuro.

Hurrying back, I had the sudden, queasy conviction that Kuro might leave while I was gone. I could picture it clearly: the empty room, windows thrown wide, where he'd stayed last night. The rumpled bed with only an imprint of his body.

I hadn't been exactly reconciliatory. What if Kuro decided that the best course was for him to disappear or become a hermit on Mount Tai? I wouldn't put it past him and his ridiculous code of honor. My heart sank; my steps grew heavy. A wrenching sadness seeped through me, like icy well water flooding the pit of my stomach. I've never been able to control Kuro, which is why I had loved him so much.

WHEN I RETURNED, Bohai had already left by mule cart (so much for my futile errand). I was putting away the rope and pastries when there was a commotion from the front shop. One of the clerks hurried to the family quarters. "*Tai furen*, there's someone you should see!"

I heard my old lady's quick step in the corridor. "Who is it?"

I had a bad feeling about this. Wiping my hands, I peeked into the reception room to find the visitor was none other than Shiro.

He draped himself, still attired in his Korean merchant's clothes, gingerly on a chair as though he felt sick. My mistress said, "Mr. Shirakawa, have you come to see Bohai?"

"Ah, yes, I was worried about him."

Lies, I thought.

"I'm afraid he's not here. He just left on a trip." My old lady hesitated. From Shiro's surprise, it was clear he hadn't heard about Bohai's stabbing two people yesterday, so she said uncomfortably, "He's not . . . well."

"I'm sorry to have missed him. As a matter of fact, I'm feeling ill myself, and came for some medicine." Shiro pressed his hand against his stomach. "I've been poisoned."

"Was it something you ate?"

"Yes." The faintest of hesitations, as though Shiro was debating what to tell her. "Please give me whatever can draw out poison."

"Oh dear!" My mistress's face tightened with anxiety as she rushed off to consult the chief clerk from the medicine shop.

As soon as she left, I went in. No point trying to hide if Shiro was here to demand things. I stood over him, bristling with annoyance. "Why did you come here?"

"How could I not? You left notes all over Oda's house saying that you were going back to the medicine shop and to meet you there."

"They weren't notes for you," I hissed.

"I know. More's the pity." He shut his eyes again pathetically. I wondered if he was running away from something. Or someone. Upon inspection, he really did look ill.

"So she found you after all," I said.

He gave a guilty start. "How did you know it was Zhou Yuling?"

"We shouldn't have left her behind at Mr. Chen's mansion when it caught fire! You ought to handle your love affairs better. Did she really poison you?"

"She tried to. Showed up at Oda's this morning in an absolute state, crying and wailing. I brought her up to the room, and that's when she found your straw shoes under my bed."

"My shoes?" I'd forgotten how I'd abandoned that pair of shoes under the wisteria vine, the first night I'd gone to Shiro's place. "Why did you keep them?"

"I thought I'd return them to you. Also, as a token of my passion. Aren't you even a little moved?"

I shook my head. One can never tell when Shiro is being honest.

"Anyway, she flew into a rage and accused me of two-timing her. Of course, you and I know that's not true—though I wish it were." He gave me a soulful glance. "I calmed her down, and she said she'd like to part ways properly. So I took her to the kitchen, and we opened a jar of wine to say farewell."

"Did you also roast her some dried squid and make noodles?" I recalled Shiro's little routine that other evening, and how practiced he seemed.

"Of course. I'm very good at frying noodles. Anyway, we drank some wine and one thing led to another—"

"In Oda's kitchen?"

"Well, that table is rather hard and uncomfortable, but one makes do. She said she would give me a nice present of silver, for old times' sake. But in the end, I believe she put something in the wine."

My ears were tingling with rage. What a stupid story! If Shiro was poisoned, it was all his own fault—how dare he come crawling here and endanger us all? I said icily, "What kind of poison?"

"She said it was *gu* poison, though I suspect arsenic."

Arsenic is a tasteless white powder—the poison of the ancients, by which emperors and scheming rivals have been dispatched. *Gu* poison, on the other hand, is made in the southern region by angry women. A legendary toxin, it's distilled by sealing venomous scorpions and snakes in a jar and leaving them to devour one another. Since it takes ten days to kill victims by rotting them from the inside, it's used to induce an unfaithful lover to return for the antidote.

Very few people have brewed authentic *gu* poison; I've never encountered its true form in all my wanderings. Unfortunately, arsenic is just as effective, except there's no antidote.

Shiro was beginning to pant a little. His face was flushed, and he really did look ill. "I'm going to die, aren't I?"

"Obviously she didn't give you *gu* poison! But I can't believe you were stupid enough to drink the wine."

"I was thirsty," he said plaintively.

"What happened to Zhou Yuling?"

"As soon as she started saying that she'd poisoned me, I hotfooted it out of there. For all I know she's still weeping at Oda's kitchen table."

"Shiro, you have been extremely wicked!"

He gave me a sad, crooked smile. "I know. I shall pay the price for it this time."

"If you could only ask her what she gave you, then you might be saved."

"She'd probably lie."

EVERY CREATURE HAS its time of death. Whether it comes swiftly or lingers is up to fate. It seemed unbelievable that Shiro was going to expire right now, but death had come to other foxes on just as short notice.* He'd caused me nothing but trouble, though to be fair, he'd also effected a reconciliation of sorts between Kuro and myself. "Ask the local doctor," I said. "He's quite skilled; he treated Kuro yesterday. And try not to move too much."

"What happened to Kuro, and where are you going?" cried Shiro, but I'd already dashed outside.

In the courtyard, I hesitated. Time was scarce, but I couldn't help myself. The thought of Kuro's empty room troubled me so much that I stopped outside his door. Silence. I pushed it open with a bang, but as I feared, the little room was empty. The bedroll was neatly rolled up and the window ajar. No trace of Kuro remained.

There was a horrible, squeezing feeling, as though someone had shoved a stone down my throat and forced me to swallow it. Treacherous tears pricked my eyes; I rubbed them away. So my premonition had been right and Kuro had indeed left. Why should that surprise me? I'd never said I wished to reconcile with him, only that I was sorry he was wounded. Two years ago, I'd told him to stay away from me, and he'd respected that, in the serious way he undertook promises. We'd likely never have crossed paths again if Shiro hadn't led

*One of my favorite uncles was killed when a giant firework he was making exploded. It was a great loss to the fireworks industry in Liuyang for the next hundred years, as he was a noted pyrotechnic expert.

me to that house in Moji. I wanted to run out and find Kuro. He couldn't have gone far if he'd left this morning.

On the other hand, Shiro might die if I didn't help him.

The way to Oda's photography shop was unfortunately too familiar now, the back alleys with their dirty puddles and roving cats. As I ran, slipping past pedestrians and dodging wheelbarrows piled with radishes, I wondered if I was a fool. Yet it was for my sake that Shiro had reconnected with Zhou Yuling yesterday, and a faithful fox ought to show gratitude. By scrambling over a couple of walls and ignoring startled shouts, I arrived swiftly at Oda's rear courtyard.

Fortunately, Zhou Yuling was still there.

Unfortunately, she looked utterly spent as she slumped miserably across the kitchen table. I had to call out several times before she turned a dazed face upwards. When she saw me, she said dully, "Go away."

"Listen," I said. "I have no interest in Shirakawa. I'm married to the other fellow."

"But your shoes were under his bed! And he was all dressed up as a Korean—*Mr. Kim*, it said on his luggage—and ready to leave." A tear ran down her face, stained with streaks of kohl. Her lip rouge was smudged, her clothes disheveled. It was a shocking change from the self-possessed, well-dressed woman who'd walked into Mr. Chen's private parlor just yesterday.

"Kim" is a Korean alias that Shiro has often employed, though I didn't mention it. I sighed. Eventually, I persuaded her to accompany me, though she wouldn't say if she'd poisoned Shiro or not, clamping her lips shut and shaking her head wildly. However, by telling her that he was dying to see her (literally), she finally agreed to go.

A sadly sinful side effect of foxes is that humans who indulge too much in our company become hopelessly addicted. As much as Zhou Yuling claimed to hate Shiro, I knew that she wouldn't be able to stay away from him. If he really died, she'd likely fall into a frenzy and follow him soon after. Even now, she was barely coherent, so I bundled her into a passing rickshaw and got us back to the medicine shop as soon as possible.

Kicking open the unbolted side gate, I dragged her into the salon where Shiro was now lying prone on a rosewood bench, attended by a pharmacist who was palpating his wrist and examining his tongue. At the sight of Zhou Yuling, Shiro's eyes widened.

"I suppose you really mean to kill me," he said to me. His words were drowned by the loud wails of his discarded lover, who flung herself upon him and had to be prized off by one of the clerks.

As I stood there, panting with exertion, I was uncomfortably reminded that wherever we go, our legacy is chaos. Having burned down Mr. Chen's mansion yesterday, we'd now brought further trouble to the medicine shop—though arguably, Bohai had done his fair share as well. Whoever says that foxes are a natural phenomenon like war and pestilence might well be right. But I'd like to think that we're merely agents of change. Foxes, while often blamed as ill-omened creatures, are the needle that lances a boil.

Gazing upon this scene, I felt the squeeze of conscience. I had set out to avenge my child, but I'd done so in a willful, fox-like manner, not so different from Shiro after all. Excusing my own behavior, I'd only drifted further from the path to enlightenment. How many years had Kuro and I tried to walk that narrow road, only to have our sins of grief and mistrust undermine us? Now Kuro was gone, and Shiro's alarmed efforts to remove himself from Zhou Yuling's embrace only made me grimace.

But I must finish the task at hand. Racing off, I leaped over potted plants and crossed several courtyards to bang on the door to Bao's room.

"Get up!" I said. "I need your help. Now is the time to use your talent."

Such words always appeal to men of integrity. Someone like Bao, who, if not for his mixed-up *qi*, might have achieved great things as a government official. The old man looked amazingly better. I wouldn't have put it past Kuro to have given him some of his own life force. Seizing his hand, I dragged Bao along hastily.

When we arrived at the salon, the situation had calmed down. Zhou Yuling was sitting in a chair, crying silently with her eyes wide open (a very disturbing sight).

"Tell the truth," I said. "Did you use *gu* poison on Shirakawa?"

"Yes," she said defiantly.

I looked at Bao. He shook his head. *False.*

Zhou Yuling's mouth dropped open. "How did you know?"

"If not *gu* poison, what did you put in his wine?"

Shiro had fallen silent. A calculating look drifted over his face as he gazed at Bao, then me.

"Arsenic," she said.

Again, Bao shook his head.

I wanted to stamp my foot. Every moment she delayed meant a step closer to death for Shiro. At the back of my mind, too, was the image of Kuro walking away. Farther and farther until he disappeared into the mist. That was ridiculous, of course. I'd no right to complain. My thoughts were getting jumbled, my chest squeezed painfully. "At least tell us whether you poisoned Shirakawa so he can make a proper repentance of his sins."

At this, Zhou Yuling burst into loud wails. "I gave up everything for him! Now my patron suspects that I've betrayed him. But I didn't poison him."

Shiro sat up abruptly. "The white powder you put in the wine—what was it?"

"Rice flour. I wanted you to suffer and be at least a little sorry."

The servants were gaping, goggle-eyed, at this drama. It was better than front-row seats at a Chinese opera. Well, what happened next was no longer my business. My heart was heavy with sorrow and anxiety. Shiro was saved, but Kuro was gone. I'd wished to break with both of them and now I bitterly regretted it.

62

It's a day of disruption, following hard on yesterday's events like a whirlwind. Being stabbed, then visited by a demon in his dreams is bad enough, but the chaos continues into mid-morning, like a flower blossoming into ever more madness.

Bao gazes at the strange assortment of people gathered in the medicine shop's salon, including Shirakawa and Zhou Yuling, whom he met outside Oda's photography shop. Gone is her fur pelisse, imported silk hose, and sleek hair. She looks desperately disheveled, ranting about poison. Bao understands that his role is to discern the truth, an unspoken communication that shivers like a lightning spark between himself and the fox lady.

No, he mouths, *no*, and then *yes*, when Zhou Yuling finally tells the truth. The tension that's been boiling through the room collapses abruptly, along with Zhou Yuling, who throws herself on Shirakawa again.

Of course it's not over. A messy affair like this that spills into other people's lives with implications of infidelity and attempted murder will fuel gossip. Bao hopes it won't impact Tagtaa's family too much. What is it about both the woman who fetched him out of his room and Shirakawa that inspires such passionate longing and disruption? If anyone were to be suspected of being a fox, he'd nominate these two. But that's ridiculous. Though even his own response of *That's ridiculous* seems overly quick to him, resembling a suggestion planted in his brain. The more Bao questions his reactions, the more muddled he becomes. It's as though he's being tricked.

That's right.

This is a different way to bend reality, not the same as the lies that make his ears buzz and his tongue numb. Bao feels he can almost grasp the tail end of it before it whisks away into confusion.

As Bao considers this, he notices Shirakawa's sharp glance.

So sharp that it almost cuts, like a chisel used to chip out the eye of a wooden statue. Shirakawa makes a brief gesture over the wailing of Zhou Yuling (now in his arms, nuzzling her face into his neck in complete abandonment of any propriety). Making eye contact with the fox lady, he flicks his chin. She looks annoyed. It's a clownish moment of irritation between two people who look like they ought to be the emperor's favorite courtier and a lady of blazing romantic possibilities.

For an instant, Bao grasps the limits of these creatures. Capable of immense deception, they're constantly tripped up by their own frivolous behavior, like a fox that gets its head stuck in a bottle. There's no real plan, despite their charming appearance. Perhaps that's the true horror.

He thinks of Feng, found frozen on a doorstep; the pork butcher's wife who was also abandoned in the snow; the long trail that he's taken, searching for any hints of foxes. Was it Shirakawa who did this or another creature like him? Even if it was Shirakawa, he won't know or care. Living moment to moment in an utterly inhuman manner, he may not even recall the women. Is this, then, the difference between men and beasts? Around and around Bao's thoughts go as he feels ever dizzier. He clutches his head.

There's a tap on his shoulder. Turning, he sees that Tagtaa has returned. "Why aren't you resting?"

Bao gestures wordlessly at the scene in front of them, and Tagtaa says, "I went to look for a doctor for Mr. Shirakawa, but apparently he's going to be all right." She puts a hand to her chest, as though she's been hurrying. Eyes bright, cheeks pink.

"Were you worried?" asks Bao.

"No, Mr. Kurosaki went with me."

And there he is. The one who saved Bao from Bohai's wild slashes—was it only yesterday? He stands behind Tagtaa, silently. It's hard to read the expression on his face. Bao's stomach contracts. Tagtaa's excited words when they were children spring to mind: *I thought he was very handsome.* Of course it can't be true, because the man who saved her sixty years ago on the grasslands could never be this age, yet the sparkle in her eye is painfully similar. Bao rubs his forehead. Forcing himself to meet Kurosaki's eyes, Bao is surprised to see his gaze rest on the fox lady. It's a look of pensive longing that Bao understands. And suddenly, Bao feels that he likes Kurosaki very much and has only good wishes for him.

"I must take my leave," Kurosaki says. "Thank you for your help."

"So soon? But you haven't recovered fully." Tagtaa looks disappointed.

"If we stay longer, you won't be able to part with us at all."

Who is "us"? Bao wonders. Obviously, it's the three of them. They're as different from everyone else as swans from geese. Shirakawa attempts to disentangle Zhou Yuling's arms from around his neck. It's not easy, as she's determined not to let him go. Her tears have stained the front of his shirt with sad, desperate splotches, and her eyes are puffy and red.

"Ah, Kuro!" he says in relief. "Tell this woman to let me go."

"Do it yourself!" snaps the fox lady. Bowing gracefully, she takes Tagtaa's hands in both of hers. "I wish you well, *tai furen*." Her eyes turn to Bao. "Are you still making inquiries about Chen?"

Bao nods. "Was Chen's death overboard an accident or deliberate?"

She says softly, "You should question Lu. I believe you're the only one who might discern the truth."

Then she's standing in the doorway, next to Kurosaki. Their alert stance reminds Bao oddly of animals glimpsed in the wild, through tall grass. Poised, watchful. Tagtaa takes a step forward. "Don't leave!" she says. "I still have so many questions. I want to talk to you more."

"Talk to the one beside you," says Kurosaki, a hint of a smile in his dark eyes. "Old friends are the best companions."

THE REST OF the day is mysteriously mundane and muted. Everyone seems to accept Kurosaki's departure along with that of Ah San, Tagtaa's servant, unquestioningly. The hazy impression is that she's returned to her hometown somewhere in the north. As for Shirakawa and Zhou Yuling, they remove themselves as well. In fact, Shirakawa is so determined to leave that his smooth charm seems a trifle strained. Concerned about Zhou Yuling's distress, Bao makes sure to get both, since she won't release Shirakawa's arm, into a rickshaw with instructions to take her home. Strangely, the more frazzled and distracted Shirakawa becomes, the more Zhou Yuling regains her self-control.

Dabbing her eyes, she says, "Come to my house, Shirakawa. Now that you're back, I'll never let you go."

"Your patron won't like it. I think we should take a break from seeing each other," he says.

"No. I can handle him. It's you I can't live without."

The gaze that she fixes on Shirakawa makes Bao feel both embarrassed and alarmed. The whites of Shirakawa's eyes show in a vaguely panicked manner. They remind Bao of an animal caught in a trap, though there's a flash of cunning in them that speaks of other options. Still, it seems like a risky relationship. Men and women can be driven to great lengths by passion. Recently, a local scandal erupted when a courtesan castrated her lover with a billhook. A shiver ripples up Bao's spine. Recalling Zhou Yuling's face, her strong-willed glance and tight grip, he thinks unaccountably of those tales of foxes and how they often result in unpleasant endings for all parties involved.

TWO WEEKS LATER, Bao sits in the courtyard of the medicine hall's private residence. The elm tree is in full leaf with the promise of early summer. Bao watches as a caterpillar slowly unspools on an invisible thread. The breeze whips it to and fro, and he moves his hand to gently divert it from his teacup. The tea is a fine blend specially mixed by a local tea merchant. Its smooth, mildly bitter finish reminds him of the tea his father drank.

Bao is now about the age his father was when he died from pneumonia after a summer chill. At the time, Bao was working as a teacher in another town. Hearing of his father's illness, he'd hastened to his bedside. All his life, Bao was slightly afraid of his father, yet as he approached him, lying in his carved bed, he was struck by how he'd shrunk. His father's eyes were bleary and unfocused. Over his labored breathing, he told Bao he was a good boy. Words that reminded Bao sadly of parting remarks to a household pet.

"Father," he said, wondering if he'd been mistaken for his older brother, "it's me, Bao." *The one who couldn't pass the Imperial examinations*, he added silently. Funny how that didn't bother him anymore.

"I always thought you had talent," his father said faintly. "What a waste that you never used it."

Those were the last words his father uttered, other than to remark that his tea was late in arriving. Over the years, Bao has turned them over in his mind, examining them like a window into a dim, unknown landscape. How should one compare being a good boy to also being a waste? Was goodness a waste in his father's mind, or was he merely wandering, his mind starved by his labored breathing?

Now, as Bao regards the tea in his own cup, he thinks of how, at the very end, the fox lady roused him from his sickbed, telling him *Now is the time to use your talent.* That, as well as the odd explanation Bao received in the middle of the night about his ability to hear the truth. They're fragments that add up satisfyingly.

He glances up. Tagtaa joins him, carrying her own teacup.

"I'm returning to Mukden," he says. "I bought my train ticket already."

"Are you well enough to travel?"

Bao's swift recovery after being stabbed has amazed everyone, including himself. The past two weeks spent as an invalid here have been almost embarrassingly pleasant. The rhythm of this house, with its well-trained servants, delicious meals, and soft beds, is a comfort that Bao hasn't experienced for a long time. There's been internal family drama, of course. The return of the master of the medicine shop from his concubine's residence caused friction, though the fact that the new baby is a girl and not a boy mollified his wife. But none of that really concerned Bao, an outsider. What's more important has been Tagtaa's quiet companionship.

"Is there a reason you must return tomorrow?"

"I have some business to tie up."

Tagtaa doesn't ask him what it is. That's what he likes about her, her straightforward, friendly gaze. He briefly considers telling her what her servant Ah San said right before she left—for Bao to investigate Lu. That's an interesting line of inquiry. He wonders why she said that.

Bao feels the familiar fuzziness in his head whenever he thinks too hard about Tagtaa's servant. More than once, Tagtaa has lamented her going. "I shall miss her so much, though I'm glad she's reunited with her husband," she says, though the truth is that neither Bao nor Tagtaa has any details beyond that. Even Bao's insight about foxes, their chaos and clownishness, has lost its sharpness. In fact, when he told Tagtaa his earlier theory that they might all be itinerant actors, she'd nodded enthusiastically and said that Ah San had mentioned an orphanage, a common origin for such artists. The peculiar, driving desire he's had to discover more about foxes, which has compelled him all his life since childhood, has vanished along with the pain in his left lung.

"May I come back to visit you?" Bao asks.

His relationship with Tagtaa's household, especially her son and daughter-in-law, has been remarkably congenial. They seem grateful he bears no enmity for being stabbed by Bohai. More than once, the master of the medicine shop has declared he's glad that Bao is his mother's childhood friend (and thus unlikely to demand monetary or legal compensation).

Tagtaa says, "I'll be waiting for you. Whenever you decide to move to Dalian."

"How did you know?" He's surprised that she's divined his thoughts. After all, there's nothing binding him to Mukden other than his older brother.

"I could tell what you were thinking. Asking questions about the city and looking up your contacts. Also, I must thank you for helping us smooth things over with the Chen family."

Indeed, Bao has been wondering if an angry envoy from Mr. Chen would appear, demanding restitution. No one has come yet, but upon contacting Hong, it seems Mr. Chen's household has been far too busy with the aftermath of their mansion burning down to even think of an escaped servant named Ah San. The cause of the fire, according to Hong, was an overturned incense burner. He made no mention of any odd visitors, including a mysterious, fox-like woman. Still, Bao keeps it in the back of his mind that he ought to interview Lu about Chen's disappearance overboard, though he's beginning to forget who told him about that.

"I promise I'll be back soon," says Bao.

Tagtaa laughs. "I can wait. I waited for you in the courtyard for days when we were children. Do you remember?"

Smiling, Bao says he does.

Epilogue

In the autumn of that year, the Dowager Empress Cixi died in the Forbidden City. Far away, in the old Manchu capital of Mukden, discussions in teahouses and the villas of the rich strategized about what was to come next. In villages and hamlets, peasants continued trundling their goods to market in wheelbarrows, swarms of locusts ravaged the southwest, and a three-year-old boy, Aisin Gioro Puyi, was installed as the likely last emperor of the Qing dynasty.

"I don't think that bodes well," said Kuro.

We were sitting on a wall near the Korean border. In fact, this whole area used to be part of the Goryeo kingdom, but nowadays nobody pays attention to that. Except perhaps foxes. After all, when kingdoms expand and recede, there's always profit to be found. It had to be done honestly, of course, but that went without saying.

The stone wall was warm from the heat of the sun and made a pleasant perch. Originally part of a ruined fort, it had long been abandoned and was now home to field mice, which scurried in and out of its crevices.

"Don't!" I said to Kuro as he eyed one of them. "You've had more than enough to eat, and besides, didn't you say we mustn't be greedy?"

In answer, Kuro merely inclined his head. It's one of his gestures that people who aren't familiar with him think are mysterious. I knew, however, that it meant he still had room for another mouse. Just as I knew it would be very hard for me to part with him. We still hadn't quite made up—or at least I hadn't. There were nights when I wept, and mornings when I didn't wish to speak to him. In the end, however, only Kuro and I had memories of our lost child. Only he had known and loved her brief existence as much as I had.

We'd both done our fair share of repenting for mistakes that led to her loss. My going on a journey to visit my grandmother's grave. His decision to go hunting and leave her alone, a hunting trip that took too long, snarled with mishaps and delays. The words he'd said to me when he'd returned late, not realizing our child had been taken: *Why are you so upset? My parents used to leave us alone for days.* My frenzied rage.

The facts were that we were both away when a hunter dug up the den and seized our child.

The facts were that infant mortality is high. Ours is a dwindling race anyway.

The facts were that I failed my daughter.

Kuro says that's wrong, and the fault is his. He says he cannot live without me, that he's tried and if I tell him to go away again, he will journey to Mount Tai and meditate in a cave until he dies. I don't think he's joking. He's quite capable of behavior like that. In any case, I've progressed far enough down this bitter path to see a little sunlight amid the thorns.

I try to remind myself that neither of us was responsible for either Bektu Nikan or the hunter he hired. On good days, I don't think about them at all. On very good days, Kuro and I recall the wide-eyed, sweet heaviness of our child and the wonder of her fleeting existence, without biting recriminations against each other.

The other day I said to him, "What exactly was that book that you wrote in Japan about—the one that made Miss Yukiko's grandfather offer you a job?"

He turned his head, embarrassed. "It was a book of ghost stories. I never expected anyone to read it."

"Ghost stories about what?" Certainly we've encountered many strange events over the years.

"The haunted temple in Daegu. The man with no nose in Qiqihar. The twenty-nine cursed steps, and the well with human hair floating in it."

I was silent for a while. Each of those tales features a missing wife or child. Kuro said, "I wrote and rewrote them for myself."

"With happy endings?"

"I believe a literary critic called it a 'forlorn and wistful collection.'"

"I never would have imagined you to have such a poetic soul."

"I was very sad without you," he said simply.

There's not much one can say to declarations like that. It's my fault for having married someone who makes me blush with his seriousness. To change the subject, I said, "You should have added the tale about Shiro and the provincial governor's wife. Now that was a scandal." Indeed, it was so notorious that Shiro had to avoid Chang'an for seventy-five years.

"Speaking of Shiro," Kuro said, "I heard that he's on his way to Formosa to set up a sugar refinery."

"How is he?" Frankly, I was surprised that Shiro had survived. The determined look on Zhou Yuling's face had suggested that she was just as capable as Mr. Chen of maintaining her own private prison. Truly, humans are fearsome creatures.

"Apparently, he's still with Zhou Yuling, though it isn't clear whether that's by choice or coercion. But Shiro can take care of himself."

Yes, he certainly could. He might even use the funds to start a real sugar refinery. Shiro is very lazy, and Zhou Yuling, despite her obsession, seemed like a capable businesswoman, so perhaps their relationship might last a little longer.

Kuro stared pensively into the distance. A magpie flashed its black-and-white wings. I said, "Are you worried about him?"

"No. I was thinking of you. Whether you might have preferred to go with him rather than me."

"Is that why you were so calm when we were all in Moji?" I recalled Kuro's stoic presence and the shadow of Miss Yukiko, who'd clung to him possessively. I really didn't like that.

"I was actually extremely upset."

"Well, your expression didn't change."

Kuro gave a wry smile. "He's always had a soft spot for you. I knew this, yet I asked you to marry me."

"Did Shiro ever say anything about that?" I scraped the mortar of the wall with my nails. It crumbled, and small bits fell into the wild grass. Yet another piece of the empire that we foxes were destroying.

"We both knew. So when you said you never wanted to see me again, I thought I might as well wish for your happiness."

"Are you saying that if Bektu Nikan hadn't been killed and Mr. Chen hadn't locked me up, you might just have stayed quietly in Moji?"

He nodded.

Annoyed yet relieved by Kuro's stubbornness, I shoved him off the wall. He gave a yelp, landing gracefully in a crouch. Picking himself up, he gazed up at me with bright eyes.

"Snow, let's begin anew. Will you walk the thousand-year journey with me?"

"Only you would propose with a moral pilgrimage," I said. "But why not? Besides, we already agreed to try not to sin too much."

Laughing, I jumped off the wall. Kuro caught me by the waist and swung me round in a circle.

"It's time to leave this area," he said. "There's a bubonic plague among the marmots, and I fear it will spread to people. If there are deaths, they may blame foxes or evil spirits. We should cross the border to Korea; we can be Mr. and Mrs. Park, two mild-mannered herbalists."

"Let's make a fortune selling rare medicine."

"No, we must give the profits to the poor."

"But we don't have any money right now!"

"You are my heart's treasure," said Kuro softly.

You can't argue with someone who says things like that; I hugged him tight, tight against the wind that was blowing from the north, and the brilliant sunlight shining on the long grass around us, so that every seed head looked as though it were made of pure gold.

AND THAT'S WHERE I must end this tale. If I told you half the things that the average fox does in a year, you could fill an entire book from cover to cover, plus a very long set of footnotes. I'm going to bury my diary under this stone wall, and perhaps, when it finally collapses, someone will unearth it. Or not. For all stories have an ending as well as a beginning. But a beginning is where you choose to plant your foot, and the ending is only the edge of one's own knowledge.

As to whether Kuro and I will manage the thousand-year journey, I don't know. But if you're at least a little fond of foxes and don't consider us a plague or nuisance, leave out an offering of fried tofu.

Who knows, we may come and visit you one fine summer evening.

Notes

Fox Spirits

I've always been fascinated by old Chinese tales of fox women (and men) who tempt and beguile humans. Traditionally, women labeled vixens were accused of willfulness, strong emotions, and licentious living. The stories told about these shape-shifting foxes are brief and elliptical; as a child I always wondered where they came from and what they were up to between these episodes, written down in Chinese literature as "histories."

Northern China is the ancestral home of the fox cult, which spread to Korea and Japan. Foxes were mentioned as omens of good fortune, with records of them dating from the Han and Tang dynasties. The transition from being regarded as celestial foxes to life-devouring demons perhaps represents two sides of the same coin—foxes as supernatural beings whose intentions towards humans are unclear. Interestingly, there are also historical parallels between foxes and foreigners. "Hu" is both a homophone for "fox" (狐) and, in ancient times, a name that denoted barbarians (胡) from the north and west of China.[1]

The fox holds a marginalized position in Chinese culture, both worshipped and exorcised, living in the shadows of human settlements. The ability to shift between human and beast forms echoes that uncertain status of in between. Said to be uncontrollable, lustful, and wicked, foxes were also considered fertility deities, healers, and moral guides. During the Ming and Qing dynasties, writers like Pu Songling and Ji Yun popularized stories of foxes and ghosts. In Chinese literature, they are often linked with romance, although it is mostly the beautiful fox woman who is "tamed" and turned into a wife or concubine who bears sons who do well in the Imperial examinations.

There are far more stories about fox women than men, perhaps because many of the stories are told from the viewpoint

1. Xiaofei Kang, "The Fox (hu) and the Barbarian (hu): Unraveling Representations of the Other in Late Tang Tales," *Journal of Chinese Religions* 27, no. 1 (1999): 35–67.

of a male protagonist, usually a scholar, who is seduced by a woman who approaches him. I've always wondered at the lopsidedness of this portrayal. If such creatures existed, what were their motivations? While researching this novel, I read many stories of foxes, including purported historic encounters from China and Japan. Some are very odd and disjointed indeed. Others seem to hint at a rich and busy life for these creatures. *The Fox Wife* explores this world that intersects tantalizingly with our own. In writing about these mysterious creatures, I also couldn't help turning it into a detective novel, with, of course, a body count. . . .

The Thousand-Year Journey

This is a spiritual pilgrimage that probably has roots in a mixture of Daoist, Buddhist, and folklore traditions, and is the belief that if a thousand years of moral study and righteous living are diligently applied, anyone or anything can refine itself. A snake, for example, who meditates for a thousand years may become a dragon, and a tiger turn into a mountain god. It was believed that many animals who lived a long life and displayed certain characteristics, such as white coloring or an unusual number of tails, were on their way to enlightenment. Even plants and natural objects, such as very old tree peonies, chrysanthemums, pine trees, and stones, could transform into humans after surviving for a long time and avoiding sin.

It's not entirely clear what lies at the end of the journey, including possible deification as a local god or sainthood. In the novel, Snow and the other foxes refer to it obliquely, as it's considered a mystery that one can begin to understand only after centuries of moral refining and the pursuit of virtue.

Footnotes and Marginalia

There is an old Chinese literary tradition of footnotes and marginalia, where people would write their reactions and comments to the text, and sometimes even poems inspired by it, and then pass the book around. In this way, literary discourse was promoted even among women who might ordinarily be unable to attend literary salons. Some of the comments were by famous people or were considered so interesting that they were reprinted along with the text in new editions. China has a very long history of printing and writing, and many of the comments spanned years and even centuries, enlightening later readers.

I originally wanted to fill this novel with Snow's personal footnotes and little backstories about what foxes might be up to, literally on the margins of society (ha ha!). However, I realized that readers might not be overly fond of footnotes, and so cut back on them. One day, perhaps, I'll be able write a book filled with short anecdotes of foxes and their mysterious goings-on.

Fall of the Qing Dynasty

The Qing dynasty (1644–1911) was the last imperial dynasty to rule China before it became a republic. It was one of only two non-Han (Chinese) dynasties, the other being the Yuan, or Mongol, dynasty founded by Genghis Khan. Like the Mongols, the Manchus, originally a seminomadic tribe from the north, eventually became absorbed by Chinese culture, though remnants of their influence remain. The *qipao*, or *cheongsam*, dress, for example, is actually in the Manchu style, as were the shaved head and long pigtail forced upon the Chinese population upon pain of beheading.

The last years of the Qing dynasty were ruled by the Dowager Empress Cixi, who resisted attempts at reform and modernization, ruling by proxy as regent. It was a time of turmoil, warlords, and rumblings of revolution. Many young Chinese scholars went abroad to study, particularly to Japan, which was geographically close and had modernized faster during the Meiji era.

Names

As is customary, the Chinese names are given with last name first. The meanings are as follows:

Bao: 包, meaning "to wrap or hide." I haven't specified if this is his first or last name, since it could be either, or even a childhood nickname, but it is the same character as Bao Gong, the famous judge who was deified as a god.

Tagtaa: Mongolian for "dove" or "pigeon."

Huang Bohai: 黄渤海 Huang is a surname meaning "yellow." Bohai means "ocean waves."

Chen Jianyi: 陈健义 Chen is a surname meaning "old." Jianyi means "strong and righteous."

Lu Dong: 鲁东 Lu is a surname meaning the ancient state of Lu. Dong means "east."

Zhou Yuling: 周玉玲 Zhou is a surname originating from the relatives of the royal family of Zhou. Yuling means "jade bell."

Shiro: 白, meaning "white" in Japanese. Also pronounced as "*bai*" in Chinese.

Kuro: 黑, meaning "black" in Japanese. Pronounced as "*hei*" in Chinese.

Snow: 雪, pronounced as "*yuki*" in Japanese, "*xue*" in Chinese.

Acknowledgments

I love stories of foxes who turn into people and their outsider take on the human world. The transformation of these ideas into this book would not have been possible without:

My incredible agent, Jenny Bent, without whom this book would have been twice the length and half as interesting.

My wonderful editor, Amy Einhorn, for her deep insights. I was worried that nobody would want to read a book written from the point of view of a fox, and am so grateful for her enthusiastic encouragement.

The amazing team at Henry Holt: Janel Brown, Mary Beth Constant, Laura Flavin, Lori Kusatzky, Meryl Levavi, Morgan Mitchell, Caitlin Mulrooney-Lyski, Julia Ortiz, Kenn Russell, Christopher Sergio, and Vincent Stanley.

Dear friends and much-appreciated readers Sue and Danny Yee, Li Lian Tan, and Suelika Chial, who have kindly read all my novels and always give terrific, unvarnished feedback. Special thanks to my midnight buddy, Xiaoyuan Tu, who was always mysteriously awake when I texted her obscure questions about animal names and other folklore. Also to my sweet and long-suffering parents, especially my mum, whose long-ago Chinese literature degree I have fully exploited over the years by double-checking my literary Chinese with her.

My friends and extended family who have supported me in my writing endeavors over the years, especially my children, who patiently listened to ever more outlandish plot ideas over the dinner table. And of course, James. Beloved first reader and first in everything. I write for you, always.

Catch for us the foxes, the little foxes that ruin the vineyards, our vineyards that are in bloom (Song of Solomon 2:15).

About the Author

YANGSZE CHOO is a Malaysian writer of Chinese descent. After receiving her undergraduate degree from Harvard, she worked as a management consultant before writing her *New York Times* bestselling debut novel, *The Ghost Bride*, now a Netflix original series. Her second novel, *The Night Tiger*, was a Reese Witherspoon Book Club pick and a Big Jubilee Read selection for Queen Elizabeth II's Platinum Jubilee. She lives in California with her family and loves to eat and read (often at the same time). *The Fox Wife* and all previous novels would not have been possible without large quantities of dark chocolate.

Yangsze is happy to visit book clubs via Zoom! You can find her on her website, yschoo.com, or @yangszechoo on Twitter, Instagram, and Facebook.